DIVINE DILEMMA

A DRAGON RIDER
FANTASY ROMANCE

TALES OF THE VANIR
BOOK III

Rochelle Wilcox

Cover Design by 100 Covers
Formatted with Atticus

Thanks to the beta readers and editors who helped make this a better book:
Cindy Ray Hale and Keele Publishing
Kaitlin Slowik
Keeya Marquez

And perpetual thanks to my alpha reader, Cynthia Davis

DEDICATION

To everyone willing to fight for what you want ...
and strong enough to take it.
This one's for you.

Vulryn's song is *Glitter & Gold* by Barns Courtney

CONTENT WARNING

This book is intended for adults only, and contains subject matter that may be difficult or disturbing for some readers.

Sensitive material includes, but is not limited to: frequent profanity, violence, torture and killing of people and dragons (but not the cat; nobody messes with Thor), sexual assault (a brief episode of withdrawn consent), emotional abuse, socio-economic power imbalances, frequent mentions of blood, and genocide (of elves).
Divine Dilemma also contains explicit, open-door sexual content.
Reader discretion is advised.

CONTENTS

GLOSSARY

Ætt: Clan/Fhord's people

Dragon's-Length: Unit of measure; sixty feet

Draikana: Female of a mated dragon pair

Drake: Male of a mated dragon pair

Draugr: Undead

Drott: Chief/leader

Dróttning: Queen

Kastali: Castle

Konungr: King

Male's-Height: Unit of measure; six feet

Meistara: Lady

Meistari: Lord

Seiðr: Ability to predict the future

Thunder: Group of dragons

Valkyrie: Shield maiden/female warrior

Vekter: Guards/police

Viku: Unit of measure; one mile

MAP

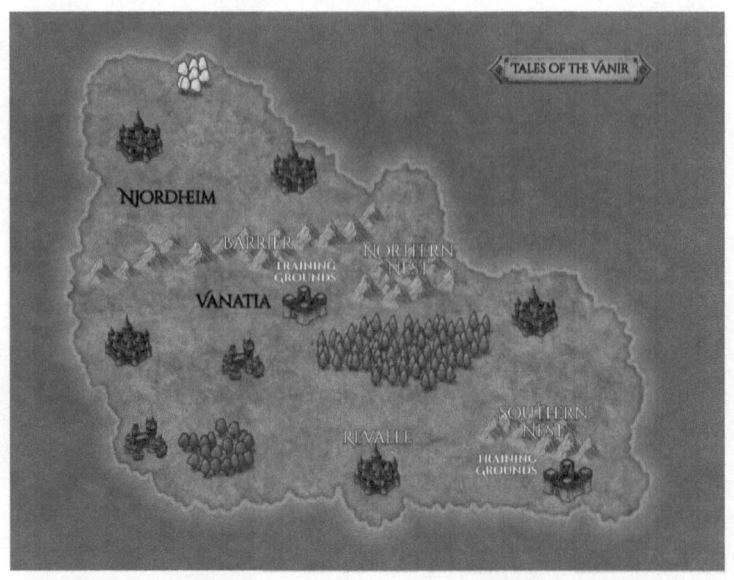

RECAP

WHAT HAPPENED IN THE LAST BOOK?

I N *FRENZIED FATE*, SIFA and Fhord are on the run, trying desperately to stay ahead of the Dróttning's soldiers
as they head north, to a spring with healing waters. They
reach it—and Astarot finally starts to return to the vigor
of a dragon who hasn't been mercilessly tortured—then
travel to a different kingdom, where the Dróttning won't
find them. Fhord doesn't fully trust Njordheim's mercurial
monarch Harald but they need allies in their fight against
the Dróttning. They decide the risk is worth the reward.

But Harald surprises Sifa and Fhord as soon as they cross
the border, accosting them with a large group of soldiers and
refusing them entry into Njordheim. He declares his disdain
for Fhord, who has spent decades serving the Dróttning, and
difficulty believing Fhord has changed. He then discloses one
of Fhord's secrets to Sifa: that Fhord and Sifa are mates. Sifa's

xii   ROCHELLE L. WILCOX

angry to have heard it from Harald and not Fhord, but recognizes its truth.

Harald proposes an exchange: Fhord and Sifa will separate, each with a different task, and if they succeed, he'll contribute his forces to the fight against the Dróttning. From Fhord, he demands to learn the Dróttning's secret to controlling the dragons. He insists Sifa remain in Njordheim, where she'll find and "tame" one of the many wild dragons in this land. Terrified for Sifa's safety if she returns with him to Vanaheim—where he expects the Dróttning to be waiting for him on the other side of the barrier—Fhord convinces Sifa to agree.

When Sifa's alone, Harald discloses a secret the Dróttning hides from everybody: that Fhord is the Dróttning's son. (We'll later learn that the Dróttning has a special connection to Fhord, allowing her to sense him and his magic from a distance.) Harald then demands Sifa fight three of his soldiers for supplies and maps. Sifa wins, barely, and Harald sends one of those soldiers (the elf Dani) with Sifa as she chases wild dragons. Sifa and Dani slowly become friends and manage to subdue a large brown dragon. He's attacked and killed, though, by a ferocious copper dragon, who Dani shoots with a dragon bolt. They trap the copper dragon, naming her Vulryn, and join together to enter her mind to try to "tame" her. (Dani also has mind magic; it's an elf thing.) But Vulryn surprises them by capturing Dani's mind, refusing to let her go.

In the meantime, Fhord reunites with Sifa's troll, his Ætt (a group of soldiers who are like family), Sifa's friends Mikkael, Johan, Liv and Frida, along with Joralf and his mate Fróðr.

Together, they go in search of the Dróttning's secret. Along the way, they're accosted by a dragon, Khirta, and her rider, who demands that Khirta kill Fhord and the others. Khirta refuses, killing her rider instead, and joining the group. Fhord and the others learn that the healing water, available only rarely in Vanatia, is part of the Dróttning's secret, but not all of it. Before Fhord can learn the rest, they're found by the Dróttning, who reveals she can shift into a massive wyrm. Fhord is forced to shift into his savage—a wolf form he rarely embodies—and kills the Dróttning's soldiers before returning to the barrier in search of Sifa.

Sifa feels Fhord's presence at the barrier and races there to reunite with him. They return to Dani and Vulryn, where Fhord helps free Dani's mind. But Dani and Vulryn have bonded and now they have to escape Njordheim because Harald won't tolerate one of his soldiers being bonded to a dragon instead of him. Along the way, Fhord and Sifa separate from Vulryn and Dani, and they are captured. Vulryn and Dani return to help free them, but Vulryn terrifies everyone, including Dani, by burning all of the soldiers. Fhord's reluctant to take Dani with them to Vanatia but Sifa won't leave her behind, so Dani joins them.

Fhord, Sifa and Dani reunite with the others, where Mikkael accosts Dani. We learn that years ago, on a mission from Harald, Dani manipulated the mind of Mikkael's lover, forcing Mikkael to kill his lover when she turned on him. Mikkael leaves the group, refusing to spend any time with Dani. That evening, one of Fhord's Ætt reveals another of Fhord's secrets to Sifa: that Fhord realized he was connected to Sifa when she first landed in Vanatia—while she was being tortured—but he refused to pursue it because he knew if he let himself get close to Sifa, the Dróttning would punish him by torturing his dragon. Sifa's angry at all the secrets Fhord's keeping from her, pushing him away just before they realize they're under attack.

Fhord reveals his biggest secret to Sifa—that he's a wolf shifter—then leaves the group to try to draw the Dróttning away. It doesn't work and Sifa's group is attacked. Johan is killed and Fhord is captured, to be taken to the southern Nest, where Tindera is being held. There, he's tortured mercilessly and learns how brutally Tindera's been tortured. Sifa, meanwhile, is struggling with her conflicting feelings for Fhord, angry at all his secrets. After talking to Toffer, though, she realizes he had reasons for everything and forgives him, finally accepting the mating bond. When she does, the connection between her and Fhord solidifies, giving her access to his thoughts, which will be critical in their rescue efforts.

They join a group of rebels to plan Fhord and Tindera's rescue, where Sifa learns that Bevin (the overseer who first connected her to Fhord) has been a secret rebel all along. He helps Sifa and Astarot get into the southern Nest, where they fight their way to Fhord. But the Dróttning returns before they can free Tindera, forcing Sifa and Astarot to carry Fhord away without his dragon.

In the final chapter, we get Dani's voice for the first time. Vulryn rejects Sifa's demand that Vulryn and Dani stay behind, determined to rescue Tindera. Vulryn attacks the Dróttning, who is in her wyrm form, and the copper dragon is able to resist the mind manipulation the Dróttning uses to control Vanatia's dragons. Vulryn carries the Dróttning away, giving Astarot and Khirta a chance to free Tindera, and then is attacked by a large blue dragon, who forces her to release the Dróttning. Vulryn lets the blue dragon go, revealing to Dani that he is Vulryn's mated dragon. Vulryn declares she will give the blue dragon a chance to prove himself worthy and kill him if he does not. Dani's worried about a connection to one of the Dróttning's dragons but can't disagree. She's giving her mate a chance to prove himself but may need to kill him too.

CHAPTER ONE

SIFA

YOU DID IT

I CAN FINALLY SEE more skin growing over all the blood and gore.

It's been twelve hours since Astarot carried Fhord from the Nest, then returned for Tindera and somehow found the strength to hoist her onto his back and haul her away too. Twelve of the hardest fucking hours I've ever lived. And I've lived through some hard fucking hours.

Fhord hasn't woken yet, but that's a blessing. Once we got back to the camp, we did the painstaking work to remove every gods-damned bolt and chain from his dragon's poor, tattered wings. She suffered it all in silence, stoic and resolved despite her agony. She's so gods-damned strong. Then we devised a stretcher for Fhord and took off. The Dróttning will recognize his presence if she's close enough when he wakes up. We can't risk her finding us, so we're traveling again.

The rebels all stayed with Bevin and Ulfhild at the camp. I'm still in a bit of shock that my former boss—the most important overseer in Revalle—is covertly supporting the rebellion, and that he and the courtesan Ulfhild are lovers. But I can't deny that we wouldn't have gotten Fhord and Tindera out of the Nest without him.

During the rescue, Bevin disappeared as soon as the Dróttning showed up, desperate to maintain the illusion that he's fully committed to her. With Fhord on that bitch's enemies list now, we need Bevin close to her. He had one of the rebels break his arm, and plans to return to Revalle alone. He's confident he can convince the Dróttning that he's as pissed about our escape as she is.

We're back to our core group. The Ætt are here, of course, since Leif, Torsten, Jorunn, and Astrid are Fhord's family. They wouldn't abandon him. My troll and cat, Toffer and Thor, refused to stay with the rebels, ignoring the risk of traveling with us. I'm worried but relieved to have them by my side. And Dani. Even if she wanted to find a home in Vanatia after leaving Njordheim behind, her dragon wouldn't let her. They're ours for now, at least.

The others surprised me. Ulfhild asked Liv and Frida to join us, and they were happy to agree. When they left Revalle, they put their bedmate days behind them and fully committed to the rebellion. I was even more shocked by Joralf and his mate Fróðr's decision. I thought that after Joralf spent two years in prison, they'd want to hide somewhere together. They're more committed to the rebellion than ever, though, and we'll be doing the most important work.

We're small enough to move without much notice, if we didn't have four dragons with us. Everyone's walking since we know we'll be able to fly at some point—hopefully soon—and don't want to abandon horses when we do. They'd be too much for the dragons to carry, along with so many people and our gear.

The Dróttning will throw everything she has at finding the traitors who stole her son from her torture chamber, so we didn't waste any time putting distance between her and us. I'm starting to think the gods might actually be on our side because as bad as Fhord and Tindera are—and they are terribly, horrifically bad—they're alive. They'll both recover.

Plus, Toffer found an enormous cave system that Fróðr swears is undiscovered. We've checked and there are no footprints anywhere. It descends at a gradual pace and will carry us far enough away from the surface to evade the Dróttning's heightened senses where Fhord is concerned. She won't be able to find him once we're a couple of vikus below ground. We're being as careful as we can—Leif is tailing the group, hiding our trail as we go—and I think we might just survive.

I've held Fhord's hand the entire time, walking next to the stretcher that hangs between Khirta and Vulryn. Khirta's uninjured and Vulryn's too strong and stubborn to let her injuries stop her. She's earned my respect—and a place at our side. What she did in Njordheim is behind us.

Astarot's helping Tindera, flying just above her whenever the cave's big enough to hold her wings aloft and apart. It's the only position we've found that gives Fhord's suffering beast the respite she needs to walk with us. Both dragons are exhausted—we all are—but they're driven. Astarot's emotions are the same mix of horror and hope as mine. We're waffling between bone-crushing despair about the Dróttning's torture of Fhord and Tindera—dragging up memories of our own torment by that bitch—and joy that lightens our souls because we are finally complete. Our mates are free to share our lives, but they are suffering while they heal.

And they are healing. I'm giving Fhord every bit of power I can muster to bolster his. It's not much since we both drained ourselves in the Nest during the escape, but it's helping. At least, that's what I keep telling myself. A good night's sleep will make the biggest difference and Toffer promises we'll be able to stop soon. He's taken charge for the time being, which feels strange. But trolls sense caves in a way nobody else can. I'm happy to follow him while we look for a safe place to rest.

"You did it." Fhord's rasp barely reaches my ears, even in the silent cave.

My head whips around almost before the words have registered in my lethargic thoughts, lips tipping up into a broad grin. "You did it, Fhord. We wouldn't have gotten out without your magic. I have no gods-damned idea how you had the strength after what you've been through, but I'm so glad you did."

"She kept me well fed while I hung there. She isn't ready to kill me yet," he whispers, his words little more than a sigh. "That's probably changed now," he adds with a smirk.

"We'll kill her first. Now that we have you and Tindera out, nothing will stop us." I feel the truth of that statement in my bones. It's as certain and undeniable as my bonds with Fhord and Astarot. I try to keep the tears from my eyes as I watch my battered, tattered mate, but I can't. "I missed you so fucking much, Fhord."

"I missed you too, rabbit. More than I ever thought possible. You are so deep under my skin, I forgot what it was to live without you."

"Never again," I promise him.

"Never again."

"You shouldn't be talking." I'm desperate to feel normal with him again, to talk and laugh like everything's okay, but he's not ready for that. "Save your energy." I squeeze his hand a bit, still nervous about causing him more pain with the pressure, but I can tell he craves my touch.

"You talk. I need to hear your voice."

"Astarot is so fucking happy." I hiccup, finally finding some control over my emotions as I let my dragon's relief at freeing Tindera fill me. "He's not a talkative beast, but he's been nagging me nonstop about figuring out some way to get Tindera to the water near the border. He's desperate for her to be healed the way he was."

"It's a long way." Fhord's voice is barely a whisper, accompanied by a shiver of pain.

"We know, and he realizes it's much too dangerous, with the Dróttning throwing every soldier she has into finding us. But it's driving him a little mad," I admit with a laugh. "The mating bond is urging him to split from the others and carry Tindera there. He's desperate to take away her pain." I can't hold back the smile as my gaze finally leaves Fhord to glance at my stalwart dragon before I look back at him. "Almost as desperate as I am to take away your pain. I've talked him down from the cliff. For now."

"Thank fuck," Fhord breathes.

"Thank fuck," I agree. "We're in no shape to fight another battle if we get caught. We'll let you both recover, then figure out what happens next."

He watches me for a few more seconds, but he's tired. His eyes start to droop, and he falls back down into sleep. Within a few minutes, he's fully relaxed and snoring lightly.

I feel lighter, freer than I have in a long time. I have no idea how long this can last, but I plan to cling to it and enjoy it while I can.

I'm struggling when Toffer finally leads us into a large cavern and announces we can stop and rest here for a day or two. I watch, clutching Fhord's hand, as Leif and Astrid make a bed for us and the dragons lead us over to move him from the stretcher.

After I make sure Fhord's sleeping soundly—I will not let him wake up alone—I ask Fróðr to show me to a pool tucked deeper in the cave where I can wash off quickly. I'll take a bath at some point, but right now, I need sleep. And to be with my mate. Dragging myself back to our bed, I ease myself down next to Fhord, pull up a blanket, and close my eyes.

Soft voices draw me from dreams of flight on Astarot's back, Fhord and Tindera by our side. I'm confused for a moment, not sure where I am, but then Fhord's scent washes over me. And it all comes back. The fight in the caves. Forcing Fhord to leave without his dragon. Vulryn's refusal to do what we asked—and thank the gods she did. If she wasn't such a stubborn beast, we'd still be near the Nest, trying to figure out how to get Tindera out.

Turning my head, I open my eyes and smile. He's watching me, eyes like emeralds sitting between his beautiful, long lashes. He looks so relaxed, and I can't imagine how that's possible after what he's been through.

"It's you, rabbit," he whispers, lifting a hand to caress my cheek. "You calm me. Waking next to you fills me with a peace, a comfort, I've never known before."

"Is that how it's going to be now?" I ask as my smile somehow grows even larger. "You'll be able to read my thoughts, answer my questions before I even ask them?"

"When you're this open to me, I can sense your emotions and the outline of your thoughts. When our emotions are heightened, like when you were battling that dragon in Njordheim, we should be able to talk to each other, at least in short bursts."

"That was real?" A wave of shock washes through me as I recall him dropping into my mind and snarling the advice I needed to take control of poor Bob, the brown dragon Vulryn killed before we captured her. "I thought I imagined it."

"Our connection is so fucking strong," he declares, his thumb stroking my cheek. "Your distress pulled me there, even through the barrier. I knew what you needed and was able to stay long enough to tell you."

"You saved our lives." I lift my hand to rest it on his. "That was gods-damned amazing." And I'm crying, because this bond I have with Fhord is the sun that rises in the morning, bringing light and heat and hope to everything in its embrace. He is the radiance in my world, the flame in my gut that burns for him alone, the joy in my life. "I love you so fucking much, Fhord."

"Fuck, do I love you, rabbit." He pauses, his gaze holding mine, eyes glowing like the morning grass. "We'll be able to shield from each other when we want to," he adds after a moment, "but I like this. Especially now. I want to experience every single emotion you do. I've dropped my shields too. Can you feel how much I love you?"

My mind reaches out to his, and I suck in a deep breath when I find him. "I've never sensed such pure, unrestrained love."

"It's yours, rabbit. Everything I am is yours. Till the end of time."

But we don't have until the end of time. My chest clenches, and I throw a shield between us, desperate to hide a fear that's been bouncing through my head since we left the Nest. Fhord doesn't know I'm aging like a human, unlike every other elf in this world. He has no idea we'll have decades together if we're lucky, not the centuries he'd have with another elf.

Now isn't the time to share that truth, though. He's suffered too much to add that burden to his others. I have to tell him soon, especially after being so angry at him for his secrets, but he needs to heal from the Dróttning's torture first. So I push the guilt and worry aside and lift myself just a bit, hovering over him before I lean forward and kiss him. His lips mold to mine, and I wonder how I ever lived without this. Without him.

Even this gentle kiss lights a flame in my center. Pulling myself away, I place a palm on his cheek, marveling at how much he's healed overnight. "I can't wait to get you alone," I whisper, my lips finding his for one more quick kiss.

"I'm so fucking ready," he groans. "For now, though, let's focus on something that will keep my thoughts away from how gods-damned good it will feel when I can plunge into you again."

"Is there such a thing?" I ask with a laugh.

He smirks and I'm home again, every part of me settled by Fhord just being Fhord. It took me years to recover from the Dróttning's torture, and I'm sure I'll see signs of what Fhord suffered in the days and weeks ahead. In this moment, though, I'm so gods-damned grateful to have my occasionally playful, always devoted, perpetually horny mate smirking at me.

"I've been thinking," he tells me after a few seconds, "about how Vulryn managed to ignore the Dróttning's command to stand down when she went into the Nest to help free Tindera."

I nod, still amazed by the fact that the Dróttning has no control over Dani's dragon. "Astarot tried to warn Vulryn before she attacked that wyrm form the Dróttning takes," I relay, my gaze lifting to find the stubborn copper beast. "He told her she wouldn't be able to do anything because the Dróttning controls all dragons in Vanatia. Vulryn laughed at him. Turned out she was right."

"It's the first time I've seen a dragon refuse one of the Dróttning's direct orders. She controls them all, and I've never understood how. It's a huge part of what gives her power. We need to figure out why Vulryn's immune."

"It surprised Astarot too, about Vulryn but also about himself. When he attacked in the cave, he felt the Dróttning's command that he fight *for* her, instead of *against* her. He resisted it—something he's never been able to do before. Which makes me wonder why the Dróttning didn't just order him to take a rider. Why torture dragons, instead of controlling them?"

"The bond is very particular," Fhord explains with a sigh. "When the Dróttning's trying to force one, it doesn't stick unless the dragon and rider both agree, of their own free will."

"A tortured dragon is acting on free will when he gives in?" I'm sure my expression reflects my skepticism because that makes no gods-damned sense.

Fhord smiles, launching a kaleidoscope of butterflies in my stomach. He's so fucking beautiful. I still can't believe he's mine. "Surrendering is a choice," he says, "even if it's an utter bitch of a choice. It's still their free will. But whatever the Dróttning does to compel compliance takes control away from them, depriving them of their ability to refuse her. And I have no gods-damned idea what it might be."

I watch him for a moment, thinking again about what Astarot told me. He's craving something, although he's not sure what. Worse—and scaring the fuck out of me—he's getting weaker and convinced he may need it to survive. But I'm not going to share that with Fhord right now either. It's not an immediate problem so we'll deal with it after Fhord and Tindera heal.

"What?" he asks, lifting a hand to caress my cheek. "Where'd you go?"

A shriek from across the cavern stills my tongue. Sitting up—Fhord popping up next to me, although the sudden movement must have killed him—I spin in that direction. I'm astounded to find Vulryn and the little green dragon, Khirta, glaring at each other, flames fluttering out of their snouts. Toffer stands between them as some kind of buffer.

"Stop," Toffer demands, his voice quivering as his gaze spins from one dragon to the other. "Please, stop," he adds in a lower voice, a plea sneaking into the words.

Vulryn scowls at Khirta, fire bursting more quickly from her. She rumbles out something that sounds like a warning—harsh and angry—and spins her head to find Dani. When their eyes meet, Dani's face lights up in shock, her eyes flicking wide as her lips tip down and she starts to shake her head. A sense of doom settles on me, driving out every ounce of hope I felt as I sat with my mate. I don't know what in Helheim could have triggered the venom spewing from these dragons, but I know it's going to fuck up our fight against the Dróttning.

"No," Dani whispers, horror clear in that one little word. "That can't be right."

Khirta screeches, her response an odd mixture of fury and despair, and the hopelessness that was trickling through me turns into a wave. Toffer's expression falls even further as he takes the smallest step toward Khirta, lifting his hand to stroke her snout as he tries to comfort and calm her.

"What the fuck's going on?" Fhord demands as he pushes to his feet, pausing for a moment to steady himself before ambling across the cavern.

Dani's still shaking her head, her gaze focused on Vulryn as they talk through whatever just happened. Finally, she spins to look at Fhord. "Tell me about the blue dragon."

"What?" Fhord's just as confused as me.

"A large blue dragon attacked Vulryn while Astarot and Khirta were carrying Tindera away. Khirta knows him. She hates him. Why?"

Fhord's head spins as he turns back toward Khirta. "Was that the dragon who hurt you?"

She squeals again, this one so full of despair, tears well in my eyes. I don't know what that dragon did to her, but it was bad. Poor Khirta's still carrying that trauma.

Fhord sighs, his lips drooping as he watches the little green dragon. "Why?" he asks, his gaze never leaving Khirta as worry and a desperate need to protect the distraught beast consume him.

"Please, Fhord. Just tell me. I need to understand why Khirta's so angry with that dragon." Dani's trying to be reasonable, but she's also walking toward Vulryn, standing with her beast against whatever Fhord will say.

Fhord's gaze spins again but this time he's looking at Vulryn. Now, he's resolved and a little angry. Dani's dragon has developed some interest in the blue dragon so she needs to hear whatever Fhord will say.

"The blue dragon, Ziselær, was given to one of the Dróttning's favorite soldiers, Matthias, about a century ago. Matthias is a cruel male. He has to be, to hold as much power as he does in the Dróttning's twisted little army. It's how he earned such a majestic beast. Ziselær resisted at first. It took a year or more for Matthias to gain the dragon's loyalty and decades to squeeze all hints of compassion and kindness out of him. But once Ziselær gave in, it was over."

"What does that mean?" Dani's words are harsh, her hand digging deeper into Vulryn's feathers.

"A few dragons and riders in Vanatia are lucky enough to bond as the fates intend. Tindera and I are one pair, and I know of two others. I suspect that's because most dragons are destined for elves, so they never even meet the rider the fates chose for them. Maybe for others, the timing isn't right, but I suspect fate brings dragon and rider together whenever it can."

"And for everyone else?" Dani's gaze hasn't left Fhord, her free hand lifting to hold the back of her neck while she nervously bites her bottom lip.

"The Dróttning offers dragons to soldiers who have pleased her—usually by their cruelty, although some earn it by increasing her wealth or power in some way. When Ziselær hatched, we all knew he would be one of the stronger beasts. So the Dróttning chose Matthias for him."

"Why? What did Matthias do?"

"Matthias is a skilled warrior. He fought by the Dróttning's side in the Downfall."

"Was that the battle with the elves? When the Dróttning took over and sent all the elves to prisons?"

Dani knows Vanatian history better than most Vanatians, but that's not surprising. The Dróttning controls information here, and Harald would want his people to know exactly how she rules Vanatia.

"It was," Fhord concurs. "Matthias was a young man then, by our standards, but far more brutal than most of the Dróttning's people. His natural cruelty serves him well in her army."

"How is he still alive?" Dani's eyebrows have pulled together, confusion written all over her face.

"The Dróttning has ways to extend the lives of her soldiers. Nobody knows how. It's one of those secrets she holds very close, like her control over the dragons." Fhord pauses, his gaze finding Khirta again for a moment before shifting back to Dani and Vulryn.

"I think Ziselær probably was a good beast before he gave in to Matthias. But those days are long behind him. When a dragon accepts a rider, he starts to take on that rider's traits and temperament. Ziselær has become very cruel over the years. He's the perfect match for Matthias now."

"And what happened with him and Khirta?"

"Ziselær wanted her, so Matthias convinced Khirta's rider to turn her over to the blue beast for a night. He almost killed her. He's too fucking big for a dragon as small as Khirta. I've heard rumors that he's cruel to the females he mounts, and it's worse when they fight him. It took Khirta a long time to fly again. She still hasn't recovered from the trauma."

"Well, fuck me," Dani croaks, her eyes wide as she stares at Khirta. "This is gonna be such a gods-damned disaster."

"What is?" Fhord's gaze hasn't left Dani and Vulryn.

Dani spins her head. I know her well enough to see how conflicted she is, how much fear and worry are building in her gut. "Vulryn says Ziselær is her drake. She thinks that means Matthias is mine. She wants to go after them, consummate our bonds, and bring them back with us."

Dani forces her lips into a half-smile at the end, but she's the only one in the cavern smiling.

CHAPTER TWO

FHORD

BAT-SHIT CRAZY

"**F**UCK NO."

I can't believe my gods-damned ears. Vulryn and the blue dragon? Fucking mates? And she thinks they're gonna just fly over to the Nest and bat their fucking lashes at those evil fucks, and everything will be rainbows and ponies?

Fuck. No.

I know we owe them. Tindera wouldn't be here if it weren't for Vulryn. But that doesn't mean they get to be bat-shit crazy. And going after Matthias and Ziselær is as bat-shit crazy as it gets.

"Do you think I like this?" Dani demands, her voice rising. "I don't want Vulryn to be mated to a dragon who would hurt Khirta the way he did." She sucks in a deep breath, then another, her fingers scratching behind Vulryn's horn as her gaze flits from one person to another. "Vulryn thinks he belongs to her. That he'll come around and join us. She's going to try, whether I like it or not."

"That bastard will *never* join us. *Never*," I spit at her. I need to be nicer, but I fucking can't. "He's been bound to Matthias too long. Whatever bond may exist between him and Vulryn will pale in comparison. Once a dragon and rider have been connected for a gods-damned century, there's no tearing them apart. He won't choose her."

I can hear Khirta grumbling in the background, an occasional whine breaking through, but I'll deal with her in a minute. Right now, I need to shut down the insanity that's coming out of Dani's mouth.

Vulryn shakes her head, dislodging Dani's fingers that had been embedded beneath her feathers. Pushing Dani to one side, she stalks toward me. Tindera's head pops up as Vulryn closes the distance between us, but I lift a hand. Vulryn won't hurt me. And she's the one I need to convince. Her eyes flash and another burst of flame flickers between us.

"He's gone," I tell her, my voice as calm as I can make it. "In the history of Vanatia, no dragon has ever betrayed a rider it's been bound to for so long. And Matthias will never turn against the Dróttning. He's too committed to her cause. Because he's an evil, manipulative bastard."

Dani barks out a frustrated laugh, striding forward to stand next to her dragon. "You're not going to change her mind," she says. "She's going to try, whether we like it or not."

"Would you expose Dani to Matthias's cruelty?" Sifa asks Vulryn from my side. "The Dróttning chose Matthias for Ziselær. They're not fated to be together, so Dani and Matthias probably aren't fated to be together. But you're just going to force your rider to accept someone cruel like Matthias?"

"She won't force me to do anything," Dani declares, her tone strident. "If Matthias is as bad as you say, I'll reject him. That won't change whatever happens between Vulryn and Ziselær."

"You don't know dragons well," I tell her, "so you don't realize how wrong you are. The fates always mate paired riders with paired dragons—like Sifa and me—because riders are connected emotionally and physically with their dragons. You'll feel what Vulryn feels. If she mates Ziselær, you and Mattias will be pulled together. Vile as he is, you may not be able to resist the draw to fuck him. And that is not a male you want to fuck."

Dani lifts her chin, blue eyes sparking. "I'm stronger than that. If I don't want him, I won't take him."

"Nobody is stronger than that," I snarl. "Maybe once or twice, but eventually, you'll give in."

"You don't know shit about me, Fhord." Dani's hand drops away from Vulryn as her dragon huffs her agreement. "We're not gonna chase them down today. Please just let this go. I don't want to talk about it right now."

Khirta whines again, drawing my gaze to hers. "What's she saying, Toffer?"

"Khirta wants Vulryn to know what the blue dragon did to her."

Vulryn's gaze softens as she spins her head to look at Khirta. I think she likes the little green dragon, though she's loath to admit it.

"Tell all of us," I demand. Vulryn needs to hear this, but we do too.

Toffer's quiet for a minute or more, his expression drooping as he listens to Khirta, who seems to shrink within herself as she shares her story with him. Tears have formed in her massive eyes by the time she's done, and it's all I can do to stop myself from striding over and digging my hands into her feathers to comfort her. Tindera beats me to it, lifting herself carefully to make her way across the cave and nuzzle Khirta.

The cavern is deathly silent, nothing but the sound of a distant drip disturbing the heaviness in the air. Finally, Toffer turns toward Vulryn. "When dragons mate, even when they want to, they hurt each other." His voice is broken but resolved. "That's okay, though. Usually, it's just scratches and bites. But the blue dragon is mean. He wanted to really hurt Khirta."

Khirta snorts to emphasize these words, her gaze holding Vulryn's, who narrows her eyes in response.

"Stop," Dani interjects. "This'll just fuck with everyone's heads. We can talk about it later. Tomorrow, maybe. Give us a minute to sit with it." She approaches Khirta, her pace slow and measured, as if she's waiting for Khirta to send her away. But Khirta wouldn't do that.

"I'm sorry about all this," Dani whispers when she's a few steps away, her hand lifting in a silent plea. "We will listen to you. We will hear you. Just not now, okay?"

Khirta holds Dani's gaze for a moment, then dips her chin, a low rattle filling the cavern around us. She looks up at Vulryn, who's watching her with wide eyes, then nods again and spins to stalk deeper into the cavern.

Fucking hell. This shitshow just turned into a gods-damned nightmare. How in the fuck could Vulryn be mated to Ziselær? The gods must have engineered this crap because they could not have chosen a more fucked-up dragon and rider to inject into this rebellion. Fucking Ziselær and Matthias. *Bastards, both of them.*

But we don't have time to dwell on this shit. *Can you move?* My eyes lift to find my dragon as I cast my question toward her.

Yes. Her answer is layered, as it always is. She can, but it will be at least a day, maybe two, before she'll be able to fly.

We should go north, find the field with the fat goats. Her lips tip up into a smile that sets my soul free. I thought I'd never see her happy again. *We both need a good bath. It'll help everyone.* I know the Dróttning isn't anywhere near us, but Tindera and I still talk in code when I don't speak my thoughts out loud. We can't risk the Dróttning hearing us somehow, and after so long together, Tindera always knows exactly what I mean.

North, she responds, before turning toward Astarot, her smile still lighting up her expression. She's such a majestic dragon. The fates truly blessed me when they gave us to each other.

"To the water?" Sifa asks as she steps toward me and reaches for my hand, linking her fingers with mine. "Astarot's excited to go there. He and Tindera have waited a long time to fly together. But are you sure we can make it? The Dróttning will be throwing everything she has at finding us."

"Toffer can lead us north through the caves for the next day or two until Tindera's ready to fly. It'll be hard but worth the trip."

"So fucking hard," Sifa agrees. "You're both up to it? You still look pretty fucked up, Fhord." She lifts her hand to caress my cheek, dark eyes soft and full of light.

"We can do it," I assure her, laying my hand on hers. "And once we're there, it'll be worth it." My gaze finds Joralf and Fróðr leaning against a nearby wall. "We need to go there anyway, start to figure out if the water is one of the keys to the Dróttning's control."

"I still can't believe it would be so simple. Plus, Astarot's convinced it's something the dragons eat, maybe along with the water, but he thinks the food is critical. He craves something so badly, he thinks it's making him weak, but he's not sure what it is. He's been in magic water a few times since we freed him and that hasn't touched the cravings."

"Magic water?" I can't hold back the smirk. "Is that how it felt when I fucked you in it?"

Sifa's eyes twinkle as she slowly turns toward me, a grin pulling out the dimples in her cheeks that I don't see nearly enough. "Enchanted? Holy? Fan-fucking-tastic? What should we call it?"

"Fan-fucking-tastic is closest," I muse, my fingers squeezing hers as I try to stop myself for reaching for her ass, "but a bit unwieldy. Maybe gods-level? Transcendent? Other-worldly? I'd be good with any of those."

Sifa's free hand rises to rest on my cheek as she draws me a bit closer. "And feed that ego even more? I think not. We'll go with magic."

"My ego—and the rest of me—knows exactly how you feel about me taking you in that water," I rumble, letting my savage rise to the surface. "How many times I made you come. How ready you were when I plunged inside you. And I can't wait to feel you quiver under my touch again."

"We'll have to send everyone away. Because otherwise, they'll all hear it when I scream out your name."

"Once Tindera and I are healed, she'll take us to a pond we found. It's secluded. Nobody will know how loud you get when I nibble on that sweet little clit, my fingers deep inside you."

Sifa sucks in a deep breath, her gaze never leaving mine. "Are you strong enough to travel today? Now?" she purrs, one hand dropping to my chest.

"So fucking dangerous," I murmur, my tongue reaching out to taste her ear as I release a heavy sigh. "We'd be leaving even if I wasn't ready," I add, my cock almost painfully hard. I can't fuck this gorgeous little elf in front of me until my wounds are closed, and I *need* to be inside her. Lifting my head, I turn toward Tindera. *Today*, I tell her.

She blinks her large eyes, as eager as I am to go. *Today*, she agrees.

"Let's go talk to Fróðr and Toffer." Turning, I tug Sifa toward the other side of the cave, growing more anxious by the second. "We're leaving today," I announce as I plant myself in front of the rest of the group. "We'll go north as far as we can before exiting the caves, then take to the air as soon as Tindera's able to fly. How far can we get before we'll be forced to move to the surface?"

I'm met with silence for a moment, a few jaws hanging open as they gawk at the gaping wounds still littering my body.

"Are you sure you're ready, Fhord?" Joralf's voice is calm and measured—the tone of a schoolmaster trying to reason with a difficult child. "Perhaps we should wait a day or two?"

"Tindera and I know what we can do. We'll leave today, heading to an area that will help us heal." I firm my jaw, throwing my shoulders back. "I ask again. How far north can we go in the caves?"

Fróðr stands, his stance as relaxed as he can muster as he falls into the role of the peacemaker in a bureaucracy that eats all the nice people alive. I still have no idea how he survived it. "Where are we heading, Fhord?"

"Nearly to the barrier," I tell him, my tone still firm. "Roughly between the northern Nest and the ocean."

"So, four, maybe five days by foot, depending on where the caves take us and how many soldiers we encounter when we're forced to move to the land."

"Tindera will be able to fly tomorrow or the next day. The dragons will carry us once we're out of the caves, as long as we can get far enough away from the southern dragons."

I can tell Fróðr's struggling to hold his tongue, but I don't care. This isn't their decision. "I know what my dragon and I can do. We're leaving now. Don't make me ask again."

Fróðr drops his chin, a palm lifting toward Toffer.

"One day of walking fast. Sun and sky summon." Toffer's gaze holds mine for a moment before spinning toward Sifa, as if seeking her approval. She nods and smiles, her eyes soft.

"We'll stop and rest there," I suggest, "then travel at night while we're above ground."

"Let's go, then," Joralf says, lifting himself to stand next to his mate.

The group moves as one, packing up bedrolls and supplies as they chat among themselves. Satisfied that nobody is going to behave like a mother hen, I tug Sifa back to our bed.

"Are you sure about this?" She's worried and I get it. I must look like shit.

"The sooner we get to the water the better off we'll be, and we will make it." I pause, lifting my hand to caress her cheek because I can't stop myself from touching her. "And I want to get as far away from the Nest as quickly as we can. We're still exposed here. If the Dróttning passed over this area, she might sense me, despite how deep we are. We'd never lose her once she started to track us."

"That makes sense. I was worried the horny savage was coming out and leading you to questionable decisions."

"Oh, that's true too. This is absolutely driven by my need to be inside you. But there's also a good reason for it."

She laughs, leans forward to brush her lips against mine, and then pushes me toward Tindera. "Go. Talk to your dragon while I gather our things. You're not allowed to do anything except walk or ride until we get to the water."

A broad grin erupts on my face as I saunter over to Tindera, who puffs out a laugh. But I know she feels the same about Astarot. They're going to fly together. Finally.

The trip north is much easier than it should be. Which scares the fuck out of me.

We leave the cavern within a day, as Toffer said we would. And then we travel without encountering a single soldier. I know the Dróttning is searching for us—she will never let me go, especially after we humiliated her in our escape—and it makes no sense for our trip to be so smooth. But it is.

We end up walking the next two days because Tindera isn't ready to fly yet. She swears she's strong enough, but I can feel her pain. She'd suffer too much if she used her wings now. But we're moving faster than any of us had expected. By the end of our second night of walking—just as the sun is lifting over the trees in front of us—she's ready to fly. We throw ourselves on the dragons, heavy but manageable for them, and they lift into the sky.

It takes another day in the air, and it's a brutal day for my poor dragon. By the time we catch our first glimpse of the field and river that could change everything, she's exhausted but trying her damnedest to hide it from me. I can feel the edges of her misery—the bone-draining fatigue of her enormous heart, the numbing ache in her mangled wings—because she's too tired to fully shield her pain.

She's always done everything she can to protect me, hiding the trauma she suffers because of my choices, and it breaks my gods-damned heart.

But we're here. It's breathtaking, shimmering with colors so vibrant and spry, I wonder if trees and flowers come to life overnight to dance in the grasses and swim in the water. With greens and blues and reds and yellows and purples so rich and luxurious it seems they must have been gifts to this world from benevolent gods, I forget for a moment what bastards the gods really are.

And then I turn to see my little rabbit's brown eyes sparkling in the sun's warm light, and I'm reminded that those same gods are fucking with our lives, trying to keep Sifa and me apart. We won't let them. We will destroy the Dróttning and live without fear of her vengeance, or we'll die trying.

"Ready?" she asks, her voice rich with anticipation.

"I have never been so fucking ready for anything," I respond with a short laugh as Tindera huffs by my side. *I'm not holding you back*, I respond, spinning my head to look at her. *Go.*

Drake. She wants to enter the water with him, but he needs help removing the supplies he's carrying.

Sifa's eyes grow distant at the same time, and she nods as he drops to the field below, landing with a gentle thud. We all scramble down and start pulling the packs with us. Within a few minutes, he's free and shaking his feathers, the red and black reflecting the sunlight to cast rainbows all around him. I feel Tindera's pride in her drake as she snorts and then leads him to the river.

"He's happier than I've ever felt him."

"Tindera too. They've waited too long for this."

"We've all waited too long. Let's go bathe you, Fhord, and then we'll find the pool you mentioned and rediscover each other."

Her voice is sultry and seductive and my cock responds like it always does. I'm bulging my pants within seconds, glancing down as Sifa's gaze follows mine. "So predictable," she whispers, winking as she turns to saunter toward the river.

I can only follow, thanking the gods, bastards that they are, for the sexy ass swaying in front of me.

Dropping into the river is unlike anything I've felt in a very long time. I'm still covered in open wounds, angry reminders of the Dróttning's wrath. As soon as the water hits a sore, it starts to tingle, the pain shifting to something akin to a tickle immediately. Laughs and giggles—actual gods-damned giggles—bubble out of me like I'm a fucking teenager.

My cock, already hard as a rock, turns into a gods-damned stone. I've got no choice but to wrap my hand around it and relieve some of the pressure that's been building for days. I don't even look around to see who might be watching because

I don't give one single fuck about that. Release is almost immediate, and I can't hold back the groan as I turn to find Sifa staring at me—well, staring at one slightly more relaxed part of me—with bright eyes and a bewitching smile.

When her gaze tracks up my chest and then lands on my face, my breath catches in my throat. She's always stunning, but in this water, surrounded by the most beautiful field anywhere in Vanatia, she is devastating. And my cock's ready to go again.

"You're healed," she whispers. "Just like that."

"Just like that." Reaching for her hand, I place it on my bare chest, every bit of ink stripped away by one carver or another. "A blank canvas, ready to mark our story in my flesh."

"I'll miss your tattoos," Sifa murmurs, skimming her fingers lightly over my fresh skin.

"I won't," I tell her, lifting her hand toward my lips to kiss each of her knuckles. "Everything they sliced off grew out of my allegiance to the Dróttning—most to celebrate scars she'd given me, others to proclaim my commitment to her fucked-up cause. I'm a new male because of you, rabbit. Let's write a new story—a gods-damned happy story—in place of that bullshit." I tug her a bit closer and give her a gentle kiss, letting my engorged cock show her what's on my mind. "After I fuck you," I add. "Because I need to be inside you right now."

"So it's time?"

"Fuck, yes, it's time."

Astarot and Tindera are beside us almost before we can ask, stretching out their wings so we can climb up as soon as we throw a few clothes on. Too gods-damned many of my dragon's feathers are still missing, but we expected that. They'll grow back, and she doesn't need them to fly. I can feel her excitement, which filters into me like a warm caress, savoring this moment in time before we fully claim our mates. It's gonna be a fan-fucking-tastic day.

Astarot takes off first. His wings stretch out as he runs a few steps to throw himself into the air, Tindera on his heels. Her joy at finally flying with her drake fills me, heightening all my senses.

And we haven't even gotten to the good part yet.

Within a few minutes, we're dropping toward the secluded valley Tindera and I discovered a few years ago. It has the same water as the river, but it's private, only accessible by other dragon riders. Sifa's screams will be mine alone. Exactly as they should be.

The dragons dump us in the small field and then launch again, flying in a few seconds. I watch them for a moment as they spin around each other, both knowing instinctively the mating dance that precedes their first joining, and then turn my eyes away. We'll *feel* the edges of their coupling—as they'll feel ours—but they won't want us to see them too. This time is for them alone.

Sifa's watching me, her eyes sultry, when I turn to her. "Take off your clothes," I rasp out, forcing my hands to rest at my sides. I want to see her bare herself to me.

And she does. She starts with her top, lifting it over her head, leaving her standing in nothing but the strap she wears around her chest, her dark, damp skin glowing in the soft morning light. I almost give in and strip her down myself but grasp my restraint just in time. My savage needs to watch her do this as much as I do.

The strap falls next, releasing the tits I've been fantasizing about for the past two weeks. They're perfect, and I can't wait to bury my face in them. Sifa gives me the sexiest smile I've ever seen as she spins—because she knows her ass is my favorite part of her sexy body—and dips her thumbs into her pants. Oh, so slowly, she shimmies as she tugs them down her long legs and then kicks them off, leaving nothing but the skimpy underwear she must have picked just for me.

Turning again, she glances down, her gaze asking whether the underwear should go too. I give my chin a sharp dip, speechless as I marvel at the show she's giving me. This time she stays put, her gaze holding mine—as long as it can—as her fingers pull down that last scrap of fabric. And I let my eyes go where they will, dropping to stare at her full breasts, then her flat, firm stomach, and the legs that go on for miles.

"Now undress me," I breathe, anxious to feel her hands on my newly-formed skin—every little bit of it.

She saunters over, a wicked grin on her face, to tuck one finger under my chin, lifting my gaze to hers. "Eyes up here," she purrs as her hands start to tug at the bottom of my shirt. I stand motionless, watching her, while she manipulates my body to slowly pull off every piece of clothing. A sigh emerges from my gut when she drops to her knees, smiles, and focuses on the cock that's been calling to her since she released me from the rack.

"It's definitely bigger," she whispers, her tongue reaching out to lick the tip and taste the precum that's waiting there for her. Her smile grows wider at my groan. She lifts one hand to wrap it around my base, moving my cock just enough to give her easy access to the large vein running along the bottom. And then her tongue stretches out again, and she runs it up and down my length, drawing shivers from me as her light touch sets off little flares.

When she reaches the tip and wraps her lips around it, taking me deep enough to feel the back of her throat, I almost come undone. The growl that rumbles out of me shakes the nearby trees, a hint of my power breaking free to echo around us. I am fire, an inferno, a blaze that will never end, and she is the match. Nothing could ever be this good. I come down her throat in hot spurts, faster than I have in centuries.

And we're just getting started. Sifa looks up at me again, licks her lips, and then rises, pressing herself against me so I feel every part of her. Drawing my lips to hers, she opens to me, sucking my tongue for a moment and then exploring my mouth with hers. I've never felt so alive, as the mating bond acts like a drum, bouncing between us with each feeling building on the other.

"Now's when things really get fun," Sifa purrs when she pulls away, taking my hand and leading me into the water.

And she's so fucking right. The sensations that vibrate through me when we submerge ourselves take my breath away, but I don't need air any more. I will breathe in my little rabbit. She'll sustain me.

"Now do I get to touch you?" I demand, unable to keep the *need* out of my voice.

"I am all yours," she tells me, lifting my hands to rest them on her tits.

I drop to suck one nipple into my mouth, and then another, moaning at the taste of Sifa on my tongue. And then I reach for her, my thumb rubbing over her clit as two fingers plunge inside. Pulling them out, I lick them, one after the other, savoring her flavor. So fucking delicious.

"I *want* to draw this out," I tell her as my fingers reach for her again, making sure she's ready for me. Because this will not be a slow, leisurely fuck. We'll go slow next time, or maybe the time after that. Right now, I'm going to take her hard and fast. "But I want to fuck you even more."

"Fuck me, Fhord. I. Am. Yours."

That's exactly what I do. Spinning her around, I press her chest down, firming the water beneath her to hold her in place. And then I drive my cock into her. I'm not gentle but neither of us wants gentle right now. We need to *feel* each other. My savage needs to *own* her. The mating bond that's been waiting for years to ripen and solidify needs to *possess* us.

I've never enjoyed a fuck so much. Just being with my little rabbit after so much time—our mating bond letting us experience each other's pleasure—would be the best sex in my long life. The water takes our pleasure and magnifies it, every wave of ecstasy ten times better.

The dragons, though. They are the gods-damned cherry on top. Because I can feel Tindera's excitement, her fervor and euphoria, almost as deeply as I feel my own. As they fly above us, finally connecting in a way they've been denied for too long, the hurricanes of pleasure washing through them add to our own. I am a boat, rocking in a sea of ecstasy, and I don't ever want to return to shore.

When I come, the earth around us shakes because for that moment in time, I don't have one little bit of control over myself. Sifa coming on my cock, her body trembling beneath mine, are the only things my mind can grasp. My hips roll with hers as I draw out our pleasure, until I collapse on her back, breathing in her scent.

"Fuck. Me." She's still panting, her tight cunt wrapped around a cock that's hard again already.

"Oh, I will," I tell her, pulling out just a bit to see if a slow, leisurely fuck could be nearly as good. "We're just getting started."

CHAPTER THREE

DANI

MAJESTIC BITCH

I HATE THE BLUE dragon already. Ziselær. And his evil fuck of a rider, Matthias.

I'm finally floating in the river we've been traveling to and it's every bit as magical as the pond where we trapped Vulryn in Njordheim. All my aches and pains are gone. My body is vibrating with life. I feel good.

But my gods-damned dragon is bombarding me with images of the blue dragon. She's become obsessed with him and his tall, ferocious rider. And handsome. I can't deny Matthias is fucking gorgeous. I've always loved dangerous men, and he looks as perilous as they come.

I can't relax with the visions Vulryn keeps throwing at me, trying to convince me to abandon Fhord and Sifa and chase down her mate.

She's so gods-damned stubborn.

He won't betray the Dróttning for us, I remind my dragon as I stand and twist my head to stare at her. *How many times do I need to tell you that? It's not going to happen.*

He will or he won't. I do not know what will be. But we will go to him and give him the chance to earn a place at our side. We owe it to our drake. And his rider.

We don't owe them, I grunt back, my voice a little too full of scorn. *Mates are a chance of fate. They don't mean anything.* I should know this better than anyone, because if I'm right about my mate, he'll never be mine and I'm pretty sure I don't want him anyway.

Fate made you mine. Does that mean anything?

She's wicked smart. And she knows it. *It means everything.*

So, we shall go to him. We shall convince him to join us. My drake shall fight by our side. If he refuses, then we shall kill him. The wyrm will have one less dragon.

I shake my head and snort out a frustrated sigh. *I don't want to talk about this right now. Let me just enjoy the water. Please.*

She dips her chin, her lips tipping in the victory she knows is coming her way. *Bathe. I will wait.*

Frustrating beast.

I drop back in, floating as I force myself to relax, starting with my toes and working my way up. I don't want to talk about Ziselær, but it doesn't stop me from thinking about Matthias. Vulryn has a memory that can capture exact images, and she keeps showing me a picture of Ziselær's rider. She's so devious.

He's ridiculously sexy—much taller than me with wide shoulders and narrow hips. His blonde hair is cut short, exposing the swirls and swooshes of the tattoos that start on his scalp and cover his neck, and probably the rest of him. Blue eyes sparked in anger when Vulryn attacked them, and since that's the only image I have of him, I can't imagine him any other way. With sharp, angular bones and a thin nose, he looks perpetually intense and driven.

I know he's evil and I want to stay away from him, but I still can appreciate the perfection that is Matthias. He's almost as impressive as Mikkael.

Not that I'll ever have either of them. Or would want one even if I could. Because I know Mikkael is an asshole, and Matthias sounds even worse. I'm better off alone. Just me and my dragon.

If she can forget about the stupid blue beast.

When Astarot and Tindera appear overhead, racing toward us like they're driven, I know something's wrong. I don't know what yet, but I'm pretty sure we're about to get out of here. Just when I was starting to relax.

They throw themselves down, wings extending as Fhord and Sifa almost run from their backs, their heads spinning as they search for someone.

They seek the land elf, Vulryn tells me. *We are leaving.*

Why do they want Fróðr? What happened that has them so worried?

The shaking of the trees before you entered the water was our male's magic. He remains … weak, she adds, as if making an excuse for him. *He fears the wyrm sensed it and does not want to risk exposing this place to her. It is to be our sanctuary.* A smirk emerges as I realize what must have led Fhord to lose control of his powers. He's a horny bastard.

My grin drops away just as fast, though, because I really don't want to leave. This river is helping to heal a part of me that broke when we left Njordheim and everything I've ever known behind. I've spent my entire life in the North, but I'm starting to wonder if I belong here in Vanatia. Whether I'll find the happiness here I never found there. That is, if we can destroy the Dróttning and end her cruel reign.

Sighing, I wade to the shore, grab my towel and stalk over to my packs. I may have no choice about going but that doesn't mean I have to like it. When I've dried off and pulled on some clothes, I track down Sifa, who's strapping a few packs to Astarot.

"Where to now?"

She looks up with a smile. "You sound as disappointed as I feel. This is a special place."

"I shouldn't be surprised," I sigh. "I suspect we'll be on the run until we kill the Dróttning. If we ever can kill that wyrm."

Sifa barks out a cynical laugh. "I suspect you're right." She glances toward Fhord, who's striding toward us, then back at me. "Joralf and Fróðr know of a place. The rebels claimed an island years ago. One of the hidden elves, someone even Joralf and Fróðr have never met, possesses magic that helps hide it. They promise we'll be able to rest there—let Tindera fully recuperate—while we plan our next moves."

"I go where you go," I tell him with a shrug. "Just point us in the right direction, and we'll follow you."

"We'll fly the whole way," Fhord says as he approaches us. I can't stop staring. He said the water would heal them but holy fuck. He's as good as new. "No delays. I want to be out of this valley within fifteen minutes."

"Does Tindera look as good as you?"

Fhord's eyebrows slam together as his gaze finds mine. "What?"

"You don't have a single mark on you. Other than your missing tattoos, it's like you were never hurt. It's gods-damned amazing."

Fhord's smile could light up a room. He shares it with Sifa all the time but rarely with others. Almost never with me. It's nice to see this side of him. "Fuck, yes, it is," he says. "But we don't have time for this. If I've fucked up and let the Dróttning know I'm in the North, we need to be far away from here when she gets close. I can't risk exposing this spot to her."

I respond with a sharp nod. "What do you need?"

"Will Vulryn take riders again?"

I turn toward my dragon, who's listening in on our conversation. She carried others here because Tindera couldn't and we had no choice, but she didn't like it. She's still annoyed that Vanatian dragons are expected to ferry people about like horses. She grunts out her disdain at the suggestion but dips her chin anyway.

I will carry you and two others until we reach this place, she tells me with a huff. *Tell our male he should not ask again. I will allow it this time because we must reach safety to find others who will help.*

She's such an uppity bitch, but gods, do I love her. I can't hold back the smile as I look at Fhord. "She agrees, just this once. She'll take two, in addition to me."

Fhord inclines his head toward Vulryn. "My thanks," he tells her. His gaze finds mine as he snaps out, "Be ready," before spinning on his heel and striding toward Khirta.

"Alrighty, then," I mutter to myself as I start to stuff things into a bag. Within ten minutes, our packs are strapped to Vulryn, and I'm watching the others clear this space, removing any hint we were here. Fróðr knows what he's doing. He's proven to be a valuable ally.

I'm relieved, for reasons I don't take time to consider, when Joralf and Fróðr walk toward us. I like the others well enough, but I'm glad the elves are riding with me. Torsten and Liv stand with Sifa next to Astarot; Tindera's taking Fhord, Leif, Toffer and the cat, and Khirta will carry Frida, Jorunn and Astrid. It's a lot for the little dragon, but probably the lightest load she could take.

"Fhord says we should fly high," Joralf tells me. "He hopes we'll sense another dragon early enough to hide, but he's worried about patrols on the ground seeing us from a distance."

Vulryn grumbles her assent, extending a wing for us to mount her. "How shall I hold you?" Joralf asks as he positions himself behind me.

"Wrap your arms around me," I tell him as I spin around and give him a quick wink. "I promise I won't bite ... unless you want me to."

His responding laugh lightens my soul. He's been through terrible torture, but it somehow hasn't darkened him. Maybe that's why I'm glad he and Fróðr fly with us. I need some of his lightness in my life. "Ah, the things I sacrifice for my mate," he sighs, his hand reaching for Fróðr's to give it a small squeeze. "It's a generous offer, but I must decline."

"Perhaps in another life." I lift my arms as he settles in behind me and watch for Fhord's signal.

When Tindera launches herself, Vulryn and the others do the same, shooting through the clouds as Joralf and Fróðr suck in deep breaths, almost in unison. And then they start to giggle.

"Is this your first dragon ride?" I shout back at them, turning to share in their joy. They both nod, exuberant bobs of their heads like children too excited to speak. "I'll ask Vulryn to make it special," I say, before looking around to confirm we're clear of the others. *Can you do some spins for our guests?*

She glances back, her lips tipping up. *Fun or frightening?*

Why would you want to frighten our friends? I demand.

Perhaps they deserve it.

These are good elves. They don't deserve it.

Vulryn snorts, her view of who deserves to be frightened a bit different than mine. But she dips her chin as I turn back to Joralf. "Hold on," I tell him as I tighten my grip on Vulryn.

My dragon doesn't waste a bit of time. Tucking her wings, she drops into a tight spiral, spinning us around like the twisters that sometimes lift homes and even people into the sky, dropping them vikus away. Joralf is tense for a moment, his arms around my waist digging into my ribs, but then his laugh fills my ears and he relaxes just enough to let me breathe.

I can't hold back my own laugh, anticipating Vulryn's moves as she opens the connection between us, leaning left or right to signal to the elves what to expect. We soar through the air, Vulryn twisting and turning as the others give her space, Joralf and Fróðr both laughing and giggling the whole time.

I feel it when her mood changes. She stiffens and spreads out her wings, her head spinning to glance at Tindera and then search the skies around us.

One of the wyrm's dragons approaches, she tells me in the voice I know too well. The carefree dragon who emerges rarely is gone. This is the predator who will kill anyone that threatens her or those she has claimed.

Are the other dragons concerned?

This one is a threat but also a friend. They do not wish to attack. We will take him down.

If they don't want to attack, they can't want you to.

They are weak. They treat their Thunder like allies. They all are enemies until they reject the wyrm. She pauses, her tone becoming more strident with her next words. *We will take him down.*

I don't try to talk her out of it. I know her well enough to realize it won't work. "One of the Dróttning's dragons chases us," I yell at Joralf and Fróðr. "Vulryn's going to attack. Hold on and duck if you have to."

I see the gulp that slides down Fróðr's throat. Joralf, though, is fearless. He's been through too much to be afraid of something like this.

Vulryn's abrupt spin takes even me by surprise. I'm thrown to the side when she makes a sudden shift to the left and down, barely holding on as Joralf's arms around me tighten and then soften at my gasp of pain. We've only flown for a few seconds when I see an enormous brown beast below us, almost invisible against the dark ground we've been flying over for the last thirty minutes.

He's huge, I breathe at Vulryn.

He is no threat to us, she responds, offense in every word. *We will take him down.*

She's spun around enough to put the sun at our back as we descend, hiding us as long as possible. We're two or three dragon's-lengths away from the other beast when he realizes he's being stalked. Twisting, his wings jerk out and flap three or four times as he tries to put us beneath him. I can hear Vulryn's laugh bouncing through our bond at his foolishness.

Hold, she tells me as she does the same, throwing everything she has into staying above him. Even carrying three times the weight as the brown dragon, she gives him no ground.

The rider looks up and I can almost hear the snarl I see ripple across her lips. Before I can respond with my own growl, Vulryn tucks her wings and dives, flaring them almost immediately as she pulls up and her claws aim for the rider. She's as shocked as I am, which makes her an easy target. With the light hold on her mount that gives a rider the most flexibility to move with a dragon, she's got no defense.

Vulryn snatches her arms and pivots in the air. As the other dragon spins to follow, my beast races away—Fhord's "No!" howling in the background—and then she lets go. We're a viku or more in the air. The brown dragon's rider is dead if her beast can't reach her.

And I'm so fucking proud of my dragon, majestic bitch that she is. My chest balloons as I savor the knowledge that I ride the most lethal dragon in this world. Not even Fhord's roar as Astarot chases us down is going to disturb this mood.

Extra goats for you when we get there, I purr, not bothering to hide the smile in my voice.

Vulryn huffs. *I did what must be done. I will be strong when they are weak.*

No wonder I love you so much.

I feel her pleasure at my words. *The fates chose well for us*, she responds after a moment, her tone holding a hint of the pride in mine.

We've flown a couple of minutes when I realize the brown dragon has returned, shooting from a cloud just above us in search of vengeance. I turn as the beast's claws stretch toward us. Joralf wails in pain when the nails scrape down his back, separating the elves as the dragon tightens his hold around Fróðr. For a few seconds, I can't move. I can't even breathe, that enormous bastard carrying away Fróðr the only thing I can see. A chill rolls down my back as I wonder what in the fuck we've done, exposing Fróðr to this monster's fury.

"No ... Vulryn ... help," Joralf pleads, wrenching me from my stupor. His voice is hollow, eyes wide as he spins in his seat. He's trembling as he scrambles away—almost like he plans to jump after his mate—and I fling a hand back, grabbing his wrist just before Vulryn pivots and throws herself at the shit-colored beast.

"We will not let that dragon have Fróðr," I screech at him. "Don't make this harder for Vulryn. Wrap your arms around me. Do not let go."

He holds my gaze for a moment, his eyes more haunted than I would have thought possible for someone who's endured so much, then dips his chin and clings to me.

Just in time. Vulryn is nearly on top of the brown dragon, who's still carrying Fróðr. The shit beast spins his head to spit flames at my dragon. He mirrors Vulryn's glare for a moment and then drops Fróðr. My stomach plummets into my feet as quickly as Fróðr plummets to the ground.

Vulryn's wings tuck in tighter than I've ever seen them, and she starts spiraling toward Fróðr, who's tumbling through the air so erratically, I wonder if he's already gone. "Please, please don't let him be dead," I mutter under my breath, although I have no idea who I'm asking. The gods abandoned me long ago and the fates already have decided whether Fróðr will live or die.

Vulryn splays her wings as we overtake him, her claws reaching for the elf flopping through the air. And then more gently than should have been possible, she wraps them around him, bringing his twisting to an abrupt stop.

Hold, she tells me, tucking her wings once more as she dives toward the ground. Above us somewhere, I hear angry bellows ringing through the air. I look up just in time to see Astarot, Tindera and Khirta digging their claws into the dragon they once called their friend.

I can't bring myself to pity them. The lines are drawn. The sooner they realize that, the better off we'll all be. The Dróttning's dragons stand with us or against us. There is no middle ground.

I watch as Tindera and Khirta seize the brown dragon's wings, splaying them out and suspending him in midair, his throat and belly exposed to Astarot. Sifa's dragon wastes no time. His beak wraps around the enemy's throat, clamping down and yanking. He nearly decapitates him, leaving shreds of skin and fur to hold the head and body together. When his captors let go, he plunges away.

Hold, Vulryn barks out one more time. I twist my head just in time to see the ground flying toward us. I'm convinced she's going to throw Fróðr but somehow, she flings her wings out in time to stop with Fróðr only inches above the dirt. Setting him down gently, she backs up a few feet, lands and extends her wings for Joralf and me to stumble down.

I watch, my heart in my throat, as I pray to gods I abandoned long ago that Fróðr is still alive.

CHAPTER FOUR

SIFA

YOU HAD NO CHOICE

ASTAROT FALLS TO THE ground faster than he ever has before, desperate to get the medical supplies we're carrying to Fróðr.

What the fuck happened? I demand, my tone harsher than I intend. It's not Astarot's fault. If anything, it's Vulryn's, but I can't blame her either. The brown dragon chased us. He would have called others and followed us until we were surrounded.

Revenge, Astarot tells me, a warble in his voice I rarely hear. Vulryn took Orme's rider and the brown dragon couldn't reach her in time, so Orme took one of Vulryn's riders. Vulryn was faster and caught Fróðr before he could hit the ground.

Are you okay? I ask, heartbroken at the despair billowing out of my dragon.

Friend. He and Orme were nearly the same age and they've known each other a long time. Orme's rider was chosen for him by the Dróttning, and she was a cruel woman, but Orme had tried to fight the evil that consumes too many dragons given to undeserving riders.

You had no choice.

Astarot doesn't respond, but he knows it's true. Once Orme's rider was killed, he became too much of a threat. Even if he had no great love for his rider, they still were connected. He'd never have let us rest.

When he lands, I grapple with the cords behind me, tearing out our supplies and falling to the ground to run the short distance to Fróðr. I almost cry in relief when I see his chest slowly rising. It's shredded, though, nearly as bad as Joralf's back. Dragons know how to carry beings in their claws without causing harm, but Orme wanted to hurt Vulryn's riders.

"He can't die," Joralf whispers, ignoring the gashes across his own back as he lifts haunted eyes to watch me drop next to Fróðr. His words are so low, I barely hear them, as if he's afraid he'll harm his mate if he speaks any louder. I reach for one of his trembling hands, which stills for a moment under my touch. He drops his gaze toward the bandages, his body completely motionless now except a single tear running down his cheek. "I've only just got him back," he croaks at last.

"We won't let him die," I assure him, forcing every bit of confidence I can muster into my words. Fear for Fróðr fills my gut—bursts of despair burning my throat as they threaten to erupt—but I force them all down. I can't let this elf see my doubt. Fróðr needs his mate's faith if he's to have any hope of surviving the gruesome injury he's suffered.

Joralf nods once then turns to his mate, gesturing with a hand that's again shaking for Torsten to lift Fróðr so he can wrap his chest wounds.

"Can I enter his mind?" I ask, holding my voice as steady as I can.

"Will it help?" Joralf doesn't try to hide the wobble in his words.

"I think so. If I can find a memory of his pain before he passed out, I may better understand his injuries."

"Do it," Joralf whispers, his head dropping so low, I can't see his face. I can sense the waves of despair rippling from him, his heart pounding under the weight of a fear so thick it feels like he'll never be able to escape it.

I shake away the dizziness that threatens to drag me under along with Joralf, sitting back on my heels so I can pull Fróðr's pant leg from his boots and touch his skin. Closing my eyes, I focus my psyche on Fróðr's sleeping thoughts. This is always strange because I sometimes have to grapple with dreams, but thankfully—or not—his mind is still.

It only takes a few seconds to find it. When the dragon reached for Fróðr, one of his claws clipped his scalp. Agony rippled through him for a split second as his head flung forward and then everything went blank.

My eyes fly open. "He got a head injury. Is there blood?"

Torsten's gaze tracks down. "I don't see any. Jorunn, come look while I hold him." He glances up, finding Fhord as he gently rolls Fróðr and shifts out of Jorunn's way. "The elf hurt his head. He may not be able to heal on his own, and we probably shouldn't move him far. How long can we stay here?"

"Not long," Fhord mutters, looking up and spinning as he searches around us. "If the Dróttning's close enough, Orme could have sent a message to her. We need to find cover."

"I know a place," Leif says, his voice low. "The barn," he adds as he looks up at Fhord. "It should be safe until he's well enough to travel."

"Can you get there without me?" Fhord's gathering a few things from his pack as he asks this, tucking them into pockets and sheaths.

"We can," Leif responds. "Why?"

"I've used a medic who lives near here. If he's home, he could help."

"Is it worth the trip?" Leif's worried. He and Fhord seem to know this area well, so his fear infects me, a buzz in my gut that makes me want to keep Fhord by my side.

"Will he survive without help?" Fhord demands, his gaze finding mine.

And I can only tell the truth, despite my *need* to hold my mate close. "I don't know. It's bad. Head wounds are the worst for elves because they suppress our ability to heal. If the wrong area is damaged, we've no more magic than humans."

Fhord responds with a sharp nod. "Then it's worth it." He turns to his dragon, who's watching him with solemn eyes. "I need to go on foot. There are too many people between here and there who could see you fly. I'll meet you at the barn."

He doesn't wait for an answer, striding over to kiss me, hard, before turning to start running into the trees. The buzz in my stomach turns into a rock as I watch him go.

Fuck, I hate this.

But I can't focus on Fhord. We don't have time to waste, so we quickly prepare a stretcher for Fróðr, which hangs between Khirta and Vulryn as it did with Fhord. They've proven they can work together, and Fróðr needs that kind of care. Within an hour, we're pulling bushes and shrubs away from the massive door leading to a large barn, then gathering inside while Leif goes back out to hide the footsteps leading here.

And we wait. Fróðr still hasn't woken, but we don't expect him to. Fhord's medic may be his only hope. And it's taking a long gods-damned time for them to get here.

I spend the entire time pacing—Astarot grumbling in my ear as he watches me—because every time I try to sit down, it feels like bugs are trying to escape from beneath my skin. I keep seeing images of Fhord when we carried him from the Nest, more blood and gore than skin. It would kill him to be captured again. It would kill all of us.

Finally, hours after he went after the medic, we hear the pounding of a horse galloping toward us. I stretch out my mind, sucking in a deep breath when my thoughts graze Fhord's.

"He's here," I announce as I stride toward the door, flinging it open. As soon as they're inside, Leif heads out to hide their tracks, while Fhord and a male I've never seen before drop from the horse and rush toward the others.

We watch in silence as the male crouches down next to Fróðr, placing two fingers on each of his temples and closing his eyes. The magic that flows out of him is unlike anything I've felt before, calm and soothing, as if the elf's injury will somehow heal itself in the warm embrace of this male's power. But I soon realize that's exactly what it's doing. This male reaches the healing capacity within each elf to boost it. Fróðr has the ability to heal that his head wound had taken from him.

It doesn't take long. Within a few minutes, Fróðr's expression changes, life flowing back into his cheeks. Joy and relief erupt in Joralf's eyes, which grow bright as a hand with just a hint of a tremble lifts to cover his mouth. He looks at Fhord and something between them shifts, as if a wall collapsed in this barn. "I am in your debt."

"We are allies. We protect each other." Fhord's words are solemn and sincere. It feels like he's making a promise to himself as much as Joralf. The moment passes quickly, though, as Fhord looks toward the door. "We should go. We're lucky the Dróttning hasn't found us yet. We don't want to be anywhere near here if she's searching."

He walks out with the medic, whispering to him before shaking his hand and sending him away, and we leave a few minutes later. The rest of the flight is smooth, thank the gods. Hours without a hint of pursuit, which makes me nervous. But anything would make me nervous at this point. I won't be able to travel these skies without fear until the Dróttning is dead. I just hope this place we're going—Lumaria, Fróðr called it—is as safe as he promises.

The sun is well into its descent when we leave land behind, Vulryn pushing herself to the front to lead us there, as she follows whatever instructions Joralf, and maybe Fróðr, give her. The burning orb sits in front of us like a beacon, throwing a harsh light on the sea that seethes far below. It's dark and empty, and the farther we get from land, the more desolate it all seems.

After an hour or so, the copper beast drops, positioning herself a dragon's-length or so above the waves. I don't know why. The sea looks the same—open and empty—but now we're close enough to see the harsh, angry crests pounding its surface. They rise and fall like a drumbeat, strumming to a crescendo then dropping to climb again. Other than the occasional breach of a fish soaring over the water, nothing disturbs the vast ocean.

Within a few minutes, though, a dense fog appears in front of us, obscuring everything on the other side of the curtain it creates. I can't recall the last time I saw such a heavy cloud sitting above the water. Chills roll down my spine, my chest starting to tingle as dread fills me. Everything in me rebels against losing myself in that mist. But into it we go.

And then we're through, and our destination rises in front of me. It takes my breath away.

It's the most beautiful island I've ever seen, a shimmering emerald sitting atop a sea so calm, it feels like we've entered another world. Spinning my head, I search for Fhord, wishing he was holding me as we experienced this for the first time. He's watching my reaction, I realize as our gazes meet, the corners of his eyes crinkling with a grin that creases his cheeks. He's so fucking beautiful, all hard planes and soft glances.

As we get closer, the island reveals itself. An enormous mountain sits in the center, a layer of snow covering its single peak, which shifts into hunter green trees and then shamrock fields. A wide river flows around it in a complete circle, a large sapphire lake the river's beginning and end. Even from here, I can see that much of the island is occupied, but its hub sits around the lake. Many, many people live here.

"It's good to be back," Torsten rumbles behind me.

I spin my head, unable to keep my jaw from dropping as I stare at him. "Back? You've been here before?"

"Aye," he tells me, winking before he looks toward Fhord and Tindera. "I'll let him tell you."

My stomach flutters, butterflies filling it, as I watch a half-smile emerge on Torsten's face—an expression that's almost as shocking as the words that just spilled from this stoic male's lips. I'm speechless for a moment, still catching up to this new piece of information about my mate. "Fhord's been here before?" I mutter at last. "He didn't say anything."

"He likes his surprises."

Twisting, I find Fhord again. His grin is even broader now as he watches Torsten tease me, and I sense his barriers drop, inviting me to ask the questions flipping through my thoughts. I have no idea how I can talk to him—what it is about this place that makes it so much easier to communicate in our thoughts, without spoken words—but I feel that ability when he opens himself to me.

You know this place?

I know it well.

How? And why didn't you say anything?

I wanted to see your face when we broke through the fog. Couldn't have you rustling around in my thoughts looking for memories of this sanctuary if you'd known.

I bark out a laugh. *Rustling around in your thoughts?*

You've broken down all my barriers, rabbit. I can't seem to keep you out, and I don't know why I'd want to. If I'd told you about this place, you wouldn't have been able to resist searching for it. It's not like anywhere else.

Even the field we just left?

Do you remember what I told you about that field? He must see the confusion in my face because he smiles again as he glances toward the lake. *The river is one of two places the Dróttning never discovered that contain healing waters. This is the other.*

The lake?

All of it. This island is magic embodied. Every bit of water circulating through it holds power.

Astarot slows, and my gaze follows the path of his descent. Already, a group has formed in the field we'll land in, eight or ten people watching as we approach. When we're close enough to see their expressions, I realize they must recognize Tindera. They're open and maybe a little excited. I have so many more questions for Fhord.

We settle about a dragon's-length away, Torsten scrambling down to go help Fróðr as he drops from Vulryn. Fhord takes the lead, his steps sure as he approaches the small group. They kneel, as one, their eyes on Fhord as their fists pound their chests.

What.

The.

Fuck?

"Stop," he snarls, glancing at me with a hint of horror in his eyes before turning back to the others. "I've told you not to greet me that way."

"We will abide by all your requests but that one," the closest male responds, a smile in his voice as he stands to stride forward and clasp Fhord's hand in his. "You always will be treated with the respect and honor you've earned when you enter this place."

"I really wish you wouldn't," my mate mutters, letting his gaze bounce around this time. Joralf and Fróðr are speechless, their jaws hanging so low it's a wonder they don't draw flies. The Ætt look like they belong. Liv and the others just look confused. None of us had any idea that Fhord even knew about this place.

"You cast the spell to hide Lumaria?" Joralf chokes his words out.

"I did."

"But ... how? And why?"

When Fhord looks at me, his green eyes are soft, moss on a spring morning. "I'll talk more about it tomorrow," he says. "I want to tell Sifa first. And I have the perfect place to do it." He turns toward the male who greeted him. "Will you arrange a meal for my mate and me on my cliff?"

I can feel my eyes widen at Fhord's question as I spin my head to look at the male. Fhord has a cliff here? What the fuck does that mean?

"Your mate?" The male smiles as his gaze finds mine. "What a lovely female the fates have gifted you."

"I am favored, indeed," Fhord declares, his hand reaching for mine to link our fingers together. "Sifa, meet Birger. He has cared for this place since we established it."

I lift my free hand, reaching for Birger's as I hold his gaze. "It's a pleasure," I manage to respond. I'm still struggling to catch up with the new information Fhord's sprung on me in the last few minutes, but I eke out a smile to accompany my words.

"The pleasure is mine. Truly." Turning toward Fhord, he dips his chin. "Will an eight o'clock meal give you the time you need to bathe and dress?"

"Eight would be perfect. Are my rooms ready?"

And rooms? Fhord has rooms here? My head is spinning with every new piece of information they're dropping. I have so many questions for this enigma I've tied my life to.

"Always," Birger responds, not a hint of hesitation in his word. He's the leader, but he defers to Fhord in everything. This place belongs to Fhord, I realize, and nobody here will dispute that claim.

"Sifa will stay with me. Place the others nearby. We have much to discuss while we're here."

"Of course."

"Where will the dragons find the herds?"

"In the east field."

Fhord turns toward Tindera. I see her nod and then feel Astarot's knowledge ripple through me, a hint of excitement with it. She'll take them to feed, then our dragons will return to carry us to the cliff Fhord mentioned. A small group emerges from our left, arms outstretched as we take the packs from our beasts and hand them off. As soon as the dragons are unpacked, they throw themselves into the sky, and Fhord tugs me to follow him.

He leads me to the town nestled around the lake, which looks as if it's been here decades, rather than years. The buildings vary in size and height, some small and a single floor, others much larger with two or even three stories. Unlike Revalle's colorful homes, simple whites and beiges dominate here. The structures are all clean and in good repair, but they're not what give this town the feel of having lived longer than it has.

The trees and shrubs, grass and flowers seem utterly out of place. They're mature—many of the trees a dragon's-length or more in height—but it's obvious they were planned to fit into the town and not the reverse. The street we're strolling down holds dozens of palm trees, spaced perfectly along its sides, each the same distance from its neighbors. Large banyans, or something similar, protect the houses, their broad canopies perfectly positioned to welcome the morning sun inside but shield the warmer afternoon rays.

I turn to Fhord to ask how the landscape could be so mature, but before I can, he leans forward and nips my ear. "I'm eager to share my space with you," he whispers.

"I'm eager to hear whatever you haven't told the others," I tell him, holding in my wonder for now. "I suspect you have quite the tale to share."

"It surprised even me when I realized what I'd done."

Fhord's rooms occupy part of the top floor of one of the larger buildings—a three-story structure that holds meeting rooms and an enormous kitchen on the ground floor. "Many people live here," he explains as he draws me up the stairs, "but I claimed the best room for myself. You'll see when we get there."

And I do. We walk into a warm, inviting space that reminds me of the rooms Fhord led me to when I first met the Ætt. It is distinctly Fhord, and I feel right at home. He strides across the room to open the curtains, revealing a large balcony, and I suck in a breath.

The lake ripples in front of us, its crystal waters the truest blue I've ever seen. Waves flow across it in a rhythm that seems too perfect to be possible. Each rise of water mirrors the others, lifting just as high and following just as closely as the ones before it.

The mountain behind it, though, is what steals my breath. It looks completely symmetrical, a cone dropped onto an island. Trees climb its sides in unnaturally precise patterns, with bright green maples and elms blanketing the surrounding ground and the first fifth or so of the mountain, and then darker pines, spruces and firs spiraling up to the snowy peak. I'm mesmerized by the design crafted by Mother Nature.

"How is it possible?"

"I have no idea," Fhord whispers as he stalks back over to me, takes my hand and pulls me forward. "It's looked exactly like this since I first saw it." He reaches for the door he's leading me to, spinning the handle to reveal a room with an oversized bath, steam rising to disappear into an open window right above it. "Which I will tell you all about when you've bathed and dressed, and I can finally share my place with you."

"Are you coming with me?" I purr, turning to saunter toward the bath, slowly lifting my blouse up and over my head to drop it beside me. I pause, spinning only my head so I can watch him as my fingers release the strings on my chest strap, letting it fall to the floor. Fhord reacts exactly as I'd hoped, his trousers bulging as one hand reaches forward to palm his groin.

"I want nothing more," he growls, stroking his growing dick over the material, "but what I want has to wait. I need to handle something first." He groans, his eyes roving down my bare back to the ass he loves to grip, as my thumbs catch my waistband and I push down my pants and underwear. "Fuck me," he mutters, spinning on his heel and striding out the door, throwing one last look back as I sway my way into the pool.

I spend too long submerged, but I can't regret it. The river in the North is life-changing, but it's cool. This water is every bit as alive and stimulating *and* it's warm. Perfectly, heavenly,

I-could-die-here-happy warm. I thought the river was the best thing I'd ever experienced. This bath is.

I'm desperate to take Fhord in here. I know it will happen. Soon. And I can't drag my hungry thoughts away from it.

Everything I'll do to him.

Everything he'll do to me.

Gods, it's going to be a good night.

But it's not like I can stay here all afternoon, waiting for him. So I drag myself out and dry off, then wander around. When I open the closet, my feet root to the floor, my eyes focused on the women's clothes taking up half the space. Not just any clothes, though. Mine, or near-duplicates of mine. It's as if Fhord examined my wardrobe and recreated it here, for my use whenever he managed to bring me.

He has so much to tell me.

I have no idea how to dress for whatever he has planned so choose a compromise—a pair of pants and a festive blouse, with sandals I could dance or climb in. After getting dressed, I dig through my packs to find a little makeup. By the time Fhord returns, I'm on the balcony, enjoying the balmy evening.

I hear him enter and stride across the room but let him come to me. When his hands land on my hips, his lips nuzzling into my neck, I lean into him, savoring his strength. We fit together perfectly.

"I couldn't stop thinking about your ass," he rumbles. "Did you enjoy your bath?"

"It would have been better if you'd shared it. Later?" Spinning, I wrap my arms around his neck, pulling his lips down to mine. Our tongues tangle as I drink him in, savoring the perfection of this moment in time.

"I've thought of nothing else since I left. That and the meal I have planned." Dislodging my arms, he takes my hand and pulls me out the door. "The dragons are ready," he tells me as his steps quicken down the hall.

"Why does it feel like you've been planning this for a long time?"

"Because I've been planning this for a long time." He turns once to wink at me, then continues striding forward, forcing me to jog a bit to keep up.

"Are we racing a clock?"

"I'm eager," he says, then falls silent. He wants to surprise me, which is cute and also a little frustrating. I don't usually like surprises. Most aren't happy.

The dragons huff as we approach, as anxious to go as Fhord is. *Did Tindera tell you where he's taking us?*

Yes. This time, though, his single word comes alone, no nuance or hidden meaning in it.

And?

Surprise. Again, a solitary word. They've ganged up, determined to keep me in the dark.

As soon as the dragons are in the sky, they aim for the mountain, spinning to the right as they get closer. If I weren't so preoccupied with whatever Fhord has planned, I'd be spellbound by the view—a kaleidoscope of stars casting their soft light onto the jewels arrayed beneath us. But I can't pull my thoughts away from Fhord and his surprise.

They carry us to a large shelf on the other side of the mountain, a vast cavern behind it. The fire at the cave entrance reveals a table sitting near the cliff's edge, two plates and a bottle of wine waiting for us. I expect Fhord to lead me there when we dismount and send our dragons back into the sky but instead, he takes me into the cave, leading me down a dark tunnel toward a light somewhere ahead of us.

We've walked fifty feet or so when the passage opens into an enormous room that looks as though it was designed for me. Everything I could want is here, but beyond that, it's perfectly my style. From the pillows to the drapes to the rugs, everything is bright and colorful and playful and happy. Even the curtain positioned next to a steaming pool would fit perfectly into my apartment in Revalle.

"What is this place?" I whisper, my heart in my throat as my eyes fill with tears. A warmth blossoms in my chest, flowing into all of my limbs, every toe and finger. I don't think I've ever felt as *seen*, as revered and loved, as I do in this moment.

"This is my homage to you," Fhord whispers, his arms wrapping around my stomach as he draws my back into his chest. "I didn't know it at the time, but I built this sanctuary for you."

"What do you mean?" My voice is a little louder now but not much. He's rendered me nearly speechless.

"You know that when you arrived here, I realized you'd come. I didn't understand what you would mean to me, but I recognized even then that if I let you, you'd matter to me. I never could have imagined how much."

"Yes, you told me." I wrap my arms around his, linking our fingers as his words mesmerize me.

"Everything changed ten years ago. Before then, I refused to see the Dróttning for what she was. She was my mother, and while I didn't agree with how she ruled this land, I didn't fight her. I believed my time would come, and I could be content until then."

"I knew that. Or most of it."

"What I haven't told you—not really—is how quickly my opinion of her changed when you arrived. It wasn't intentional; my thinking just evolved. I realized I support the rebellion. For the last eight years, I've been welcoming rebels to this island, a place I'd discovered more than a century before that and hidden from the Dróttning. At first, Birger alone was aware of who protected it, and he became my overseer. When we needed more leaders, we brought in others he and I could trust."

He pauses, squeezing me a bit tighter as he nuzzles my neck for a moment, drawing a moan from me as he reminds me with his words and his lips that he belongs to me. Just as I belong to him. "We had one agreement beyond the secrecy," he continues. "This cavern is mine. It's off-limits. Nobody knows it exists except Birger and a few people he trusts to care for it. Even now."

"But ... why?" I still haven't turned to look at him. I don't think I could hold back the tears, and I don't want to cry right now. That will come later, when I let myself revel in all that Fhord's done for me and for the rebellion that matters so much to elves like me.

"I didn't know why at first. I only knew I needed a place to express this new part of me—a vivid, vibrant, vivacious being that suddenly emerged in my core. I started by moving the stone to expand the cavern that had been much smaller. That took a long gods-damned time. I couldn't do much and risk alerting the Dróttning to this island's existence, so I went slowly, shifting bit by bit until it was large enough. For us, as it turned out."

He smiles, nudging me a bit to walk around the cave, his arms still wrapped around me as he matches my pace. "When I started decorating it, I didn't recognize myself. I wondered if I was finally losing my gods-damned mind. I am not bright or lively. Not like you. But I couldn't stop. I knew, somewhere deep in my soul, that this space needed to look exactly like this."

Now, he pauses again, spinning me around so his gaze can hold mine. "On our trip to the northern Nest, I knew why I'd chosen these colors, this look. All those years, without even realizing it, I was creating a space to share with my mate. A space you would know belongs to you as much as me." He leans forward for a kiss, gentle and sweet and full of so much love, I can't stop the tears that fill my eyes.

"I built this for you. Some part of me knew, even when I refused to accept it, that I would share your life, and you would love it."

Holy fuck, this male. If I hadn't already accepted the mating bond, I'd be fully lost to it now. Because Fhord's right. I love this place, and I can't imagine loving him any more than I do in this moment.

CHAPTER FIVE

MIKKAEL

SHE'S NOBODY

⚬

"WHEN HAVE I EVER disappointed you?" My fingers are sliding up her leg, searching for the holy land as her eyes narrow on mine.

"Who in Helheim is Dani? You never answered me last time."

Fuck. Me. I will never live that down. Especially with myself.

I was balls-deep in this gorgeous female, rocking her gods-damned world, when that northern bitch invaded my thoughts, turning my cock into a steel rod. For reasons I will never understand, I let her stay, imagining her blue eyes drinking me in. Gripping her auburn hair in my fist. Wrapping her long, luscious legs around my ass. Driving deep into her warm, tight pussy.

I was riding the wave of the best orgasm I've ever had when Dani's gods-damned name slipped from my lips.

Fuck me.

Really. Just … fuck me.

I was even more horrified than the blonde currently letting my fingers creep toward paradise. For a solid week after that, I stayed away from females. No fucking way that was gonna happen again. I can't let that shrew anywhere near me. Even my fantasies.

But my cock was having none of that. I've been dipping my stick for the last week or so, and I haven't slipped once. This female in my hands knows how to ride cock. I'm anxious to feel her walls tighten around me as I prove to her that she's the only thing I care about. At least, right now.

"I told you she's nobody. I want you. Only you."

She smiles, her legs widening just a bit as my thumb rubs over her clit and then dips inside. I pull it out and suck on it like a drooling toddler, eager to taste her again. She takes my hand and draws my thumb to her mouth, reminding me how gods-damned talented her tongue can be. And my cock starts to throb.

I'm dragging her upstairs before she can drop my thumb, climbing a few steps above her so she can keep swirling her tongue around it. As soon as the door is closed, I push her down to her knees, releasing my belt and pulling out the cock that's been demanding her attention since my fingers landed on her leg.

She doesn't waste any time, sucking me in as my hands wrap in her hair and I set the pace. She gags once or twice but she's been sucking cock long enough to know how to take me deep and she does. The ripples of pleasure turn into waves, and I am reminded again that I'm the luckiest gods-damned male in this shitty land.

Because the rebellion sent me to an island full of hungry women and they are eager to eat me up.

This female—Bodil, I think her name is—has my cock in her mouth and her hand wrapped around its base when she looks up at me. Her eyes, blue as the sky above, smile as her tongue spins around my tip and once again, Dani's image erupts in my thoughts. The eyes aren't exactly the same, but they're close enough to drag her into the middle of what should be an earth-shattering orgasm.

So I step the fuck back. "On the bed," I snarl, "on your knees." I'm gonna fuck her, but this'll be the last time. I will not give that northern bitch space in my thoughts, even if it means giving up a female who knows how to please a male.

She grins—she likes when I ride her like this, if I'm remembering her and not some other female—and rises gracefully to stride across the room. Stripping to reveal generous breasts and a lovely tummy, she crooks a finger to urge me forward then turns and crawls onto the bed.

I don't bother taking my clothes off. There's only one part of me that needs to be bare right now. Striding over, I pause a moment to appreciate the thick ass raised high for me, my fingers sliding up and down her wet pussy. I push two in, playing with her a bit as my thumb finds her clit and rubs on it. She's moaning and rocking her hips in a few moments, more than ready for me.

Drawing my fingers out again, I lick one before leaning over and pushing them into her mouth. She knows what I want and starts sucking on them, just like she does my cock, as I thrust into her.

Fuck, she feels good. For a female that beds as many males as she does, she's tight, wrapping around my cock like a sleeve. I set the pace, slamming into her as I play with her clit. This will be as good for her as it is for me. I've never left a female unsatisfied, which is why so many are eager to share my bed.

That and my massive cock. That helps, I'm told.

The wave of ecstasy is cresting, release just within my reach, when the female turns to cast those bright blue eyes at me, a smile on her face. Suddenly, I'm fucking Dani again. And I can't get myself to stop. So I give in.

Closing my eyes, letting her image stay in my thoughts, I imagine it's her. The cock that already was fully engorged expands again, drawing a groan from beneath me. A surge of pleasure rolls through me, setting every nerve on fire, and I don't think I've experienced anything this good since the first time I came with Dani's picture in my mind.

I rub the clit in my fingers more quickly, determined to rock Dani's world, and her moans grow more intense, her thighs banging against my balls in just the right way. We fall over the cliff together, ecstasy pounding through me, as we both collapse.

I catch myself just before Dani's name rolls off my lips. And feel like I've been dropped in a frozen lake.

What the fuck have I done? I let myself come to thoughts of that witch again.

Good as this female is, it's not worth it. If I bed her again, she'll be blindfolded. Which she'd probably like anyway.

"That was good, Mik," the female purrs, pulling my arm to wrap it around her. "Stay with me. We can do this all night."

That's the last gods-damned thing I need. I give her a little squeeze, nipping her neck quickly, and push away. "Wish I could," I tell her—because a little white lie comes in handy once in a while—but I need to get out of here.

She rolls over, palming her big tits as she watches me tuck my cock back into my pants, and smiles. "Soon?" she murmurs.

"Soon," I promise—another little white lie she'll appreciate right now—as I lean down to take a quick kiss.

And then I turn and stride out the door, throwing a "thanks" behind me as I go.

Why Dani? Of all the females in this land, why the fuck does my mind have to fixate on her. She's gorgeous—exactly my type, with those sparkling eyes, thick hair, rich as a chestnut, and legs that go on for days—but this world holds many gorgeous women. I don't even like Dani. She's fucking evil and just plain mean.

But ever since she appeared in Helga's room—and then somehow convinced me to kiss her instead of kill her like I should have—she's been stuck in my thoughts. I'd almost pushed her out completely when she showed up again, Fhord and Sifa having decided she should join our merry band of rebels. Now I can't get rid of her. She's haunting me, demon that she is.

I need a gods-damned drink. In a different inn. Because I cannot see this female again. Even if she is a great fuck and probably willing to wear a blindfold, I won't do anything that drags Dani back into my sex life.

"Mik," I hear when I walk into a pub a few blocks over. "Been wonderin' where you disappeared to."

"Bjorn," I call, happy for the distraction as I stride over and plant myself in a chair across from him. "It's been a minute. How's business?"

Bjorn sells weapons on the mainland. He's got great contacts in the Dróttning's ranks and manages to avoid suspicion by feeding their dark demands. People will overlook a lot when they need what you have to sell. And Bjorn's blades are as sharp as they come.

"Always good," he tells me. "The tighter the Dróttning squeezes, the more I sell. Nobody's got the balls to face her, but they all wish they could. Everyone but the dragon riders. Those bastards won't ever turn on her."

"You never know," I tell him, recalling my awe when Fhord and Sifa appeared with their dragons and a couple others in tow—before I realized Dani rode one of them. "Rumor has it some dragon riders may be sympathetic to our cause."

"Fuckin' Fhord? That dick?"

"You know him?"

"We all know him. He's like this with the Dróttning," he says as he raises crossed fingers to wave them in front of me with a sneer twisting his lips. "He won't ever turn on her. People say he's lived gods-damned centuries and been loyal to her the whole fuckin' time. He ain't never changing."

"I'm not so sure. He may not be the male you think he is."

"I'll believe it when I see him squeeze the life out of her cold, dead eyes. Until then, I don't trust him or any other dragon rider. And I'm not alone." Now his voice is low, like he's sharing a secret he's afraid someone might hear. "There's others like me on this island who know them dragon riders won't never give up their beasts. And everyone knows the dragons all belong to her. We're not gonna let them betray us."

I watch him for a moment, surprised by how cynical he's become. Or maybe he's always been this way. Shaking my head, I tell him, "I think you should give them a chance, but you do whatever the fuck you want. I'm here until the rebellion calls me back to the mainland. I won't be seeing any dragons anytime soon."

"You ain't heard?" Bjorn's eyebrows slam together, sitting like a caterpillar above his ruddy eyes.

"Heard what?"

"He's here. That gold dragon showed up with three others yesterday. They're eatin' our goats while fuckin' Fhord takes the best room at the common house. Like he's a snot-nosed prince or something."

A tremble rushes through me, my heartbeat kicking up like a gods-damned schoolboy anxious to see his first crush in class. I reach for Bjorn's ale, sucking down a big gulp as his eyebrows somehow creep even closer together. "What the fuck?" he demands, his hand shooting out to swipe his glass away. "Get yer own."

"Fhord's here with three other dragons?" I ask, still trying to convince my heart to calm the fuck down. "Have you seen them?"

"Saw 'em come in. Nearly shat myself. Ain't no dragons flyin' above Vanatia but the Dróttning's. But then they started sayin' it's Fhord and some rebels. Joralf broke free from the Dróttning's prison, if you can believe it, along with his mate, and a couple of Ulfhild's girls. Some are even sayin' Fhord found this island and gave it to the rebellion. But I don't believe that shit for one minute. If he did, he's prob'ly just try'na trap us here so she can kill us all in one fiery attack."

"One of those dragons copper, like a bell?" I ask when he finally shuts the fuck up. He nods and my chest deflates, but I'd have been surprised if he'd said no. "Well, I hope to the gods you're wrong about Fhord. Pussy on this island is too good. I'd hate to see the Dróttning ruin it."

"Ain't that the truth?" Bjorn shoves his palm into his groin, a wide grin erupting as he glances at the staircase. "I got someone waitin' for me," he adds. "I think I may go take a taste."

"Enjoy," I tell him as I crook a finger at the barmaid. "I'm sure I'll be finding my way up there soon."

The girl—Dahlia, I think—is another female I've lost myself in, trying to forget about Dani. I've enjoyed her bed a few times, but today, I'm not in the mood. My mind keeps replaying my last few seconds thrusting into Bodil with Dani's image in my thoughts. I'm growing hard just thinking about it, and I need to stop this shit.

Dahlia plops down on my lap, rubbing her ass on my cock, and I wrap my arms around her. Maybe I am in the mood. She's got brown eyes and darker skin like me—nothing like Dani—and could be exactly what I need.

But then the door opens and a breeze carries in a scent I'll never forget, a mix of citrus and sandalwood that's so enticing, I almost could forget that it wafts from a bitter, rotten female. Like they've got minds of their own, my eyes lift and find her. And my gods-damned heart stops—as if it's waiting for her to see us too—and then starts to race when her gaze catches mine. Sifa, Fhord, and his people shuffle in behind her, but I barely notice them. She's all I can see.

I'm so fucked.

Dani's as surprised as me, an expression that almost looks like longing appearing for the quickest moment, before a mask of disdain drops. She sneers at me, turning to say something to Sifa, and then stalks to a table on the far side of the room. She's as gorgeous as I remember, and I can't help but notice how many males in the room stop whatever they're doing—talking, flirting, drinking, walking—to turn and stare.

Mine, something inside me rumbles, but I shove that shit down deep. She's not mine. I don't want her.

Sifa watches Dani for a moment then turns to me, giving me the prettiest smile I've seen since I got here. I used to wonder what it was about Sifa that drew me to her. It wasn't sexual, which is strange for me because normally I'd want a woman as striking as her.

I figured it out after a couple of years of working with her. Something about her when she arrived—a hopelessness and despair, this feeling that she was out of place, somehow—spoke to my soul. I've been lost in this land all my life. It's never felt like home. Getting to know Johan helped. And then Sifa came along, a kindred soul, and I stopped feeling so alone. She's my sister now. That's why I dragged Johan along to join Sifa when Fhord's people showed up.

I wonder if Johan's with them. Guess I'll know soon.

"I had no idea you'd come here," Sifa says when she's close enough to be heard over the chatter around us. "How'd we end up on the same remote island at the same time?"

"Didn't you know?" I ask as I finally pull my head out of my ass and push Dahlia off my lap. She smiles and winks at me—a standing invitation—walking away as I rise and wrap my arms around Sifa and then smirk at Fhord, who's glowering at me from across the room. "This is where they send the rebels they're trying to hide, or maybe just to get away from."

"I didn't know this place even existed until yesterday when the dragons brought us. Imagine my surprise to learn Fhord's the reason everyone's here."

I pull out a chair for Sifa, gesturing for her to sit as I catch Dahlia's gaze and throw up two fingers. I hope the ale's colder than Bjorn's glass was. Dahlia knows how I like my ale, so it should be.

"It's true, then?" I ask when we're both settled, sitting close to each other so we don't have to yell over the laughing patrons around us. "Fhord's the founder everyone knows exists but nobody's seen?"

"So he tells me. Apparently, he discovered the island a long time ago and hid it from the Dróttning. He started bringing rebels here years ago. They've built it up quickly."

"How'd he do all that without the Dróttning finding out?"

"He's done a lot behind the Dróttning's back. He's been supporting the rebels in his own way for a long time."

"Well, shit. I guess I owe him an apology."

"Like I owed Bevin an apology when I found out where his loyalties lie?" Sifa's eyebrow quirks up in the charming way it always does when she's calling me out for something. Usually, it's little things. This one's big.

"He told you?"

"He got us into the southern Nest, helped get Fhord and Tindera out."

"How'd Fhord end up in the southern Nest?"

"You missed a lot." Her face drops, grief sneaking into her eyes as she holds my gaze. "Do you know?"

A chill rolls through me. I'm not sure what she's talking about, but I can tell from her expression it's bad. "What happened?"

"I hate having to tell you this." She pauses, reaching for my hand as her eyes start to shimmer. "The Dróttning discovered us on our way back. She was traveling with a large group of soldiers. We were trying to escape through a cave, but they found their way in, so we doubled-back and attacked them." One more pause, a tear rolling down her cheek. "Johan didn't make it out," she tells me at last.

"Fuck."

For a moment, I can't move, ice moving through my veins to freeze me in place. Johan's my brother. I never connected with another soul before him. I don't remember anything about my childhood, but since my earliest memory at fifteen years old or so, I've felt like I didn't belong. I was an orphan living in one of the shittiest homes around—part of life around here—and never felt like I fit. I've always been a lion in a pack of wolves.

Johan changed that, pulling me into his life to become my closest friend other than Sifa. He's one of the best males I've ever met. Everything about him is good. He doesn't fuck with people the way I do.

Was, my fucking mind pipes up to remind me. Johan *isn't* anything now.

If the gods weren't such absolute dicks, he'd be alive and stunned by news of my death.

"I shouldn't have left," I mutter when I finally find my voice.

"It's not your fault. You couldn't have stopped it."

"Of course it's my gods-damned fault. I convinced him to join Fhord's people and go to you. And then I fucking left." When the reason hits me, my world turns red, a wave of fire pulsing down my back into my fingers and toes. With a stiff neck and straight spine, I slowly turn my head to find Dani. If

I could kill her right now, I would. "Because of her," I add in a voice so low, I don't expect it to reach Sifa's ears.

But it does. "It's not her fault either, Mik," she urges as she gives my hand a little squeeze. "Johan died for a cause he believed in. It was an honorable, brave death."

"A cause I abandoned because of her." I look at Sifa, not bothering to hide the self-loathing she must see all over my face. "I've been fucking my way across this island, not doing shit since I got here. Now Johan's dead, and fucking Dani's here to make sure I know how crappy my decisions have been since I left Bevin's bar." Standing, my chair clattering behind me, I glance at Dani one more time and then back at Sifa.

"It's time for me to go. I can't be on the same island as her."

"Give it time, Mik. I think she's leaving soon anyway. Let yourself grieve before you do something foolish."

"The only foolish thing I've done is letting that northern bitch get under my skin and leaving Johan behind because of it. I need to make it right. I'm going back to join the fight."

I spin on my heel, not bothering to look at Sifa's face because it would break my heart. She's right. I know it deep in my bones. But it doesn't matter.

Johan's dead and somebody has to pay.

CHAPTER SIX

DANI

HE HATES ME

I WANT TO GO after him. It's fucked up because he hates me, and I really should hate him. But I can't. He means something to me, and it twists my insides to see his anger and hatred.

Sifa sits alone, her gaze fixed on the door, for a long time. Finally, she stands and walks over, so much sadness in her eyes I wish I could take her pain. I'm not normally emotional about others—I haven't had a friend since my Academy roommate fucked me over with one of our instructors—but Sifa brings out strange feelings in me. Like I'd sacrifice something important if it would further her cause.

I don't like it. I much prefer myself as the heartless bitch everyone in Njordheim knows me to be.

Fhord hands her his whiskey when she sits next to him and she throws it back, sneering a bit as it burns its way down. "More?" he asks, his hand reaching for hers.

She nods, and he glances at the empty glasses on the table, then catches the barmaid's eye and gestures for another round. It's the harlot who was perched on Mikkael's lap when we came in, and I almost give in to my need to fuck with her by dropping memories of some of my more depraved kills into her thoughts. But that would mean I'm jealous. And I'm definitely not jealous of some random female who may have caught Mikkael's eye.

"Vulryn keeps nagging me," I announce to the table when conversation lags. "We'll leave soon."

"You're going after Ziselær and Matthias?" Fhord demands, his mouth a thin line as his eyes spark.

"We are. She needs to try, and I'm starting to think it makes sense."

"They will *never* betray the Dróttning. They'll just kill you. You're too valuable to us to let that happen."

"It's not your decision, Fhord. We're going. You can help by telling us what to expect—how we might get through to them—or you can wash your hands of us. Those are your choices."

Fhord glowers at me, his gaze never leaving my face, until the barmaid brings our drinks. When she finally draws his focus away, he grabs a drink and turns back to me. "You hold my greatest secret," he says at last, lifting an arm to gesture around him as the whiskey sloshes around in his glass. "Leaving now to chase them down would threaten everything. You have no idea what he's capable of. How he'll hurt you in service of the Dróttning."

"We'll never betray you, Fhord. I'd have thought you'd know that by now." My voice is bitter, but I don't try to hide it. "We've proven ourselves allies. Fuck you for suggesting otherwise."

Sifa places her hand on his shoulder, giving him a gentle squeeze, and Fhord inhales deeply. I can see him trying to capture his raging emotions. Finally, he wins.

"You have proven yourself," he agrees, and I stop myself from responding flippantly because fuck, yes, we have. "I don't suggest you'd betray us willingly. But I know Matthias." His voice drops now, his gaze holding mine as he bites out the next words. "He *will* hurt you. He'll do anything he must to get the information she demands. You're strong, but I don't know if anyone is that strong."

And now I'm pissed, because they were that strong when the Dróttning held them, but they think I'll crumble. "Did Sifa give in?" I growl. "Did you? You've both been tortured and protected your secrets. Why can't you trust me to do the same?"

"She's right, Fhord," Sifa says, her voice calm and very fucking reasonable as she takes his hand and draws his gaze to her. "They're going to do this. We need to trust them."

I take a deep breath and try to reel in my anger, see my decision from his perspective. He's worked hard to create this sanctuary, but my dragon and I are about to carry his secret into the most dangerous place in this land. And I can't deny that I know next to nothing about dragons and the emotions

Vulryn's mating bond will provoke in me. He'll see, though. We'll prove our loyalty with actions, not words.

"Fuck," Fhord mutters. But the anger is gone. This is frustration. Resignation. "I don't like it."

"I don't either." Sifa turns to me, her eyes sad. "You're part of our lives now. We expect you to return to us. With or without Ziselær—we don't care—come back to us when you're done."

"I will. You're part of our lives too. This fight is ours as much as yours. We'll join you and help you win."

Sifa drops her chin once. "I know you will. And Vulryn," she adds with a laugh.

"That beast of mine has claimed you and she's not letting go," I agree with a smirk. "Even if I didn't want to come back, she'd bring me. She's got a bit of an attachment issue."

"A bit?" Fhord's eyebrow pops up, his head tilting as he matches my smirk.

"Maybe more than a bit. It makes her a loyal ally."

"That it does." He lifts his glass, gesturing toward the others. "You're one of us," he tells me, his glass pointing at Sifa and then each of his Ætt. "So you get our traditional farewell to a member leaving on a journey of sacrifice and uncertainty."

"Do I have a choice?" I'm not sure if I like the looks on their faces. They're all a bit too eager for whatever Fhord plans to do. Except Sifa. She looks confused—probably never subjected to the farewell because Fhord's smart enough to stay on her good side.

"None," he responds with a wink. "But I promise it won't hurt." He looks at Torsten, who sneers in response, before adding, "At least, not too much."

"Great," I mutter, lifting my whiskey to join in whatever they have planned.

"I'll go first because ..."

"He always does," Leif interjects with a grin. "The perks of being the boss."

Fhord tilts his whiskey toward Leif. "Because I get those boss perks." And then he grows solemn, his gaze more intense than I've ever seen it. "I owe you a life, which I promise to repay at your call." His gaze flicks outside to where the dragons wait as he adds, "You and Vulryn."

He turns back to me and continues in the same somber tone. "I don't think Tindera would have survived much longer. She is free only because your dragon—stubborn bitch that she is," he adds with a smile full of affection, "refused to listen to me. And I thank the fates every day that she did. You freed my dragon. I owe you a debt I will never be able to repay. Call your marker anytime, anywhere, and I will come."

I drop my head and stare at the table because I will not let this crew see me cry. But, fuck, I've never felt such a rush of gratitude for mere words. The part of me that long ago abandoned the idea of being loved, a part I thought dead and gone, is back. I belong with these people. And they belong with me. It makes me happier than I would have thought possible.

Finally, I lift my eyes and hold Fhord's gaze. "I think we're even. Harald would have killed me and Vulryn."

"You're not tossing off my debt to you that easily. Call and I will come." He turns toward Sifa, but she shakes her head, so the whiskey glass tips toward Leif before Fhord lifts it to his lips to toss it back, then turns the glass upside down on the table.

"I'm gonna be crying before this is over, aren't I?"

"Only if we do it right," Leif tells me, the tavern's soft light casting shadows on his dark eyes and tawny skin. "Torsten's never cried, but Torsten doesn't cry. The rest of us blubber like babies when it's our turn." He watches me for a moment, although I'm sure he knows what he's going to say.

"We were four for many years—Fhord, Torsten, Jorunn, and me. I was the one who got nervous when Astrid joined us because what we had worked. I don't like to fuck with things that work. Now we're seven, fucking with more things that work."

Pausing again to look at Astrid, Sifa and then me, he nods once and then continues. "But I'm not nervous anymore. We're more complete now. We're more capable now. And that will be even more true if you manage to turn that blue dragon and bring him to us. You trusted us, and because of you, we're complete again. So I owe you my trust. Whatever happens, I trust that you will make the right decision, and I will support you without question. Starting today."

I smile when Leif turns to Fhord, throwing his shoulders back and jutting out his chin. He somehow rises even taller in his seat, his long, lanky frame firm and strong. "She's got my trust in this," he declares. "That ferocious beast she rides is gonna chase down her drake, and we'll do whatever the fuck we can to help her make it work. They've proven themselves to us. We owe it to them."

I don't drop my head when the tears fill my eyes this time. My chest grows warm as I let his words wash through me, glancing around to see the others—even Fhord—nodding their heads as their gazes hold mine. Something about Leif makes it okay to be vulnerable. I turn back toward him and whisper my thanks. He tips his whiskey toward me and then Jorunn, sucks it down, and thumps the glass on the table, upside down like Fhord.

I'm seeing the pattern here.

Jorunn and I haven't spoken much and I'm not sure what to expect from her. Her coloring is similar to mine—auburn hair and blue eyes—and I suspect she could beat Torsten in battle, despite his size. She's as solemn as Fhord and doesn't smile much.

"They're emotional bastards, aren't they?" she asks at last, tipping her glass toward Fhord and Leif.

"I'd never have believed it," I respond with a smirk.

"Leif, maybe, but not Fhord."

"Never Fhord," I agree.

"I am not emotional." Jorunn glances toward Astrid before adding, "With most people."

"Noted."

"My debt is more practical. Your beast is a weapon we needed, and still need. So I owe you a blade."

"I have a blade," I point out, gesturing toward the knife on my belt. "And a sword in my room."

"Not like the blade I'll bring you. Choose your weapon—sword, knife, ax. Whatever you want. I'll have it made for you by the best bladesmith in the land. It will be unlike any you've wielded before."

I like Jorunn. She's practical and pointed. "I could use a better sword."

"Everyone could use a better sword. Before you leave, show me what you're using and tell me what you don't like. I'll have your blade waiting for you on your return."

"Thank you," I tell her. "I can't wait to wield it."

She dips her chin once, points her whiskey toward Astrid, then drinks it and bangs her glass on the table.

Astrid's always been more open and friendly than her lover, so I'm not surprised when she starts with a broad smile. "This is only my second farewell," she tells me as she reaches out to take my hand and give it a little squeeze. I resist the urge to pull away—she's much more touchy-feely than me—and force out a half smile. "We haven't done this for Sifa yet, so you get the debt I'd planned for her."

"Lucky me, I think?" I can't hold back the grimace, or the apology that probably fills my eyes, as I glance at Sifa.

"It's yours," she tells me with a shrug, "whatever it is."

"Oh, don't worry. It's nothing grand. Just my way of saying thanks for joining me in this group that took me in and made me theirs." She releases my hand to take Jorunn's, who doesn't shrink back the way I did, then smiles again, her purple eyes sparkling.

"I was alone before I found Jorunn, and she brought me into this group. I don't think I loved her yet, but it didn't take long. She gave me her trust and then everyone else did too. She's my best friend, but it's different, you know, than with other friends. You get from girlfriends something you don't get from lovers." Squeezing Jorunn's hand, she holds her gaze for a moment then turns back to me.

"You and Sifa have brought a different kind of friendship into this group. I love all these oafs, but I've missed having girlfriends. You've given me that again, even if we haven't had enough of a chance to get to know each other, and I'm grateful. So that's my oath to you. I am your friend. When you need someone to turn to—when you need to complain about Fhord or gossip about Torsten—I'll be there for you."

"I haven't had a friend since I was a teenager. I wouldn't know where to start."

"You're doing great so far. Just be yourself. I like the sorta grumpy, occasionally funny, always sincere person that you are. I'm your friend, and I accept every part of you."

"Thank you, friend." My eyes are watering again and I'm ready for this to be over. It's too much emotion for me in one sitting. If they ever do this again, I'll ask them to spread it out over a couple of meals. That might work.

"That goes for Sifa too," Astrid adds as she glances at her. "It's kind of a two-fer."

"I thank you too, my friend." Sifa's smile is broad and genuine.

Astrid gestures toward Torsten, then lifts her glass to her lips. But she's not a fan of whiskey, apparently. She pauses for a moment, her expression already puckering, then tilts the glass back. Her throat doesn't move yet, though. Instead, she seems to consider whether she's really going to swallow. When she glances toward Fhord, her eyes widen and she gulps it down, her face twisting even more. "I hate whiskey," she sputters after a moment, then plops her upside-down glass on the table.

"I'm practical too," Torsten says, not wasting any time. "You brought us another beast willing to carry your allies, and I owe you a beast." He pauses as my eyebrows tip together, then gestures toward Fhord. "He rides Sigurd when he can't ride Tindera, or she's needed elsewhere. Sifa rides Hilde, although she's an old girl and may soon retire to pasture again. You need a horse. I'll find that beast for you."

"I can get a horse if I need it," I sputter, unsure what use I'd have for one. "But I don't know why I would. Vulryn can carry me where I need to go."

"You need a horse," he insists, brown eyes narrowing. "Dragons cannot always take to the skies. Sometimes they must walk, and you'll ride a horse when they do. But it can't be just any horse. It must be trained to be carried when your beast flies." I shake my head, but he raises a finger, silencing me. "And it must be worthy of you, a fearless warrior and deadly dragon rider. I owe you a horse," he says in a tone that brooks no disagreement, "and a horse you will have."

Lifting his glass, he tips it at Sifa, throws back the whiskey and slams it down. Not a drop reaches his thick, red beard, and he definitely doesn't wince as it slides down his throat.

"I wanted to go last because I'm new to the Ætt, but also because while I'm new to you, it feels like you've been part of my life forever. Maybe it's because I've walked through your head..."

"Ya' think?" I ask with a laugh, leaning back as the memories of those strange and frightening days spin through my mind.

"That's probably it," she agrees with a wink. And then she grows serious, holding my gaze. "I owe you my life, and my trust and friendship, and probably a blade and a horse too. But those are taken so I'm going with this." She pauses, looking at Fhord as they have some silent conversation. He gives a barely perceptible nod, and she turns back to me.

"You gave up your home for us. I realize you think you didn't have a choice, but you did. You abandoned everything you knew and joined a cause that isn't yours, giving us loyalty and commitment we haven't earned. I'm grateful. Fhord is grateful. Astarot and Tindera are grateful. You'll always have a home with us."

And I'm crying again. They are hitting every soft spot I possess, finding spots I didn't know existed.

"This will be a physical gift and a promise. We'd like to give you a space to claim as yours. It can be here. This island is safe and Vulryn can bring you anytime you want to come home. Or we can find a place in Revalle or somewhere else. But we want you to know you'll always have a place that's yours alone."

"That's too much," I tell her. "You don't need to do that for me."

"We do and we will." She glances at Fhord again, then continues. "And here's the promise. Like the others have said, we're family now. You have a home with us, wherever we are. We'll prepare a room for you in the Ætt's hideout in Revalle and the other places they've claimed. You'll always be welcome there. You belong to us and we belong to you."

I suck in a deep breath, looking around at this group who have become the most important people in my life. I don't know how it happened, but I'm grateful it did.

Sifa tips her glass to me, drinks it like the bad bitch she is, and sets it down on the table.

"I'm not much for speeches," I say as I lift my glass, "so I'll keep this short. You're the family I never knew I needed. As Sifa said, Vulryn and I belong to you, and you belong to us. Thank you."

Now it's my turn to drink, and it feels important, like a door has opened and I'm stepping through with this little gesture. A few months ago, I would have stopped. Maybe I wouldn't have joined them. But bonding with Vulryn changed everything. I've realized I need connection—I need family—as badly as she does. And I'm so fucking happy this one has claimed me. I follow Sifa's lead, throwing my drink down and setting my glass on the table.

We chose well, Vulryn purrs.

We leave the next day, after Vulryn speaks with Khirta and learns what an evil fuck her drake is. Neither of us wants to wait. I had all the emotion I could take last night, and I need some space to breathe while I process everything. So I put it out of my mind, focusing on the dragon beneath me, the cerulean sky above, and the dark, angry waves below. An odd sense of peace settles on me. Chaotic as my life has been since the Monarch sent me with Sifa, I feel like I'm exactly where I should be.

He comes. We're close to shore when Vulryn's words drop into my thoughts.

Ziselær? That doesn't make any sense. *Why in all the worlds would he be here?* I demand, a seed of worry sprouting in my gut. Its tentacles wriggle into the cynicism I keep buried deep inside to start to drag it to the surface. I know we're doing this, but I don't see how it turns out well.

He seeks me.

Do you mean he can sense you? That he knows where to find you?

He is ours. We are connected. She's got a satisfied tone to her voice. The blue dragon might be off to a good start.

And if we'd stayed on the island, could he have found us there?

Perhaps. I am unfamiliar with this bond. I do not know how distance will affect it. She's quiet for a moment, then adds, *He is angry.*

Okay, maybe not such a good start after all. *Why is he angry?* I ask, trying to keep the blossoming angst from finding its way

into my words. My heartbeat is picking up, and I do not want
Vulryn to hear my fear.

*He knows that as he can sense me, I can sense him. He cannot
hide from me.*

So, why's he coming?

He comes to kill us. Vulryn's tone is so matter-of-fact, I spew
out a laugh.

And that doesn't bother you?

*He does not know me. And he cannot kill me. He is not yet
strong enough.*

Yet? What the fuck does she mean by that?

When he chooses me, I shall teach him to fight.

Does he know we're coming from an island? I hope not. We
can't give Matthias or his dragon any bit of information that
might lead back to Lumaria.

*Perhaps. I do not share his thoughts, and he has not chosen to
speak with me.*

What do we do?

We meet him in the sky, where draikanas meet their drakes.

Fuck me. That doesn't sound good. *And what if he tries to
kill us?* A gods-damned warble sneaks into my words. I need to
get my shit together.

*We stop him. We are not ready to die. But he will not choose
to kill us. Not yet. He will want to know me first.*

How can you be so sure?

He is mine and I am his.

I can see them now—Ziselær and his cruel, magnificent rider. They're flying fast, as if anxious to end our lives, but Vulryn

keeps the same pace. She's cool as fuck, and I wish I could be so chill.

Ziselær comes in hot, literally. Flames spurt from his mouth, laying a path nearly a dragon's-length that he flies through as he draws closer. He looks angry, as if the fates fucked with him when they chose Vulryn for his mate. But Vulryn's still calm and resolved.

She spins when his flames get close enough to reach us, launching herself up and back. Before he can respond, she's at his back, throwing out flames of her own. This was just a demonstration, though. She's not going to hurt him. She just wants him to know she could if she wanted.

He twists his wings, slowing him down enough to nearly retake his position. Nearly.

Vulryn tucks her wings, plummeting to the ground in a move we've practiced a lot but which most other dragons with riders can't do. The pressure is too great, and I've nearly been thrown off more than once. Ziselær follows, apparently oblivious to the risk he's taking with Matthias.

When Matthias's grip on his dragon fails, sending him tumbling into the sky, Vulryn is there to rescue him. She pivots in the air, reaching him before the blue dragon can, and wraps her claws gently around his torso. When she has him, she throws all her speed into reaching the mainland, racing there before Ziselær can challenge her and potentially put his rider at risk.

He's on our tail, nearly on top of us, when she makes it, spiraling down to a remote beach with no escape except by air or sea. And then she slows to set Matthias down gently, flapping her wings to push us far enough away from the pissed-off asshole to ensure he won't reach us before Vulryn can get airborne if she needs to.

"What the fuck was that?" Matthias demands, stalking toward Vulryn and me. The tattoos on his neck ripple as his veins and muscles pulse, and I wonder if I've seen anyone quite this mad. Ziselær reaches land and settles in behind him a moment later, every bit as angry as his rider.

Ridiculous. We're just trying to get some alone time.

"They're mates," I scream at him, as Vulryn extends her wing and I dismount to stand next to my dragon. "Vulryn wants to talk to Ziselær."

"That's not the way to do it," he barks at me. He takes another step closer, but Vulryn spits out a few flames, stopping him in his tracks.

"How the fuck should we have done it? You came here to kill us. Should we have asked your permission?"

Quiet, Vulryn tells me, her voice as cool as ice. *I would speak with my drake.*

Ziselær must have relayed the same message to his rider because Matthias's eyes go distant for a moment, then he nods his head and takes a step back, waving his arm toward us.

The next five minutes are tense. Matthias's hand never leaves his blade—he's probably not as quick as me—and my gaze never leaves him. We both stand ready to attack if our dragons give the word. But they're too focused on each other.

The snarls and growls, with an occasional shriek, when they first start talking eventually become howls and yips. And then silence, as they seem to agree to actually speak with each other. By the end, Ziselær's anger has disappeared, and Vulryn is settling into a heady sense of victory.

She's won. She always wins. We're going to trust Ziselær and Matthias, and go with them to the Nest.

I hope to fuck we survive it.

CHAPTER SEVEN

FHORD

HER NAKED BODY

I WAKE UP WITH Sifa in a bed. Her naked body is wrapped around mine, head on my chest, her arm and a leg flung over me. Her scent fills me as I pull her closer.

I'm so fucking hard. It's not just about the sex—although that's better than I could have imagined, and I'll be thrusting into my little rabbit the moment she opens those beautiful, brown eyes. This is only the second time we've woken together in an actual bed, in my space. A room that belongs to me, and now her. She became part of my world so quickly when I finally gave in to the mating bond, it seems strange that she's just now becoming part of my home, too.

But that's not right. Home is wherever she is. This is just a place. Home is any bed she's lying in, any cave we find along the way, any field sprouting with life.

She's my home, just as Tindera is.

Still, it feels so gods-damned good to have her here. I wish we were in the cavern I created for her. I think she loves that space as much as I do, and my savage preens himself about that. He drove it more than me. His *need* to make a nest for his mate was too great to ignore, even if I didn't realize at the time what we were doing.

We were too tired to go last night, but we'll fix that tonight. I want to wake up there tomorrow.

When she moves, my cock twitches, urging me to wake her up and take her. It's not going anywhere, though. It'll be ready for her when she's rested enough. We're just gonna stay right here and the fucker is gonna wait. We'll be deep in Sifa soon enough.

My savage is at peace for the first time in a long time. Sifa and Tindera are ours and we're theirs. He's never felt so satisfied with his life. So complete. His calm soothes something deep within me.

But then Sifa's eyes fly open, and she sits up with a sharp gasp, her fear and pain exploding inside me in a burst that seems to trigger every nerve in my body. Her face twists, agony written in the creases along her brow and around her lips, and her hands clutch her side just as Tindera's terror drops into my mind.

Drake. Astarot's been shot with a dragon bolt. She doesn't know how the fuck it happened—where the bolt came from—but he nearly fell from the sky, injuring himself more when he landed. They're in a field a viku or so away and she needs us there now.

I throw myself up in bed, my cock deflating like a popped balloon. Sifa's staring at me, confused, as her eyes spark with her dragon's pain. "What happened?"

"Astarot's been shot. He's injured in a nearby field."

Sifa's wide awake now, her brows pulling together as she casts her mind toward her dragon. She's quiet and still for a moment, and then her face twists with even more concern. "He's hurt badly," she breathes, her voice shaky. "How do we get there?"

"Tindera won't leave him. Khirta will need to carry us there."

She nods, throwing off the covers despite pain that must be rattling through her. We both dress quickly, wordlessly roaming the room to gather the clothes we left strewn across the floor last night. I grab a suture kit—which I never should have needed on this island—and within a few minutes, we're racing down the hall. She ties her hair back as we run, and with no stray curls to soften her expression, I can see how worried she is. How much pain she's in.

It fucking guts me that this happened here. We're supposed to be safe on *my* island.

Khirta's still sleeping, but she shakes it off, extending a wing for us and throwing herself into the sky as soon as we're settled. The field Tindera described is just a few minutes away, but it's a long few minutes. Sifa's quiet in front of me, and I can feel her mind casting toward her dragon. I don't think he's responding.

Which has me fucking worried.

Sifa's gasp when she catches sight of Astarot sends a chill down my spine. I feel her grief—probably remembering the bolt that nearly killed him in the forest before she was taken to the northern Nest—and desperately wish I could take it from her.

I don't feel grief. Not yet.

All I feel is anger.

Rage.

Fury.

My ears are pounding, blood racing through every part of me as my fingers itch to wrap around a throat and squeeze the life out of whoever attacked him. Somebody on this island—my island that I opened to these wretches—attacked Sifa's dragon. They could have killed him, or maybe Tindera, if the bolt had hit the right spot. Astarot's being tortured again, the pain of his wound drawing a low keen from him.

We can't trust a single person in this gods-damned place other than the few I've hand selected over the years.

We're going to heal Astarot, and then I'm going to break some gods-damned heads figuring out what the fuck happened. Why someone would shoot down one of our dragons. And how many others want to do the same.

"How do we get him to the closest water?" I snarl as Khirta lands and throws out her wing for us to race down.

"We need to get the bolt out first," Sifa suggests, fear twisting every word. "He thinks maybe he can get there on his own once he's free."

The arrow didn't puncture anything important—thank fuck—but it's barbed, and we could easily kill him as it comes out if we're not careful. Sifa's entire body is trembling as she leans into his massive chest cavity, guiding the sharp tips out as she struggles to not cause him more pain. Tindera's fear is a constant presence, and I can't do shit except pull slowly, painstakingly, on the shaft while Sifa maneuvers it.

It takes ten minutes to pull the bolt out of Astarot. Ten of the longest gods-damned minutes in my life. But—another hearty thank fuck—Astarot passed out a few minutes in and didn't wake up. Sifa sucked in a deep breath when he did, free of his shared agony, and continued to yank at the metal embedded in her dragon.

Finally, Sifa moves the bolt past the last dangerous spot, and I can wrench it free, tossing it far away.

"That was fucking exhausting," Sifa mutters, her shoulders slumping as she looks at her passed-out dragon. Bone-crushing fatigue and despair emanate from her, seeping into my bones. This was supposed to be the one place I could bring my mate and our dragons and know we were safe. "At least he didn't feel most of it," she adds after a moment. "It would have been so gods-damned painful if he'd been awake."

I take a deep breath, dreading what we're about to do, but at least he's still unconscious. "Let's sew him up. Maybe you'll both get lucky and he'll sleep through that too."

She dips her chin, turning her haunted eyes toward me. "I'll hold him together while you do the stitches," she murmurs. "I think my touch will help him."

"I'm sure it will." I pause for a moment, reaching out my hand to caress her cheek. "He'll live. We'll get through this."

"I know," she says as she reaches up a hand to rest it on mine. "And I know now's not the time to think about this, but what does it mean that he was attacked? Is there a traitor on the island? More than one?" Her eyes water as she glances at Astarot and back to me. "He should be safe here. We all should be."

One little spark and my temper's flared again. I can feel it rumble up and down my spine, looking for an outlet. "I don't know who to kill for this, but I promise you, someone will die. Maybe many people. They will pay."

"I know," Sifa whispers. "Let's just do this and get him to the water."

Sewing up Astarot takes even longer than pulling the bolt out did. We start inside because he won't be able to move if we don't—fixing an organ I think is the equivalent of his spleen with hastily drawn stitches, before turning to his skin.

It's firm and slippery the way dragon skin always is and if it weren't for Sifa pulling the edges together, this would take a long fucking time. But we work as a team, our thoughts bouncing off each other so we don't need to speak. He sleeps the entire time, thank fuck. Within twenty or thirty minutes, we've patched him up enough to travel. We don't wake him yet, though. His body may need the rest before he moves again, and we can't risk screwing this up.

So we sit there, waiting impatiently, for another hour. Tindera's moved to the other side of the field, where she can pace without disturbing him. She's frantic because he should have sensed the attack and avoided the bolt. She suspects something else is wrong. That's a conversation for another day, though. First, we have to get him healed.

Finally, Sifa looks at me. "He's waking up," she breathes, the crease between her brows relaxing a bit as the tension that's been vibrating through Tindera starts to ease.

Just as Astarot's eyes open, I see Leif and Torsten riding toward us from across the field. Something hangs between them, although I can't tell what yet. Bastards have come to help. The first smile since launching out of bed this morning teases at my lips. They're always there when I need them.

Pain, Tindera tells me as I force my gaze away from them and look at Sifa and her dragon. They're talking about something—probably what it'll take to get Astarot to the water—and I wish I could take away the agony rippling through both of them, echoes of their pain digging into my side and squeezing my spine in a harsh grip. It's a long distance to the closest river if we have to walk.

But then the horses get closer, and I can see why they're walking instead of galloping. They have an enormous bucket of water sloshing between them. Leif is grinning like a child on a Yule morning, offering a gift to his parents.

I have no gods-damned idea what he thinks will happen. We're too far from any river or lake for the water to have an effect. Its power slips away the further the liquid strays from its source. They know the magic well enough to realize that.

"Not sure why they're here with that," I mutter to Sifa as they get closer.

"Guess we'll find out soon," she grits out, one hand on her belly and the other on Astarot's snout.

"You're probably wondering what we're doing," Leif yells when he's close enough.

"Crossed my mind."

"The water shouldn't work this far away from the river."

"Also crossed my mind."

"But it will." Now Leif's smile grows even broader.

"How the fuck could it? Magic doesn't work that way." I'm confused as fuck. They're smarter than this.

"One of the elves who arrived recently has a rare magic. I didn't even know such a thing existed. She's part dwarf and uses that ancestry to make vessels that can hold power for a short time. The strength of the magic will dissipate, but slowly. She suspects it will only work well here in Lumaria because this island is so imbued with the healing water. It's beneath our feet—deep in some places, but there. So it does work here, she assured me."

"Why have I never heard of this?"

"Like I said, she hasn't been on the island long. She mentioned it to me yesterday when Birger introduced us. She wanted me to let you know about it." He smiles. "What better time than now, right? When Toffer woke me up this morning to tell me what happened, I tracked her down and got this." His chin juts toward the bucket, one eyebrow lifting toward his hairline.

"And you think that'll help Astarot?" Sifa's voice holds hope I'm not letting myself feel. 'Cause Leif's right. I've never heard of this kind of magic before.

"She promises it will. We'll pour it on. It should heal him enough to get him into the air and to the river a mile or so from here."

"In Njordheim," Sifa adds, "we pulled water from a lake to pour it over Vulryn's wound. It helped—not like her dunking into the lake would have, but her wound closed more quickly than it would have without it."

"Just try it," Torsten grunts. "Brought it out here. May as well use it."

Practical, as always.

I nod. *Can you lift that barrel to pour the water over your drake?*

Yes. My dragon's as skeptical as me but willing to give it a try.

"Put it there," I tell them, gesturing toward a spot far enough away for my beast to lift it smoothly. "Tindera will take it. She'll be able to get high enough and have better control than we would."

They set it down, managing to not spill a drop, and Tindera hovers over it to clutch the handle with her claws. I've never seen her fly so carefully, her wings moving the air around her just enough to get her aloft. The surface is nearly glass—shockingly still—as she lifts it and carries it to her drake. It ripples a bit when she shifts claws, holding the handle in one while the other grasps the rim to slowly tip the bucket and rain the water over Astarot.

Surprise bursts from Sifa and Tindera at the immediate relief, my own pain almost disappearing as I let out a sigh that seems to start in my gods-damned toes to whisper up and out of me. The barrel must have some effect, because the water should be impotent by now. And then I *see* it healing Astarot, the stitched area seaming itself together just like it would if he were soaking in the river.

Well, fuck me. That's gods-damned miraculous.

"It worked," Sifa breathes next to me, her eyes brighter than they've been since we got here. "I still feel some pain, but hardly any. He's nearly healed."

I lift a finger to tuck a lock of hair behind her ear and caress her cheek. "We'll go to the river, get him fully healed, then find the bastard who did this."

"Fuck, yes, we will." Her eyes are feral, and I wish I could take her right here, right now.

Instead, I turn to Leif and Torsten. "I knew there was a reason to keep you around." My grin tells them just how thankful I am.

"Gotta make ourselves useful," Leif responds with a smirk.

"Thank you," Sifa tells them, her voice rich with emotion. "We both would have been miserable as he dragged himself to the nearest river. I am in your debt."

Torsten guffaws as Leif shakes his head, his gaze never leaving Sifa's.

"We are in your debt, Sifa," Leif tells her, every hint of levity gone from his gaze. "It took the boss a while to realize it—it took all of us too gods-damned long—but we needed you to break us out of the half-assed support we'd been giving the rebels. We needed to go all in, break free of the Dróttning. You got us there."

"Is that where we are?" I demand, anger over the attack on Astarot filling me again. "Even after what happened this morning?"

"Don't change nothing," Torsten mutters, his gaze holding mine. "We gonna let the bite of one snake stop us? Turn us away from what we know we gotta do? Fuck, no. We're in. We're all in."

"What if it's more than one snake?"

"We'll find 'em and root 'em out. Cut off the damned heads. Still don't change nothing. We're in."

"This is a death sentence for you if we lose." Now my burst of fury is gone. This shit is serious. "I'm in. I've made my choice, and I'll never regret it for one second. But I can't ask you to fight the serpent with me."

"Fuck you." Leif doesn't get angry often, but he snaps these words at me now. "Seriously, fuck you, Fhord. Do you think, after all these years, we'd abandon you? Now, when it really matters? When we finally might be able to change everything, free this land from the Dróttning? We're in. We've always been in. We're not gonna fight you about it."

Something inside me unfurls at his words, as if a coil, tightly wound around an important but undiscovered part of me, suddenly released. Relief washes through me. I don't know why. My Ætt have been by my side forever. They never would abandon me. But Leif's heated declaration, joined by Torsten's enthusiastic smirk, confirms what I already know. If we're going to defeat the Dróttning, I need them and they're not going anywhere.

Leif turns toward Astarot, who's standing to stretch his wings. "Our job here is done," he announces with a grin, striding toward his horse and throwing himself into the saddle. "See you in a bit," he says to Sifa, pointedly ignoring me. And then he yanks the reins, nudges the horse with his heels, and gallops away.

"We're in," Torsten repeats before mounting his horse and following Leif back to the city.

We watch them for a few moments before Sifa speaks. "You're not surprised about that, are you?" Her voice shimmers with her laugh.

"Guess I needed to hear it from them," I respond as I take her hand and draw her up and toward me. "We're all fucking crazy for doing this."

"We are," she agrees with a dip of her chin.

"We're gonna regret it."

"Probably."

"But I wouldn't change a thing."

"Me either." She lifts her hands to rest on my cheeks, drawing my lips toward hers.

And my cock springs to attention, filling the limited space between us. I groan—because even that little amount of pressure feels so fucking good—and I feel Sifa's smile as our lips pull apart.

"Fuck me, Fhord," she whispers, reaching forward to untie my trousers and wrap her hand around my bulging cock.

"Thank fuck," I whisper, untying her pants to drag them down while she wiggles free of them. I wrap my hands around that perfect ass and position her just above my cock, driving into her as she wraps her legs around my waist. "Gods damn, rabbit," I rasp. "You are perfect."

"Perfect for you," she breathes as she starts to move her hips, nibbling on my ear as she takes me as deep as she can.

I'm still for a moment, just thanking the fates for this female they've gifted me. And then I fuck her.

Sometimes when we fuck it's slow and sweet. I want to eat her up, luxuriate in her body and feel everything while we make love.

And sometimes we just fuck. This is a fuck. We've been doing a lot of that lately, too desperate for each other to go slowly. I'm moving her up and down on my cock as I plunge into her, fast and hard. She's holding on but also matching me thrust for thrust. I release my grip on the wall in my mind—something we've both erected to give ourselves a little bit of privacy—and feel her do the same.

Only fucking Sifa with all our walls down gives me the pure delirium that's rolling through my body right now. It's not a wave. It's a gods-damned typhoon, every nerve in my body vibrating with ecstasy.

Fucks with Sifa are fast, and this one's faster than most. We're both so wound up—we need this so badly—we let our bodies guide us, not holding back at all. Within a few minutes, she's starting to tighten around me, her breathing building into the pants that always pull my orgasm out of me. So fucking sexy.

We come together, Sifa's tight cunt wrapping around me as she starts to tremble, leading me into an orgasm with her. Slowing down, she rides my cock as our releases vibrate through us, drawing every bit of pleasure we can out of each other. When I'm done pumping my seed into her, she rests her hands on my cheeks one more time, pulling my lips down to hers.

"Fucking perfect," she whispers, wiggling her hips one more time as she smiles.

"Fucking perfect," I agree.

I wish we could stay here together, just my little rabbit, me and our dragons.

But the revolution awaits. And whether we like it or not, we've got a big role to play.

CHAPTER EIGHT

MATTHIAS

SHE'S NOT MY TYPE

I CAN'T BELIEVE I let Ziselær convince me to bring the dragon and her rider back to the Nest.

What the fuck was I thinking? I'm in charge in this bonding. *Me.* Not my gods-damned dragon. We went out there to kill that bitch of a beast and her female. Now they're coming home with us. Vulryn is Ziselær's draikana, and he's convinced he can turn her into a valuable ally.

They'll be in a cage and the Dróttning will be happy with our gift. I just hope I can convince her not to torture the dragon. She'll want to but that would piss Ziselær off. He never really wanted to kill Vulryn, and I should have known he'd convince me to keep her alive. The mating bond is strong in dragons. Much as he dislikes the idea of being bonded to a northern dragon, he knows it's her or nobody. And he wants to try.

I hate the idea of a northern dragon more than him because Vulryn bonded with a northern soldier. Which means Dani and I will join too, sooner or later. I've seen enough mated dragons to know their riders always end up together. The emotions that consume the dragons suck us in too.

She's not my type—Dani's an uppity cunt, like most female dragon riders—but she's pretty enough, with clear blue eyes and thick auburn hair I can wrap around my fist as I pound into her. Plus, her tits look fucking fantastic under the tunic she's wearing. Dani may not enjoy the fuck, but I'll make sure I do. That's all that matters anyway. She's a prisoner, and she'll take whatever I choose to give her.

For now, though, she'll just sit her ass down in her cell. When Ziselær decides to take his draikana, I'll take Dani. In the prison. And then I'll leave her there because that's where she belongs.

Alarms sound as we return with a dragon on our heels. The sentries know every beast in this land, and they saw Vulryn come here with Fhord and his little band of traitors. They also realize Vulryn's ferocious and fucking dangerous. She's taken down a couple of our strongest dragons.

The Dróttning should be in the Nest, so she'll get my gift soon. She hasn't left since Fhord blasted his way out of here, throwing every resource into searching for him, that elf, and the rest of the rebels. I've served her for many years, and I've never seen her so angry. She'll peel Fhord's skin herself when she gets him back. He got away with too much for too long. That shit's over.

I'm the fiercest, most loyal, dragon rider in Vanatia. And now I'm bringing her the beast that helped rescue Fhord and

Tindera, carrying my liege's wyrm form from the Nest so others could free them. She'll finally give *me* the respect I've deserved for decades.

She raged for days about their escape. So much blood. Any soldiers who survived the traitors' attack paid for their failure on the rack or in the dragons' feeding grounds. Ziselær reveled in a hearty meal—a shithead who'd fucked my favorite whore, although he knew I'd claimed her—a treat he rarely enjoys since humans aren't often sacrificed to the Thunder.

The Dróttning's waiting for us when we arrive, the smirk I've come to recognize when she's feeling particularly vengeful teasing the lips she always paints black. A red dress covers her as normal, curving just slightly around her small breasts and hips.

"Where are the others?" she demands as Ziselær settles near her, Vulryn close on his heels. I glance back at Dani as we both dismount and almost laugh. She's not nearly as nervous as she should be. The Dróttning will fix that soon.

"We didn't find them. These two arrived from the sea alone."

"From the sea?" The Dróttning's steely gaze shifts to Dani, her lips pursing together. "Why were you at sea?"

Dani cocks her head, narrowed eyes holding the Dróttning's for a moment as a little smile plays on her lips. "Vulryn was craving fish. We hadn't yet found one to her liking and would have soon returned to our hunt if Ziselær and his rider hadn't found us."

"Your invincible dragon was unable to catch a fish?"

Dani shifts her head to the other side now, a little sneer erupting as she rolls her eyes. I'm surprised for a moment that she's still alive after such disrespect, but my liege needs information from her.

"As I said, we hadn't yet found the fish she craves, one of those spearfish that like to jump from the water. Vulryn grew thirsty—a need she hasn't yet slaked," she adds with a pointed scowl at the Dróttning, "so we headed for the shore and found Ziselær. Fortuitous."

"Why in all the worlds would it be fortuitous?"

"Because Vulryn and Ziselær are mates," Dani explains as if to a child, prompting the Dróttning's gaze to spin toward me, the glare in her eyes one most people dread. "Vulryn and I are here to find out if Ziselær wants to explore the mating bond."

"So, you hope to join us, abandon Fhord and his elf?"

"We haven't decided yet. We may go back to them." Her gaze shifts to me and then my dragon, and back to the Dróttning. "Or maybe not. We'll have to see."

"So little loyalty," the Dróttning muses, flicking her gaze up and down Dani's frame.

"My loyalty is to Vulryn. My commitment is to meeting her needs. It's why we abandoned the Monarch and came here. If she needs to be here with Ziselær, this is where we'll be."

"If I allow it." The Dróttning's eyes flare as her lips thin.

Dani watches her for a moment, the smirk I already recognize playing at her lips, before dipping her chin once. "If you allow it."

Now, I'm even more pissed at the gods who paired my dragon with Vulryn. Dani's an obnoxious bitch, and she's gonna get herself killed. Fucking idiot.

"Take them to their cells," the Dróttning barks out, throwing the briefest glance at a nearby soldier.

He drops into a deep bow and gestures toward another guard as Dani sneers at her.

"You're putting us in a cell?"

"Cells," the Dróttning clarifies. "You will not be allowed the privilege of sharing a cell."

"I'm not going into a gods-damned cell." Dani's grimace is unspeakably rude. The Dróttning desperately wants information from her, or she'd have a sword through her eye. She's gotten more leeway than I've ever seen the Dróttning give anyone. Except that traitor Fhord.

Vulryn rumbles, drawing Dani's gaze to her. Dani's eyes glint as she speaks with her dragon, shaking her head twice before finally spitting out, "Fine."

"You may put me in a cell for now," she mutters, slowly turning toward the Dróttning. "But if you hope to earn my loyalty, you won't keep me there long."

"Stupid girl," the Dróttning declares. "If I want your loyalty, I *will* have it." She turns to the guard. "I'm done with them. Take them away."

I can't hold back the smile as I watch Dani stalk away, while her dragon struts. She's weak, letting her dragon lead her. It will be easy to control her. To take what I want, when I want.

This could be a satisfying turn of events, after all.

I look at the Dróttning, ready to request my leave, but before I can, she gestures toward her rooms. "Follow me." She doesn't wait to see my response—she never does, because I'll be dead if I do anything but comply—turning to stride down the hall.

Smiling to myself, I follow close on her heels. She'll reward me well for this gift.

She doesn't pause as a guard swings open the door to her rooms, stalking to her favorite chair to spin abruptly and drop into it.

My steps slow when I see her face. She doesn't look nearly as pleased with me as she should. She's clenching her hands as if she's stopping herself from throttling me, her nostrils flaring in and out slowly.

Throwing out her arm, she gestures impatiently toward the chair across from her. "Sit."

I dip my chin then lift it. I've done nothing wrong. I have no reason to fear her, I remind myself as I plant my ass into the seat.

"When did you know Ziselær and that orange dragon are mates?"

Shit. Maybe I fucked up after all.

"Ziselær has suspected Vulryn is his mate since they fought on the day Fhord escaped."

The Dróttning's eyes narrow as she holds my gaze.

Gods damn. I think I fucked up.

"Why did I learn this from the dragon's rider and not you?" I recognize this cold, heartless tone. It almost always precedes torture or death, often both.

Bloody Helheim. I definitely fucked up.

I suck in a deep breath, gathering my words to convince her she has my eternal loyalty. "Ziselær was unsure. We've been searching for the dragon, hoping to confirm his suspicion before I bothered you with it. I would not take your valuable time with an unfounded belief."

She's silent for a long time, watching me, measuring my words and my commitment to her. She sees so much and must know by now I would never betray her. I'd sooner take my life or my dragon's than lose her trust.

When she speaks, her tone is low and flat. "I do not appreciate being taken by surprise. You should have told me as soon as Ziselær encountered that dragon."

Lifting a fist to my chest, I drop to my knees in front of her. "My apologies, my liege. It will not happen again."

Her silence doesn't last as long this time. Gesturing me up after a few seconds, she nods. "If it happens again, you'll be on the rack."

"And I'll deserve it."

Her gaze spins in the direction of the cages holding Vulryn and Dani, as if she could somehow see them from here, and back to me. "When you arrived, I intended to torture them. Drink their blood. Suck them dry. I've been craving their death since they helped that ingrate Fhord escape. I will have it. The rider *will* die; we shall see about the dragon. But we'll use them first. Torture isn't always the way."

I don't let my relief show. If she realized how badly Ziselær wants to know Vulryn, she'd use it against us. We'd be the ones suffering, despite our loyalty. Never letting my gaze stray from hers, I give her a small nod. "How may I serve you?"

"Give them what they want. Your dragon will have time—let's say, two weeks—to secure the orange dragon's loyalty, her oath to me. She will eat what I choose for her and drink from the water I provide. She may fly with Ziselær when I decide it's time, not before." Her eyes narrow, an expression I know well. She won't debate her demands. "The dragon will learn what it means to swear fealty to me. If she does, she may live."

"And her rider?"

"We'll kill her after we extract her knowledge. She's one of Harald's soldiers and an elf. Fhord and his dragon escaped because of her. We cannot permit her to roam this land." She pauses, a smile twisting her lips as her gaze grows distant. "I will enjoy teaching her what happens to those who defy me."

Nodding her head, she looks at me again. "First, though, we'll try to win her loyalty too. I believe she's flighty and easily moved. She may give us what we need without a fight. Then we'll kill her. And perhaps I'll let you choose Vulryn's new rider, if you succeed."

"I would be honored, my liege." My mind bounces around the women I would choose from—the cunts that pretend they don't want me. I'd have fun taking one of them while Ziselær takes Vulryn.

"Please me and I may permit it." She lifts one hand to gesture toward the door. "Leave now."

Rising quickly, I drop into a deep bow and then stand straight, giving her the respect and fealty she deserves. "I will not let you down."

"No, you will not."

She doesn't expect more from me, so I don't dawdle. Turning, I stride toward the door as a guard swings it wide for me and into the hall.

Time for Ziselær to meet his draikana.

His grumble of pleasure when I find him and tell him what the Dróttning decided pisses me off. He was a sentimental bastard when the Dróttning gave him to me, but I fixed that shit. It took a long time to break him. He's been *my* dragon—ruthless and fearless like me—for longer than he wasn't. I'll let him be sentimental this one time, but if I see it again, I'll do whatever I must to stomp out any softness he may be feeling about his draikana. Vulryn and Dani are weak. We won't let them infect us.

She must stay in her cell for now. If she satisfies the Dróttning that she'll be loyal, she'll be allowed to fly with you. The Dróttning will want to know what you learn from her. Vulryn and her rider will need to tell the Dróttning where the rebels are hiding to earn her trust.

Ziselær, normally talkative, is silent for a long time. *Fly*, he says at last. He thinks they'll need to consummate their mating bond before Vulryn will betray the rebels.

Stubborn fucking bastard. I step into Ziselær's path, forcing him to lift his wings to keep from running into me. Spinning, I let him see the side of me he dislikes, even after all these years. *I didn't ask for your opinion*, I rebuke him. *She will give us what we need whether she flies with you or not. If she doesn't, she'll die. Those are the Dróttning's commands. We will comply.*

He snorts, his eyes flaring. He may not be able to break her—especially not in two weeks, without consummating their bond—but he knows he has no choice. I am his master, as the Dróttning is mine.

Comply, he declares, his voice fierce. We will do what we must to compel Vulryn to bend to the Dróttning.

Damn straight we will.

He's strong now, and gods-damned lucky the Dróttning paired him with me. He'd have been spineless with another rider.

Turning again, I continue stalking down the hall toward Vulryn's cell. When we get there, I take a minute to look at her before opening the gate for Ziselær. She's a fucking gorgeous beast, her feathers a rich color that hovers between red and brown, sparkling when one of the lamps flares to cast its light on her. She's asleep, and her expression is softer than it's been before. Every time I've seen her, she's looked either angry or flirtatious.

Ziselær grunts, nudging me with a claw.

Impatient? I ask with a laugh.

Draikana, he complains. He wants to touch her, to feel her snout rub against his.

Should I stay, or lock you in with her and leave?

Go. He doesn't hesitate. He wants to be alone with her. Of fucking course he does.

I unlock the gate and swing the door open, smirking as Vulryn's eyes open and she watches in silence while he prowls toward her. *Go*, Ziselær says again, turning to glare at me.

Calm the fuck down, I tell him as I swing the gate closed and twist the lock. *Don't kill each other.*

He doesn't respond, just watching me in silence. Part of me wants to stay just to show him I can, but I told him he could have this. And we need Vulryn on our side. So I turn on my heel and leave.

I don't want to watch them anyway.

I'd rather go fuck with Dani. Show her what life's gonna be like between us.

She's asleep too, so I pause to watch her. Now that I'm really looking at Vulryn's rider, I see she's more than pretty. I'll enjoy fucking her, fisting that thick hair as I shove my cock through those pretty lips, watching her blue eyes water while I fuck her mouth so deep she can't breathe. I bet she's shit at sucking cock, but I can fix that. She'll be a pro before I'm done with her.

Her eyes pop open, alert and wary, as if she feels my stare. Sitting up abruptly, she plants her feet on the ground and glares at me. "What the fuck do you want?"

"Ziselær is with your dragon. I decided it's time for us to get to know each other."

"Fuck you. I don't want you anywhere near me while I'm trapped in this cell."

"That's not how this'll work," I tell her, steel in my voice. "The Dróttning wants you here. She's being gods-damned generous, though. You've got a bed and a blanket, despite the fact that you helped the Dróttning's two favorite prisoners escape. That's not something we usually give our enemies. You'll also be fed well."

"How kind of her." Dani's tone is sharp, a blade poised at a throat.

"Kinder than you deserve. If it were up to me, you'd be dead. But she thinks you'll come to your senses and join our fight. You and your dragon could be valuable allies."

"We came to you voluntarily," Dani yaps, "and this is how you treat us. Locking us up like gods-damned prisoners. This is not how you gain our loyalty."

"Make no mistake," I growl. "She will have your loyalty. The only question is how much pain you'll suffer before you pledge your blade to her."

Dani stands, stalking over to stand as close as she can with the bars between us. She says nothing for a moment, her narrow eyes and thin lips telling me how angry she is. When she speaks at last, saliva sprays from her mouth. "I will never pledge my loyalty to a ruler who must torture me to extract my oath. Tell her to kill me now if that's her plan."

"Not yet," I hiss, wiping some of her slobber from my cheek. Reaching out before she can move away, I grasp her by the neck with my free hand, holding her in place while my spit-covered finger pushes into her mouth. She bites, hard, and I smile, removing my finger when she finally releases it and sucking it into my mouth. "I'm gonna taste you first, feel what it's like to fuck Vulryn's rider while Ziselær takes her. If you haven't sworn loyalty by then, I'll kill you."

"I will never fuck you," she snarls as she wrenches herself away from my grip. Those pretty little eyes flash the kind of hatred that stirs my cock, her fists clenched as she throws her shoulders back. She sure as fuck doesn't mean to give me a better look at her tits, but that's what she does. And they really are magnificent tits.

I reach out again, but she steps back, smacking my hand before I can wrap it around her throat. "Foolish girl," I drawl, my cock jerking again as I let my gaze roam down her body and back up. "You're in the Nest now. You belong to the Dróttning. We'll be fucking before the month's done. You'll want it as much as me, but I don't give one little shit whether you do or don't. Your body's mine and I will take it whenever and however I want."

She's still for a moment, the only motion a chest that rises up and down with her harsh breaths. I watch as she forces herself to relax, tension leaving her shoulders as a smirk lifts her lips. "I'll bite off your gods-damned cock before I let it touch me," she promises, resting her hands on her hips.

And my cock jumps again. This is gonna be fun.

"You'll change your mind," I hurl. "No rider can resist the pull of their dragon's mating bond. Maybe you'll even like it. But I don't give a fuck whether you get off or not. I will fuck you. And *I* will like it."

Turning, I stride away. She spews a few threats behind me, but I don't turn around. She'll learn soon enough that everything we do is on my terms. And she'll be grateful for every minute I give her.

CHAPTER NINE

DANI

HE HURT ME

*H*E *HAS COME TO me.* Vulryn's ridiculously happy with herself and I can't help but smile. We've been here two days—two painfully boring days—and this will be Ziselær's third visit.

And are you pleased with him?

For now. He is a splendid drake. Strong and sure. If he gives me what I demand, we will be a good pairing.

And if he doesn't?

As I said, then we will kill him.

How? We're both trapped in a cell.

Do you still have so little faith in me? If I say we will kill him, we can and we will. He is impressive but southern beasts are weak. He is no match for us.

I shake my head, although I have no idea why. Nobody can see me. I'm just talking to myself. I'm alone and will be for a long time.

Matthias is staying away, thank the gods. He's every bit the bastard Fhord and Sifa described. But I've realized Fhord and Sifa were right that we'll probably end up fucking anyway. I already feel Vulryn's attachment to Ziselær, and how it connects me to Matthias.

It doesn't help that he's so striking, or that I haven't had sex for a very, very long time. I'm a normal girl who likes sex. Even bad sex has always been good for me. I can get myself off if the male doesn't try. I'm also up for almost anything. It wouldn't take much for Matthias to turn me on, and I don't know if I'll be able to resist him when Vulryn flies with Ziselær and her lust feeds mine.

I need to make sure it's just sex, that I resist the draw to be with him beyond that. I'll be damned if I'm going to let Vulryn's emotions twist mine. I can't ever let myself start to think I might actually like the bastard.

I sigh, wishing I had a book as I look around my cell. They're feeding me well, as Matthias said, so I'm healthy enough to exercise. And that's pretty much all I can do. Three times a day, I go through my training regimen. I'm sore—I usually do this only daily, so I'm pushing myself—but I like the burn. It reminds me I'm alive. For now, at least.

My back is turned away from the door when I hear his grunt. And smell his stench. The ugly guard who's taken an interest in me. He's tall and broad with pale skin, thin lips, and sunken eyes, and he's spent the last two days leering at me every time he passes by.

"What the fuck do you want?" I demand, not bothering to turn around.

"I like the show," he mutters, his voice low.

I'm guessing he's already groping at the unimpressive bulge in his pants. He doesn't try to hide his reason for watching me, but why would he? I'm sure the Dróttning doesn't give a fuck what he does. I'm a prisoner and she'll probably feed off my misery and pain, no matter its source.

Spinning around, I lift my chin and sneer at him. "I'm done exercising. You can leave."

"I like the show even if you're not moving. You're a pretty thing."

"I'm also a mean thing. Savage. I'll kill you if you try to come in."

His gaze slips up and down my body, insects crawling over my skin. I want to cringe away from him, but I won't give him the satisfaction. Instead, I plant my feet and hold my ground.

"Little thing like you?" he huffs. "If I want you, I'll take you. Nothing you can do to stop me."

I really wish I could play with his mind a bit. They strapped the manacle Sifa and Fhord mentioned around my throat before they threw me in this cell. I feel like they ripped away part of me—maybe the most important part, other than my bond with Vulryn—and that's even more annoying than being trapped here. Thankfully, this manacle is less powerful than the one Fhord described. It doesn't quell my bond with my dragon. The Dróttning wants us to talk. She thinks I'll be more malleable. I'd be going crazy without Vulryn in my head.

Sneering—making sure the guard sees the badass bitch the Monarch drove me to become—I stalk forward as I hold his eyes, stopping close enough to grimace at his breath. Ugh. Garlic and liver and ... dirt? This is absolutely the most dangerous part of this man. "Try me," I purr. "I could use the distraction."

And he does. The bastard eyes me up and down, pausing at my breasts for way too long, and then pulls out a fucking key. My heart is a racing horse in an instant, my fingers flexing as I back up and start to bounce on my toes. He's big, but if he's assigned to the prison as a guard, he won't fight well. They wouldn't waste a warrior's talents here.

Vulryn must sense the shift in my emotions. I feel her mental caress a moment before her words drop into my mind. *What is happening?*

A guard wants to try his luck with me. Don't worry. I'll handle him.

You are strong. He will fail.

He will.

I back up, preparing myself for whatever he plans. He looks more confident than he should, and I wonder for a moment if I've misjudged him. His gaze holds mine as he raises a hand to caress an amulet of some kind pinned on his coat, smirking as the pain hits me.

It's unlike anything I've felt before, as if my spine suddenly turned into a corkscrew and started spinning in place, wrenching bones and nerves and muscles as it gathered them all like string. I collapse to my knees, trying to breathe through the agony, but it's captured my lungs too, squeezing every bit of air out of them.

WHAT IS HAPPENING?

Vulryn's scream echoes through my mind as his hand drops, freeing me from whatever just happened. I fall to the ground face first, my nose slamming into the rock. *He hurt me*, I moan as I inhale blood and gunk, coughing it out and searching again for air to fill my desperate lungs. *I don't know how. I've never felt such pain.*

"I'm gonna fuck you, and you're gonna lay there and take it. If you try to fight me, I'll give you pain again."

Flipping over, my feet coming up to hold him away, I snarl my response. "Fuck. You."

He shakes his head, his lips twisting into a cruel grin as he lifts his hand, stroking the ornament on his coat to twist my body again. I curl into a ball, struggling to find my way around this agony. A sane part of my brain knows it's entirely mental, and that I should be able to stuff it in a box and ignore it. But my mind is too consumed by pain to do anything but survive.

The guard drops his hand again, releasing the amulet's grip on me and reaching for my feet as he barks out a laugh. "You're fucking sexy when you're rolling around on the ground," he sneers, pulling at one ankle while his other hand grasps at the other and shoves my legs apart. "I'm gonna take what I want. This is just foreplay. I get harder every time I see you squirm."

My drake will tell his rider. He will come.

Not Matthias. Please. That fucker will probably watch and laugh. Just ... let me deal with this.

The male hurts you. My drake's rider will help you. I will make sure of it.

No. Please.

She's quiet for a moment, resolve echoing through our bond. Because she's a stubborn bitch. *It is done*, she tells me after a few seconds. *Protect yourself until he arrives.*

I don't have the energy to fight her and this bastard at the same time. He's still standing there, watching me try to catch my breath, my legs splayed out in front of him like I'm a gods-damned roast chicken. "I'm gonna let go now and you're gonna take these pants off." His gaze wanders up, stopping again at my chest. "And the shirt. I wanna see those titties."

I brace myself for what's coming next and wrench my ankles away from him, pulling back a knee and pounding a kick into his balls just as he reaches up for that fucking ornament. He barely grazes it, sending a hint of pain toward me, before crumbling to the ground, both of his hands slamming into his cock.

Before he can gather his wits, I launch myself at him, reaching for the amulet, but then yank my hand away as a flood of pain washes through me.

Fuck. Me.

Now my thoughts are scrambling, searching for some way to get the amulet away from him without torturing myself. He's moving too quickly, though, his gaze finding mine as a cruel smirk twists his lips. I kick out again, punching away the hand reaching for the amulet with the first kick and breaking his nose with the second one—because if I'm gonna have a broken nose, he sure as fuck will too.

Now he's pissed. He spins away from me as his hand reaches up again, slapping over the talisman—or whatever the fuck it is—before I can stop him.

I'm on the ground again, my body twisted into a knot as I try to find some air in a room that's become a vacuum. A detached part of my mind watches as he drags himself up, leaning over me and spewing out the blood flowing from his destroyed face.

And he just stands there.

His hand splayed across the amulet.

His lips twisted into an ugly sneer.

His blood running down his chin to drip onto my lips and nose and eyes.

While I count down the seconds until I die. Because I can't fucking breathe.

And nobody can survive this kind of pain.

Finally, he pulls his hand away, resting his palms on his knees as he leans over and spits in my face. *The fuckwad.*

"Take off your gods-damned clothes now. Or I will fuck you while I twist your insides."

But I can't move yet. I'm still struggling to fill my lungs as the remnants of the pain ripple through me.

"Now," he howls, kicking me in the ribs and setting off another fire, this one thankfully isolated to just one place. "Take. Off. Your. Clothes."

I smile instead. Because he hasn't wrung the fight out of me yet.

"I will not," I growl. "If you want me naked, you'll need to strip me yourself. You won't, though. Because the second you get close enough, I'll bash in your cock again. You won't be able to get my clothes off while you push that gods-damned button on your coat."

This time I'm ready for the pain. I don't flinch, holding his steely gaze as the Dróttning's fucked-up magic feels like it's ripping my spine out of my back. I clench my teeth and ignore my need to breathe, refusing to show him the weakness he demands.

"Fine," he yells after a few seconds, throwing up his hands and releasing me from the pain. I'm sucking in a breath of air when he leans forward, one hand whipping out to grab my wrist as the other fumbles with a pair of cuffs at his back.

"Did the Dróttning give this prisoner to you?"

Matthias's tone is cold. He's relaxed, standing in the open doorway to my cell with his hands resting on the knives at his belt. The guard's eyes widen as a pulse starts to beat in his neck. He doesn't move, and I almost laugh as he struggles to mask his fear.

"I'm guessing the answer's 'no'," I gasp through my stuttering breaths, "if his reaction to your question is any indication." Despite the pain still echoing through me, I can't keep the smile from my words or my lips.

"Shut up." The guard's grunt barely reaches my ears. He straightens and turns around slowly, still clutching my wrist in his meaty paw.

"He wants me to shut up," I purr, my gaze lifting to find Matthias. "I wonder why."

"Did he hurt you?" Matthias's voice is freezing now, not even a hint of emotion in his words.

"That button on his coat—he used it a lot. And I think he broke my fucking nose."

Nodding, Matthias shifts his gaze back to the guard. I'd be shitting myself if he looked at me like that, a tic in his jaw and every inch of him clenched tight, ready to pounce. "The Dróttning has forbidden use of the talisman for torture," Matthias reminds him as he takes a heavy step forward. "It draws from her magic, which angers her when done without cause."

"The bitch fought back. I had to restrain her."

Matthias sneers, probably pissed off about having to come save me. But he's much more pissed at the fucker that just tried to rape me, forcing him to come to my aid. And I'm gonna enjoy every second of his revenge.

"Stand up and face me, guard."

The guard's fear disappears, replaced by rage. And now I like the fact that Matthias is a gods-damned asshole. Because this male is going to regret coming after me. He just doesn't realize how badly yet.

"You know my name, dragon rider," the guard says as he finally releases my wrist.

"You think too much of yourself," Matthias responds with a vicious smile. "I don't retain such meaningless information."

"This one is mine, dragon rider. I won't fight you for a female again."

"Didn't go well for you last time, did it?" Now Matthias's grin is genuine. There's an interesting story here.

"You got lucky," the guard mutters. "I'd have had her if you hadn't come along."

"She didn't want you any more than this one does. She wanted me though. She was grateful when I put you in your place." Now Matthias's gaze flicks toward me for a moment, then back to the guard. "I think this one will be too. I'll enjoy her thanks."

"Fuck you, Matthias." If he thinks this gives him a pass into my pants, he can fuck right off.

Matthias's eyes go hard, little blue rocks sitting in a fierce, angry face. "I'll get to you soon," he tells me. Turning back to the guard, his expression relaxes. "Now, where were we?"

"I was telling you to stay the fuck away. This one's mine."

"That's where you're wrong." Matthias prowls forward now, planting himself directly in front of the guard. They're nearly the same height and build, but Matthias is so much *more* than the guard. It's not just his looks, although that helps. Matthias is healthy and vibrant, where the guard is old and weak. It's no contest and the guard must know it. "I brought her here, and she's mine."

The guard's not ready to give up so easily, though. He swings, one hand punching into Matthias's ribs and the other pounding his jaw. The guard almost loses his balance but manages to hold himself up, planting his feet as his arms swing back into position, ready for the fight he's trying to start.

Matthias doesn't flinch. He stands there, a rock, and spits in the guard's face. His hands are loose on his sides, as if the guard isn't worth even the effort of a punch. "That's all you get, guard. If you try again, I won't hold back."

The guard's really pissed now, his jaw clenching as his nostrils flare. His right hand flails out again, but Matthias is ready for him. The dragon rider's left hand rips up, catching the guard's fist inches from his nose. He squeezes, drawing a hiss from the guard, followed by a whimper. In seconds, the guard's on his knees, his free hand trying to peel Matthias's fingers away. But Matthias's hold just tightens.

The first crack echoes in my little cage, the guard's squeal bouncing around behind it. Matthias smirks as his hand tightens even more, snapping what sounds like every bone in the guard's hand. By the time he releases his grip, the guard is on the floor, clutching his hand next to his stomach as he screams like a stuck pig.

"Was that the hand that hurt you? Or do I need to punish the other one, too?"

"That's the one," I say, "although if you hadn't stopped him, he'd have done that and worse with the other."

Matthias watches me for a moment, then reaches for one of the knives on his belt. Handing it to me, he gestures toward the still-screeching guard. "Take a finger. For your troubles."

"A worthy gift." Matthias may be an evil bastard, but I'm wondering if we're the same kind of evil. I take the blade and kneel down next to the guard, yanking his left hand toward me as I examine my options. His eyes are saucers as he watches me, whining as tears roll down his cheeks.

"Please," he mumbles, his gaze holding mine. "I won't do that again. I swear."

"A pinkie, then," I announce, swiping the knife down to slice off his smallest finger, "because you apologized so nicely."

He squeals again, plucking his hand from my grip to tuck it into his stomach along with the other one and rolling away. I expect him to drag himself up after a few seconds, but he just lays there, the squeal turning into a wail and then a whimper.

I look up at Matthias and smile. "He's not much without his little button."

"Never has been," Matthias grunts, spitting at the guard one last time. When he looks back at me, his blue eyes are clear, no anger sparking in them. He holds my gaze for long seconds, then extends a hand to pull me to my feet. "I'll ask the Dróttning for permission to move you to a room. You'll still be a prisoner but no longer subject to weak males like this."

"Why?" He hasn't let go of my hand and I don't mind. I like this version of Matthias, gods help me.

"Ziselær has grown fond of Vulryn. He hopes to please her. While you're unhappy, your dragon is unhappy."

"Will the Dróttning care?"

"She wants your loyalty. I'll convince her this is the best way to earn it."

"And if I never give her my loyalty?"

"You'll die, and perhaps your dragon. Ziselær will grieve, but his commitment is to the Dróttning and me. He'll continue to serve in her army, as will I."

"And what must I give for her to trust me?"

"The rebels," Matthias responds with a shrug, his voice flat. "Fhord, his elf, and their dragons to start. The location of their refuge. Everyone else you know who supports the rebellion. She'll require everything. If you don't give it to her, she'll kill you."

Dropping my hand, Matthias reaches for the guard's feet, flipping him onto his back to pull him from the cell. The guard lets himself be dragged, still clutching his hands to his stomach. Matthias pauses just long enough to lock the door behind him when they're in the hall, then drops one of the guard's feet, hauling him with the other. I watch as it bounces along behind them, the guard too broken to resist.

When they walk around the corner and out of sight, I reach out to Vulryn. *Thank you. He saved me. I'm okay now.*

Vulryn doesn't respond with words. Instead, I hear her snort of approval, followed by a quick caress of love.

I love you too, I tell her as I lay down, facing the door to think through everything I've learned.

CHAPTER TEN

SIFA

JUST BETWEEN US

"Who the fuck would have attacked one of our dragons?"

Fhord called for his advisors to gather as soon as we got back. Our good moods from the river Astarot bathed in—and everything that happened before that—disappeared when we walked in the door and found them bickering. They spin toward him, apologies in their eyes, when we slam into the room demanding answers.

"We're conducting a search," Birger assures, hands splayed on the table in front of him. "We'll find the weapon and bring whoever wielded it to justice."

"But why?" Fhord's voice vibrates with his anger. I can tell from his posture—rigid shoulders and a straight back—that he's trying to control it, without much success. And I can't blame him one little bit. I'm struggling to hold back the fury that flamed inside me when we found them like this, more focused on whatever squabbles they have with each other than the traitors in our midst. "Why would someone attack our dragons?"

"Are you truly surprised, Fhord?" An older female named Gerta asks this question, her tone soft. "You're easily recognized in Vanatia. We few have known your truths, but most have always believed you to be a committed ally of the Dróttning. She commands the dragons, and they've done much harm to the rebellion. It can't be easy for people to change views of you and your beasts that they've held for a very long time."

"Rebels fear the dragons, and for good reason," another offers. "They've never before been our friends."

A frustrated sigh erupts from Fhord as he plops into a chair, reaching for my hand to pull me down next to him. He turns toward me, frustration written in every line of his face. "You know this world well. What should we do?"

"What can we do, except stay the course?" I demand, squeezing his hand. Hopelessness tries to suck me in, but I push that shit away because I will not let that bitch win. "None of this will be easy," I remind him, my voice rising. "The Dróttning has fucked every person in this land in one way or another. Why in all of Helheim would they trust us? But we don't have a choice. It's her or us, and it has to be us. So we'll root out the bastards that did this, rip every rotten one of them from the ground, and then finish it with her. Put her in the ground."

The door opens, and my gaze snaps up to find the Ætt entering the room. Something in me relaxes at their presence.

They keep Fhord sane, and I've found myself relying more and more on them too. Nods and smiles greet them, Birger standing to wave toward some of the empty seats at the table.

"Thank you for joining us," he tells them as he catches the eye of the man who led them in. "Show the others in when they arrive," he says. "We'll be here for a while and none of us have eaten. Bring bread and cheese, and some wine and ale."

The man dips his chin, closing the door behind him.

Fhord lifts one of his eyebrows as he turns back toward Birger. "Others?"

"A few of your allies," he explains, "with interest in our work and perhaps knowledge to offer."

Fhord cocks his head. "If we don't know anything about the attacker, what is there to discuss?"

"We can do nothing about that until our people find the weapon. We should focus on other important matters." He smiles, a playful look dancing across his face. I don't know how he does it, but he sucks some of the tension from the room. "It's time to plan the revolution," Birger says with a wink. "We've been waiting for you to be ready. I never suspected a mate would be the cause, but we're all happy the time has come."

"And you're sure we're committed, even after one of our dragons was attacked?"

Birger watches Fhord for a moment, and I wonder how much he sees with his wise eyes. Finally, he looks around the room. "Everyone here has been supporting the revolution in one way or another for many years. You, Fhord, have done and sacrificed more than any of us."

"I've been the Dróttning's trusted soldier for every one of those years, save the last few months."

"Do you think I don't realize what that has cost you? We've needed someone in her inner circle, who could play her game and convince her of his loyalty." He pauses again, holding Fhord's gaze, his eyes fierce. "I know what you've had to do to hold her trust. I know how much your soul has withered over these many years."

When Birger turns toward me and leans forward, his expression shifts, his chin lifting along with the corners of his lips as his eyes grow bright. Even his voice changes, the somber notes giving way to words that would glimmer and sparkle if they could take form. "How hard has it been to play the Dróttning's games since your mate entered this world?"

As I watch Fhord's spine stiffen in his stubborn refusal to acknowledge what a *good* male he is, I feel Birger's question in my soul, that part of me that belongs to my mate. I'd been so angry with him, never once considering the cost for this selfless soldier to play a necessary role to protect those he loves.

In a ridiculously short amount of time, Fhord's life has been flipped upside down. He abandoned everything. The Dróttning tortured him and his dragon mercilessly. He can never return to the Nest and the life he's lived for centuries. All because of me. Still, his steps haven't faltered once. Instead, he's expanded the net he casts around everyone who's found a way into his heart, tugging each of us into his steadfast embrace.

But then the flame I hold for him stutters, flickering inside me, as I recall that I hold the biggest secret between us, as bad or worse than anything he kept from me. He still has no idea our time here is limited because I'm aging like a human. I promised myself I would tell him as soon as he healed, but I haven't. He needs to know he put everything at risk for a mate who will be gone in what will feel like a blink of an eye.

"It doesn't matter." Fhord tells Birger, dragging my thoughts back to this room. He sits back in his seat, releasing my hand and crossing his arms over his chest.

Guilt and dread wash over me, but I push them aside again. This isn't the time or place to bare my soul. We need to deal with this first.

"It does matter," I interject, my hand reaching for Fhord's as I try to pull him—and myself—out of this funk. "He's sacrificed more than most, and I wish others realized it. But I can't blame them for not knowing our secrets."

"Indeed," Birger agrees, sitting back. He opens his mouth to speak again but is interrupted by a sharp tap at the door, which then swings open to reveal Mikkael, Frida, Liv, Toffer, and even Thor.

"The whole gang," I murmur as I smile at my happy troll and the grumpy cat draped across his neck, Thor's legs hanging down over Toffer's shoulders.

Birger nods at me. "Everyone may have something to offer. Mikkael could be particularly helpful since he didn't arrive with you, so most on Lumaria have no idea of your connection. He shared his thoughts about the shooter with the guards searching for the weapon."

"I'm not surprised."

Mikkael smirks at my words as he plops down, leans back and kicks his feet onto the table, ignoring the stares leveled at him by a couple of the advisors. "Just like me to be in the middle of the shit," he agrees.

"What do you know?" Fhord's always direct and to the point where the dragons are concerned. And he's still a little suspicious of Mikkael.

"The night you came to the tavern with that northern bitch..."

"Dani." My tone is sharper than I intend, but he needs to get past this. "Her name's Dani, and she's an important part of our team."

"I know her name," he responds, his voice flat. "I also know she left, which is the only reason I'm still here." Shaking his head, he drops his feet to the ground, leaning forward to rest his elbows on the table. "Anyway, before you got there that night, I was talking to Bjorn, the weapons seller. He said something about dragons and their riders I barely noticed at the time. But then Astarot was shot, and I realized I needed to talk to Birger."

"What'd he say?" Fhord's leaning forward too, his eyebrow drawn together, lips a flat line.

"He said they didn't trust any of you—that dragon riders all are loyal to the Dróttning—and they weren't going to give you a chance to betray everyone."

My stomach clenches. I know what Mikkael says is true. I told Fhord the same thing a few minutes ago. But knowing that people in this town are cocky enough to spew their venom aloud—that they're spouting their hate in taverns, not just whispering it behind closed doors—drives home how entrenched they are. We may end up fighting them as well as the Dróttning.

"Fuck," Fhord mutters. He watches Mikkael for a moment before turning toward Birger. "Do you have Bjorn?"

"We do."

"Is he talking?"

"Not yet."

"Sifa and I will get what he knows." He glances at me, his eyes fierce, as he stands.

"Give us a chance first, Fhord." Birger's adopted his "reasonable steward" voice. I barely know him, but I already recognize it.

"Why the fuck should I do that?" He's tugging on my hand, but I stay put. I'm not ready to go yet.

"Let's hear what he has to say, Fhord," I murmur, mimicking Birger's tone. "Before we do something we may regret."

"Why?" Fhord's still standing, a grimace on his face as he cocks his head to the side, but he's not pulling on my hand anymore. "Why should we give them a chance?"

"Bjorn is well-known and liked," I remind him, trying my damnedest to keep a level head. One of us has to. "If we want the rebels to trust us, we start by winning over people like him. We don't know if he's directly involved. If they find the weapon among his things, we'll rip his mind apart. But if it's not him, we'll have a better chance of persuading others if we can convince him to join us."

Fhord's eyes narrow, suspicion rising in his face. After a few seconds, though, he sighs. "I hate it when you make so much sense. Because I really need to rip someone apart and I was hoping it would be him."

"Patience." I draw him back down into his seat, then reach for his cheeks as I turn his gaze to me. I let his presence calm me, remind me what matters. "I promise you can kill whoever shot Astarot. My gift to you."

"You always know exactly what to give me," he responds with a smirk as he leans forward for a kiss. And the rest of my angst sputters out. We've both survived so much. The fight ahead will be fucking hard, but we can do hard things. And we will do this.

"None of that," Torsten barks at us, a grimace twisting his ruddy features. "Let's get on with this. We're here to discuss the revolution. So talk." He gestures vaguely at Birger, leaning back in his seat.

"Direct as usual," Birger says with a nod of his head. "And correct. It's time to get focused." He turns toward Fhord, a question in his eyes. "Was I wrong about your commitment?"

"You weren't. We need to weed out the rebels we can't trust, but we can move forward with making plans, if we keep them limited to this group."

"Are we agreed? These discussions are for us alone?" Birger's gaze flicks around the room, getting a nod from everyone before moving along. "Good. We've believed for many years that we should focus on freeing the elves first, then use their help to wrest the dragons from the Dróttning's grip. We no longer think that's the best path forward. We'll need more dragons if we're going to free the elves."

"We're freeing the dragons first. But how? And why?" That's my preference for a lot of reasons, but I don't understand why their views have changed.

"The 'why' is you, Sifa. Or, more accurately, your dragon," he adds, and I can't hold back the smile at the mention of my brave, loyal beast. "He and the little green dragon are lighting a fire of discontent in the Thunder. Many are happy with the Dróttning, but many more are not. We think it's time to reach out to those who aren't and turn them against riders they despise."

My soul feels lighter knowing that others see Astarot's strength and are anxious to follow him into this fight.

Food, Astarot rumbles into my thoughts, reminding me about his constant *need* for some meal he's been craving and how weak he's getting because he's gone too long without it.

"Astarot doesn't think we're ready. We need to figure out first what the Dróttning feeds the dragons."

"What do you mean?"

"The dragons need two things to survive—water, like we find here, and something else. Astarot's had a craving he can't satisfy, even with the water. We're just starting to recognize the second need. We haven't explored it yet."

"Tell me about this food." One of Fhord's advisors speaks up now, leaning forward with an intense look.

"Astarot's been away from the Dróttning's control longer than any dragon we know."

"Other than Vulryn," Fhord interjects.

"Right," I agree as I tilt my head toward Fhord. "Longer than any southern dragon."

"What does he need?"

"The Dróttning serves all her dragons some kind of green gruel. Astarot suspects it's made from a moss, but he doesn't know. They get it every few weeks and always want more than she gives. Astarot has vague memories of disliking it when he was a hatchling but that didn't last long. By the third or fourth time she offered it, he enjoyed it. He particularly loved the way it invigorated him, which lasted until the next feeding. It's been part of his diet since then."

"And why is he focused on this?"

"He's started to crave it. Desperately. At first, he wasn't sure what his body demanded, but he's become more focused on the gruel." I pause for a moment, turning toward Fhord as I push my fear for Astarot to the back of my mind, then back to the female questioning me. "And it's more than just a craving. He's losing strength. He believes he needs it to survive, that he'll continue to grow weaker until he falls to another threat that shouldn't be able to touch him, like the bolt."

"What do the other dragons think?"

"Khirta is developing minor cravings but nothing as fierce as Astarot. Tindera hasn't been away from the Dróttning long enough to notice a difference."

"The Dróttning fed this ... gruel ... to Tindera, even when she was being held and tortured?" This question is from Joralf. "She didn't withhold it as part of the punishment?"

"To our knowledge, no dragon has ever been denied it," Fhord tells him. "No matter how angry she is with a dragon, she always gives it to them."

"But Vulryn's never had it? And doesn't crave it?"

"Both true statements," Fhord agrees with a dip of his chin.

Joralf leans back, his gaze bouncing between Fhord and me, before landing on Fhord. "You've spent a lot of time in the Nest. Do you have any idea what it is?"

"I've never paid any attention to it; never had any reason to. But the Dróttning's good at hiding shit, making it seem meaningless. And as close as I was to her, she kept many secrets from me."

"Okay, maybe we can get at this another way," Joralf muses. His body is still reclining, but I can see his shoulders draw tight. "What does she feed those whose lives she's chosen to extend? We've long wondered if it's related to the power she holds over the dragons."

"I don't know." I feel Fhord's tension as Joralf dances close to a secret he's been keeping nearly since he could talk.

"But you must," Joralf insists, sitting up to stare at my mate. "You can't be an elf—not as close as you've always been to

the Dróttning—but you've lived for centuries. Only the Dróttning and those she chooses live so long."

Fhord's answer comes more slowly this time, an uncertainty
that probably tastes like dirt in his mouth washing through
him. Finally, he sighs, his gaze holding Joralf's. "I don't need
any substance for my long life," he explains as eyebrows around
the table slam up at his admission. "I'll live as long as her,
maybe longer."

"Then what are you, Fhord? How have you lived so long?"
This question from the older female, Gerta, pisses me off a
bit. It's terse, a hint of distrust hidden in its depths, despite
what Fhord has done for every person who's safe on this island
because of him. I have to stop myself from pointing out that
Fhord doesn't owe her or anyone else an explanation.

Birger does, though. "You don't have to tell them, Fhord."
His voice is tinged with concern.

"They should know who I am—what I am—before they
fully commit to our cause with me."

"It's none of their business." Now Birger's voice is strident,
almost angry. "Tell them if you choose, but not out of some
false sense of obligation. What you've done here is more than
enough to earn the loyalty of every rebel across Vanatia."

"It's time," Fhord murmurs, reaching again for my hand.
"I'm half elf," he says after a moment drawing my gaze toward
him. But I shouldn't be surprised. He possesses strong mind
magic. Of course he's part elf. "I'm told my father lives in one
of the elven camps," he continues, "but my mother has spent
my life working to turn me against him and all elves. It wasn't

until Sifa arrived that I started to really question everything she said. All that she did. I kept this secret for her, but that shit's behind me."

"And who is your mother?" This demand's from Mikkael. He's facing Fhord, his arms folded tightly across his chest and his feet planted in front of him. "Or should we guess?"

"It's exactly who you think, Mikkael," Fhord tells him in a flat voice. "The Dróttning's my mother. She was joined to an elf before the Downfall and refused to send him to prison for many years later, hiding him from everyone. I believe she sent him away shortly after I was born. I've never met him, so I don't know for certain."

I glance around the table at the mix of acceptance, confusion and anger. Nobody's talking or even moving, other than Birger, who's leaning toward Fhord, his gaze open and accepting. The Ætt look defiant, their shoulders back as if they're daring anyone at the table to question Fhord's commitment to the rebellion. Liv, Frida, and many of Fhord's advisors are confused, although their expressions quickly settle into acceptance.

Mikkael and a few others, though, look pissed. And now the emotions that have been swinging wildly within me since I woke up this morning settle on rage. At Mikkael—who's supposed to be one of my closest friends—but even more at these males and females who have taken so much of what Fhord has given to the rebellion but would still dare to question him.

We're all sitting with the bombshell Fhord dropped on us—as I struggle to hold my tongue while some of them process and hopefully get past their anger—when the door swings open, the man who was supposed to be bringing break-fast stomping into the room.

"We've got them. Two of Bjorn's people, but we don't think he was involved. We received several reports of them bragging about it afterwards. They haven't admitted it yet. Their rooms are being searched."

"Can I rip open *their* heads?" Fhord snarls, the corners of his lips tilting up just a bit as he tries to temper the relief I feel rippling through him at this news.

"Only if I can help." I don't try to hide the anticipation that flares inside me at the thought of watching Fhord take vengeance on the bastards who hurt my dragon.

"Wouldn't do it without you." This time when he leans forward, Torsten doesn't stop him. "So gods-damned dangerous," he whispers before his lips find mine. It lasts just a moment, but it's a moment I need.

"Let's go rip open some heads," I murmur as he stands and reaches for my hand.

But he pauses before we move away from the table. "Birger, Sifa, and me. Nobody else."

"Me too, Fhord." Mikkael's on his feet and striding toward the door before we can stop him.

"Why the fuck should you be there?"

"No, he's right, Fhord." Birger gestures Mikkael toward the door. "He's been here long enough to get to know this group. He could be helpful."

I squeeze Fhord's hand, drawing his attention toward me. "Mikkael's good with people. He could help."

"Fine," Fhord agrees. "But you don't say a word unless I ask for it."

Mikkael sneers at Fhord but gives him a sharp nod, then turns to follow us into the hall.

Birger's man leads us down a few flights of stairs to a basement I didn't know existed and through a hallway with cages that remind me too much of the Nest. He opens a door to reveal a man and a woman hanging from chains suspended from the ceiling, their feet barely touching the ground.

"Aw, fuck, Dahlia," Mikkael sounds disappointed when his eyes land on the woman. Blood covers her chin, but her eyes tell me there's plenty of fight left in her. She's pretty and I'm not one little bit surprised that Mikkael knows her. "What have you done?"

"Why are you with the dragon riders, Mik?" Dahlia's voice is cold, angry, and a little hurt.

"Why are you here, Dahlia? What the fuck have you done?"

Dahlia opens her mouth but closes it just as fast, looking at the man hanging next to her and then around the room. "Nothing," she declares, lifting her chin as she throws her shoulders back. "They've got the wrong people."

"Many people heard you talking about what you did." Birger slides a chair across the room—its feet squealing the entire way—and plants himself in front of the pair, leaning back to look them in the eyes. "We know it was you. We want to know why."

"Even if it was us," the man blusters, "why would we tell you? Dragon riders all stand with the Dróttning. You aren't our allies. I don't know how the fuck you managed to convince so many people you are."

Fhord's hand on Birger's shoulder draws his gaze. "They won't give you what you want. Can Sifa and I do this our way?"

About gods-damned time. Fucking with this couple won't ruffle feathers the way it would have with Bjorn, and we need to know if he's involved.

"Of course," Birger agrees, rising to offer his seat to me as Fhord drags over another.

Fhord drops into his chair and reaches out, linking our hands as I feel him drop his walls and I do the same. *Everything they know*, he whispers, opening his power to me. I don't need it—the mating bond has made me strong—but I take what he offers so he can join me as we dig into Dahlia's brain.

I feel his laugh when the first of Dahlia's thoughts filter into ours. She's still focused on Mikkael, pissed at how eager she was to fall into his bed the last time he asked. But I push that memory aside—Mikkael is like a brother to me, and there are some things I never want to see—and start to dig for her memories of the rebels who told her to attack us.

It's not much, unfortunately. Images of the man sitting next to us bounce through her mind, but I can't find anyone giving them orders directly. It's always a note left beneath a mat or passed in a tavern. The man received this one, with instructions on where to find the weapon. She's always paired with him. This group of rebels consider themselves an elite force, demanding secrecy of everyone who supports them and giving them minimal contact with other members.

So I approach it differently. Since her mind's malleable enough to compel, I build a memory of a note instructing her to tell us who introduced her to this group. There's always a "who", even if they're sometimes not easy to find. I drop it into her memories and watch as the emotions flutter over her face. Tight eyebrows and thin lips reveal the confusion washing through her, followed by the wide shoulders and smirk of defiance, and finally a relaxed posture as acceptance takes over.

When she turns toward me, her partner hisses her name, but Fhord's not putting up with his shit. He stands and his fist swings toward the male's temple, knocking him out before he can say another word.

It's no wonder I love you, I purr. *You always know just what to give me.*

I aim to please. Dropping back into the chair, his hand reaches for mine as I look back at Dahlia. The confusion that tried to take hold when Fhord punched her partner disappears again, and she gives me a wide smile.

"I've been wondering where to find you," she announces, bobbing her head up and down in excitement. "We don't meet many others."

"They're very careful with their information. We all know how important it is."

"We do," she agrees. "You'll keep this just between us?" Her gaze bounces around the room before she adds, "And these nice males?"

"It'll be our secret," I assure her.

"Good, because nobody else knows he supports the rebellion. The Dróttning would have one of her dragons rip him to shreds if she knew."

"I promise. Just between us."

She nods. "I found out when he called me to his house one day. You know, his wife stopped pleasing him a long time ago. And he pays well."

"A good male, no doubt."

"One of the best. Even if he is a little ... little." Her wide eyes turn to Mikkael, gazing at his face before tracking down to the dick she probably knows well. "Nothing like you, Mik."

"I aim to please, Dahlia," he tells her with a wink. "Who's this lonely male with the little prick?"

"You all should know him," she says, nodding her head as she looks at each of us again. "Everyone in Revalle does. Bevin's never liked him, but he's tight with the Dróttning."

And then my memory drags up the little dick she's talking about. Liv's bouncing on him, bored out of her mind, and I'm pissed because I did not get up early to see that. "Aksell," I mutter, drawing everyone's gaze to me.

"You do know him!" Dahlia exclaims just before Fhord's fist slams into her temple, sending her to the same place as her partner.

"She could have more to say, Fhord," I remind him as he pulls his hand away from mine.

"I've heard everything I need. It's time to go back to Revalle."

CHAPTER ELEVEN

MIKKAEL

READY TO GO

I'M READY TO GO.

I stayed a few days, even after learning what happened to Johan, because that northern bitch left. I didn't know where she went and didn't want to risk running into her at one of the rebel camps, so I gave her a chance to get farther inland before returning to the fight. But I've been here too long. The Dróttning made this war personal, and I need to chase Johan's vengeance.

I have no idea how. The Dróttning's responsible and she's the one who has to pay. I should stay with Fhord and Sifa. They'll get me closer to her than I could get on my own. But they're also close to Dani. They brought her into their fold, made her part of them. I'm not ready to spend so much time with people who are connected to her.

They can take me back to the mainland and drop me with one of the rebel groups. I'll figure out from there what I can do to help.

How I get revenge for Johan.

I don't even bother to say goodbye to anyone. Nobody here matters to me. Johan's gone, and I can't be with Sifa's group right now. I've always been alone, and I'll be alone again. It's probably exactly what I need.

"Ready?" Sifa's voice in my doorway draws me from my pathetic thoughts.

"Who's going with us?"

"Just the Ætt, Toffer, and Thor. The others are staying for now, to give Fhord's advisors their insight on other possible traitors. We'll drop Toffer and Thor at home, and I'll check on Halla and Sagga."

She smiles, and for a moment, I reconsider my decision. Sifa's always helped me stay centered. Her friendship might be what I really need. But then my traitorous thoughts drag up Dani's image, a flicker of hope rustling through me when I realize I could see her again if I went with Sifa and Fhord. So I shove that idea away. I need to get some distance between me and everyone connected to her, get my head on straight.

Instead, I try to focus on the things that matter. "Before I came," I tell Sifa, "I touched bases at the tavern, made sure they're still getting meals."

"Thank you. I hope you know how much it means to me that you and Johan took such good care of them."

"I know how important it is—how important they are." I watch her for a moment, but Dani's image appears again in my mind. Before I can stop it, a question tumbles from my lips. "How can you be friends with her?"

Sifa knows who I mean. Her eyes are so kind. They brighten with her mood, garnets framed by her thick lashes when she's happy and a deep bronze when she's angry. Right now, they look like tiger's eye, rich with shifting colors. She holds my gaze for a moment, then walks over to sit next to me on the bed.

"I've walked through her mind. I know she's a good person." She pauses, making sure I'm listening to her next words. "Dani and Vulryn will be important to our fight. Vulryn's independence from the Dróttning is going to help us break free. And she's a brilliant fighter. She's already taught our dragons so much."

"If she's so important, why did she leave?"

"She's also ridiculously stubborn." Sifa's lips twist into a rueful smile and she casts her eyes down at the ground. "Vulryn's bonded to one of the Dróttning's dragons, a massive blue beast who attacked us when we were rescuing Fhord and Tindera. The dragon mating bond is strong, and Vulryn wants to explore it. She and Dani went to find Ziselær and his rider."

"What does she think she can do?"

Sifa barks out a laugh as she looks at me again. "She insists she'll turn him or kill him."

"And you trust her? She holds the rebellion's biggest secret."

Sifa nods slowly, never letting her gaze stray from mine. "She's committed to us. We can trust her."

I stand, stalking over to the window to stare out. "I think you're wrong. She'll never put your interests before hers. She's going to betray you."

"And I think you're wrong, but we'll find out soon. She found Ziselær quickly. We got word that they turned themselves in to the southern Nest and are being held as prisoners."

"Then we better get the fuck out of here. If Dani's in the Dróttning's hands, she already knows where to find us and is organizing an attack. I don't want to be here when it comes."

Sifa watches me in silence for a moment, her eyes inscrutable. When she stands, she shakes her head a bit, a little frown playing across her lips. "Like I said, we'll find out soon. That's not why we're leaving. Aksell's causing problems again. We're going to go make him pay for Astarot."

"Aksell was behind the rebels who shot your dragon?"

"Seems he's behind more than we realized. It's time for his reckoning."

"And Dani won't be involved?"

"She's in the Nest. We're hearing that she won't be let out anytime soon."

I can't keep the smile from my face. Aksell is a bastard, and I want part of him. "Then count me in. I've been trying to get a piece of that asshole for a while. The leaders weren't ready to take him out yet. They wanted to watch and see what he did. If the time's come, I want to be there."

Sifa smiles and waves her hand toward the door as I grab my bag and toss it over my shoulder. Casting one last look around the room, I stride out, eager to get back into the fight.

Vanatia never changes. Revalle's always the same when I return, but somehow, I'm surprised every time. It feels like time is paused in an error—some mistake cast in stone ages ago—and it's waiting for the right moment, when everything will go back to normal. The way it should have been. I've known as long as I can remember that it would come, although I have no idea when or how.

The dragons go straight to a rebel hideout a few vikus away from Revalle, where they'll wait along with Fhord and the Ætt for Sifa's message. Our beasts will stay in the hideout tonight while the rest of us track down Aksell to either kill him or take him with us, depending on where he is and what or who we find with him. Seizing him is a declaration of war the rebellion's been avoiding but there's no reason to hide any longer. The battle lines formed when Fhord announced his allegiance to Sifa.

I tag along with Sifa, eager to see Halla and Sagga. After feeding the mother and daughter for so long, I've become nearly as connected to them as Sifa is. And I know they're essential to her in some way, beyond her affection for them. She's never told me exactly how or why, but Sifa needs them safe.

Before we go find them, though, we take Toffer and the cat to her apartment. As I follow them, my thoughts shuffle through all that's happened in such a short time. It's only been a few months since Sifa left on a mission with an asshole of a dragon rider, anxious to get it over with and return home.

Now, that asshole is half of her soul, a dragon owns the other half, and her home is on an island she never knew existed.

Sifa's rustling through her closet when the strangest sensation washes over me—a familiarity, combined with a tug unlike anything I've ever felt before. My gaze snaps to the nearby window just in time to see a large blue dragon fly past, slowing to a near stop as his head swings in my direction. He can't possibly see me. It's the middle of the day and too bright outside for the apartment to be visible. Still, it feels like he's looking right at me.

"Sifa," I call as a *need* to go present myself to him washes through me. "I'll be back in a few minutes. I need to take care of something outside."

Her head pops into the doorway, a smile on her face as she relaxes in her home. "We'll be here. We can't get Aksell until tonight, so we have plenty of time."

I give her a tight smile and spin toward the door but Toffer's there, Thor still wrapped around his neck like a gods-damned scarf.

"I need to go, Toffer." I place a hand on his arm—the cat throwing his bitch face at me as he growls deep in his chest—to try to nudge the troll and his cat-scarf out of the way. He doesn't move. Instead, he reaches up for my shoulders, standing directly between me and the door as he looks at me with wide eyes.

"The dragon's in a dangerous dilemma."

"What?" I like the troll but sometimes he makes no sense.

"Murder mate, at master's mark?"

What the fuck? "Toffer, I really need to go."

"The dragon's in a dangerous dilemma," he repeats. Toffer's words are sharp, insistent.

"Sifa," I yell, my voice a little frantic. "Toffer's trying to tell me something, but I don't know what the fuck he's talking about. Can you help?"

She strides into the entry, her gaze bouncing from the troll to me, and back to the troll. "Tell me, Toff."

"The dragon's in a dangerous dilemma," he explains. He looks grateful for Sifa's presence.

"What dilemma, Toff?"

"Murder mate, at master's mark?"

Sifa's eyebrows slam together as her head cocks to the side. She stalks over to the window and I follow, wondering if there's any hope of finding the blue dragon now.

"Have you seen a dragon, Mik?"

"A large blue dragon," I tell her. "It's why I was leaving. I think I'm supposed to find it."

"Fuck." Sifa spins, her hand reaching for me before she stops herself. "Can I see?" she asks. "I'll just look for the dragon. Nothing else."

I nod because what else can I do? Whatever is going on has Sifa and her troll freaked out.

Her eyes go vacant for a moment, and I feel the smallest whisper at my mind. I wouldn't have noticed it if I didn't know she intended to start digging around in there. I focus on the image of the dragon, making it as easy for her to find as I can. Her face drops when she sees him.

"Fuck," she repeats, twisting to look out the window again. "What's going on, Sifa?"

"It's Ziselær," she tells me. "He's the blue dragon Vulryn says is her mate." She pauses, looking back at me. "Don't go."

"I'm just gonna go look," I respond with a shrug. "No harm done."

Now she turns to face me, and I realize she's worried. Her eyebrows have pulled together again, little lines forming between them, her lips pursed as if to say something she can't yet voice. "Do you know dragons are required to kill their destined riders if they come across them?" she asks at last. "The Dróttning wants no competition for their loyalty, so if they ever discover the rider fate intended for them, they kill them."

"What the fuck does this have to do with me?" I demand as my arms fly up. "I just want to go look at the dragon. I don't see them often."

"If you sensed him, he could be yours. Mik, that's not a dragon to test. He hurt Khirta. Fhord says his rider, Matthias, is a cruel bastard and they've been together long enough that Ziselær has taken on Matthias's cruelty. If you're his rider, he'll kill you."

"I'm not his rider, Sifa," I bitch as I spin around. Throwing a glance behind me as I stride to the door, I force out a little smile. "Don't worry. I'll be right back."

I slam the door behind me, my *need* to find the dragon urging me into a run. I'm outside in seconds, my feet flying down the road as I follow an invisible thread that connects me to him. My thoughts play around with the possibility the dragon is mine. That I'm somehow the fated rider for the majestic beast that seemed to look straight at me. That he'll kill me if I find him.

But I can't stop. If he's mine, I have to see him. If death is the price, I'll pay it. If he's not, it's enough to look at him, and maybe understand what's drawing me in his direction.

I've run for a viku, maybe more, when I turn a corner into one of Revalle's larger parks and see him fifty feet away. My senses are tingling, every nerve in my body attuned to him. I barely notice the bright sky, casting dark shadows in the space between us, or the low hum of the people walking nearby. I can only see him and the rider that does not belong on his back.

Blue is such a weak word to describe him. He's the sea at dusk, as the sun's rays cast their softest light over the shifting waters, revealing the sapphire and azure that dance in the waves in those few minutes when day shimmers into night. Mixed in are navy and cobalt and even a hint of the morning sky, his feathers all melding together in a tapestry that is both organized and chaotic. And so fucking beautiful, I wonder if anything could ever compare.

He's just as large as I thought. Broader than any dragon I've seen, he looks as if he's all muscle in a body that must stretch at least seventy feet. If he turned, his tail could reach and even wrap around me, pulling me toward him for the death I now know he's supposed to give me. Because he's mine. I've never been more certain of anything. Or more proud. I'll never ride him but to know that the fates destined me for this beast humbles me in a way I couldn't have imagined.

Nothing. I hear his word rumble into my mind, but it's not intended for me. He's ignoring me, telling his rider—Matthias, Sifa said—that there's nothing to see. That I'm nothing of concern. He's trying to protect me.

Matthias isn't convinced. He spins on Ziselær's back, searching for whatever is distracting or disturbing my dragon. I can't hear his words, but I feel Ziselær's conflict. This dragon faces a dangerous dilemma, as Toffer tried to warn me. Because the rider the Dróttning chose for him will force him to kill me if he realizes I'm here.

As Matthias turns my way, I step backwards and find shade to hide in next to the building. I don't want to put Ziselær in that position. He's satisfied with his rider and safe as a member of the Dróttning's Thunder. That's all the happiness he'll have. And it's good enough.

But Matthias's gaze stops when it passes over me, as if he can see me shrouded in the shadows. He remains astride my dragon for a few moments before tossing his leg over and starting to climb down.

Nothing, Ziselær repeats, frustration seeping into this word. He wants Matthias to believe he hungers for his mate. That his desire to leave this park relates to Vulryn alone.

Matthias still isn't convinced. I can see him grimace at my dragon from here and feel Ziselær's frustration, a flutter in his stomach that reminds him of the wings of hatchlings as they search for air to lift them. Matthias snarls a word or two at Ziselær and then spins and prowls toward me, his long strides covering the fifty feet in less than a minute.

"Why has my dragon taken an interest in you?" His voice is brittle, a sheet of ice on a winter day.

I know the smart move—what I decided to do a few seconds ago because it's best for Ziselær and it's definitely best for me. I *should* play dumb, pretend I don't know what the fuck he's talking about. Walk away from my dragon alive, knowing he'll have a content life with the rider the Dróttning chose for him.

Still, something inside me refuses. The part of me that recognized Ziselær when he flew past the window and dragged me into the street then to this park—a whisper deep within from the fate that decided I should ride this glorious beast—refuses to deny our connection. It'll be my death sentence, but I should be dead anyway. I'll be damned if the last thing I do is deny my dragon.

So I smirk, giving him the fuck-you look that's gotten me kicked out of a lot of taverns—and invited into a lot of beds. "My dragon," I growl as my hand reaches out to pick a feather from Matthias's riding jacket. I lift it to the light, smiling as it reflects sapphire in my hands, and drop it into my pocket.

His punch catches me by surprise. I thought there'd be a little foreplay before we got down to business. But I am nothing if not prepared for anyone who's determined to roll around with me. His strike sends my head swinging to the side, but I'm still standing.

And now I'm angry. Because this fucker has been riding my gods-damned dragon. I plunge my fist into Matthias's gut, laughing as he leans forward, and dance back to measure him.

But then Ziselær roars from behind me, sending trickles of flame up and down my spine.

"Burn him," Matthias sneers, planting his feet as he glares in my direction.

Go. Ziselær wants to leave. He doesn't want to kill me. Images of Vulryn filter into my mind and I understand. Vulryn is his mate and that bond is good. She's found and unleashed a part of him he thought died long ago, brought joy he hasn't experienced in decades back into his life. Maybe the bond with me is good too.

"It's okay," I say, my heart in my throat, as I turn to look at him, ignoring the bastard at my side. "It's enough knowing you're mine and I'm yours. The Dróttning will punish you if you defy her. Take my life. I'll be proud to die by your flame."

Matthias laughs. "You heard him, Ziselær. He's a stupid fucker, but he's right about one thing. The Dróttning will make you suffer if you refuse this command. Burn. Him."

My dragon stands there, unmoving, for longer than I expect. Flames ripple from his snout a few times but not enough to reach me. He doesn't speak and I can't feel his emotions. He put up some kind of wall between us, and I wonder if that same barrier stands between him and Matthias too.

I feel more alive than I have in a long time, balancing between life and death in my dragon's shadow. But then Ziselær's eyes grow wide in alarm—*Move* blasting through our bond—and I spin just in time to dodge the blade Matthias had flung at me. Ziselær screeches at us, throwing himself into the air as fire ripples into the space between Matthias and me. He's pushing us apart, isolating us, and now Matthias is well and truly pissed. He's spewing threats at Ziselær, but the dragon isn't stopping.

When nearly a hundred feet separate us, Ziselær pauses and his gaze spins to mine. *Leave*, he demands, this word angry and imperious. He extends his wings and swoops into the air again, his claws reaching for Matthias to carry him away, who curses at his rebellious dragon as he writhes futilely.

I can only watch as my destined fate soars away with the male who took my place.

CHAPTER TWELVE

DANI

I WON'T BETRAY THEM

MATTHIAS IS GRUMPY AS fuck when he appears at the door of my cage, howling at the guard like a rabid dog. He's a sexy dog—his short sleeves showing off even more of the elaborate ink on his skin—but a dog nonetheless.

The female watching me today snaps back but does as he demands, swinging the door wide and handing a small set of keys to him. He grunts out a peremptory "Follow me" and turns to stride down the hall, looking back once to repeat his command. I shake myself out of my shock and move my feet. I don't know where he's taking me, but unless it's the rack, it's better than this place.

The guard follows as Matthias leads us through a series of tunnels and finally to a door with two other guards posted. They pound their fists to their chests and then one turns the handle, revealing a large room as it swings wide. Matthias stalks in, stopping in the center to spin around and scowl at me.

Well, fuck you too, Matthias.

I don't know what pissed him off, but I don't care. I think I've been upgraded. There's no window, but that's no surprise. We're in caverns, so I suspect none of the rooms have a view. It's spacious, with a bed covered in pillows and blankets, and even a couch, chair and table between them. A door to the left is open enough to reveal a bathroom. It feels like a palace after the cage I started in.

"This is your new prison," he confirms for me. "You will stay here, guarded by soldiers loyal to me. None will touch you."

"This is nicer than I expected. Why?"

"Your dragon demanded it," he complains, blue eyes sparking with a flame I don't see often.

"She has no sway here."

"Ziselær beseeched me after your attack, and I spoke with the Dróttning to relay his request. She approved that request today." I get the sense he regrets it, that something has changed in the day since he stopped—and then punished—the guard who tried to rape me. But I also know he won't tell me. I'll ask Vulryn when he leaves. Perhaps she knows.

"It looks too ... comfortable. Spacious. I'm wondering why the Dróttning would give this to the dragon rider who helped Fhord and Tindera escape."

Matthias's lips pinch together in a sharp line as his jaw clenches. "Don't play the fool. We both know why the Dróttning has you here instead of on the rack. And we also know your time here is limited. If you don't give her what she wants, you'll suffer her wrath."

I cock my head, a smile teasing my lips. "How long do I have?"

"I don't try to predict the Dróttning's actions. You're here now. You'd be wise to make your decision soon. Fhord and Sifa do not deserve your loyalty. The Dróttning does."

"And if I give them to you, she'll give me my freedom?"

"Not just them. When the traitor Fhord and the elf Sifa hang on the rack and you've revealed all you know about the rebels—where they're hiding, who's involved, how many there are—then the Dróttning will start to trust you. If you don't give her everything she wants soon, you'll be the one hanging on the rack. She'll get the truth from you that way, but you'll never earn her trust."

"And she'll never have my dragon."

Now it's his turn to cock his head. His lips twist into a smirk, and I hate myself for noticing how fucking hot he looks when he's being an absolute asshole. "Foolish, foolish elf. All dragons bow to the Dróttning in Vanatia."

"Except Vulryn. And Astarot. And Khirta. And now Tindera. I think your leader's losing her touch."

He ignores my taunt as he stalks toward the door. "It's only a matter of time until Vulryn bows to her," he says as his hand rests on the doorknob, his gaze spinning back to find me. "If you don't join your dragon, the Dróttning will give her to another rider." Now he smiles. "I know who will ride Vulryn, and I hope to fuck you forfeit your bond with your beast."

"Vulryn will never bow to the Dróttning."

"She will." With that, he opens the door and leaves, slamming it behind him.

"Asshole," I mutter, turning toward my new room with a smile. *Thank you.* I really love my dragon.

It is fitting. I will not let you be harmed. He must protect you.

Much as I'd like to believe that, I think it's up to the Dróttning at this point whether I'll be harmed or not.

My drake and his rider must protect you. I will not let you be harmed.

She's such a bad bitch. I think she actually believes what she's saying. It doesn't matter—the Dróttning's gonna do whatever she wants with me—but it's sweet. I'll enjoy having a room while I can.

Why is Matthias in such a bad mood? He was nicer to me when he saved me from the guard, but he was a real asshole just now.

He is angry with my drake. It will pass.

Why would he be angry with Ziselær? I thought that after a hundred years, they agreed about everything.

Vulryn laughs, satisfaction in every note. *My drake has accepted me, and he is pleased with the fates' choice. He wonders how it would feel to be ridden by the male the fates intended, rather than the male the wyrm chose.*

My dragon doesn't often render me speechless, but she's done it now. I'm not sure what to think. *Why would Ziselær be wondering something like that?*

He encountered his destined rider and refused to kill him. My drake's rider is angry but has not told the wyrm. He fears losing the wyrm's trust. My drake's rider will punish my drake, but he has not yet.

Matthias plans to punish Z7selær? I demand, my voice warbling. *Is your drake concerned?*

My drake is pleased the wyrm does not know. He will accept his rider's punishment.

What happened when Ziselær found his destined rider?

The angry male was with the starry female, the troll, and the feline …

I'm sorry, what? Why are you talking about them?

You asked. Vulryn's response is matter-of-fact, and a rock drops into my stomach as understanding washes over me.

Is Mikkael the angry male?

Yes.

Mikkael is Ziselær's destined rider?

Of course. He is your mate, and so he must be my drake's destined rider.

Fuck.

Me.

I knew it. Deep inside, where secrets hide until they're pushed into the light of day, I knew what the fates had done to us. Mikkael's my mate. And because they always pair dragons and riders, it makes complete sense that Mikkael would be Ziselær's destined rider.

But seriously.

Fuck.

Me.

This just got so much more complicated.

Shall I continue?

I guess I should know everything. Please, fuck up my world a bit more.

Vulryn is quiet for a moment—a rare pause for a beast who loves to hear herself talk—but must decide to ignore my little outburst. *The angry male was with the starry female...*

Can we call him something else?

He is an angry male. It fits him better than any other words you could choose.

Let's just call him something else. Please.

The amorous male? Or perhaps the wanton male?

A laugh erupts from me before I can stop it. *Where did you come up with those names?*

He is well-known in the pretty place for his proclivities. Those names also suit him.

And how the fuck do you know that?

The troll learned many things while we stayed in the pretty place. He speaks with the clover dragon often.

So Mikkael's exploits are the talk of the town, and Toffer and Khirta are gossiping about them too?

The angry male is well-liked by the local females. They are eager to discuss his ... attributes and talents.

Stop talking, please. I do not need to know about Mikkael's attributes or talents. Let's call him the wanton male. And we'll make sure he knows his nickname if we ever see him again.

Serves him right, the dick.

Not that I'm thinking about his dick.

Or how many females he stuck it into in Lumaria.

So, Mikkael was with Sifa and the others, and then what happened?

My drake flew past the window and felt his presence.

Ziselær realized he was passing by his destined rider?

Yes. He grew curious and slowed his flight to remain nearby. He wanted to see the male the fates had chosen for him.

But he's committed to Matthias.

That remains true. He will not betray the rider the wyrm chose for him. That bond is too deeply embedded within him.

Why did he want to see Mikkael?

He is pleased with our bond. As the fates chose you well, they chose my drake well. He hoped to see who the fates had selected to ride him.

What did he think?

The fates chose well. The wanton male is strong and smart. Reckless but smart.

Why reckless?

He chased my drake and claimed him.

What do you mean, "claimed him"?

My drake's rider confronted the wanton male, and the wanton male declared that my drake belongs to him.

Fucking Mikkael. Of course he did. He's such an arrogant bastard. *He should be dead. Why isn't he dead?*

My drake would not kill him.

He defied the Dróttning?

Yes.

Why would he do that? I thought he was fully committed to Matthias and the Dróttning.

He is. But he remains curious about the wanton male. And he knew it would displease me.

Why would he believe that?

You are mine, and the wanton male is yours.

Did he realize that I know Mikkael? And we hate each other? A small part of me rebels at my words, but I squash that shit. There is no future for that asshole and me.

Vulryn scoffs. *You do not hate the wanton male.*

I know who I hate and who I don't. Mikkael's a dick and I definitely hate him.

Still, the wanton male is yours. My drake did not know of your past, but he knew the fates had connected you and that it would displease me if he killed the wanton male.

He defied the Dróttning for that? My heart warms at the commitment Ziselær already feels for my dragon.

He is a good drake. As I said.

You're sure Matthias isn't going to tell the Dróttning? She can't know about Mikkael.

His rider will not tell the Dróttning. He knows what he must do.

What does that mean, "He knows what he must do"? I don't want to know the answer, but I ask anyway.

The wanton male is your mate. My drake's rider knows he must secure his place at your side instead.

Fuck off. I don't want Matthias at my side.

That is where he belongs. We do not follow the path the fates set for us, but on any path we follow, our riders must be joined.

And what if I don't want him?

Then we shall kill my drake and his rider and return to our male, the starry female, and the others.

Vulryn's words shake me because of what she's not saying. *Are you suggesting that if I accept Matthias, you want to stay here in the Nest? Under the Dróttning's control?*

I suggest nothing. Whether we are here or there, my drake's rider belongs at your side.

I won't betray them. My voice is smaller than I want, a knife slicing through my gut at the thought of giving in to the Dróttning's demands and turning our friends over to her.

We shall see what comes. Vulryn's cryptic response does nothing to soothe my nerves.

For the first time since we bonded, I'm afraid of what my dragon plans to do.

I'm asleep when Matthias returns to me. The daylight doesn't reach me here, so I have no idea how long I slept, but I'm more rested than I have been since we turned ourselves in. I feel good.

The smells coming from the tray a guard brings in behind Matthias wake me right up as he sets it onto the table in front of the couch. They gave me food in the cage, but none of it was very good. Grains and beans with an occasional slice of bread filled my belly. He just brought me a feast.

I can't see what he brought—all the dishes are covered—but I can smell it. Pork and gravy, rolls, some kind of vegetable I don't recognize, and a bean stew. My stomach is grumbling frantically by the time the guard steps out and closes the door behind him.

Neither of us speaks a word as I find the stew and dish a bowl for myself. The beans in the cage were edible; this is mouth-watering, and I love a good bean stew. Some kind of meat floats in it, little drops of fat hovering on the surface, with carrots and onions and the same green vegetable he's brought as a side dish. It's the perfect temperature for me to dip in a spoon and enjoy it now, so that's what I do.

Matthias doesn't join me, but I don't care. We're not friends—and I don't plan to be more than an occasional fuck when our dragons fly—so I don't need him to share a meal with me. I plow through two heaping plates, adding gravy as I go along because I love that shit, and then lift the last cover to find dessert. A chocolate cake with strawberries and cream.

Does he know I love chocolate and strawberries?

I have watched you eat. I told him what would please you.

You really want me to like him, don't you?

Our riders must be joined.

She's such a stubborn bitch. But if this is how she woos me on his behalf, I'll enjoy it while I can.

When I've eaten more food than should be possible—Matthias's face having relaxed into something very close to a smile as he watches me—I sit back, wishing for whiskey or ale to top off my meal.

"Next time, bring a drink with you. You could at least join me in that."

"Do you want me to eat with you?" One eyebrow lifts, setting a little fire in my belly. I may hate the bastard, but I can't deny he's fucking gorgeous.

"I want you to drink with me or at least bring me a drink."

"What would you drink?"

"Whiskey or ale. But not the dregs they serve in the cheaper taverns. Something you might drink."

He nods, standing to stride toward the door, opens it a crack, and murmurs something to the guard. Closing it, he catches my gaze as he turns back toward me, a little smile lifting his lips. "I will have a drink with you."

"Why are you being so nice to me?" I know what Vulryn said, but I want to hear it from him.

"Our dragons are mates. Ziselær is ... enamored ... with Vulryn. He wishes to please her."

"You told me the Dróttning will just kill me and give her to another rider. And you'd prefer that rider. Why not just get it over with? Rip off the bandage?"

Matthias watches me for a moment, his expression more relaxed than I've seen it. I know he can be cruel and wonder if he's showing me a true side of himself or if this is an act, presenting something he thinks I want to see. When he answers, his tone is measured, as if he's proposing a cease-fire to an enemy.

"The fates did not choose me for Ziselær, and it took many years to gain his steadfast loyalty. He suffered and so I suffered because even in a bond such as ours, I feel my dragon's pain. Perhaps that is the path you and Vulryn will choose. But

Ziselær would rather his draikana have her destined rider and I agree. If we can avoid the years or decades of training, it will be better for our dragons. And better for me."

"What's better for me doesn't matter?"

"You are a means to an end. Luckily for you, you're a pretty means to an end or you would already be on the rack."

"So you're willing to fuck me for the dragons? But you wouldn't if I were plain? You don't care for your dragon quite enough for that?"

"You and your dragon took the Dróttning's prize, a male who has been by her side for centuries. He and his elf are free—and they're strong enough to do tremendous harm to the Dróttning before she can subdue them—because of you. You're here because the Dróttning values my loyalty, and I asked her to give you the opportunity to swear your allegiance to her."

"Despite all I've done, you'll join our lives together because I'm pretty? That can't be enough."

"You're bonded to a dragon worthy of Ziselær. Vulryn is strong and sure. The fates do not choose weak riders for such beasts. If you commit yourself to the Dróttning—help her recover the traitors and destroy the rebellion—you and your dragon will be worthy soldiers in our fight."

A knock on the door interrupts my next question. Matthias doesn't move, grunting "Come" loud enough for the guard's ears. The door swings open and a guard enters with a tray holding a rich amber liquid in a beautiful carafe and two glasses. He places it on the table, bows deeply, and leaves without anyone muttering a word.

"No thanks?" I ask as Matthias leans forward to give us both a generous pour.

"He is beneath me. He doesn't expect my thanks, and I'd kill him if he did."

"You are quite the prize," I mutter, reaching out for my glass.

He doesn't give it to me, though. Instead, he rests both glasses on his knees, watching me. When he speaks, his tone has shifted to the commander I've seen too much of already.

"Vulryn refuses to eat a food the Dróttning offers her. She must eat everything our liege demands. If she doesn't, she *will* be tortured and eventually killed."

I hold his gaze for a minute or more, not sure what to say. Finally, I smirk at him. "I don't tell Vulryn what to eat. If she doesn't want it, she won't have it."

"That's not an option. The Dróttning allows no defiance of this command."

"Why the fuck would it matter what food Vulryn eats?"

"All dragons must eat this food. She may choose anything else, but she may not refuse this."

"Why? Tell me why I should try to convince her to eat this food?"

"Because the Dróttning requires it."

"But, why? Will it make her stronger? More agile? What's so special about this food?"

"It doesn't matter," he snarls, rising to tower over me. "We do what the Dróttning demands. We don't question it. We don't need answers. It's enough that she demands it."

"*We* don't do what the Dróttning demands," I bark as I stand and close the distance between us, making sure he knows I won't cower to him. "If she wants Vulryn to eat some special food, we need to know why. What this food will do to her and why it's so important."

"Just stop being such a stubborn bitch and have her eat the fucking food. This only works if she eats the food. The Dróttning will only trust her—she'll only trust you—if this food runs through Vulryn's veins."

I stalk around him toward the door, swinging it wide. "Take the whiskey," I growl at the guard. "I don't want his gods-damned bribes."

Matthias prowls toward me, pausing inches away to grasp my chin and drag my gaze to his while both guards scramble in to retrieve the trays.

"Vulryn will eat this food," he tells me, his eyes hard. "If the Dróttning must kill you to secure your dragon's compliance, she will. And she will fucking love it. Because you are a thorn in her side she aches to remove."

He releases my chin with a shove and strides out the door without looking back. One of the guards slams it closed as soon as he's through.

Good fucking riddance.

I turn back toward the room, my thoughts spinning.

That was an interesting exchange. I need to figure out a way to reach Fhord and Sifa and make sure they know what the Dróttning requires in order for Vulryn to stay here.

CHAPTER THIRTEEN

SIFA

OUR PATHS WILL CROSS

"**Y**OU CLAIMED HIM?" My voice is harsher than I intend but holy Helheim. I thought Mikkael was smarter than that.

He gives me one of those smiles he always offers when he's pissed someone off and is trying to win their forgiveness. "It was a decision made in the moment," he explains with a shrug. "I expected to die, by Ziselær's fire or his rider's blade. I couldn't let denying my dragon be my last action in this world. He deserves my loyalty, even if I'll never ride him."

"He doesn't deserve anything," I chide, fear for this idiot of a friend pushing aside any sympathy his charm drags from me. "He belongs to Matthias, and he's become a cruel beast. You're gods-damned lucky he didn't kill you. You won't be so fortunate next time."

"He fights for the Dróttning because that's what all dragons do in this land. That doesn't make him cruel."

"No, that's what Matthias has done to him." I pause, wondering how I can make him understand he *must* stay away from this dragon he's claimed. "You don't know what he did to Khirta, do you?"

Mikkael's lips tip down at the edges as he drags a hand through his messy hair. "The little green dragon who killed her rider in the cave?" he asks after a few seconds.

"Yes, her."

"What did he do?"

I pause before answering, making sure I have his full attention. "Matthias has a lot of power in the Nests," I tell him at last. "The Dróttning likes him. Other riders offer him things to try to get close to him. Khirta's rider offered his dragon to Ziselær because the blue beast wanted her." Mikkael's expression shutters. He doesn't want to hear this about the dragon the fates chose for him, but I'm not going to spare him any details. "He's too big for her. You can see that, right?"

"Of course he's too fucking big for her," Mikkael mutters.

"But it wasn't only how roughly he mounted Khirta that fucked her up. He was deliberately brutal. He hurt her in other ways. It took her a long time to recover physically, and I don't think she's ever recovered emotionally." One more pause, because this part is important. "There was no gods-damned reason for Ziselær to be so cruel to Khirta, Mik. Fucking Khirta, the sweetest dragon in Vanatia. He did it because he wanted to, or his rider wanted him to and he does every single fucked-up thing Matthias demands of him. He's gone. He's not yours."

Mikkael sucks in a deep breath, and then another, casting his eyes down to the ground as his fingernails drum on his thighs in a fast, jerky rhythm. "He belongs to Matthias," he says at last, looking at me again.

"He's fully committed to his bastard of a rider. You won't break him away. It's never happened before, and you won't get a chance to try because the Dróttning will kill you if she ever learns of your existence."

His gaze drops to the floor one more time, shoulders drooping. He stays that way, motionless, for a minute or more. Finally, he lifts his head. "Thank you for telling me. I needed to know."

I nod as tears fill my eyes, wishing I could give him some hope. I can't imagine watching another rider astride Astarot, knowing he would never be mine. Closing the distance between us, I pull him into a deep hug. "I'm sorry," I mumble in his ear.

"Me too," he responds as he clings to me. "Me too."

When he pulls away, I can see something has changed. His jaw is tight, little wrinkles around his eyes like ripples in a pond. "It's time to go. This shouldn't happen. Dragons should be with their destined riders. We need to fix it."

"Fuck yes, we do."

"I'm gonna go track down Bevin, figure out where I can be the most help." He pauses, a smirk lifting his lips. "Stab Aksell once or twice for me."

"I will. Our paths will cross again soon."

"We're connected, Sifa. I'm not sure how or why, but I know we are. Our paths will always cross again."

I lift my hands to hold his cheeks, making sure he sees the light he brings to my eyes, the ease I feel in his presence. "Always, my friend. Always."

"Give Halla my love. I'll see her next time." He leans forward to kiss my forehead, holding me for a second more before stepping back and spinning away. "Be well, elf," he says as he strides out without looking back.

"Forever a faithful friend." Toffer's voice from behind me is sad. Mikkael's been a steady presence in his life too. Neither of us likes to see him suffer this way.

"He is the best of friends." I turn and smile at Toffer, who has Thor wrapped around his neck like always. "Just as you and Thor are. What's up with you two?" I ask, a smile teasing at my lips.

"Comfortable cats are cute," Toffer responds as he twists his head enough to kiss Thor on the top of his head. But the cat does not like kisses, which Toffer knows. He bats at the troll, claws extended just enough to leave a mark.

"Mean, miserable mate," Toffer murmurs with a smile. He reaches up to scratch the cat behind his ear, drawing a purr and, I'm sure, forgiveness.

He's been speaking more in alliteration lately and I'm not sure why. It's usually a way to deal with strong emotions, but I don't sense any of those right now. I need to watch him, make sure he doesn't feel lost as our little world grows into something very different and much more dangerous.

"Really, though?" I push gently after a moment. "You hated each other forever. Then you get a little alone time and you're best friends. What happened?"

"Change is challenging even for chums. Alone we accepted our alliance."

"So, all along, I just needed to disappear for a couple of weeks to get you two to work it out?"

"Time tests all tension."

"And what now? Do you want to stay in Revalle or come with us? It'll be dangerous and you'll be much safer here."

Thor chirps once, and Toffer gazes at him, his lips still tipping up at the ends. When Thor's gaze finds me again, Toffer's does the same. "He agrees we should go. We'll wander with the warriors."

"We love having you along, but are you sure?"

"The caves call to the curious with hidden holes and halls."

"You're probably right that we'll need your help again with the caves. You've come in very handy already."

"Trolls and their tricks are terrific." Now Toffer's smile is broad, his eyes twinkling.

"That they are," I agree as I reach out to scratch Thor behind the ear. Spinning around, I take a step toward the bedroom to keep packing but realize my usual meeting time with Halla is approaching. Mikkael arranged with another friend, Freya, to meet Halla at the same time to deliver food. I don't want to be late.

"Can you finish here?" I ask, turning back to Toffer. "Pack your stuff and make sure we've gotten rid of anything that might spoil. I'll finish packing when I get back. It won't take long."

"Go. Get to the girls."

"Thank you." I stride out the door, suddenly anxious to check in with Halla and Sagga. It's been too long.

After picking up their meal for the day, I go to the place Halla and I always meet. I know she should be waiting, but I'm still relieved when I see her. Eyes wide as she catches sight of me, she leaps to her feet, closing the distance between us in a few seconds. I lift her in my arms and swing her around, my heart tripping over itself at the emotion Halla never let herself show me before.

"I've missed you so much," she whispers as I stop spinning and just hold her, my arms tugging her closely into my chest. "Mama said you'd be gone a long time but that you'd come back. I didn't think it would take so long."

When I lean back to look more closely at her, a wave of emotion washes over me. It took me a long time to realize it, but she's more important to me than I ever thought possible. I'm grateful to the gods—bastards that they are—that she came into my life when she did. She's another reason I can't leave this world, no matter what it will cost me to stay here.

"I've missed you too," I whisper as I drop her to her feet and take a step back. "Have you grown while I was gone?"

She drops her eyes to the ground, a little smile drawing out her dimples. "Mama says I have. I feel taller."

"I think you're going to be very tall," I tell her, making sure the wonder I sense in her presence fills my words. "Much taller than me."

Her head whips up, eyes wide. "But you're so big," she whispers.

"You'll be bigger. I'm sure of it."

"I hope so. Then I'll be strong enough to help Mama with everything."

"You're going to help more people than your mama. I'm sure of that too."

She sighs, dropping down to the steps to stretch her feet in front of her. "I wasn't sure when you were going to come back," she says as she watches me sit next to her.

"I'm sorry I was gone for so many weeks."

"Mama said you would be. And she didn't worry about you. It just seemed like you'd never be back."

"I'll try not to stay away as long this time."

"Mama said you'd be leaving again soon." Her voice is sad but resigned. "Maybe for longer."

"Gods, I hope not." I think a hint of desperation sneaks into my words, despite my resolve to stay upbeat.

"Mama said it's okay. What you're doing is important." She pauses for a moment, her eyes searching mine. "She said it matters to us too, but I don't know why."

"Your mama does," I tell her. "She understands more than I realized before."

"She was right?"

"So, so right."

"And you're gonna change everything?"

"I hope so. Me and a lot of other very good people." I glance at the bag in my hands. "Roast chicken tonight," I murmur, trying to distract myself from the future staring me in the face.

"Mama will be happy. It's her favorite."

"I know. Has Freya taken good care of you and your mama?"

"She comes every day, just like you did. If she can't come, she sends someone." Halla casts her eyes down again, a little tear dropping onto her cheek. "Ms. Freya's so nice—almost as nice as you—but I miss Mr. Johan."

"Mikkael told you?" I'm surprised, but I shouldn't be. Halla and Sagga deserve to know. Of course Mikkael told them.

"Mama knew. Mr. Mik told me what happened when I asked him."

"Johan was very brave. He died fighting to help us. He was doing what he loved."

"I know. I still miss him."

"Me too."

We sit in silence for a few minutes, simply enjoying each other's company, but eventually Halla rises. She has more words from Sagga for me, I can tell.

"What does your mama want me to know?"

"Mama said you met someone important while you were gone. You've taken different paths and you both have things you must learn before you meet again. Do what the fates command. Your destiny will be clear when they bring you back together."

"Thank you, Halla. I think I understand that better than many of your mama's words."

"There's more. It's about Mama and me, but I don't understand it."

"Maybe I will."

"Mama said our time hasn't come. We aren't ready yet, but Mama will know when the time is right, and she'll get word to you."

"I do understand. Thank you."

"Will I see you again tomorrow?"

It breaks my heart to hear Halla so sad. "I will try," I tell her, "but I don't know yet. If I can find you before we leave again, I will."

She leans forward to wrap her arms around me, squeezing as tight as she can. And then she lifts the bag in both hands, turns, and takes one step down the stairs. Pausing one more time, she whispers, "Be safe, Ms. Sifa," then walks away.

Fuck. That hurt more than I expected. But Halla's strong, just as I'd hoped. She'll be everything we need her to be when the time comes.

A wave of déjà vu washes through me as I stare at Aksell, one of Ulfhild's girls bouncing up and down on his puny little prick like it's worth the ride. He's blindfolded and tied up—because of course he is—and her back is turned toward us, so we can stare as long as we want. The problem is we're struggling to hold back our laughs at the exaggerated moans bouncing around us.

Leif loses it first, doubling over at one particularly lusty groan, sending the rest of us into fits as the girl flings her head around and throws one leg over Aksell, releasing his little stick-dick with the smallest "pop" possible.

"Are you one of Bevin's girls?" Fhord demands, striding forward to yank her away from Aksell and shove a blanket into her hands. He hands her off to Astrid, who helps the girl cover herself while her brain catches up with the sudden shift in energy in the room.

When the bedmate turns to Fhord, understanding finally filtering in, she gives him a shaky nod of her head, then looks back at Aksell and the miniscule member now flopped between his legs. "Bevin?" she mumbles, tightening the blanket around her. "I work for Ulfhild, not Bevin. She sent me here."

"You can speak freely in front of him," Fhord tells her. "If he leaves here tonight at all, it'll be as our prisoner. And that will only happen if he convinces us it'll be worth our trouble to keep him alive."

"Fhord," Aksell snipes, jerking at the ties binding his wrists to the bed, his head spinning in the direction of Fhord's voice as veins bulge in his neck and his face reddens. "I'd recognize the traitor's voice anywhere. You'll get nothing from me. Fuck you and every one of you treasonous bastards."

"Here to drag you to Helheim with me," Fhord responds with a wave of his hand and a mocking bow. "After we find out what you've been doing."

"Fuck. You. Can't make it any plainer than that. I will never help you."

"We're going to destroy that bitch. You know that, right? The Dróttning's powerful, but she won't be able to stand against Sifa and me, and the legion we're gathering to take her down."

Aksell's lips twist into a sneer, his chin jutting out as his body relaxes. "You're a fool," he spits. "She's even more powerful now than she was when you betrayed her. I gave her a new weapon, and he's more dangerous than you could imagine. You won't beat him. Nobody can."

"What the fuck are you talking about?" My tone is sharper than I want. Something about Aksell's warning sends a chill down my spine, a kernel of fear settling deep inside. My head tells me he's bullshitting us, but my gut warns me he's not. That we all should fear this new "weapon".

He turns toward me, his shoulders and expression relaxing even more. "You'll see, elf. I suspect you've met him before. I wish I could be there to see your expression when he sends you to Helheim, where you belong."

Fhord snarls, snaking out his fingers to wrap around Aksell's throat. I grasp his wrist, drawing his gaze toward me.

"Not yet," I murmur, jutting my chin toward Ulfhild's girl. "We should send her away before we get started."

He nods, squeezing Aksell's neck once and then dropping his hand. "The dragons fly," he says as he glances at the bedmate, pausing for her to finish the phrase all rebels know.

"Free at last," she responds, her gaze never leaving his.

"Anything we should know before you go?" I demand, anxious to get her out of the house so we can dig into Aksell, force him to tell us more about this supposed weapon.

"He's got something hidden here," she tells me. "I'm not sure what or where, but he got nervous when I wandered over to that corner." She lifts her hand to point toward the closet that seems to be Aksell's favorite hiding place.

"Thank you. Tell Bevin we have Aksell. Now the fun starts."

"Good. The dragons should be free."

"They will be," I promise with a smile. "Soon."

She nods and drops to gather her clothes, disappearing into the bathroom alone as Leif and Jorunn reinforce the ropes on Aksell's wrists and bind his legs. By the time she's slipping back out and moving toward the door, we're ready to get to work.

"Do I need to watch for any servants?" she asks before opening the door.

"They're all asleep," Jorunn tells her. "They'll be out for a while."

"Thanks for getting here before he bored me to death. This is my first time with him. I've heard rumors, but I never thought they were true. You should take his cock this time. Put him out of his misery."

"I should have done it last time," I agree. "Give Ulfhild—and everyone who suffered through Aksell's pitiful peter—my apologies."

She dips her chin and opens the door just enough to exit, carefully closing it behind her.

"Let's take off his blindfold," Torsten grunts. "I want to see his eyes as we gut him."

Jorunn leans forward and rips it away—chunks of hair coming with it—pulling a scream from Aksell.

"That?" She spews out a laugh, reaching out to grab another clump of hair and tear it out. "You'll have reason to cry soon," she tells him as she shoves his hair and the blindfold past his teeth and follows it with a pair of his underwear sitting on the ground, a little brown smudge appearing for a moment before it's lost in his mouth. I can't stifle the shudder that rolls down my spine.

"Losing a little hair?" Jorunn adds as she steps back. "Not a good reason to bawl like a gods-damned infant."

"Boss," Leif says as he walks up with a satchel in his hands, leafing through the documents inside. "You should see this."

Fhord takes it from him, reaching in to pull out the stack of papers and set them on the bed in between Aksell's spread legs. "Oh, fuck no," he mutters as he accidentally glances up. "Can someone cover that, please. Like Ulfhild's girl said, we need to put this man and his pathetic pecker out of his misery."

Astrid laughs as she steps forward, a teeny doily she swiped from his dresser in one hand. She lays it across his boyhood, smirking as it covers him up. "We really should just cut the thing off. It can't be much use anyway."

Fhord isn't even listening, though. He's flipping through the files Leif found, a wicked grin emerging on his face. "We came on the perfect day." He turns to catch my gaze, gesturing me forward. "Dig into him a bit," he asks. "Figure out how recent this information is, and whether there's anything it's not telling us."

I pick up a few pages and my lips tip up too, as I wonder whether the gods finally are starting to smile on us.

Aksell has just given us the name of every dragon in Vanatia suspected of sympathizing with the rebellion, along with details about their riders and the reasons the Dróttning suspects them. To her, it's a list of beasts to watch, and a guide for anyone she trusts enough to gather more information.

For us, it's salvation. The army we need and haven't yet begun to gather.

For the first time since I met Fhord and joined the rebellion, I think we have a chance.

We might just win this thing.

I might have a future with Fhord after all.

For the short time I'll live in this land.

CHAPTER FOURTEEN

FHORD

WE'RE DONE

I'M ENJOYING KILLING AKSELL more than I expected to.

Sifa and I couldn't get into Aksell's mind—his shields are impossibly strong—so we're doing this the fun way. The bastard hasn't told us a single gods-damned thing about this supposed weapon, but I didn't think he would. His defiance just adds to the joy rippling through me as we take his life. I don't know what about the process is so satisfying with this asshole but shoving my blade into his guts, shaving his penis away bit-by-bit, lopping off his fingers and toes, is really soothing my savage and me. I've killed a shitload of assholes and it never felt this good.

I'm sure it's because he arranged for that female to shoot Astarot and is behind much of the dissent and unrest among the rebels. Idiots think he's an ally, but he's been trying to weasel his way into the Dróttning's inner circle as long as I've known him. Pretending to support the rebellion so he can offer the fools he ensnares to that bitch on a gods-damned platter. He deserves every bit of pain and terror he suffers.

It's more than that, though.

This is the first thing Sifa and I have done together to truly advance the rebellion. It feels romantic, as fucked-up as that is. We're bonding over Aksell's squeals and screams. With every squirt of blood we draw, every organ we yank out, every limb we hack off, I fall more in love with her.

I want to send my Ætt away and take her on Aksell's bed. I won't because I don't think she'd enjoy that nearly as much as me, but fuck do I want to.

"Where'd you go?" Sifa asks as she folds her crimson hands around me, leaning her forehead against my back.

"Into your pants," I mutter, reaching around to plant my wet hands on her ass.

"Thank fuck," she murmurs, plastering herself just a bit closer.

"Thank fuck for what?" I turn to capture her lips with mine, unable to resist when she's wrapped around me.

"It's not just me. Because right now, I want nothing more than to take you in my mouth and…"

"We're done," I bark, striding forward to swipe a blade from Torsten's hand and run it across Aksell's throat. "We aren't getting anything else from him. You all clean up. Sifa and I are going to the apartment. Give us a couple of hours before you come back."

I spin to grab her hand, dragging her toward me and into the hall as I ignore the laughs that follow us. We're covered in blood, but I don't give a fuck. It's the middle of the night and this is Revalle. We can disappear into hidden corners while we're in the estate area. Once we get away from here, nobody would dare look at us too closely. It's easy to lose an eye or a limb if you let it wander in this place.

We're across town in minutes, running hand in hand most of the way. Just as I'm reaching for the door to The Lucky Duck—the abandoned tavern the Ætt and I claimed when we got to Revalle—Sifa steps in front of me, resting her hands on my cheeks. "This is the first place you brought me," she murmurs, reaching up to kiss me. "By the gods, you pissed me off, but as much as I despised you, I desperately wanted you, even then."

"I was so angry at fate for giving me a mating bond I thought could never work. Now, I've never been more grateful. Thank the gods—bastards that they are—that fate wouldn't take my 'fuck no' for an answer."

"Thank the fucking gods."

"If you don't let me open that door, I'm gonna take you right here, right now. I'd hoped to go slowly tonight, but I'm gonna lose every bit of self-control if you're not naked soon."

Sifa lets go of my cheek to reach for the knob and open the door, clutching my shirt with her other hand to drag me in behind her. When I step out of the way and slam it behind me, she dances back a few feet and pulls her shirt over her head, dropping it to the floor as she spins. Tossing the sexiest fucking look I've ever seen over her shoulder, she starts to traipse upstairs, dropping clothing as she goes. By the time she gets to the second floor, she's completely naked and I still haven't moved, other than rubbing my throbbing cock like a gods-damned schoolboy.

"I'll meet you in the bathroom," she purrs as she sashays out of sight.

I've never reached the second floor so quickly. Or raced to my bedroom. Or gotten undressed. I think my savage must have pushed his way out to give me a kick in the ass. He's so fucking impatient where our mate's concerned.

Sifa turns her head to glance at me as I step into the bathroom, dragging the sponge slowly down her arm and then dipping it into the basin of water sitting in front of her. I step close enough for my cock to get some relief as it strains into her ass, taking the sponge from her hands and ringing it out. And then bit by bit, I clean every part of her, following the sponge with my lips and my tongue.

She doesn't move as I take care of her, giving me complete control to move her as I need to erase any hint of Aksell from her skin. As I work, cherishing my mate, I feel my savage settle inside me. We needed this, more than I realized. It calms us, helps us focus, to have this moment of time with the female the fates chose for us—the female we chose after realizing we can't live without her.

When she's clean, I drop the sponge in the water, take her shoulders, and gently spin her around. "I need to wash up before I can join you in bed, but I need a taste of you first." Dropping my fingers to her pussy, I can't hold back the grin when I realize how wet she is for me. I swipe through her a few times before lifting my fingers to suck them one by one, savoring the flavor of her juices.

But that's not nearly enough. Pushing the basin out of the way, I grasp Sifa's ass and lift her onto the table, pulling her forward just enough to bare her wide for me. And then I drop to my knees and feast.

She's midnight on a bright, starry night, the glorious flower that emerges when the sun has crossed to the other side of the world, stunning the creatures of the dark with her beauty. I hold her gaze for a moment as my tongue explores her, dipping inside and then focusing on her clit as my fingers take its place. She's so gods-damned spectacular, her eyes barely open as she watches me, little moans and sighs emerging every few seconds from those luscious lips.

I can't hold back the smile when her orgasm starts to build, gasps filling the space around us as her hands clasp the edges of the table. "Oh, fuck, Fhord," she breathes, her voice sending another jolt of need to my demanding cock, "that is so fucking good."

"Come for me, rabbit," I command, my fingers finding that spot inside that always makes her quiver as my tongue swirls around her clit.

And she does, trembling as her hands delve into my hair and her pleasure ripples through her. I can't look away as I slow down, licking and sucking to draw out every taste of her I can get, letting her fill a hole in me that always forms when it's been too long since I savored her this way.

When she releases her grip on my hair and lets out a long, deep sigh, I suck her clit one more time for good measure, then stand and kiss her. She opens to me, her tongue reaching between my lips as she explores my mouth the way I just explored her.

"Go to bed," I whisper when she leans back, her brown eyes sparkling at me between her thick, lush lashes. "I'll clean up and join you soon."

"Don't be long," she purrs as she reaches into my pants and wraps one hand around my cock, stroking up and down before she catches the drop of moisture at its tip and lifts her finger to her lips. "It's my turn to taste you." Dropping back to her feet as I step back, she spins and struts out the door. I can't drag my eyes away from her, utterly besotted by the magnificent creature who will share the rest of my life.

My savage is rumbling inside me, demanding more. My cock also wishes I'd hurry my ass up, but after tasting my little rabbit, I'm in control. If that's all I get tonight, I'll go to bed happier than I deserve to be, and sleep like the satisfied male I've become since she tamed me. I take my time cleaning, giving her a chance to sleep if she wants.

Still, my cock gives a throb of relief when I walk out of the bathroom and see Sifa lying on the bed utterly, divinely naked, her gaze firmly on me and the eager bastard pointing directly at her. She doesn't move for a few seconds as I stand watching her, but then one hand lifts, a finger crooking to call me to her before it drops down to slide over her cunt. She's still so fucking wet for me.

"You didn't think you were done, did you?"

The groan that starts deep in my gut and rolls through me answers her question better than words could. She smiles as she draws her hand up and over her belly, pausing at her tits to cup them the way I fucking love and then twirl her finger around each nipple, finally lifting it to her lips to suck it in.

"That's mine," I drawl. "Every single drop of it."

"You took your time, Fhord. I had to start without you."

"Again," I tell her. "More slowly this time."

She does as I ask, dragging her fingers back down to her wet cunt and spending a little more time there, plunging them deep inside twice before running them along her belly to those dark, firm nipples, and then lifting them up toward her lips.

"Stop," I rumble. "That belongs to me." Prowling forward, I crawl onto the bed, hovering just over her, no part of our bodies touching. Taking her hand, I suck her fingers into my mouth, moaning as I taste her again. "This is mine tonight. I will not share, even with you."

She stretches beneath me, pushing her hips up just enough to graze my cock, which trembles like a leaf in the wind. I'm completely at her mercy—despite my demanding words—and she knows it. "Take it, then," she breathes as she slowly drops her ass back on the bed. I reach for the blindfold on the table next to the bed, wrapping it around her eyes as a smile tilts up the corners of her lips.

"My savage needs you," I tell her, "if you'll have him. I won't shift. I'll still be me, in the form you know. I'll just loosen my restraints a touch, begin the very start of the shift. My claws and my fangs will grow and I'll give him some control. He'll tell you what he requires to claim his mate. But it'll be me fucking you, Sifa. It'll be me plunging into you and when I come, that will be all me."

I'm watching her as I ask and I don't see a hint of fear or concern. Her hands lay loose on the bed, her body relaxed beneath me. "I trust you, Fhord, and I trust him. Take everything you want, any way you want. But I want to see you. I know what you and your savage are, together. You don't frighten me. I belong to him too."

Fuck me. I worship this woman. She is everything I need. Everything my savage needs.

And so I take off the blindfold and then draw him up, reminding him what he can do and what he can't. Holding back the shift when it's gone just far enough for him to join me, I savor his excitement at taking part in this, and finally getting from our mate something the most primal, wild part of him demands.

We are two now. We rarely exist like this because it requires so much of us to balance on this wire. Yet, it feels natural. Although we've never done something so intimate in this form—we would not want this with anyone except our mate—deep inside, we know this is how it must be when we take Sifa together for the first time.

Our gaze roams over our mate as blood pounds through our cock. We want to plunge into her, but we cannot move too fast. We cannot let ourselves lose control. First, we will touch and taste her. Then we will fuck her.

We reach out one claw, running it gently along her cheek and jaw, a wave of satisfaction rolling through us as she trembles at our touch. We lean forward to taste her neck, letting our canine draw a single drop of blood, smiling as she whimpers in delight.

She is our mate, and she is eager to share every part of her with us.

Our lips and tongue roam down her body, pausing at her breasts to suckle and then draw a bead of blood from each, satisfied growls filling the quiet room with every sigh and moan our mate gives us. When we return to her cunt, wet and ready for us, we feast. We have indulged once already tonight, but we will never tire of the musky flavor of our mate's arousal.

Her hands are in our hair, frantic and needy, but we do not let our mate come this time. When ecstasy fills her, it will be on our cock and we will join her, as it must be this first time. Just as we feel her near the cliff that will carry her to her pleasure, we pull away, our lips and tongue and teeth grazing her skin as we find her lips again.

"I need you to fuck me, Fhord. I need all of you." She lifts her hips again, reaching for our needy cock.

And we realize we cannot wait any longer.

"Present," we snarl, knowing instinctively she will understand.

And she does. A wicked smile curves her lips, her dark eyes sparkling like a newborn star, as she drags one finger down our chest and then turns over. Leaning back, we watch in satisfaction as she rises to her knees, giving us everything we need, exactly the way we need it. We run the tips of our claws over her ass, her trembles filling us with pride.

She is a worthy mate.

Taking our cock in one hand, our other hand grasping her hip, we drag its tip gently along her cunt, groaning as her wetness coats us. She pushes back a bit, but we clench her side. "No," we tell her, our voice heavy with our desire. "We must fuck you."

She sucks in a deep breath, steadying and stilling herself as one of our hands returns to her cunt. We play with her, circling her clit with our thumb and driving two fingers inside of her to make sure she's ready for us. And then we plunge into her in one thrust, lighting an inferno inside as the feel of our mate on our cock pulsates through every part of us.

Her gasp of surprise, followed by a low moan, fills us with a desperate need, but we will not rush this. Slowly, savoring every inch of movement, we pull out and then push back in. Her hips start to roll, demanding more, but we squeeze, telling her what we need. We must control this.

"I'm trying, but I need you to fuck me. Hard."

"We will fill you, our mate," we grunt, holding her in place, our cock deep inside. We've only begun but already we can feel the change—how large we are growing—and we know we must be careful. We will not hurt our mate. "You will have everything you need."

She inhales again and I sense her confusion as she, too, realizes that we are more than we ever have been before. "Are you ... getting bigger?"

"We will grow as we take you." Our voice is deep, a feral mix between man and beast. "We will go slowly. We will cause you no harm."

She nods, stilling every part of her body except her cunt, which tightens around me. "Take what you need."

A howl rustles through us as we lift our other hand to her hip, seizing her tightly. We pull out again, letting the sensations shiver through as every part of our body feels the pleasure rippling from our cock. Rolling our hips as we push in—drawing a moan from our mate that we feel deep in our bones—we find our rhythm and fuck her, our entire body throbbing with the shared frenzy of this joining.

Carefully, struggling to maintain the balance between man and beast even as the beast side of us pleads for more, we release a small part of our hold on our savage, letting him feel every bit of the pleasure that ripples from our skin. This is what he needs to bond with our mate and fully connect. After tonight, we will be everything we can be together.

Our mate must sense the change. The sounds we are drawing from her pause, a question rising in her mind for a moment. But we thrust into her again, answering her. We are as we always have been. We are two and she belongs to both of us. As we belong to her.

Pushing in once more, knowing she is ready, we abandon thought and reason as we set ourselves free, letting instinct guide us. Rolling and rocking our hips as we thrust in and out, we acknowledge the mating bond as it rises to take over. Our mate sucks in a deep breath beneath us as she feels the same thing, recognizing the change occurring within us.

Seconds or minutes or hours carry us through the fervor of our pairing. We know only her, and the pleasure we give to and take from her. We feel only her, her tight cunt embracing and claiming our cock. We are only hers, the bond we have with her eclipsing even our bond with our beloved dragon. We are nothing without her.

When our orgasm comes, we can't hold back any longer, but we know—in that place we share with our mate, where we alone exist—that she is ready to join us. Releasing all restraint, we roar through our climax, preening with pride as our mate trembles beneath us, her orgasm tearing through her along with ours. We are ripped into pieces, our separate beings gone now as we become one.

She collapses on the bed, and we fall beside her, an arm and leg splayed across her back and thighs as we breathe through the waves of pleasure still rushing through us. We can't move. We can barely think. We know only our mate, and the feel of her body beneath ours. Nothing else matters.

When my savage lets go, slipping back into the part of me where he rests, I take a deep breath.

"Is he satisfied?" Sifa's whisper fills me with such love, I wonder how I survived without it.

"He didn't know before tonight what it would be to join with his mate. I've lived a long time, rabbit. I've known much joy in my life. My savage, though, has been restless all those years. Through every moment of pleasure, every taste of happiness, every rush of desire, something has been missing. That part of me has never been satisfied before. He's never been complete before."

I roll onto my back, shifting her toward me so I can look in her eyes. She's so perfect for us. Even from his near-slumber, my savage's rumble of fulfillment shivers through me. "We have never felt so whole. After centuries of needing more—an itch we could never scratch, a hunger that wouldn't be satisfied—we have enough. We have everything we could ever want. You are all we'll ever need."

"I felt it too," she tells me, lifting her hand to trace her finger over my jawbone. "I thought our mating bond already was all it could be. But we needed him. He's part of us. He needed to mate with me."

"I didn't realize it either. This is new to me too." I pause, holding our gaze. "Thank you for trusting us, rabbit. For giving yourself to us."

"I gave myself to you a long time ago, Fhord. We're just discovering all the different ways you can take me."

"This was the best discovery yet."

"You're right. So what's next?"

I know she's asking about everything we just shared, but I don't answer that question. Instead, I smile at her, running a thumb along her cheek. "Tomorrow, we start fighting back. I spent a little time with Aksell's list, and I know which dragon we're going to approach first. She's close."

"Do you think we've got a chance at turning her?"

"I don't know, but if we can turn enough, everything will change."

She nods, her eyes bright. "Tomorrow, then. We truly take the fight to the Dróttning."

I smile, leaning in for a kiss. "Tomorrow," I agree, "the revolution begins."

CHAPTER FIFTEEN

SIFA

THE TRUE COST

"WE CAN'T TAKE YOU with us." It breaks my heart to see Toffer so sad at being left behind, but this trip is too dangerous and uncertain for him to come.

"Khirta can keep us close." He watches me for a few seconds, adding in a plaintive voice, "Trolls are terrific at talking."

I exhale slowly, fighting the part of me that wants to give in. He's been my closest friend for a decade as we've searched together for a path home—the only way we know to regain the long lives we'll both lose if we stay here. Now, I've all but abandoned that search, the fight against the Dróttning pushing everything else aside. I've got Astarot and Fhord, and he's embraced our new family, but he still needs me. And I still need him.

Not for this, though. I steel my shoulders and draw him into a hug. "You might be able to help," I whisper, "but it's still too risky. Astarot and Tindera know this dragon and they'll try to convince her. If she turns on us, we can't have you there.

She's bigger and faster than Khirta. The other dragons could get away, but Khirta might not be able to escape. And then we'd lose both of you."

"And Thor," Toffer mutters as I release him and lean back to hold his gaze.

"Why Thor? He wouldn't need to go even if you were."

Toffer's eyebrows shoot up, forming one massive caterpillar above his eyes. "Abandon our ardent ally?" he demands, his voice shrill.

"It's dangerous. Even if we let you go, why risk Thor too?"

"Cats are cunning communicators." He lifts a hand to stroke the ever-present cat wrapped around his neck, staring at him with soft eyes and a half-smile.

"Well, it doesn't matter. You can't come. Stay here, and I'll get you when we're done."

"Your word we'll go with when you wander?"

I sling my bag onto my back then stride over to Toffer, wrapping my arms around him. Thor's purr as he nuzzles into my ear calms me, as it always does. "I promise. We won't leave without you."

"Speed and safety to my sidekicks."

"We're your sidekicks?"

Toffer nods, a teasing grin lifting his lips, before his eyes narrow, lips forming into a thin line. "Reprieve will return when you reappear."

I pat his cheeks, unable to keep the smile from tipping up my lips. "I can't wait." Dropping a kiss on his nose, I pet Thor one more time, then spin to leave. It's time to go turn a dragon.

Fhord and Sigurd are waiting for me when I get back to The Lucky Duck. "No Hilde?" I ask, searching for the loyal beast that came out of retirement for me. "She's still got a few good runs in her."

"Not this time. We'll ride together." He smirks, pleased about something he wants to surprise me with.

The round of drinks before Dani left Lumaria bounces through my mind. "Torsten didn't get me a horse, did he?" There's only one reason we'd share a mount from here.

Fhord's face drops, and I know I'm right. He recovers quickly, though, apparently resolved to keep up the ruse.

"Why would Torsten get you a horse?" His voice is smooth as honey.

I cock my head at him, giving him my don't-fuck-with-me face—a look he knows well.

"Okay, Torsten got you a horse. But you need to act surprised. He's as excited as Torsten ever gets about anything."

"So he might smile? His eyes might soften a bit?"

Fhord scoffs. "Fuck, no," he declares in a dismissive tone. "I've never seen Torsten smile—well, once, but I wasn't supposed to be *there*—and today won't be the day. He may frown less. Or maybe not. It's hard to predict."

"I thought it might be too much to ask for. But why would he get me another horse? I love Hilde."

"It's time for Hilde to retire for good. She's gotten slow. We won't be able to move at her pace as we chase the dragons. You need a new horse."

Now he's the one wearing the don't-fuck-with-me face, and I know I've already lost. But I also know he's right. I should have gotten a new horse after my first trip with Hilde. She has the spirit of a warrior but the body of a nag. We're lucky she got as far as she did. It's time.

Torsten's nowhere to be found when we arrive at the rebel hideout to get our dragons, though, so any introduction to my new mount will wait. I'm relieved, but I'd never tell Fhord. I don't like gifts, and I'm glad to put this one off to another day. We've got something more important to do today.

Astarot nudges me as I walk over, eager to chase the dragon Fhord chose. *Stubborn*, he tells me. He doubts we'll have any luck with this beast.

Stubborn could be good. If she resisted the Dróttning and the forced pairing, she might be easier to turn.

Stubborn, he repeats, because he's the most stubborn dragon I've ever met.

I smile and scratch behind his horn, happy to be with him again. *I've missed you*, I whisper before turning toward the leg he extends toward me.

Weak, he tells me. He's getting worse, growing more desperate for the mystery food the Dróttning gives her dragons. And more convinced that's important to her control over the Thunder. He can't think of another Vanatian dragon who's gone without it, and he's spent his long existence believing—like everyone else—that it's nothing more than a treat the Dróttning provides.

That alone should have told us it's important. The Drót-tning doesn't provide treats.

Fhord's checking with a couple people loyal to him at the Nest to figure out if we can get some for you. He doesn't think we'll get more information about what's in it—it's a secret the Dróttning holds too closely—but if we can get a sample along with some for you to eat, we might be able to figure it out. We're working on it, I promise.

Time. He still has time. It's a fierce craving but not yet a need.

"Ready?" Fhord's already astride Tindera, who's watching us with the flirtiest look I've ever seen on a dragon.

Have you and your draikana been having fun? I ask, trying desperately to keep the laugh from my voice.

I expect a little embarrassment, but I clearly don't know my dragon well enough. He turns toward me, cheeky bastard that he is, and winks. *Fly*, he announces, shaking his feathers and then turning to preen them a bit. They've been making up for lost time. And who can blame them?

I'm glad you're enjoying your time together, I tell him as I climb up and settle in for the ride.

He grunts, a throaty sound that's clearly intended for his draikana, not his rider, and turns toward Tindera. She tosses her head, the corners of her lips flickering, and then launches into the sky. A dragony laugh rumbles from Astarot as he follows her.

We fly high, too close to the Nest to risk being seen, Fhord and I both whispering out our minds to search for anyone else in the sky. We're alone, though, the afternoon sun beating down to cast harsh light on the land far below. Especially from this height, it reminds me so much of Midgard—rich clover fields leading to hunter green mountains with a turquoise ocean in the distance. Vanatia and Njordheim could be any other island in the middle of one of the oceans back home.

I'm no closer to getting there than I was when I met Fhord, but I'm not sure how much I care. I can't leave my mate or dragon, even if it means I'll live decades instead of centuries. It'll be worth it. I'd rather live a year with Fhord than a thousand years without him. I just wish I could find a way to get Toffer home.

My head spins to find Fhord as the guilt ripples through me. I dread telling him that his time with me will be so short. I've been berating him for his secrets while keeping this one. He deserves to know I won't share his long life. It's horrible timing but there will never be a good time.

Close. Astarot's message from Fhord drops into my mind. We'll land now and walk the last half-viku or so. If we approach by air, she'll attack before we get a chance to talk to her.

And Fhord's sure her rider isn't with her?

Alone, he confirms. Tindera relayed that one of Fhord's people saw her rider at the Nest. This dragon's always craved solitude so she flies by herself once or twice a week.

How do we stop her from reaching out to her rider before we've had a chance to talk to her? If she does that, we're fucked. They'll send every dragon in the Nest to capture us.

Alone. This time, the word has a different meaning. Tindera and Astarot will approach her alone. Tindera thinks she'll be open to talking. She hopes so.

I hate this idea. The last time I sent Astarot alone to talk to someone, hungry trolls surrounded him, demanding dinner. That one turned out okay—barely.

The dragons tuck their wings and streak to the ground, extending them at the last minute as they reach a small field, hidden in the shadow of the mountain we've been flying toward. It's covered in fluttering shapes as the wind rustles the leaves of the surrounding trees, giving it a sinister feel. Or maybe it's just me. I can't shake the feeling that this is a bad idea. That this dragon won't be turned, and we're about to get fucked.

It's too late, though. We're committed and we'll face the same risks with every dragon we approach.

Astarot flares his wings at the last second, stopping his descent as he settles to the ground. Spinning his head to look at me—my somber mood filtering through to him regardless of my efforts to keep my gloom and doom to myself—he grumbles as his wing flares out for me to descend. *Hope,* he says, his thoughts filled with the optimism I can't find inside myself.

I know, I tell him, climbing down to rest my forehead against his cheek as my hand reaches for his favorite spot to scratch. *I'll get over this. I promise.*

He nods as he pulls away, turning toward Tindera. Together, they stride into the forest in search of the beast who could destroy us with one thought.

"We need to do this." Fhord's arm wraps around my back as he pulls me into him. "Is it this dragon in particular that has your head so messed up?"

"I have no gods-damned idea," I respond with a laugh.

But I do know, I realize, and it has nothing to do with the dragon. "That's not true," I tell him after a moment. "I've been keeping something from you. It's not intentional; I just never thought of telling you, despite what a big fucking deal it is. And then the Dróttning captured you, and there hasn't been a good time since we got you out. But there's no good time." I'm sure he can hear the despair in my voice. I don't try to hide it.

"It can't be that bad." Fhord tugs me a bit closer, turning to give me a little kiss on my forehead.

"Have I ever told you why I was so desperate to find a way home?"

"No, but I get it. You don't belong here. My gods-damned mother hunts and imprisons elves. Of course you want to go home. Or you did."

"I did. I can't leave now, no matter what it will cost me."

"We're not going to let her capture you again, Sifa. That won't happen."

"That's not what I'm talking about," I tell him, pulling away so I can face him as I admit my greatest secret. "I've lived hundreds of years, Fhord, but I don't have hundreds more. I'll live decades, if I'm lucky."

"That's silly, rabbit. Elves have long lives. We'll have centuries together."

"We won't. This world changed my aging process. When I arrived, I looked fifteen. I've been here ten years, and I've aged just like a human every one of those years. Toffer too. We had long lives in our world, but we lost that when we came here. I have the lifespan of a human. And I'm so fucking sorry I never thought to tell you this. You deserved to know I'm going to be a drop in the bucket of your long life before you tied yourself to me as firmly as you have."

Fhord's eyes grew wide while I talked, but now they narrow, his nostrils flaring as he takes a step back. And my heart breaks. This is so much worse than any secret he held from me. I've broken his trust, and I don't know if I'll ever get it back—if I even deserve to get it back. I'm holding my breath, waiting for him to say something, and he's not. I can't read his expression or find a path into his emotions. He's already erected a wall between us. And who could blame him?

Come. Astarot's command drops into my mind. *Now.*

Fhord's gaze lifts toward the dragons at the same time as mine. He nods but reaches out to grasp my wrist before I can walk away. And then the wall between us drops and I feel his love embracing me, a never-ending, unflappable commitment to this bond between us. The knot that had formed in my stomach unwinds as he lifts a hand to grip the back of my neck, locking his gaze with mine.

"I don't know why the fuck you wouldn't live as long as me, but it doesn't change anything," he snarls, the devotion I feel rippling through our bond stark in his voice. "I belong to you, and if we only have fifty years together, I'll be grateful for every gods-damned day—every single hour—that I'm with you. But you're a fucking elf and you will live the life of a fucking elf. We'll figure this out or we'll die trying. Together."

Tears fill my eyes, and I shake my head, lifting one hand to caress his cheek. "I love you so much, Fhord."

"I love you. Now shake off this bullshit mood and let's go corrupt another dragon." He leans down for a quick kiss, hard and fierce, then takes my hand, links our fingers together, and starts striding toward Astarot and Tindera. I trail along behind him, thanking the gods, bastards that they are, for giving me this unshakable male. I don't deserve him, but I'm sure as fuck gonna keep him.

The dragon, Iyanshe, is a gorgeous beast. She's black—unusual for Vanatian dragons, from what I've seen—but her coat shimmers with a rainbow of other colors. In this light, I see gold and tangerine and a yellow that reminds me of the lemons that grew outside my window as a child. She stands nearly as tall as Tindera, her eyes rich as a plum on a bright summer day as she watches us approach.

Listen, Astarot tells me. Iyanshe will hear what we have to say, although that means nothing. She could be gathering information to carry back to the Nest. But she hasn't turned on us yet—Astarot's sure she sent no messages back to the Dróttning—so that's something.

As we approach, I free my thoughts, letting them filter toward Iyanshe. I'm not sure how I know, but I can speak with her, if she'll let me. I've only been able to communicate with Astarot and, to a lesser degree, Tindera, but as my mind brushes against hers, I'm certain. Maybe it's the mating bond or my connection with Toffer, or just something about this dragon. Whatever it is, it will come in handy.

"You've known Tindera and Astarot for many years," Fhord says, striding forward so we're standing between them. "They haven't made this decision lightly. It's required sacrifice and pain, but they don't regret it because our fight is worthy. You deserve to have your destined riders. You deserve to live as free beasts, not bound by the Dróttning's commands and whims."

Dagny. Her rider's name drops into my head, and I feel her conflict. "She's been with Dagny for decades," I tell Fhord, his eyes growing wide as his head spins. I smile and nod, confirming his suspicion. He responds with the most brilliant, carefree grin I've ever seen on him. This could change everything.

"And you love her?" Fhord's voice is soft as he looks again at Iyanshe.

Devoted. "It's complicated," I explain, my gaze never straying from the conflicted dragon. "She's as committed to Dagny as any dragon is to her rider. She does love her, but she also fears and distrusts her. Dagny supports what the Dróttning did to our dragons. Iyanshe does not."

Tindera and Astarot growl out their agreement together. No dragon should be tortured the way they were.

"You would get to decide, Iyanshe," Fhord reminds her. "I don't know who the fates chose for you, but you can choose to stay with Dagny or not. We fight for you to have that control."

Dangerous. "She's worried." I take a step forward to make sure she knows I'm talking to her. "We're all worried. We've all suffered. I'm an elf and if I'm caught, my life will be over. But the Dróttning has hurt so many dragons and people—she's done so much harm—and we can't let it go on any longer. If we have to give our lives for this battle, we will. We'll have worthy deaths and be proud of our place in the fight."

Rider. A wave of desire rushes through me. Not sexual, like she might feel for her drake. This is familial, the ache a dragon has for its unclaimed rider. "She saw the male the fates chose for her," I say as I glance at Fhord. "He didn't see her—she didn't let him—but that's part of her conflict too. She doesn't want to be forced to choose between them. She can't betray either of them that way."

I'm turning back toward Iyanshe when I sense the shift in her emotions. A wave of fear rushes through her, followed by an enmity so deep and pronounced, it feels like it belongs to someone else. Iyanshe's eyes flare and a flame erupts from her snout as she takes a step forward, her tail jerking angrily behind her. Tindera and Astarot rise on either side of me, spitting out fire to fill the space between us, but I barely notice them.

My mind is still wrapped in Iyanshe's as anger and hatred push out every bit of uncertainty I found there seconds ago. And I realize these emotions aren't Iyanshe's. I've gotten a window into the Dróttning's control of these beasts. Fhord told me before that she searches randomly for dragons, checking in on them when they don't expect it. She just touched on Iyanshe's thoughts.

I have seconds, if that, to stop the Dróttning from learning everything. I plunge deeper into her mind, finding every memory of the last few minutes to rip it out, leaving an empty hole in its place. My heart is pounding like a drum, a rolling measure as I search, followed by a harsh boom to accompany every image I wrench free. Within a few seconds, I'm clenching my teeth, my breaths rasping in and out of my open mouth, as I fight against a beast determined to stop me.

But I'm stronger than her and I will not let the Dróttning win this. She can't know what we're doing. She'll entrap or destroy every dragon whose loyalty she questions if she does.

I feel Fhord's hand rest on my lower back, pulsing some of his strength into me, but it barely registers. My grasp on my body is tenuous, every bit of my attention focused on Iyanshe and the unintentional threat she poses. My thoughts are still spearing through hers, catching glimpses of her life as I probe for any hint of our appearance this morning and rip it free.

When she collapses, I know I'm done. I also know I've hurt her—maybe destroyed her mind with my violent, ruthless attack—and part of my heart breaks at what I just did to this majestic, conflicted beast.

"The Dróttning invaded her thoughts while we were talking." My whisper fills the empty space between us, heavy and dark. "I tried to remove Iyanshe's memories of us, but I think I ripped out part of her mind. It happened so fast." I look up at Fhord, tears blurring my image of him. "I think I hurt her. Badly."

"You had to do it, rabbit," Fhord whispers to me, tugging me into his side as he kisses me gently on the forehead. "Dragons are hearty beasts. She should be okay."

He's right.

Still, I feel utterly defeated as the possibility that I harmed her—a painful reminder of the true cost of this war we're about to wage—weighs down my soul.

CHAPTER SIXTEEN

DANI

SLOP

*T*ODAY WE WILL FLY. Vulryn's got that arrogant, self-satisfied smirk in her voice, and I wish to the gods I could see the look on her face that always accompanies it. She's very cute when she smirks.

Why in all the worlds would they let us fly? I haven't turned on our friends, and they don't have any reason to think I will.

The wyrm believes I have eaten her ... slop ... three times this week. She thinks she now controls me and that I will lead my drake to our male and the others. If her voice is any indication, Vulryn's smirk is even deeper now. She's so fucking happy with herself.

A food...

Slop. It is no food.

Okay. You think this slop gives her control over all the dragons in Vanatia? And she's so convinced you'll betray Fhord and Sifa because of it, she's gonna let us fly? That sounds crazy and impossible.

It is possible, she tells me, a hint of impatience in her tone. My brash beast doesn't like being questioned. *I smelled the slop when she first offered it to me and understood. It grows in the North, in a place where few tread. The beings who occupy that land wield strange magic. The plant is their god. That is why I refused to eat it and have pretended since you told me of the demand from my drake's rider.*

What does that mean, it's "their god"?

I have watched them as they bow to it. Vulryn snorts her disdain with these words. *It is their god.*

Maybe their magic's just odd. It could have nothing to do with the plant.

Similar beings live in other parts of the North. They have no such powers. It is the plant. Now Vulryn's voice is firm. She *really* doesn't like it when I disagree with her on things she alone knows. 'Cause my dragon's a magnificently uppity bitch.

Okay, so the plant gives them strange magic. What does that mean, and how could the Dróttning use a plant to control dragons?

I know not how the wyrm uses the plant to control the Thunder, Vulryn declares huffily. *I can only tell you what I have seen. When these beings eat the plant, they become as one. They engage in odd rituals at their leader's command. I have seen them take their own lives when their leader commanded it.*

Like the plant somehow gives him control over them?

That is how it appears. I know not how it works. I know only what I have seen, and that I recognize the smell of that plant in the wyrm's slop.

We need to get out of here, tell Fhord and Sifa what we've learned. It may be the key to defeating her.

We will leave today when we fly.

Are you done with Ziselær? Already? A wave of shock ripples through me. I'd resigned myself to being here for weeks, maybe months.

I am ready to leave. He is mine. He will come to me when the time is right.

Is he going to betray the Dróttning? Already?

I do not believe he is ready to reject the wyrm. But that time will come. When I leave, he will know that our bond is stronger than any other bond in his life. And then he will do what is right.

How can you be so sure?

He is my drake. He will come to me when the time is right. She pauses a moment, then adds, *If not, we will kill him. That has not changed.*

I wish I had even a smidgen of your confidence.

That too will come. Her voice is so smug, and I don't think I could love her more.

So, we'll just leave?

His rider will try to contain us, and my drake may comply at first. They will not stop us.

And do you plan to let him mount you?

He will not yet have me, Vulryn purrs. *We will fly as one when I know he will not betray me, and after you take his rider. Only then will he truly be my drake.*

The urge isn't killing you? I thought the need to fly with your drake would overwhelm you.

I am stronger than my urges. I will not fly with him until he is mine, and not the wyrm's. Now her voice shifts, steel infusing every word. *No drake of mine will bow to the wyrm. I will not allow it.*

It's no wonder I love you, my badass bitch of a beast.

She doesn't respond, but I can almost feel her preening herself. She was strong before she found Ziselær. Now, she's gods-damned invincible.

This will be a fun day.

Matthias invades my space barely an hour after Vulryn tells me her plans. He's as sexy as usual, tight leather revealing every bulge and muscle in a body that I try my damnedest to ignore. Today, he's decided to be nice, probably because his dragon wants to mount mine, and thinks Ziselær's path to Vulryn runs through Matthias and me. I prefer this over the raging asshole—and we'll never escape if he knows what Vulryn thinks—so I'm happy to go along.

"Did your dragon tell you what the Dróttning decided?"

"That our dragons will fly today?"

He nods, cold blue eyes flickering over me in what can only be disappointment or impatience. "The dragons wait for us in the courtyard. Why aren't you dressed?"

I look down at the pants and tunic I choose every day, unsure what he thinks I should be wearing. "Do your females wear dresses when they fly?"

"Of course," he declares, his tone strident. "When their beasts will join in the sky, they come prepared."

"You're looking for easy access? You think you're going to fuck me, and you're bothered you may have to move my pants out of the way?" I can't keep the disdain from my words, but I don't give a shit. Presumptuous ass.

He takes a deep breath, as if he's trying to stop himself from turning into the bastard that is his natural state of being. "It's just a fuck, Dani," he says, his voice softening a bit. "You won't be able to resist. I don't want to take it from you, but I will because I'll have as little control as you. Please change your clothes."

That's probably as nice as I'll get from the male. "This is how I ride. I'm not going to dress for sex with you." Smiling, I pat his cheek as I whisper. "You still need to romance me, big guy."

He reaches for my arm, pulling me closer as he holds my gaze. "You need to understand what's going to happen," he says, his voice almost reasonable. "Ziselær and Vulryn are mates. When they fly together for the first time, our *need* to join them will overwhelm us. You'll want it every bit as much as me. Change your clothes."

"I don't plan to fuck you, but if you're right, we can take a minute and take off my gods-damned pants. This is how I ride. Let's go and get this over with."

"Stubborn fucking female," he mutters as he drops my arm and swings his in the direction of the hall. "Don't blame me if you have to fly back here half-naked."

Didn't you say Matthias planned to woo me? Try to get me to like him so you and Ziselær can be together?

Vulryn's quiet for a moment. Finally, she responds in a voice filled with frustration. *My drake's rider is a difficult male.*

Difficult is one way to put it, I gripe. *Thank the gods Ziselær won't be mounting you today because I do not want to be fucked by this male.*

Thank me, not the gods. They have no more control over me than the wyrm.

I bark out a laugh, drawing Matthias's sneering eyes to me. Smirking at him, I walk a little faster, giving him my back. *Thank you, my beautiful beast.*

I will not have him harm you. My drake will wait. And he will want me more.

"Left," Matthias grumbles from behind me. He lets me lead, grunting directions as we go. Within a few minutes, we step into the sun, and I pause to breathe, savoring the feel of its rays on my face.

"I've been trapped underground for too long," I say to nobody, because I'm definitely not talking to Matthias.

He answers, though, because he's a bastard. "And back underground you'll go when they're done. Be grateful the Dróttning allows this."

"Fuck the Dróttning," I mutter as I stride toward the patch of copper sitting amongst the rocks, her feathers bright flames in the sun's embrace. Matthias stops at the entrance to speak with one of the guards, but there's no way I'm waiting for him. I want to feel my dragon's touch again.

Vulryn snuffs as I approach, extending her snout for the scratches she loves. Working my way from the tip of her nose to the backs of her horns, I whisper my love for her as she relaxes and revels in my touch. *Ready?* I ask as she extends her wing.

She turns to look at me as I climb up and then casts the cutest side-eye ever at Ziselær, who snorts in response. *Ready.*

Settling in, I watch as Matthias jerks a nod at the soldier he's been speaking with and then strides toward his dragon. He barely acknowledges him—no ear-scratches for his mount—stalking up the extended wing without a word or even a glance. Asshole.

They launch before us, throwing themselves into the sky. Vulryn watches them for a moment—her pride at her drake billowing around us in a cloud that feels like I could touch it if I tried—then throws her head back and follows. And I'm at peace, finally. She's been my dragon for such a short time, but this already has become my sanctuary. Nowhere else, nothing else, can touch the tranquility that fills me when I fly with Vulryn.

We head west, toward the ocean where we met Ziselær and Matthias after leaving Lumaria. *Are we returning to the cove?*

My drake would take me back there. He hopes to fly over the ocean. She pauses for a moment, and I get the sense she doesn't want to add the last reason. But she does, a hint of apology in her voice. *And you will be trapped there. His rider demands a secure location.*

It's okay, I tell her. *I wouldn't expect anything else.*

I will fly with my drake, but he will not take me. Then I will retrieve you and we will leave them.

Are you sure?

This is how it must be.

We're silent after that, the steady beat of Vulryn's wings the only noise that interrupts my thoughts. I'm not sure if we're doing the right thing. Vulryn is sure Ziselær will follow her at some point, but they've spent so little time together. What if it's not enough and we've done this for nothing?

But that's not right, I realize as the cove comes into view. We had to do this for Vulryn to recognize the food ... okay, slop ... that's so important to the Dróttning. Maybe we've accomplished everything the fates intended, and it really is time to go join the fight. As long as we can get away from Matthias.

Within a few minutes, the dragons are soaring out over the ocean, circling back to the cove that will hold Matthias and me while they fly. I hadn't noticed at the time how beautiful it is: deep red cliffs, shimmering like Vulryn's feathers when the sun hits them just right; a beach so white, from this distance it seems like the gods themselves visited to remove any blemishes; a pool so clear and crisp, I can see its bottom; and bright green shrubs sprinkled everywhere that sand meets stone. In this light, it feels magical, and I wish this could be where Vulryn and Ziselær come together.

Vulryn stretches her wings as her path takes her over the beach, settling gently on the sand and spinning her head to watch her drake land behind her. His gaze never moves from hers, and I can't imagine how we leave here today without Ziselær taking Vulryn. I've never seen two beings who desire each other more than these two.

Have fun, I tell her as I grab my pack and climb down her extended wing.

Be safe, she responds. She still doesn't trust Matthias.

Always, I say before striding toward the shore, pulling off my boots and then my pants and shirt, dropping them as I go. I catch Matthias's gaze as I start to strip—his expression a mix of shock and a desire I didn't expect—but ignore him. I came prepared to swim. He's not seeing any more than the undergarments that cover everything I need them to.

The water is every bit as warm and relaxing as I'd hoped. I'm floating just below the surface, gazing up at frolicking dragons, when I hear Matthias splashing through the waves. Turning to watch him prowl toward me, a resolved look on his face, I hold back the groan that wants to emerge. He can swim if he wants to. It's a big ocean.

Before he reaches me, though, Vulryn's voice drops into my head. *The sun beast and the fire beast approach with their riders.*

What? That can't be right.

Her response holds a hint of impatience as she repeats her warning. *Our male and the starry female approach on their beasts.*

Why in all the worlds are they coming here?

They come for us.

Why? How do they even know we're here?

I recognized their presence and called out. They will ensure we can leave. My drake will not try to stop me if we leave with them.

That makes sense. It gives Ziselær a great excuse for not stopping Vulryn. *How long until they arrive?*

Turn to the north and you will see them.

She's right. Almost as soon as she's said the words, Matthias's gaze snaps up, his eyes searching for the dragons Ziselær must have warned him about. "Out of the water," he snarls, pushing through the waves more quickly to reach for me.

"Fuck off, Matthias. I'm not going with you."

"You will come with me now or we will take Vulryn and leave without you."

"Vulryn's not coming either. We'll leave with Sifa and Fhord."

"The fuck you will. Vulryn belongs to the Dróttning now. She's already been ordered to answer to me, as the Dróttning's second. She'll leave you here."

"You don't know shit about my dragon. But you'll find out soon enough."

I'm stalking toward the shore to wait for Vulryn when Ziselær's squawk echoes off the surrounding cliffs. I haven't heard such anger in a dragon's cry since Vulryn killed hundreds of soldiers in Njordheim. Looking up, I see him and Vulryn hovering just above the water, a dragon's-length between them, chattering at each other like they did when they first met in this cove.

Vulryn's emotions fill me—anger, regret, and resolve spinning together in a chaotic stew.

Vulryn and her drake are still howling at each other when Sifa and Fhord get close enough to see us. So they have a clear view of Ziselær breaking away from his fight with Vulryn to swoop toward me, clutching my arms in his claws and launching us both into the sky. My stomach hurls into my throat and it's all I can do to keep from spewing my last meal all over Ziselær's claws.

Vulryn's angry scream shatters the air. The regret that had been at the center of her feelings disappears, replaced by a rage and betrayal so deep, my own anger is eclipsed by her pain. I spin my head to see her racing toward us, eyes flints of steel, as Astarot and Tindera spear toward Matthias.

"They will kill your rider," I shriek at Ziselær, making sure Vulryn also catches my words. "Turn around before it's too late."

But it's already too late. Tindera reaches Matthias first, grasping his arms the way Ziselær grabbed mine, and flying straight up, Astarot on her heels. As Ziselær spins to return to his rider, Vulryn's bitter howls battering him, Tindera and Astarot stop their ascent to hover in the air. Astarot takes Matthias's legs in his claws, suspending him between them. A few flaps of their wings and they'll rip him apart, permanently ending the long life the Dróttning has given him.

I can feel Ziselær's desperation, rippling through his draikana to me. He screeches at the other dragons, dropping me to plunge to my death as he races back toward Matthias. I try to catch my breath, but nothing works. My lungs feel like rocks, too heavy and full to let air seep in, while my heart beats like a hummingbird's wings. I'm searching for my dragon, desperate for one last look at her before I die, when her command breaks through my hysteria.

Spin, she roars. I'm not sure how the fuck I do it, but I pivot in the air just in time to watch her soar under me, pounding out whatever dregs of air my lungs still hold as I collapse on her back.

Hold, she pleads, her voice cracking with a fear I didn't know she could feel.

I grip handfuls of feathers, clinging with every ounce of strength I possess as she struggles to control her descent. She somehow manages to do just that—badass bitch that she is, thank the fucking gods—slowing us enough to land with two small bounces. Turning toward me as soon as she's steady, flames flickering to the beach beneath us, she extends her wing like she always does.

A rogue giggle erupts as I catch her gaze, because that was the most unhinged minute I've ever lived. I can still see a hint of desperation in her eyes, but mostly she's pissed. She watches me for a moment and then turns to find Ziselær. He's hovering near Astarot and Tindera, squawking at them as they appear to be debating whether or not to kill his rider.

When they move, it's sudden. The dragons release Matthias and attack Ziselær, barring any path he might have to save him. Now, I see the vicious blue dragon who charged Vulryn when we freed Fhord and Tindera. Ziselær is savage, attacking the other dragons with a cruelty he's been hiding since we found them in this cove. He's outnumbered and can't win, but he's determined to do some damage before they kill him.

Vulryn's emotions swing again, the rage she felt when her drake attacked me giving way to fear. *Stop*, she demands, throwing her words at everyone who can hear her. And they all comply, pausing in the air to turn toward her. Ziselær watches her for a moment, his eyes still flashing a deep, intense hatred, then tucks his wings to shoot toward his rider, who's bobbing in the water beneath them.

I watch him drop, unsure how Matthias could have survived but certain he did. Ziselær would have sensed his rider's death, but Vulryn hasn't felt the wave of grief that would come with that loss.

He lives, Vulryn confirms, watching her drake gently lift his rider from the waves and soar back to the beach. *My drake shares his pain. It is deep and intense.*

Why did Ziselær go after me? He must have known the others would stop him.

My drake's rider demanded it, and my drake had no choice but to heed his command. The wyrm's magic controls him. For now. His rider did not expect the others to attack the way they did. He believed the wyrm still wielded some influence over the fire beast and the sun beast. He will not make that mistake again.

We should kill Matthias. He's a cruel man. Ziselær will suffer, but he'll survive.

My drake wants his rider to live. He has chosen him. He will suffer too much if his rider dies.

"Are you okay?" Sifa's voice draws my attention to her, and I smile.

"I have no fucking idea," I respond with a laugh. "That was quite the entrance."

"Just in case you've forgotten how batshit crazy it can be when we're together," she tells me with a wink.

"No need to remind me," I assure as I finally feel steady enough to climb down from my dragon. "Vulryn doesn't want to kill Matthias," I tell her as I stride to her side.

"We have to kill him, Dani."

"Ziselær's too connected to him. Even after what just happened, Vulryn doesn't want to inflict that kind of pain on him."

"She's got quite the soft spot where he's concerned." Sifa's smirking now. She gets it. Dragon bonds are intense.

"For a beast as ruthless as she can be, she's got a huge fucking heart," I agree.

Sifa turns eyes filled with love toward my dragon. "I think those go hand in hand," she murmurs. Looking at me again, she quirks an eyebrow. "What do you want to do?"

What do we want to do? My gaze finds Vulryn as I ask.

He lives. We will stay with my drake and his rider in this cove while he heals.

"Vulryn wants us to stay here with Ziselær and Matthias. We'll all leave when he can ride again."

"I doubt he'll heal." Fhord's matter-of-fact in his assessment. "He's human, and those are life-threatening wounds."

"He doesn't heal the way we do?"

"No. Whatever the Dróttning gives her soldiers can extend lives and accelerate healing a bit, but it doesn't change their mortality. Most die from injuries like this."

We will stay and help him heal, Vulryn announces, staring at Ziselær even though she's talking to me.

No, we won't. I don't even like Matthias. I'll be gods-damned if I'm going to hang out on a remote beach with him while I nurse him back to life.

We will stay. When he is healed, we will leave.

And fuck if that isn't exactly what we do. Vulryn and I tell Sifa and Fhord about the wyrm's slop—giving them the missing link they've been searching for, they explain—and where they can find more. They leave us a tent, bedding, food and water, promising to check on us in ten or twelve days to find out if we need anything else.

And then I watch as they disappear on the horizon, wondering what the fuck I've let my dragon talk me into, and whether we'll survive this next episode of insanity.

CHAPTER SEVENTEEN

MATTHIAS

YOU HAD A CHOICE

WHY THE FUCK DO I smell the ocean?

I haven't opened my eyes yet. Every gods-damned part of me hurts and I can feel sun blazing down all around me and sand beneath me. I never wake up in the fucking sun. Or near the fucking ocean. Or on fucking sand.

Hurt. Ziselær's word seeps into my mind, as if he'd prefer not to give it to me. I don't know what's happened to him since he found his mate, but I don't like it. I spent a century beating any semblance of a heart out of the beast. Dragons need to be ruthless to survive in this world. Then that copper dragon showed up and suddenly he's as weak as he was when the Dróttning gave him to me. We've got some work to do when we get back to the Nest. From wherever the fuck we are.

I finally open my eyes—the pounding in my head shifting from a steady beat to a gods-damned melee as I do—and look down at myself, then up at my dragon and the cove around me. Vulryn and her rider sit about a dragon's-length away, their eyes focused on Ziselær and me, a tent and some supplies next to them. Nothing I see tells me why I'm a broken-down bag of bones lying in the sun near the ocean on a patch of sand.

And then it comes back to me in a rush—my dragon's flight with his draikana, those gods-damned traitors appearing out of nowhere to attack, and all of them turning on me. Vulryn was supposed to heed my command, defend Ziselær and me. She should have protected us. Instead, she sided with Fhord and his elf and saved her rider. It shouldn't be possible.

Why did your draikana defy my order to attack?

Devious. I hear way too much pride in that word. He's impressed with Vulryn's trickery. Bitch pretended to eat the food the Dróttning demanded, so we'd think she'd been turned. I don't know how the fuck she did it, but somebody will die for this. The soldiers assigned to guard Vulryn were supposed to watch her eat.

How did she know not to eat the food?

North. Apparently, whatever is in the Dróttning's food grows in the North. She recognized the scent and had seen it being used there.

And now the traitor and his elf know, because Dani sure as fuck told them. I need to alert the Dróttning. Her greatest secret—one she's kept for hundreds of years—is now in the hands of her enemies.

Why did your draikana and her rider stay?

Help, he tells me. They thought I'd die without care, and they were probably right. That drop into the ocean fucked me up badly. Soft-hearted idiots. I'd have left me to die.

We need to leave. Now.

Ziselær's head spins toward me, his eyes narrowed as a flame whispers through his teeth. *Stay*, he tells me. He wants me to believe it's for me—that I'm not strong enough to go—but I can sense another reason hidden in his response. Vulryn isn't coming back with us, and he's not ready to leave his draikana yet.

If your draikana refuses to return to the Nest, we'll go without her and come back with enough dragons to hunt her down. You belong to me, and I belong to the Dróttning. We will kill Vulryn and her rider if they defy her. Don't make me punish you.

Stay, he repeats, focusing on my broken body. Images of me as he pulled me out of the water flitter through my mind, followed by the bruised, bloody near-corpse he brought to shore. It's a gods-damned miracle I survived. Those bastards must have some use for me yet.

But I don't bow to the gods. I bow to the Dróttning alone, and as I watch Vulryn and Dani—defiance and resolve in their eyes—my thoughts tremble with the realization that I am fucked. Utterly, completely, irrevocably fucked. My threats to Ziselær are empty because I'm not leaving the Nest for a long, long time. I will suffer my liege's wrath when we return. I fucked up badly in letting Vulryn deceive us.

We're leaving. You will convince your draikana and her rider to return with us. The Dróttning will punish both of us if they refuse. I don't try to hide the rage in my voice. My dragon should have known better. He should have recognized his draikana's trickery. I'm gonna beat that soft heart out of him when we get back to the Nest.

No. This one's just a word, no additional meaning with it. But I don't need more. I'll punish his disobedience, and he knows it. That hussy of a beast has got him all twisted up if he's willing to defy me so he can spend more time with her.

I want to berate him for it, but Dani chooses that moment to rise and stalk over to us. I am not ready to deal with this shit, but deal with it, I will.

"How long have we been here?" I grimace at the fist that forms around my heart when I spit out those words. Fucking Helheim, that hurts. "And how far did I drop?"

Dani smirks as she sits next to me, my cock jerking—shooting a flame through my battered body—because she's too gods-damned cute for her own good. But she's just a fuck when our dragons fly, I remind myself. Whatever happens here over the next few days isn't going to change shit.

"You slept two days after dropping"—her eyes drift up as she pauses for a moment, smirk deepening—"much too far. I'm shocked you survived." Her gaze swings to me and my gods-damned prick twitches again. Everything on me except my cock feels broken or battered, and it's decided to react to a couple of smirks from this rebellious cunt. Ziselær's needs must be fucking with me.

"I'm going back to the Nest. You'll help me mount my dragon."

"The fuck I will." Ziselær joins in, grunting his concern. "We saved your life because your dragon doesn't want to lose you.

We won't let you die now. Ziselær won't take you until you're ready to travel."

"He's my dragon. He'll obey my commands."

"Maybe, maybe not. It doesn't matter." She shrugs, her eyes still playful. "I won't help you mount, and you won't get up there on your own. When you're strong enough to climb your dragon without my help, Vulryn and I will leave. We won't go back to the Nest with you. Our dragons will fly together only if you come to us." One eyebrow pops up, her smirk dropping away. "If you know where to find us," she adds in a melodramatic voice.

I can't drag my gaze away, unsure what game she's playing. "You should have let me die. I'm as good as dead anyway if I return to the Dróttning without you and your dragon."

Dani snorts out a laugh, looking at our beasts for a moment and then back at me. "Tell the happy couple that," she declares, her arm swinging toward them. "I wanted to kill you. Your dragon disagreed and mine went along. They decided we'd stay long enough to make sure you heal. What happens when you return isn't my concern. I hope she does kill you. Then I'll have done what my dragon asked, and your death won't be at my hands."

My head cocks to the side, an unwanted smile forcing its way out. I truly do not understand this female. "You had a choice," I point out. "You didn't need to do as your dragon asks. You chose to stay."

"Don't flatter yourself. I'm here because Vulryn's my ride out of this cove, and she's a stubborn beast who wants to please yours." She stands, stretching to look around. "You need food if you're going to heal. Wait here," she adds with a wink.

And that's how the next three days go. I'm healing gradually, but I am healing, able to start moving around slowly. Dani feeds me and reminds me that she hates me and is only helping because our dragons are mated. I want to hate her too. I hate everyone. But I find that I can't. There's something charming and quirky about the way she sees the world, how she moves around in it.

On the third evening, as I'm sitting at the water's edge, watching Dani like I always do—our dragons flying somewhere like they always do—I realize what it is about her that fascinates me. I've spent my life conforming to the Dróttning's needs and demands. I thrive because I have done exactly what's expected of me at every step, in every decision. I am who the Dróttning wants me to be, and I'm satisfied with that life.

I don't know what Dani's life was like before Vulryn, but I do know that since meeting her dragon, Dani has done the exact opposite of me. Dani left everything she knew to follow her dragon, and she seems satisfied. More than that—I think she's happy. She destroyed her relationship with the northern Monarch, but I haven't seen a hint of regret over her decision.

"Do you miss your home? Your life before your dragon?" I ask as she brings me a bowl of fish stew, made exactly the way I prefer it.

She cocks an eyebrow at me—probably surprised I'm speaking with her about something besides food and other demands—and turns to look at our dragons. Her gaze follows their dance in the distance as her lips lift in a charmingly care-free smile. "How could I, when I have her?"

"Were you unhappy with your life in the North?"

Dani watches me for a moment, her lips tipped down just a touch, but before she can answer, all Helheim breaks loose. A gods-damned tentacle whips from the ocean to grab me by the ankle. I catch the shock in Dani's eyes just as it wraps around my leg and starts to pull. I'm pain embodied, every battered bone in my body stretched and twisted by the monster drag-ging me toward the water.

Flipping over—which hurts so fucking bad I can barely breathe—I scrabble for anything to grasp onto on this sandy, empty beach. For just a moment, I see Dani's hesitation, her wish she could let me die. But she shakes her head and launches toward me, gripping my hand to try and pull me away from whatever attacked me. I can't help at all. The agony rippling through me, every inch of my feeble body a blazing fire, has left me searching for the air I need to survive.

"Do you want to live?" Dani screams as one hand holds me and the other reaches for the knife on her belt.

I can't answer her. The weight on my chest won't let me do anything but gasp for breath.

"Decide now, Matthias. Do you want to live, or should I let you go?"

We're moving toward the water too fast and there's nothing she can do. Even if she had the strength to hold on to a tree or a rock, there aren't any. It's a ridiculous question because I'm dead already.

But I want to live. My gaze catches hers and I nod.

Fuck yes, I want to live.

She dips her chin in response, giving me one more tug before she releases my hand and launches herself at whatever is twisted around my leg. Her blade starts hacking at it—green pus oozing from the gash she's opening—but before she can free me, another fucking tentacle whips up from the dark waves. It loops around her, yanking her away from me as it pulls both of us toward the water.

Because of-fucking-course it does. This bastard's born to attack. We're no match for it.

Part of my mind senses my dragon's desperation as it races toward us, but I know he won't make it. I catch a glimpse of Dani struggling against the creature that'll be eating us both soon, stabbing at the tentacle twisted around her, and some perverse part of me hopes she finds a way to free herself. That she lives. It's good I'm about to die because the Dróttning would kill me for even thinking something like that, vengeful cunt that she is.

When the monster drags me into the waves, I focus again, sucking in a breath of air just before I'm submerged. I have no fucking idea how I'll survive this, but I can't give up. I'm not ready to die yet.

I twist in the water, reaching down to try to pry the tentacles away, but even that's impossible. My bruised ribs bitch at me, and they're the least of my problems. We're sinking so fast, it's all I can do to keep my gods-damned mouth shut and stop the ocean that is pressing in on every part of me from spilling into my lungs.

My only hope is the dragons—Dani sure as fuck can't do anything else to help me—but they're too far away to reach me in time. For a moment, grief fills me, my soul aching. But it's gone just as quickly, anger taking its place. My thoughts reach for Ziselær. *Where the fuck are you?*

Close, he yells, desperate for me to hold on a little longer.

You failed, I tell him, rage at my dragon pounding through me. *You were supposed to protect me.*

Hold! His response is shrill, more fear than I've ever sensed from my beast. It took many years for him to cling to me, but he did. He's mine in every way. That pretender we discovered in Revalle could never be the rider I've been to him. He was right to choose me, even if he refused to kill the bastard.

I'm barely conscious when I feel Ziselær spear into the water, his draikana close behind him. My mind barely registers my dragon's fight with the beast that's dragging me down, or Vulryn's claws closing around me to pull me away from the monster. As I slip away, I realize I'm free, but too far gone to survive.

A few more seconds and I might have lived ...

The hammering on my chest wakes me. In a haze, my thoughts cloudy and lost in fog, I feel someone's hands beating at my tortured ribs, followed by the softest lips imaginable landing on mine, to push air into me. And then I'm spewing up water and gunk and mucus and anything else my lungs have sucked in. The pain I felt before is a whisper of the torture rippling through me now. I am one gigantic nerve, triggered and shooting flares of agony through every muscle, every bone, every bit of skin.

What the fuck was I thinking? I don't want to live if this is the cost. Especially if I'm just going to return to the Nest and have the Dróttning torture and kill me for losing her prize captives. *Let me fucking die already*, I demand of my dragon.

Live, is his response, the bastard. They fought that beast and pulled me away from him and saved me, whether I wanted it or not. He *needs* me to live. I never did manage to beat that heart out of him.

But he's right. I'm not ready to die. Now that my mind's worked through the agony of my near-drowning, as I'm gasping my way toward survival, I know I want nothing more. And I'm not sure what that means for me. Because the Dróttning's going to kill me and torture my dragon when I go back to the Nest.

Taking in one more deep breath, I open my eyes to see Dani leaning toward me, her face a few inches from mine, eyes as bright as the sky behind her. Her braid, the color of the bark on the maple tree that guarded my home as a child, rests next to my cheek and I have to stop myself from reaching up to take the end and twirl it around my finger. My heart beats a dozen times before I can move.

"I told you to let me die," I say at last as she sits back on her heels, her gaze never leaving mine.

"And then you said you wanted to live. I trust your second answer the most. When death calls for us, we choose life if we've any left to live. You must have something to live for."

I can't drag my eyes away from her. "You risked yourself to do it."

Her responding smirk lights a flame somewhere deep inside me. "My dragon would have kicked my ass if I'd done anything else. That sea beast isn't nearly as vicious as an angry Vulryn."

"Thank you." I lift my hand to rest it on her cheek, the feel of her skin next to mine reward enough for the pain that whispers through me when I move.

"Don't get all sentimental on me," she laughs. "I'd just started to like the old, grumpy Matthias."

"Had you now?"

"Only a bit," she assures me, sitting back farther to put some distance between us. "But don't let it go to your head. I still hate you, even if a small part of me has learned to tolerate a small part of you." Her gaze lifts, and she stares at the ocean for a few seconds. "What the fuck was that?"

"A kraken, I suspect. It never used to appear in our waters, but over the last decade, maybe more, it's been showing up more frequently. They don't often attack on land, but they've been known to when they can't sate their hunger with sea creatures."

"Fuck me. I've never even heard of them. What other creatures haunt Vanatia, flinging themselves from the sea to suck you down with them?"

"Jörmungandr is rumored to still live, although he may be a creature of myth. The Kraken, though, is very real."

"What's a Jörmungandr?"

"A serpent, born of the chaos god and a giant. His siblings are wolves. I suspect they all were created by imaginative storytellers to frighten difficult children."

Dani cocks her head at me, her eyes narrowing. "A near-death experience—well, two near-death experiences—suits you," she says at last. "You're much more agreeable than you've ever been."

I'm silent for a long time, my thoughts flickering through the events of the last few days. She's right. I feel different. I'm not sure if it's because I nearly died, twice, or because she's saved me both times. Whatever it is, I am calmer, less restless, than I've been in years. I like it.

"Maybe it's a change for the best," I tell her, turning to look at the water that sucked in one male and spit out another.

CHAPTER EIGHTEEN

DANI

NICE

M ATTHIAS HAS BEEN ... nice. I don't trust this change in him one little bit.

It's been four days since I saved him—for the second time. Fhord and Sifa have checked on us once and will again in a few days, but I don't expect them to come retrieve Vulryn and me for another week or more. We're going to stay here until they come, and then follow them to do whatever the rebellion needs from us.

In the meantime, the tall, frustratingly sexy dragon rider has kept me confused and adrift. He's been charming—who the fuck might have guessed he had it in him?—and grateful for all I've done while we've been here.

Even his cock has shown its appreciation for me on more than one occasion. Which is a sight for my sore, sex-starved eyes. Because Matthias has quite the cock. It takes some effort to drag my gaze away from it whenever it decides to announce itself in the midst of one conversation or another. He knows it too, a sultry smirk lifting his lips whenever he finds me caught in a trance by his considerable cock.

It doesn't help that Vulryn needs Ziselær like she needs air to breathe. Her urge to fully mate with her drake has magnified my growing desire for his rider. Fhord and Sifa left a single tent—the fuckers—so I've slept a few feet from Matthias since we were able to get him inside. The first night, I offered to give him the space and sleep on the sand, but he grabbed my fingers before I could leave, tugging me down next to him.

"I promise I won't bite," he murmured with a smile as he released my hand and rolled over and away from me.

It's not his bite I'm worried about. At least, not yet. His scent—a rich maple, as if he was born of the forest—and the *feel* of having him close are driving me mad. I find myself imagining him plunging inside me, and I've had to stop more than once from giving myself some relief.

Our dragons fly at night, and while Vulryn's kept her promise and stopped Ziselær from fully claiming her, they've gotten much too close for comfort. Ziselær was initially apoplectic, then penitent and contrite, over his decision to heed Matthias's command and attack me. He begged Vulryn's forgiveness, and she's convinced he'll never do something like that again, even if Matthias demands it. She thinks he's more hers than he's ever been.

Now, every time our beasts get frisky, Matthias and I follow, me in my mind, him in his blankets. His breathing changes when our dragons' flight starts to affect me, slowing down at first but eventually quickening, punctuated by an occasional grunt he's trying to hide. He makes it even harder to ignore my needs—and I really need to get laid—*because* I know what he's doing. His hand's been getting more action than I've gotten in ages.

Tonight will really test me. Matthias needs a bath. His stench has taken on a life of its own and is about to start joining us for meals. And the bastard convinced me he needs help. I know he's right. He'll be able to drag himself to the water, but he's not yet steady enough to hold himself up. And if I don't support him, he won't be able to twist quite as far as he'll need to get all the parts that stink. So my arm is wrapped around him and we're hobbling to the pool a dragon's-length away. Where he'll clean the cock that's captured my attention too many times.

I'm trying not to think about it.

"I'm gonna owe you even more than I already do," he promises, his voice low, as I drop his fresh clothes in the sand and help him the rest of the way to the water.

"So, so much," I agree. "That whiskey you teased me with at the Nest will be mine, and a few more like it."

"That's it?" he asks with a chuckle. "A bit of whiskey?"

"A lot of whiskey. For a start."

"What else?"

I turn to him, his question taking me by surprise. He sounds serious, as if he'd like to give me what I request. So I decide to make this one good. "Freedom. We won't be going back to the Nest with you. You need to let us go. We'll find you and Ziselær when they need to fly together."

He doesn't shut down the way I'd expected him to. His gaze stays on mine, eyes solemn. "I don't think I can give you that," he says as he lifts a finger to tuck a strand of hair behind my ear. "Although I'd like to."

"That's where you're wrong." I make sure he's steady, stepping back while I hold him with one arm and help him remove his shirt with the other, dragging the sticky, sweaty fabric over his head to toss it a male's-height away. "You don't need to choose the Dróttning over us. Lie to her. Do whatever you must to protect us when our dragons fly together."

He looks down, one side of his lips tipping up as my hands reach toward his hips. He lifts his head to give me a full smile, cocking an eyebrow in question.

"Yes, asshole, I'm going to strip you. I'm just working my way down to it."

He winks as he tucks his thumb in his waistband and pushes his pants over his ass, revealing a cock standing at full attention. I suck in a breath, "Fuck me," tumbling out of my mouth as I fight to drag my eyes away from his pride and joy.

"Better be careful, dragon rider," he rumbles as he wraps a hand around his cock and squeezes, drawing a touch of pre-cum from the tip. "You keep looking at me like that, and I *will* fuck you. Fierce and fast. This is just from the thought of being stripped and bathed by you." Reaching up to rest a knuckle under my chin and lift my gaze to his, he adds in the sexy voice he's using with me more and more each day, "Just imagine how hard I'll be when you're lying beneath me, begging for my cock."

And just like that, I'm soaking wet, my pussy pulsing as she reminds me it's been too long since she's had company. I take one more deep inhale, all my focus on keeping my hands still and away from the cock they're desperate to touch. And stroke. And then position in just the right place...

Matthias's low chuckle drags my thoughts back where they need to be. Breathing out, I bend down—fighting the urge to taste the little bead at the end of his cock as his hand drops to the back of my head—and lift one of his feet, and then the other, to drag his pants away. He nudges me forward just a bit, his invitation clear, but I shake my head.

"That wasn't an offer," I mutter as I stand and wrap my arm around him again to lead him into the pond.

"It sure as fuck looked like it. I think you want to taste me nearly as much as I want to taste you. Fuck if I didn't almost come from seeing you on your knees in front of me. Gods-damned beautiful sight."

"Not one you'll be seeing again." I think. I hope. Maybe. "Especially if you plan on turning us over to the Dróttning. Vulryn and Ziselær will need to fly together, but I'll stay away when they do." I grin, looking up at him, because my pussy is still throbbing and I can't drag my thoughts away from his proud peter. "Although it'll be a shame if I never get to feel you come inside me."

His grin matches mine as we shuffle into the warm water, some of my tension floating away as soon as the pool wraps around us. Matthias pauses when he's submerged to his chest and I hand him the soap, watching as he rubs it over his rippling muscles and tight abs, then down the "V" leading to the cock that holds so much of my attention.

"And what if I promise to keep your secret, for now, at least?" he asks as he strokes himself, our gazes both transfixed by his hand sliding up and down. "Will you let yourself feel the rush that comes from fucking while our dragons fly?"

Stepping into him, standing just far enough away to touch only where my hands rest on his waist, I gaze up, letting him see the truth in my words. "I want to fuck you, Matthias. But not if you're going to turn on me when we're done."

He nods, leaning down to brush his lips against mine, sending a burst of need directly to my core. "I promise I won't stop you and Vulryn from flying away when we leave here. I owe you that, at least."

"It's not enough," I whisper as I lift my hand to rest on his cheek, "but it's a start."

He nips at my bottom lip, his mouth lifting into a teasing smirk. "I can't wait to fuck you, Dani," he drawls as he looks down to watch himself relieve the pressure on his cock. Within a minute, lines of cum spurt out and drop toward the pond's floor. We step back in unison with a laugh before finishing his bath in silence.

The rest of the day passes quickly, both of us trying our damnedest to ignore the tension we built in the water. I can't stop thinking about him as I lay in my blankets that night, wondering how in all of Helheim I'm going to sleep. Just like the last two nights, Matthias is chasing an orgasm, and I want nothing more than to join him. Instead, I'm lying here trying to stanch the burning that started in my belly and expanded quickly, setting every part of me on fire.

And I realize it's not worth fighting any longer. It's just sex and I know by now that it'll happen, as everyone's said. When our dragons fully mate, I won't be able to resist the draw. I can barely resist it now. It's been too fucking long since I felt a man inside me. And Matthias is too sexy to ignore.

"I get it," I whisper, trying to keep the croak from my tone as his breaths slow. Turning over to face him, I smile at the back of his head, wondering whether I really want to do what I'm considering. "I feel their need. It makes me want you in a way I haven't wanted anyone for a long time."

When he turns toward me, it's slow and he doesn't try to hide the cock that pops his blanket up like the tent around us. His smile is wicked, and I'm reminded of the Matthias I knew in the Nest. But this Matthias isn't mean. He's playful and flirtatious and more restrained than that Matthias would have been.

"We're gonna fuck eventually, Dani. If you want to start tonight, I think it'll be good for both of us."

"And what happens tomorrow?"

"Tomorrow is the same as today. Our dragons are mates. We're tied together unless that changes. We fuck when we need to fuck. Nothing more, nothing less."

"And when I start fucking other men? Will you care?"

"I don't want a mate, my randy Dani," he croons with a wink. "Just fuck me. We'll worry about tomorrow, tomorrow." When I don't move, he lets his gaze wander down my body, pausing at my breasts and again at my core. "I've been wanting to taste you for days," he adds as he lifts his eyes to hold mine. "Come here. Let me taste you."

"You're still healing. What if I hurt you?"

"Tonight, you're in charge. I'll just lie here, and you can take what you need. As long as I can taste you first."

How the fuck do I say no to that? I toss off my blanket, lifting my nightshirt up and over my head and pulling off my underwear. And then I look at him with a smile, wondering what in all of Helheim I'm doing, before I cross this divide between us.

His grin is predatory, blue eyes bright. He throws off his own covers, revealing the cock I'll have thrusting inside me soon, and my center vibrates at the thought. *Fly with your dragon*, I tell Vulryn as I move toward him. *I'm taking Matthias tonight. Thank you for waiting.*

Her grumble of approval echoes inside me. These extra few days bound Vulryn and Ziselær together even more tightly. She's ready to fully mate with him, and I'm ecstatic she's going to chase her pleasure as I chase mine.

I don't waste any time, settling my legs on either side of his head and dropping down as his hands rest on my hips to position me just where he wants. His tongue reaches out first, firm and strong as it plunges inside and then takes up residence in my midst, sucking and licking and teasing me until I'm vibrating from all the sensations Matthias is unleashing.

I hear his laugh, a low purr that only adds to the fires he's setting, as he pauses a moment, lifting his eyes to find mine.

"You are so gods-damned delicious, dandy. I'm gonna fuck you with my fingers first so I can feast here before my cock gets wet."

"Yes, please," is all I can say in response. Because that sounds fucking amazing.

He laughs again, sending another little tremor through all my favorite parts, as he thrusts two fingers inside me, watching my reactions as he stretches them out and searches for the spot that will make me vibrate. When he finds it—my whole gods-damned body quivering to his touch—he smiles like the cat that caught the mouse, his fingers playing in just the right place while his mouth focuses on my clit.

My first orgasm hits me out of nowhere, my body so desperate for release that it washes through me in waves that seem like they'll go on forever. "That was quick," Matthias rasps from his spot between my legs, barely pausing as he continues to pull sensations from my body that I'd nearly forgotten I could experience. "We'll go a little more slowly for the next one."

Is this the same male who said he couldn't care less if I enjoyed this? I'd have jumped him days ago if I'd known what I had to look forward to.

The second orgasm comes more gradually, as he promised, building from the fingers and tongue that are still focused on my core. He's more leisurely now, his free hand finding my tits to play with one and then the other, tweaking my nipples in just the right way. He said he would draw this one out and he does. It starts as little fires where he's touching and licking and sucking, growing ember by ember, flame by flame, into a climax that rustles through me, leaving sparks to flicker away as he slowly pulls his fingers out and licks them, one by one.

"I think you're ready," he rumbles as he lets go of my hips, his hands resting on my waist to gently nudge me back. "Fuck me now, Dandy."

I grin like the randy female he's decided will be my nickname, working my way back along his perfect abs and then dropping down in one thrust to plunge his *enormous* cock inside me.

"Fuck. Me," I whisper, unable to drag my gaze away from the glorious male lying beneath me.

"With pleasure." His hips roll and he's off to the races, thrusting in and out in a rhythm that syncs perfectly with mine. In a corner of my mind, I feel Vulryn chasing her own pleasure, just adding to all the sensations Matthias is drawing from me, but I push that away. This is her time with Ziselær.

And my time with Matthias.

His hips pivot and roll and sway as he fucks me, watching my face the whole time with lidded eyes. "Play with your clit, Dandy. I'm nearly there and I want to watch you as you come on my cock."

I groan as my fingers find my favorite spot and swirl around my clit. He's so gods-damned gorgeous. His teeth nibble his bottom lip as his dick discovers the place inside me that makes me see stars, and he shifts his hips just enough to brush it with every thrust.

"Come now," he growls when I feel him tremble and start to release.

And I do, this orgasm rolling through me like a storm.

When we're both done and exhausted, I collapse next to Matthias and he lifts a finger to stroke my cheek, his eyes still heavy. Leaning forward, he kisses the other cheek then leans closer to my ear, his breaths still heavy. "Thank you for giving me a taste, my randy Dani," he purrs before rolling away, giving me his back as I move to my own bed. "Let me know when you want to go again," he adds without looking at me.

He never kissed my lips, but I don't want that. Lovers kiss and we aren't lovers. This is sex with some bonus foreplay that I enjoyed more than I expected. Still, it feels off. Insufficient. My mind drags up Mikkael's image, reminding me he's my mate, but I push him away. Matthias rides Ziselær. That's not going to change. I'm bound to Matthias and lucky he's a good fuck.

My thoughts reach for Vulryn, wondering if she's back, and I feel her soaring to the cove. She's fulfilled, complete, for the first time since I met her. I hadn't seen it before. I don't think either of us realized something was missing. But it was. She's different, happier, now.

Smiling, I spin away from Matthias, focusing on his smell as I try to forget about the obnoxious male—my gods-damned mate—that keeps worming his way into my thoughts. But much as I try to push him away, Mikkael's face is the one I see in my mind's eye as I drift off to sleep.

I feel Matthias's gaze on me when I wake up. My back's still to him—I don't think I moved at all overnight—but there's a heaviness in the tent, a steadiness to his breathing, that tells me he's awake and watching me. Casting out my thoughts, I find Vulryn swimming with Ziselær as they hunt for their breakfast, savoring her joy for a few moments. When I spin, one corner of Matthias's lips lift, his eye crinkling with his half-smile.

"I'm not sure how I've slept through your snoring these past few nights," he murmurs. "You could wake the dead."

"Happy to give you the tent," I remind him, "if it's that bad."

"And miss out on my randy Dani? I'd give up a lot of sleep to be able to taste you … and fuck you … again."

"It was … tolerable." I can't hold back the smile that emerges as I remember the three ground-shattering orgasms he gave me last night. "I might be convinced to go again. If I find myself particularly needy."

"Good to know. I'll make sure and take advantage again when you're at your neediest."

"Always the best time." My smile drops and I watch him for a moment, an unsettled feeling blossoming inside me as I compare this Matthias to the one I thought I knew. "Who are you, Matthias? The evil, cunning bastard who faithfully serves the Dróttning, or the charming dragon rider lying in this tent with me right now?"

He shrugs, his expression blanking as his body stiffens. His gaze holds mine for a few seconds, and I wonder if he's considering my question, or deciding how he should answer it to best persuade me he's changed. When his narrowed eyes soften, one side of his lips curving up, he lifts an arm to rest it under his head, settling in for whatever he's going to say.

"I always have been what I need to be to survive," he answers at last. "The Dróttning requires cruelty, and I became a cruel man, demanding brutality from all who serve me. It's worked well and I've thought little about those I hurt along the way. It's a harsh world. If not me, someone else would have harmed them at the Dróttning's command. She rewarded me well for it. Ziselær is the envy of most dragon riders, and I'm revered in the Nest."

"But..." I prompt when he's silent for too long.

"Perhaps two near-death experiences in two days—and being saved both times by someone the Dróttning plans to kill—has opened my eyes."

"So she does plan to kill me?" I'm not surprised, but I never expected him to admit it so freely.

"You're an elf. No elves are free in Vanatia. Even if she wanted to let you roam her land—but I assure you, she doesn't—she couldn't violate her own law in that way. She's our leader, but her place in Vanatia is secured through an iron fist, without the threat of those who might coalesce to challenge her."

"Would her people turn on her?"

"The ruling council has many members eager to take power. If they were able to turn others against her, they might be strong enough to take over. And she's terrified of what would happen if the elves found a way to break free. She managed to take control because she found a way to manipulate the dragons, turn them against their riders. She's kept the elves bound and powerless since then. If they had access to their magic—or if the dragons broke the Dróttning's chains on them—they could combine to destroy her. She must maintain her grip on the dragons, and she can't have even a single elf walking free, threatening her hold on power."

"But whether the Dróttning *could* make an exception for me doesn't matter anyway because Vulryn and I helped free Fhord and Tindera." This isn't a question. I know the answer.

"She'll destroy you for that," he confirms. "You're alive and here with me now because she needs your knowledge. Once she gets it, you'll be dead."

"Why hasn't she sent dragons to bring us back? We've been gone a long time. She must be searching for us."

"She told me to do what I must to break you," he tells me with a rueful smile. "She knew we might be gone for a while."

"Is that what you're doing now? Breaking me? Through worlds-shattering sex?"

"It's the best way I know of to break someone," he answers with a smirk.

"Why are you telling me this? You must be betraying her faith by revealing it to me."

"I know you won't be coming back to the Nest with me, and I no longer want to take you. I'm not even sure if I'm going back. I've caught glimpses of a life outside of the Dróttning's iron fist. I think I want to explore it. And if I go back, I'm dead anyway. As I recently discovered, I'm not ready to die yet."

"What would you do? You don't plan to join the rebellion, do you?"

"I'm not foolish enough to believe they'd trust me. And my feelings for Fhord haven't changed, although I can perhaps understand better why he betrayed her." He shrugs, his lips quirking up. "I'll hide. It's hard to do with an enormous fucking dragon, but we'll figure it out."

"And, what, Vulryn and I should track you down occasionally so they can fly together?"

"Our dragons' needs will bring them together. They'll find each other when they must. It's more than they'll get if I return to the Nest." He pauses for a moment, his gaze never leaving mine. "I don't want Vulryn to be Ziselær's enemy. I don't want you to be mine."

"I'm not sure I believe you. You just told me you are whatever you need to be to survive, and the Dróttning told you to break me in any way you can. What if that's what you're doing now?"

"I'm not foolish enough to believe you'd trust me, either. If I decide to betray the Dróttning, you'll trust me in time. And I promise to never tie you up when you come for the occasional fuck while our dragons fly. Although I wouldn't mind if you tied me up once in a while."

The grin that splits his cheeks goes straight to my core, which erupts at the alluring dragon rider a few feet away. He tosses his blanket off, revealing a cock ready to be ridden, and

I don't waste any time accepting his offer. Because Matthias may be a cruel bastard—I haven't figured out what or who he is—but he knows how to make me come and I need the release I'm getting from him right now.

The next few days are the same. Matthias heals, and we get to know each other, physically and personally. And I like him. I didn't think I would, but I find my walls breaking down, bit by bit, every time we talk. Every time he's unexpectedly gentle with me. Every time I see his cocky smile. And yes, every time we fuck. We do that a lot.

Vulryn, chatty matchmaker that she is, argues his case more than I'd like. She's absolutely besotted with Ziselær and never wants to leave him. She's also resolved to return to our found family, to fight with them against the Dróttning. She wants her drake to come with her, which means the dragons are determined to convince Matthias and me that he can be trusted to join us.

When Fhord and Sifa show up, twelve days after leaving us in this cove for Matthias to heal, I'm ready to believe him. Which terrifies me. Because I know, deep down inside, that he's a devious bastard. I can't let him betray our friends. And I have no idea what in the fuck I'm going to do.

CHAPTER NINETEEN

SIFA

ODD AND UNEXPECTED

I HAVE NO IDEA what happened to Iyanshe, whether or not I destroyed her mind.

We left with the black dragon collapsed on the ground. I couldn't sense any thought or emotion from her. That doesn't mean she's gone—she could be so deeply asleep that her brain's at rest too—but I wish I knew for certain. And we haven't been able to find her since. Fhord's allies in the Nest are trying to get us information, but the Dróttning trusts nobody. Secrets are safer now in Vanatia than ever before.

Everything about the Dróttning is so fucking frustrating.

We're heading to Dani instead of searching for Iyanshe, then we'll go meet Khirta, Toffer, and Thor to try to go north without disturbing the barrier. Toffer wonders if he can find a cave system deep enough to completely bypass it. It's worth a try because we must go to Njordheim to search for the plant Vulryn described, but Harald is probably out for our blood.

It's been twelve days, and while we've twice flown close enough to let our dragons connect with Vulryn—make sure Matthias hasn't tried to kill them—we haven't faced Ziselær and his rider yet. The reports they're getting from Vulryn are odd and unexpected. It's time to figure out what's happening in that cove.

When we get close enough to see them, Dani and Matthias are sitting together on the shore, their fingers linked, watching us soar in. Matthias looks relaxed and whole, not a hint of animosity seeping out of him. He gives us a smile that seems out of place on his harsh face as he stands and reaches for Dani's other hand, pulling her up beside him and releasing her with a laugh at something she says.

Odd and unexpected, as the dragons said.

They stride toward us when our dragons settle in the cove, extending a wing for us to climb down. At one point, Matthias reaches out, a pinkie wrapping around Dani's for a moment as he turns to smile at her and she responds with a grin.

Expected, Astarot tells me, having changed his mind now that we've seen all of them together. We left them alone for twelve days, their dragons getting closer the entire time. Vulryn and Ziselær have flown together. Even the strongest riders can't resist that pull. Of course they came together too.

But Matthias is an ass. This male does not behave like the cruel bastard Matthias has always been.

Ziselær. Mating Vulryn has changed his dragon. Drastically. In a matter of weeks, Vulryn's drawn out the part of Ziselær that Matthias thought he destroyed. And it's affected Matthias in ways none of us anticipated.

"I wasn't sure what we'd find," Fhord says when we're close enough to speak to them, his voice tight. "Never thought I'd see this."

Matthias's gaze is guarded. Neither of them trusts the other. But it's not aggressive, for now at least. "Our dragons flew. It brought us together."

"That and another near-death experience," Dani adds with a glance at Matthias.

"Another?" Fhord's eyebrow pops up as his gaze bounces between them.

"A kraken decided to try its luck." Matthias turns toward Dani with a look that could only be described as admiration, his head tilting closer to her as a smile lights up his face, little wrinkles forming around his eyes. "Dani threw herself at it, buying me enough time for our dragons to get back. It was shortly after you left so I was still pretty fucked up, but she took care of me." Now he looks at Fhord and me, his eyes a little more serious. "I'm a new man," he adds in a low voice.

Fhord's quiet for a long time, just watching the male who was desperate to destroy all of us less than two weeks ago. "Let Sifa see," he says at last. "Give her access to your thoughts so she can confirm the change you claim."

Now it's Matthias's turn to stare in silence at his nemesis. When he speaks, his tone is reasonable. It feels fake. "I'm not ready to do that yet. I don't know if I'm going to betray the Dróttning. If I return to her, I can't have given away any of the secrets your elf would find there." He looks at me, his lips set in a thin line. "If I decide to leave the Dróttning, I'll let you see enough to believe me."

"As I expected. If you're still straddling that fence, you're no ally." Fhord's voice is cold.

Matthias scoffs, his laugh harsh. "You straddled that fence for a decade, Fhord."

"I waited for the right time to start this war. The time is now. Choose a side."

"Give him a minute, Fhord." Dani's words cut off whatever Matthias was about to say. "We both know how hard this decision is. Let him decide when the time's right for him."

"We're leaving with Dani and Vulryn," Fhord growls. "You're either returning to the Nest or you're not. You're not gonna hide in a fucking cove." He pauses, looking at me and then back at Matthias. "One thing I do know is you're not coming with us. I don't trust you, and I doubt I ever will, especially if you refuse to let Sifa see for herself."

"Let's compromise," Dani suggests. "Leave the rebels for a while. Let's go chase the Dróttning's slop together. Give Matthias a chance while we're doing something that won't reveal any rebellion secrets."

"And give him a chance to fuck us on this critical thing?" Fhord snarls. "No gods-damned way."

"I have some."

Everyone turns to stare at Matthias as his soft words break through our escalating emotions.

"You have some?" Dani seems bothered by his admission, as if she's surprised that he'd keep it from her.

He dips his chin. "I told you she doesn't expect us back right away. Dragons never skip feedings. Ziselær and I brought some in the event our dragons need it."

"My dragon needs it." Now I'm taking a step toward him, the possibility of relieving Astarot's suffering driving me on. "But how can we trust that it is what you claim?"

Astarot and Matthias snort at the same time. "The dragons know," Matthias says as Astarot spins his head toward me, his agreement dropping into my thoughts. "I'll give Astarot what we need when we go someplace else. I don't care where the fuck it is—and I don't want to meet anyone from the rebellion—but it's time to leave this cove, and my dragon wants to stay with Vulryn."

"You could have left already," I point out. "Why stay?"

"I've been able to travel for a day or two at most, but where would I go? Ziselær isn't ready to leave his draikana, so I'm not going back to the Nest yet. Dani's going with you, and you know where to go. I don't. I haven't spent a decade scouring this land for dragon havens like you have."

"No." Fhord's strident in his refusal, turning toward Matthias with eyes as dark as the forest. "We go from here to meet someone who will help us search." Now he turns to Ziselær. "He rides Khirta," he says in a flat voice, his disdain for Matthias and his dragon written in the harsh lines around his lips and eyes.

The blue dragon shrinks into himself, a response I've never seen from such a beast. His eyes shutter as his head falls, shoulders drooping. Vulryn responds to the emotion billowing out of her drake immediately, taking a step closer to nuzzle her snout into his neck.

Matthias watches us for a few moments, his face blank as he speaks with Ziselær. Twice, he turns toward his dragon and shakes his head before returning his gaze to us. When he focuses on us again, I see an expression I wouldn't have imagined from a rider reputed to be cruel and callous—regret.

"Ziselær has wanted to apologize to Khirta since that unfortunate night..."

"Unfortunate?" Fhord spits out. "That's what you call it?"

"Let me speak." Matthias's voice is cold, but I hear a hint of a plea in it.

"He attacked her brutally. Tindera nursed her wounds, and I still don't think she's recovered. It was not an 'unfortunate' night. Fuck you for dismissing her pain and your dragon's role in it like that."

Matthias is silent for a few seconds before sharply dipping his chin, a concession he probably rarely gives. "Ziselær would speak with Khirta if she'd allow it. He will offer his wings to her if she needs them to be whole."

What does that mean? I've never heard that term before.

Punishment. Astarot's response is measured, as if with those few words, Ziselær has earned back some of the respect he'd lost. The blue beast would give Khirta free access to his wings, allow her to attack him in any way she saw fit.

Is that an unusual offer?

Rare, he tells me. Dragons protect their wings at all costs, given how sensitive they are in certain spots. This penance is offered within the Thunder only to right a grievous wrong.

"I'll believe it when I see it." Fhord's back is stiff now, his jaw clenched as he glares at Ziselær.

"Take us," Matthias responds with a shrug. "This is a sacrifice he's wanted to make since that night. Give him the chance to atone."

Vulryn yowls at Astarot and Tindera, who spin their heads toward her in response, puffing out fire. Tindera's eyes narrow on the copper dragon as her tail twitches like a bug dancing around a flame.

"Vulryn has called in her chit," Dani explains. "Tindera and Astarot owe her. Tindera wouldn't be free if it weren't for her. Ziselær needs this. Vulryn demands we be taken to Khirta." Now she turns toward Fhord, her expression shifting into that of the soldier I met in Njordheim—resolved and stubborn as fuck. "And you owe me, Fhord. A life, right? Matthias's is the life I choose."

"Fucking Helheim," Fhord declares, throwing his hands up as he spins and stalks toward the shore. He drags his fingers through his hair before rubbing both palms on his thighs, then resting them on his hips. He's as still as the trees behind us, no breeze to lift their limbs.

Walking over, I wrap my arms around him and rest my cheek on his back. "Maybe this would be good for Khirta," I offer. "Damaging his wings could help her fully heal from his attack."

"Or seeing him—knowing that Dani and her dragon have fully mated with those bastards—will just traumatize her more. She's suffered enough already." He pauses, lifting one of his hands to cover mine as I feel his shoulders relax, just a bit. "What if it's a trap," he asks at last, "just to lead the Dróttning to Khirta and expose one of our caves? One thought directed to that bitch, and we'll be running for our lives again."

His question spears into my gut, dragging memories with it, but I push them away. I won't give the wyrm any more control over me. "We've run before, and we'll run again. We can't let fear of exposure to the Dróttning stop us. And what if it's not a trap? If Matthias could be turned, we'd have an enormous advantage in this fight. Much as you know about the Dróttning and her forces, there are gaps he can fill."

Fhord's silent for a long time, watching the waves. Finally, he tugs me to his side, turning as he lifts my chin and catches my gaze. "I can't ask Khirta to pay our debts to Dani and Vulryn." His voice is so soft. I rarely hear hesitation or uncertainty in his words, but if anyone can bring it out, it's the little green dragon. He's aggressively protective of her.

"Let's ask her," I suggest. "We can get close enough for the dragons to reach out, let Khirta decide whether she'll see him or not."

His hesitation lasts only a few seconds this time. He glances toward Matthias and his dragon and then back at me. "You're right. She should decide."

We break down their camp quickly, eager to travel inland and get this over with. While we pack, Ziselær is quiet, solemn, and Vulryn never leaves his side. Our dragons are tense. It feels like the unknown copper dragon we turned in Njordheim has returned. They don't know what to expect from her—whether twelve days with Ziselær has softened her commitment to the family she'd claimed—and they've both erected shields around their thoughts, communicating with their mate alone.

Before we go, though, the dragons hunt together, searching as a team for the large spearfish Vulryn seems to always crave, especially during the fish's mating season. I watch them soar above the waves, finding several nearby and cooperating to trap them. And I'm struck by how easily they all set aside the emotions surrounding Khirta and support Vulryn. They have a bond that transcends borders, binding them to each other.

"It must have been miserable for Vulryn to live alone all those years."

I realize I've voiced my thoughts out loud when Dani turns to me, a faraway look in her eyes.

"It's why she's clung so fiercely to you and Fhord and your dragons. She craved family more than food." She turns to look at her dragon and then back at me. "She'll never let you go. You're hers as much as I am."

"And she's ours. We'll get through this thing with Khirta ... and then figure out how we deal with the Ziselær thing."

"At least it's never boring."

"And that's a good thing?" I ask with a laugh.

"It is," she assures me. "We're no longer playing the games orchestrated by crazy, power-hungry monarchs. Us, our dragons, we get to choose what we will and won't do. Who's worthy of our support and who's not. I'd much rather live that life than play Harald's predictable, petty games."

"You're right," I agree after a few seconds of watching her. "It is a good thing."

The dragons return ten minutes later, grinning over their large meal. And we go to Khirta.

We're more than a viku away from the cave Khirta, Toffer, and Thor are waiting in when the dragons pause in the air, hovering as Astarot and Tindera reach out. They let Vulryn hear them but not Ziselær. Khirta gets to decide whether the blue beast sees or hears her ever again.

Astarot's mood shifts as they talk. He begins the conversation cautious but open, gradually growing more tense with flashes of anger bouncing through him. Twice, he barks at Vulryn—Tindera joining him—as the copper beast and her mate hiss in response.

But then something changes. Fhord senses it too, his eyes lifting to find mine when Astarot's emotions flare into shock and acceptance. He holds his position in the air, glaring at Ziselær, who responds with a bleat that almost sounds like an apology.

Stubborn, Astarot tells me. Vulryn argued Ziselær's cause aggressively, even when Khirta made clear she didn't want to see him. Eventually, Khirta gave in, prompting an apology to

Astarot and Tindera from the blue dragon for imposing on Khirta's will the way he did.

Which is fucking confusing. This sounds like a completely different dragon than the one who attacked her so mercilessly.

But Khirta agreed, so we're doing this. The dragons turn as one, covering the remaining distance quickly. The area looks deserted, as it should. All of the refuges Fhord found in his years exploring this land—and the many Fróðr pointed us to in places even Fhord never identified—are well-hidden. Thank the gods we live in a land full of caves and caverns. We'd never survive without them.

We land and enter the cave quickly, our eyes adjusting to the dim light as we look around. Toffer stands in front of Khirta as if he's protecting her, Thor his permanent adornment.

"Caution with our comrade is compulsory," he warns, his voice low.

"We know. Thank you for protecting Khirta." Dani can't keep the hint of a plea from her voice. This matters to her more than she'd ever admit.

"Thank you for seeing us, Khirta," Matthias says as he and his dragon approach slowly. "Ziselær has offered you his wings, and we won't take that back. But we'd like you to know why he did what he did. And how much he regrets it."

Khirta's snort of disdain echoes around us, ricocheting off the walls to remind everyone how ridiculous Matthias's statement is. Ziselær hurt her intentionally. No apology will fix that.

"Our little love listens," Toffer says when Matthias is silent for a few seconds.

"Your rider was a dick," Matthias says, and I have to hold back the laugh his words prompt. Because Matthias was—and probably still is—the biggest asshole around. "He complained to many people about having been paired with such a small dragon," Matthias continues in a measured tone as he takes a single step forward. "It angered the Dróttning. She decided to show him what it was to have a weak and broken beast. She knew your rider admired me—he'd been trying to win my favor for a long time—so we were tasked with destroying you."

Ziselær takes another slow step forward, closing some of the distance between him and Khirta. She watches motionless, letting him approach as her eyes flicker occasionally to Astarot and Tindera. Khirta fears Ziselær, but she also knows she's safe here. Our dragons would never let the blue beast harm her again.

"Her command was straight-forward. Hurt the green dragon but don't let it be known the Dróttning was involved. She does that a lot—harming people or beasts without admitting it. The Council doesn't like her personal reprisals, so she hides them."

"It's true," Fhord interjects. "I've been asked to fuck with someone who angered her, just to satisfy a twisted need for vengeance about some bullshit or another."

"Your rider was a bastard, and I'm glad you killed him. He deserved that and worse. I knew he'd give me what I asked, and he did. We told the Dróttning what we planned, and she connected with Ziselær to experience it with him."

"Also could be true." The anger in Fhord's voice has disappeared. I think he believes Matthias. "She always joined us through Tindera when she ordered me to punish someone."

Matthias pauses, his gaze swinging around the room before landing again on Khirta. "We planned to beat you but not nearly as badly as Ziselær did. He didn't intend to mount you. The Dróttning insisted. But even that wasn't enough, although we all knew how much it would hurt you. We had to do more. The Dróttning demanded everything that happened. Every single gods-damned thing. I've never defied the Dróttning. I couldn't do it then. So Ziselær did what he had to do."

Ziselær takes one more step forward, getting far enough away from the others to drop to the ground and fully extend his wings, which he does. He rests his snout on the ground, his eyes never leaving Khirta.

"None of this makes it right, and we don't ask your forgiveness. Ziselær hurt you, and he wants you to take your vengeance. We'll leave after that if you need us to. We'll figure our shit out and never cross your path again."

Vulryn sniffs her dismissal of Matthias's words. Ziselær's gaze flashes to her for an instant, his eyes narrowing, then returns to Khirta. The copper dragon snarls in response before falling into silence.

"Step aside, Toffer," I urge my troll. "Ziselær won't hurt Khirta. We wouldn't let that happen. Let Khirta go to him and take her vengeance if she chooses."

Toffer does, shuffling toward me, hesitation in every step.

But Khirta doesn't move. Her eyes fill with tears she manages not to shed, holding them in as she stares at the beast who hurt her so badly. She's still, other than a chin that trembles occasionally and two swings of her head to look at Tindera and then back at Ziselær. And then she screams, anger and hurt and betrayal in that single wail, and spins to stalk deeper into the cavern.

She doesn't come back that night, and we don't go after her.

CHAPTER TWENTY

MIKKAEL

WORST HAUNTED FOREST EVER

HOLY HELHEIM, DO I hate that northern bitch.

I definitely do not want to fuck her. I don't ever want to see her again. But for some gods-damned reason, I can't fuck anyone else without seeing her face. It was bad before I found Ziselær and realized I was destined to ride a dragon who's mated to her dragon. That seriously screwed with my head. Since then, I've been obsessed with fate's utterly fucked, completely farcical choices for me.

I'm supposed to be chasing Johan's vengeance. He was my best friend, and he deserves that and more. Instead, I'm bouncing from one bed to another, trying to find someone who will hold my interest. None do. Every single time I stick my cock in a random female, Dani's face erupts in my brain, pushing out everything else. I can't stop. I need her like I need air to breathe. So I fuck another Dani stand-in, hating myself for it when I inevitably moan Dani's name as I come.

I started blowing it off a dozen females ago, pretending it's too hard to remember so many names, so I decided to call them all Dani. Now they go along. Because I've apparently become an even more incredible fuck since I gave in and let myself pretend everyone is her.

The mating instinct's such a bitch.

Okay, maybe I do want to fuck Dani. But I'll never stoop that low. Fate can fuck all the way off.

Bevin can see how messed up I am, so he decided to take pity on me. I'm going to travel alone for a while, chasing rumors about a rare plant Sifa learned about, that may be critical to the Dróttning's control of the dragons. Vulryn recognized it from the North, but we'd rather not send anyone there for a lot of reasons. Fróðr's people found hints of its possible presence here in Vanatia, and my job is to slink around the country searching for it.

It's perfect for me. Far from any females—because every single one reminds me of Dani in some way or another—so I can refocus on what's important. If we can take even some of the dragons away from the Dróttning, we'll be one step closer to destroying her. That's the only thing that matters now.

At least, that's what I keep telling myself.

Today's hunt has me heading north. If I can move fast enough, I should get to my next destination by sunset tomorrow. It's a shorter trip than it would be for others because I'm planning to pass through an area most avoid. Since I'm a thwarted dragon rider wannabe with a death wish. Gloson's forest stands between me and my destination, and I'm too lazy and reckless to avoid it.

I don't really believe in the ghost pig that keeps everyone out. The Dróttning has been known to plant tales warning of danger to protect an area she wants others to avoid, and I suspect that's what's going on here. Which makes me want to explore it. If the Dróttning created the stories about Gloson, she's hiding something here. I'm searching for things she hopes to hide and can't think of anyplace better than a pig-haunted forest.

So in I go.

It's disappointingly unremarkable at first: trees that look just like the ones I've been riding past for days; flowers wearing cherry-red and periwinkle and marigold that sparkle no more brightly than any blooms I've seen before; shrubs so plain and nondescript, I could have planted them in my yard at home.

Boring.

It's a poor effort by the ghost pig so far.

My horse doesn't agree. Since we crossed the invisible barrier into the pig's forest, he's been prancing around like he's being attacked by a swarm of enormous, blood-sucking ants. It's all I can do to keep him moving forward, and I'm starting to wonder if I would have been better off going around. Finally, though, he realizes he has no choice. We get far enough into the forest that even this daft creature knows he's probably as close to the exit as he is to the entrance, and he resigns himself to his fate.

Still nothing spectacular.

Worst haunted forest ever.

The grunts catch me off guard. We're a few hours into the forest and suddenly surrounded by pig sounds. It feels like a drove of swine all around us. My horse doesn't like this development. He's still dancing through the trees like bugs are crawling up his legs, but now his head spins constantly as he searches for whatever the fuck is making the noises freaking him out.

He could be right.

Maybe this isn't the *worst* haunted forest ever.

I nudge him a bit, ready to move a little more quickly toward the exit, and he doesn't need to be asked twice. In an instant, we're racing over the dead leaves and branches at our feet, jumping over any stump or bush that gets in our way, spinning around trees that seem to appear out of gods-damned nowhere. And the fucking pigs are right behind us. The grunts turn into squeaks and squeals and honks as a stampede follows our race to safety.

It's not just one ghost pig. I hear hundreds, maybe thousands, all chasing us as if we're the only meal they'll have all year. Maybe we are. Who the fuck knows what a ghost pig eats.

Twice I catch a glimpse of a pig, always alone, as if it broke free from the others just to fuck with us. It's enormous, white as fresh snow with spikes running all along its back like the razor-sharp tips of a hundred blades. But that's not what freaks me out. His eyes do that. They're red as blood, shining so bright, they cast a crimson glow on the nearby trees. And he's so fast that I know he's playing with us. If he wanted to catch us, he could.

Gods-damned horse was right.

This is absolutely the worst, most horrific, never-come-here-if-you-value-your-life haunted forest ever.

I'm so fucked.

The horse's hooves slip twice as we race across the uneven ground below us. Each time, I barely hold my seat as he scrambles to right himself and then bucks once or twice. If he can throw me, he might be able to beat the pig and the bastard knows it. I'm holding on for my life because if he can throw me, his speed won't matter. He just needs to be faster than me, and he sure as fuck is.

As we twist around another tree, a field opens up in front of us. It's spectacular, the colors I'd been craving all displayed here. Flowers that are marigold elsewhere are gold here. Cherry-red blossoms glitter like rubies in this garden. Periwinkle blooms are the sky on a still winter evening, as clouds erupt with the last of the sun's light in a brilliant purple display. I wish I could slow down and appreciate it, but we've got a pig on our tail and the bastard's hungry.

The horse finds speed I didn't know he could muster, flying across the grass like it's a road. And then the asshole finds his resolve. Tossing his front legs into the air, nearly toppling himself over, he finally manages to throw me. I grapple for the saddle, desperate to hold on, but he timed it right. I was ogling over the gods-damned flowers and let my guard down.

I land on my back with a groan then scramble up, spinning my head to find the closest pig. None of them are near enough to see but that doesn't mean shit. This is a game and I'm their quarry, sitting in the middle of the field like a duck waiting to be shot. Twisting again, I find a dense patch of forest and start sprinting. If I have any hope of living, I'll need to climb a tree or do something the pigs can't do.

Before I can reach it, though, one of the pigs saunters into the field in front of me. I swear I can see a smirk on his snout, lips tipping up as he reveals the teeth that look every bit as sharp as the blades across his back. My heart is pounding so hard, it drowns out every other sound. I'm terrified to look away but the idea of other pigs creeping up on me sends tremors down my spine.

Risking it, I twist my head, searching for other swine. But there's not a single other beast in this field.

Turning back, I plant my feet, resting my hands on my blades. The pig's not moving any faster, savoring this moment before the kill. When he's less than a dragon's-length away, he attacks.

Nothing has ever moved as fast as this pig. Before I can draw my blades, he's nearly on top of me. I barely manage to shove one between us, but it doesn't slow his attack. He's a stuck pig—literally, with a knife jutting out of his chest—but he doesn't even flinch as jagged teeth snap at my throat. I swing my other knife up, managing to shove it into his throat and get a second to breathe as he throws himself backwards to drag his neck over the ground, dislodging my blade.

It barely slows him down, though. In an instant, he's back on top of me, my arms struggling to hold him away, unable to reach for the knives I didn't have time to pull from my boots. Images start to filter through my mind as I realize I'm about to be killed by a gods-damned pig.

Fucking serves me right.

I deserve to die for letting myself be trapped by a swine in the worst haunted forest ever.

Dani and Ziselær push out the other images flashing through my thoughts, different pictures of them bouncing around as I'm reminded that I don't have a reason to live anyway. Another male rides my dragon, and I don't want the shrew the fates chose for me. Still, I wish I could see them again before I die.

I swear I see a smile on the pig's face, his crimson eyes glowing, as his snout drops toward my neck. I close my eyes, oddly calm as I wait for his teeth to rip out my throat, when I hear the screech I've been dreaming about. The pig is ripped away from me, globs of blood splashing over my face, as my eyes fly open to see Ziselær flinging himself into the air, the pig in his claws. I almost can't breathe as I watch my magnificent beast drop the pig on the other side of the field and turn to me, flames billowing from his mouth.

He's still hovering in the air, Matthias's angry shouts beating down on him, when the pig stands and throws himself at me. Before I can scream for my dragon, the swine's halfway across the clearing, his eyes growing even brighter than they did before. Ziselær doesn't pause as he ignores the bastard on his back and races the pig to get to me.

I dart to the left, closing a little of the distance between me and my dragon, but it won't matter much. The pig is so fucking quick, I don't think Ziselær has a chance. At the last second, though, he finds a burst of speed, reaching me just in time to grasp my arms and wrench me into the air, the swine's teeth barely missing my boot.

Fuck. Me.

Worst haunted forest ever.

"Turn the fuck around and drop this bastard," Matthias is bellowing. "I won't hold back this time. I'll tell the Dróttning what you've done, and she'll destroy your ass. She may even take your gods-damned wings. Drop. Him. Now."

Ziselær warbles in response, an apology so heartfelt I almost wish he'd drop me. I've seen my dragon twice and both times, I've exposed him to the Dróttning's wrath. If I survive this, I need to disappear and never put him in this position again. But he flies on, grief billowing from him, infusing our bond, as he defies Matthias's order.

We've traveled less than a minute when my heart drops. A copper dragon emerges in front of us, her gods-damned rider watching Ziselær with her jaws open so wide, her chin nearly reaches her chest. When my gaze finds Dani's, she clasps her teeth together. Even from here, I can see the harsh lines around her mouth as her lips dip into a deep frown. Her blue eyes sparkle like the sky.

And my cock twitches. Treasonous bastard. It's always had a mind of its own.

Astarot, Tindera, and Khirta appear behind the bitch and her dragon, their riders just as shocked as Dani. If I could shrug my shoulders, I would. I'm as horrified by this as them and there isn't a gods-damned thing I can do about it.

We fly for a few more minutes, aiming for a meadow with a narrow creek running through it. Ziselær sets me down and then backs away, landing as far from me as he can without dumping his rider in the midst of the trees. Even from here, though, I can hear Matthias's angry taunts. He's so fucking pissed.

This day just got a lot better, despite the hag climbing down the wing of the copper dragon and striding over to Matthias. I'm ready for her to slap him or do something else to show how fucked-up it is that he ordered Ziselær to drop me. We are mates, after all, even if we do despise each other.

Instead, she stands between us, giving me her back, and wraps her arms around Matthias's neck, trying to draw his lips down to hers. He resists for a moment, his gaze holding mine, but she places her hands on his cheeks and forces him to look at her. When he gives in, his shoulders relax, and his lips find hers.

This time, the cock twitch is outrage, my heart zooming like a gods-damned dog chasing a rabbit it will never catch as I feel my body tense. She's ours. We're supposed to be fucking her, not that usurper. It almost takes more self-control than I possess right now to stop myself from stalking over and dragging her away, mounting my dragon, and taking both of them out of here.

And I don't even like the bitch. Thank the gods. Because if I wanted Dani, Matthias would be a dead male, and my dragon would be burning me alive.

The mating bond is so fucked.

I cling to that last dreg of restraint, watching as they whisper something to each other, their gazes occasionally spinning toward me. Fhord, Sifa, Toffer, and the cat join me in silence, Sifa wrapping her arm around my waist to give me a quick hug as I rest my arm on her shoulder. She understands.

Perhaps five minutes after we landed, Dani and Matthias walk over to join us. Well, Dani walks. Matthias stomps, anger in his flaring nostrils and the heavy pound of his feet. She looks just as unhappy, but she's resigned. He's still ready to fight, and I can tell before they say anything that he's decided to bring the battle over here.

"The Dróttning will fucking kill me if she finds out Ziselær saved this asshole's life." Matthias's voice is sharp as a knife.

"All the more reason for you to join us, I guess," Fhord tells the usurper with a smirk. "My mother," he adds with an even wider smirk, "will flay you slowly when she learns how little control you have over your dragon."

Matthias's pupils blow wide, his hands clenching as a pulse starts to beat in his throat. And I hate Fhord a little less. If he'll join me in fucking with Matthias, he may end up being an ally after all.

I've got to be the lesser of two evils compared to Matthias. Even if Fhord despises me too.

"We can't kill Mikkael, and you know it." Sifa interjects before Matthias can shove aside his rage and respond. She's the first to argue my cause, like the perfect friend she's always been. "Like it or not, Ziselær created a bond with Mikkael when they met, and he chose not to kill him. That's why he was able to defy your commands to kill Mik, twice. And it's the only way he could have sensed Mik's distress from so far and gotten there in time to save him." She glances toward my beast, eyes wide as she murmurs, "I've never seen a dragon fly so fast."

"He'll suffer for a while, but that's just the gods-damned price he has to pay for refusing to do his duty the first time," Matthias blathers. "We cannot let Ziselær's fate-chosen rider live."

"Well, we're sure as fuck not gonna let you kill him," Sifa growls back, as I turn to wink at the usurper. "Mikkael's one of my oldest friends. He has our protection."

Matthias's pupils blow out again—and now I'm smirking too, because it makes me very fucking happy to see how thoroughly this conversation is fucking with the bastard. He jerks his head toward Sifa, glaring at her like she spit poison at him. "What the fuck did you just say?"

"Mik and I have been friends for years." Sifa's voice is more measured than Matthias's, but she's nearly as angry as him. "He's ours and we won't let you touch him.

"You're telling me this now?" Matthias demands. "Didn't you think I deserved to know something as gods-damned important as the fact that you're friends with the asshole the fates chose to ride my dragon?"

"Why the fuck would we tell you that?" Fhord yells at him. "So you can track him down and kill him when Ziselær can't stop you? We didn't know we'd find Mikkael here. The gods are manipulating all of us, and this is just part of their fucked-up game."

"You want me to just let him go?" Matthias asks, his eyebrows shooting nearly into his brow. "He leaves and there's nothing I can do about it?" He turns toward Fhord, eyes flashing. "I don't think you know shit about your *mother*," he says, a shit-eating grin on his face, "because she'll sure as fuck reward me if I carry his sorry ass back to her."

"You're not taking him to the gods-damned Dróttning," Sifa declares, her dark gaze landing on the usurper, "and we're not gonna just send him on his way, either. He's here alone, without a horse or supplies. We're hundreds of vikus from any town. We need to take him with us, drop him someplace where he can replace whatever he's lost."

"Fuck, no." Dani, Matthias, and I bark our responses together, our gazes spinning toward Sifa and then at each other.

"We can't travel together," I explain, squeezing Sifa's shoulder. "You know my history with Dani. We can't be around each other."

"What choice do we have?" Sifa steps in front of me, her chin high as her eyes spark. "Do you want us to leave you here? Or maybe you think Ziselær is going to abandon his rider of a hundred years and escape with you."

"Of course not," I scoff. "I just ... there has to be another way."

I turn toward Dani and Matthias to see them nodding their heads. At least we can agree about this.

"What do you propose?"

Sifa's adopted a very measured, extremely reasonable tone because she knows she's won already. There's nothing else we can do. My horse is long gone, probably still fleeing from evil pigs. If we happen to find him, they can drop me off. Right now, though, they either leave me here or take me with them. I can't think of another gods-damned thing to suggest.

Dani glares at me as we resign ourselves to the inevitable and I crawl up behind Sifa. I can only watch in silence as *my* mate leans up on her tiptoes to kiss the bastard who stole *my* dragon, and that fucker stalks over to the beast that belongs to *me*, climbs up and launches into the sky.

Fuck.

My.

Life.

Chapter Twenty-One

Dani

A Twisted Turn

W ELL, THIS WAS A twisted turn to the day.

I can't stop myself from occasionally glancing over at Astarot and the male sitting behind Sifa. My mate. A bastard who despises me. Twice, Matthias caught me staring at Mikkael, his eyes narrowing when I turned to see him watching me. The asshole has returned. Just when we were making progress.

Sifa's in the lead and she hasn't changed course at all. We're still heading toward our next destination, as if we're going to just add Mikkael to our little outing and bring him along with us on our trek to the North. I'd rather be buried alive than spend days in a cavern with Mikkael and Matthias. I can't imagine how we'd get through this without one of them killing the other.

Ziselær must be torn to shreds at this screwed-up turn of events.

How's your drake?

Vulryn doesn't answer right away, perhaps asking him what he'd have her say. Sifa told me about some riders—Matthias probably among them—who demand access to everything their dragon knows. I'm not one of those. I love the fact that Vulryn's her own being with her own thoughts and secrets. She continues to choose me, not because she has to, but because she wants to.

Finally, her voice more somber than I've ever heard it, she gives me a single word. *Resolved.*

For the first time ever, I don't know what she means. So I ask, although I can tell she's hesitant to say too much. *Resolved about what?*

Again, she's quiet for a long time. *My drake will not betray his rider. He feels the pull to his destined rider, but he will not be swayed. If his rider demands the death of the wanton male, he will comply.* Another long pause before she adds, *I do not agree.*

I don't want to take Mikkael's side, but Matthias and Ziselær need to know how much harm that would cause. *Sifa and the others won't let him. If he tried, it would destroy any hope of Matthias joining the rebels.*

I have told him. Still, he is resolved.

I'll talk to Matthias, make sure he knows he has nothing to worry about. I won't betray him for Mikkael. He needs to back off.

My drake will not ask this. You must.

I will.

We don't talk again during the long flight to the cavern we'll sleep in tonight. I'm dreading it, the tension that filled my chest when I spoke with Vulryn stubbornly forcing its way down to twist my stomach too. I hate the angst and anger that seeps from Mikkael, like a stench that follows him around. But he's with us for now at least. Maybe Matthias and I can disappear into the cavern for the night and pretend it's just us.

I miss the cove already.

When we land, Matthias gestures for me to wait and I do, joining him after we've both unloaded our dragons and they've left with the other beasts to find a nearby herd. He's still angry about Ziselær, and I realize I should be dreading spending time alone with him as much as Mikkael. This is the old Matthias, and I hate it when he reappears.

"As soon as they get back, we're packing our gear onto our dragons and leaving. My dragon can't spend time with that bastard. It's too fucking confusing for him." His voice is terse, a commander issuing a decree to a soldier.

But I'm not his soldier and I'm not ready to leave. "No, we won't. Vulryn and I will stay tonight. I'll talk to Sifa and Fhord, figure out what they plan to do with Mikkael, and decide tomorrow whether I stay with them or go." I pause for a moment, watching his eyes flash. "Mikkael hates this as much as we do. He hates me. He won't want to spend any longer than he must in the same cave as me."

He smirks, a mean grin I haven't seen for a while. "What'd you do to him?"

"It was a long time ago and it doesn't matter. Just know he has good cause, and I despise him as much as he despises me. They'll drop him somewhere tomorrow or we'll leave."

"I don't like it." His hands are on his hips, shoulders thrown back as he towers over me.

"It's one night. But if you don't want to stay, don't. Our dragons will find each other soon enough. There's too gods-damned much tension in this group already, with you and Fhord's constant dick-measuring contests, and I just want to take a bath and sleep this fucked-up day away."

Turning, I stride into the cavern, not waiting to see if he follows.

Mikkael is nowhere to be found, thank fuck. I join Sifa near the fire, kneeling as I watch her feed vegetables into a stew she's preparing. My stomach rumbles, reminding me it's been too long since I ate.

"How can I help?"

"I've got this," she tells me with a smile. "Mik went into the cavern on the left by himself, but the pool's in the one on the right. Go take advantage of it. I'll send Matthias your way when he comes in."

"Thank you. For everything."

"You don't have to thank me, Dani. We're in this together, and I know this is messed up for everyone. Let's just get through it and focus on what matters—destroying the Dróttning so no dragon is ever placed in a position like Ziselær again."

I can't hold back the vicious grin that splits my cheeks. "Fuck, yes," I snarl.

"Fuck, yes," she agrees.

Nodding, I stand and go dig out what I need to unwind in a bath, hopefully let go of all the shit we've gathered on this trip. I feel myself relax when I see the steam billowing off it. Gods, do I love the elf and her mate. I should have known I could count on them to bring us to a hot pool.

It's just as wonderful as I'd hoped, a perfect temperature and even a few ridges on the sides to sit on. I close my eyes and lean back, enjoying the peace of this moment.

Matthias's smell reaches me before he does, the maple I've grown to love wafting into the cavern to surround me. Smiling, my eyes still closed, I wait for him to drop into the water beside me. He surprises me, though, resting his legs on either side of me and giving me a little nudge forward to draw me into his lap as he sits down where I was.

And then he really surprises me when his fingers go straight for my pussy, brushing through me before thrusting inside, as his lips find my neck. "I haven't gone this long without tasting you all week," he whispers as he pumps in and out, his teeth nipping at my ear. "I considered leaving for about a minute and then I decided I needed to come in here and fuck you instead."

"Good fucking decision," I breathe, reaching behind me to squeeze the massive cock digging into my ass.

"The best," he groans, reaching for my hips to spin me around, resting my legs on either side of him as he leans forward to kiss me. As I open to him, our tongues tangling, he positions himself at my entrance and drives into me, drawing a sharp gasp as he spreads me wide, sending flickers of pleasure up and down my spine.

My hips start to move with his as his hands delve into my hair, holding me in place while he moans into my mouth.

"What the actual fuck?" Mikkael's voice bounces around us, bitter words echoing through the cave.

I spin my head, moving one of my legs to shift away from Matthias, but his hands drop to my hips, holding me in place. He's still hard inside me as he smiles and looks past me to the angry male on the other side of the pool.

"Get the fuck out," he bellows. "We're not done yet and we don't want an audience."

"Riding the dragon the fates chose for me didn't make you feel man enough, huh?" Mikkael's tone is cold, sneering. "You decided to fuck the female the fates chose for me too. You're so gods-damned desperate to be me. Fucking pathetic."

Matthias responds by forcing my hips to move up and down, fucking me as he watches Mikkael.

"Stop." My plea is a whisper, barely loud enough to hear over the water sloshing around us. I try to push away, but he holds me in place, his cock somehow growing even larger as he grinds into me. I'm frozen for a moment, horrified by a side of Matthias I haven't seen yet and wish I never had.

"I'm not done," he growls, still not looking at me. "I'm enjoying Mikkael's jealousy. He'll never have what I do, and it's fucking killing him."

That yanks me out of my stupor. "I'm not putting on a gods-damned show for him," I snap, shoving off Matthias to stumble back into the pool. I can feel heat flowing into my cheeks as tears form in my eyes, but I push that shit deep down inside. I refuse to show that part of me to either of these males. Instead, I drop down to hide the naked body I don't ever want Mikkael to see and spin to face him.

As much as I hate it—and I really fucking hate it—the heart I'd frozen toward Mikkael melts a little as I sense the disparate emotions raging through him. He's barely holding himself together, a need to destroy Matthias coupling with a craving for me that's so intense, I feel it at my core, along with a hatred so fierce, it would burn me if I could touch it.

His expression doesn't give any of that away, though. He's got a playful smirk on his face, as if I don't mean shit to him and he couldn't care less what he just saw.

Maybe Matthias was right. I can't be around Mikkael. This is too gods-damned difficult.

"Get the fuck out, Mikkael," I spit out. "There's no show here. Go creep after someone else."

"Don't let me stop you. I'll hold off on bathing until we get to the next cave. Wouldn't want to drop into that cesspool now." Winking at me as he tosses out a smirk that probably lands him in a lot of beds, Mikkael spins and strides away, never looking back.

I suck in a deep breath and start to move toward the side of the pool—I'm ready to put an end to this bath and this night—but Matthias reaches out to grab my hand, pulling me toward him as his other hand lands on my ass.

"I'm not done yet." His voice is mean. I think the bastard actually thinks I'm gonna finish what he started.

"I'm done. Let me go." I tug on my hand, but he holds on, still pulling me forward. So I slap him, the sound ringing around us. "Get your gods-damned hands off me."

He does at last, his gaze holding mine. "I'll let you go this time, but this won't happen again. If you insist on staying with these people ... with him ... I *will not* let him fuck with us. He needs to know you're mine."

I can't drag my gaze away from him as I realize he didn't seem surprised when Mikkael interrupted us. "Did you know he was coming in here? Is that why you came to me, looking to get fucked?"

Now he smiles, standing to stare down at me as one hand reaches up to stroke my cheek and the other wraps around his rigid cock. "He needs to know you're mine," he repeats in a cold voice before turning away from me and pushing up and out of the water. "Have a good bath," he adds as he pulls on his pants and stalks away.

I can't move. These fucking males. I don't want either of them. I just want to ride my dragon in peace.

And bathe. Since they're both gone and probably not coming back, I sink back into the water and close my eyes, leaning back against the wall.

Mikkael was wrong, but Matthias was completely fucked-up. Holding on to me like that, acting like he had the right to take what I no longer wanted to give. I can't be with a male like that.

Did he hurt you?

My lips lift in a smile despite the bullshit of the last few minutes. Gods, do I love my dragon.

He pissed me off, but he didn't hurt me.

Should I punish my drake?

I can't hold back the snort. *I appreciate the offer, but no. This is between Matthias and me. You go fly with Ziselær if you want.*

His rider took him. I will stay with you.

Matthias left? Do Fhord and Sifa know? I still don't trust him. That reality settles on me like a cold bath, sending a shiver down my spine. My first thought at learning he left was that he might be betraying us. A couple of good weeks can't erase all I know about his past.

The starry female asked me to speak with my drake. I will tell you if my drake's rider orders him to leave this place.

Thank you, my beautiful beast.

We will not let him harm us. The wyrm will not find us here.

I sink down again, but I'm too riled up to relax. Instead, I rush through cleaning everything and get dressed before tracking down Sifa.

"Do you want me to go after him?"

"We thought about it," she tells me, her gaze sharp. "We don't trust him as far as we can throw him, but we trust Vulryn. She'll tell us if Matthias directs Ziselær back to the Nest."

"I think he just needs some space from Mikkael. Thanks for giving it to him."

"We get it. This sucks. We couldn't drop Mikkael off today—there was no rebel camp close enough—but we will tomorrow. He doesn't want to be with us any more than you want him here."

"Probably less than me. He hates me with a burning passion."

Now Sifa smiles, her eyes soft. "The mating bond inspires strong emotions. He can't love you, so he has to hate you." Pulling me into a hug, she whispers, "Will you be okay? You're probably wishing you'd stayed in Njordheim at this point."

"Not even an impossible mating bond could drive me back to the Monarch," I assure her as I settle into her embrace. "This is my home. You're my family. Mikkael and I will figure it out. You're part of both of our lives, and we're gonna run into each other. We'll make it work."

She leans back, watching me for a moment before nodding her head and letting me go. "We'll eat soon. Go be with your dragon so she stops worrying about you."

Matthias strides back in before I go, though, ignoring me as he heads directly to his pack to pull out a large pouch, then turns to come over to me and Sifa. "This is all the mash I have available…"

"Mash?" Sifa glances down at the large bag in Matthias's hands and then back up at him.

"It's the food Astarot's craving. We call it mash in the Nest. I can't give it all to you. Ziselær will need some soon. But I brought enough for two dragons, thinking Vulryn would eat the mash too. This is her share. Your dragon can have it."

"I've been thinking about it," I interject as Sifa reaches out for the pouch. "Maybe you shouldn't give him any. See how long he can go without it before it's critical."

"He's weak already. He doesn't move as quickly as he should. While we're evading the Dróttning, he needs to be at his best."

"Something Vulryn said has been bothering me. That, and our dragons' reactions to the Dróttning's commands in the Nest when we freed Fhord and Tindera. It must be important that she doesn't have any control over Vulryn, and that Astarot was able to resist her command. What if not eating the mash is the reason?"

"That's a fucking stupid idea," Matthias butts in. Because he's determined to piss me right off today. "The dragons need it. The Dróttning wouldn't give it to them if it wasn't important."

I spin to face him, letting him see how angry I am right now. "I didn't ask your opinion. Sifa's dragon isn't your concern."

"Don't be a bitch, Dani."

"Then don't be a bastard, Matthias."

"Oooh, I like this," Mikkael purrs as he enters the cave. Because he's determined to piss me off too. "A little tension in paradise? Can't keep my female happy, huh, Matthias?"

"I'm not your female!"

"She's not fucking yours!"

We both yell our responses, voices loud and a little crazed. I'm frustrated, but Matthias is pissed. He's definitely going to kill Mikkael if we stay around him too long.

Mikkael just smiles and winks at me. "I'm not yours, but you sure as fuck are mine and we both know it." Turning, he swaggers away, enjoying this whole shitshow way too much.

"Ignore him," Sifa mutters, shaking her head as she drags her gaze away to glance over at Fhord, then looks back at me. He stands and walks over, wrapping his arm around her as he joins the conversation. "Tell me what you think about Astarot and this mash," she asks.

"Vulryn told you and Fhord the basics about this plant we're looking for, but not everything. She said the beings who eat this stuff in the North are devoted to it like it's their god. She described a compulsion to follow their leader that she observed only in this group. She said they do horrific things to themselves at his command, like they have no control over their own actions."

"Maybe that's how these beings are," Fhord suggests. "It could have nothing to do with the plant."

"I said the same thing. She's sure it's the plant, and she was a little pissy when I refused to believe her," I add with a smile at the snarky beast. "She told me similar beings live in other places in the North, but they don't behave the same way. She thinks it does something to them, makes them do what their headman commands."

"There's something like that in Midgard," Sifa says, her voice low. "It's a yellow flower. When you inhale it, you're easier to manipulate. Maybe this plant is an exaggerated version of that, imbued with the land's magic."

"And the Dróttning found a way to control it, maybe intensify its effects and tie the dragons to her." Fhord's nodding, his eyes wide as he leans in closer to us. "That could explain a lot."

"Even if that's true," Matthias snarls, "it doesn't change anything now. Astarot is suffering. This would help him."

"What if his body grew to expect it, to need it, and he's suffering as his body rids his system of that unnatural demand?" Sifa turns to look at her dragon and then back at Matthias. "You've seen it—drunkards who can't stay away from the tavern, choose ale or whiskey over their own family. It happens in my world too. People start taking substances and suffer when they can't get them. These urges are always temporary, even if the people think they're dying at the time. Like Astarot thinks he's dying."

"You think a gods-damned food could give the Dróttning control over these headstrong beasts? That's fucking crazy." Matthias seems angry about this conversation, like he's personally invested in Astarot eating the mash.

"Calm the fuck down, Matthias." I grip his arm to drag his gaze toward me, letting him see my anger. "I told you this doesn't involve you. Why do you keep pushing yourself into the middle of it?"

"If I'm joining you—and I'm definitely not liking the idea after hearing this ridiculous bullshit—we'll need every dragon we can get. I won't sit here and listen to you condemn Astarot to suffer and maybe die because you want to chase some bullshit theory. Give him the fucking mash, and let's go find more plants to make the shit ourselves."

Astarot growls from behind me, so close I can feel his breath on my neck. Sifa looks up, and we all watch as she speaks with him.

"He's taken this decision from us," she says after a minute. "He'll do whatever he must to break free of the Dróttning, so he thinks it's worth a try. He doesn't want to eat the mash. Maybe that will change, but for now, he'd rather see how long he can go without."

"Fucking idiots," Matthias gripes, twisting to stomp away from us.

I watch him go, wondering how in all the worlds we spent nearly two weeks together. He's nothing like the male who laughed and lounged with me on the beach, worshiping my body like he could never get enough.

And right now, I can't stand the idea of being connected to him for eternity.

CHAPTER TWENTY-TWO

MATTHIAS

MESSAGE RECEIVED

I KNOW I FUCKED up.

After nearly two weeks of winning Dani's trust, getting where I need to be with her, I've blown it in a few minutes. I let myself get carried away by rage and my *need* to put that arrogant bastard Mikkael in his place. Fucker thinks Ziselær and Dani are his, and I'm the imposter.

They're mine. They'll always be mine.

I flew with Ziselær just to put space between me and the fraud Mikkael. When I came back, I found Dani asleep by herself, her blankets wrapped tightly around her, mine lying a few feet away.

Message received.

I'll fix it with her tomorrow. Right now, I just need to sleep off this fucked-up day. *Tell Vulryn I regret what I did. I'll make it up to Dani in the morning.*

Ziselær doesn't respond for a moment as he speaks with his draikana. Finally, he tells me, *Necessary*. I *must* make up with Dani, according to him.

Fucking dragon, thinking he can tell me what I can and can't do.

I like Dani and I'm glad Ziselær's happy, but I need to fix this shit. This won't work unless I remind them who's in charge. I'll deal with it after we get rid of Mikkael and the rest of them. Dani and Ziselær don't act like this when it's just us.

She's still sleeping when I awake, her back turned to me. Spinning in her direction, my cock throbbing as my thoughts fixate on waking up next to her in the cove, I resist the urge to drag her toward me. That would piss her off, and I need to start the day right. So I go to Dani, standing to pull my blankets over and lay at her back. Wrapping my arm around her, I let her scent wash over me as I close my eyes.

It takes a while for her to move, although I can tell she woke up a few seconds after she felt my embrace. She doesn't push me away, but she also doesn't hold me the way she would have yesterday. Finally, she pulls an arm out of her blanket and lays it on mine, intertwining our fingers.

"I'm sorry," I whisper in her ear, drawing her a little closer as I give my cock a hint of what it's craving. "That bastard Mikkael makes me crazy. He's skewed Ziselær's emotions and it's getting to me. I won't act like this when he's gone."

"You need to control yourself when he's here," she whispers, steel in her voice. "If you join us in fighting against the Dróttning, we'll see him sometimes. He's a reckless bastard.

You can't be too." She's quiet for a moment and then adds in a harsh tone. "And what happened in the pool yesterday can't ever happen again. I won't allow anyone to treat me like that."

I push down the ire that rises in my gut, trying to force its way into our conversation. Now's not the time for that. I'll deal with her and the dragon after we get rid of the others. So I don't respond; let her think she's won this time. "I want you alone again," I tell her instead. "I can't be myself around any of them."

She turns, holding my gaze, focused and intense. "Get over it," she tells me, "or go back to the Dróttning. Those are your choices."

"And what does Vulryn think about that?"

"She agrees. We're both committed to them." She smiles, her eyes softening as she glances past me toward our dragons. "She's committed to her drake, but she's a loyal beast. What she has with Ziselær will never override the promises she'd already made to Astarot and Tindera. They're family as much as he is."

"That's it, then? You've made your choice? Both of you?"

"We made those choices long before Vulryn and Ziselær found each other. The only question is how you and he fit into our lives—as part of this group, or as occasional visitors when our dragons fly together."

"And what of our choices? Our loyalty to the Dróttning?"

"She doesn't deserve your loyalty and you know it. Vulryn and I will never swear to her. That won't change."

"And what of you and me?"

"We've always known this is just a fuck. It's a gods-damned good fuck, but a fuck nonetheless. You reminded me last night who you really are. I won't take a man like that for a partner."

"What if I want to be better?" I lift her chin, my thumb caressing her cheek. "What if I want it to be more?"

"Then be better and we'll see." She leans forward to kiss me, a smile emerging as her lips press against mine. "Vulryn still wants us to be more than just a fuck. I'm not opposed to it. Like I said, it's a gods-damned good fuck."

"You know it," I whisper, digging my hands into her hair to hold her in place. "You'll have none better."

She lets me kiss her but pulls away after a moment. "Nor will you," she says as she pats my cheek. "And this ... arrangement ... will be better soon. Sifa said we'll drop Mikkael off somewhere along the way."

"Thank fuck."

"I agree. Thank fuck."

Everyone eats breakfast quickly, gathering our things to take off just after sunrise. Mikkael rides with Sifa again, and just like yesterday, I watch Dani. She keeps her gaze away from that bastard for the most part, but I still catch her looking for him. And every single gods-damned time, her expression changes, her lips parting as she lifts a hand to play with a necklace she always wears. Even her shoulders relax.

He's doing the same thing, twisting occasionally to look for Dani, nodding his head when he finds her.

I doubt Dani knows she's doing it, but I sure as fuck don't like it.

The third time Dani turns toward Mikkael, I nudge Ziselær to overtake Vulryn, planting himself between her and Astarot. I'm there every time the bastard turns around to search for *my* female, making sure he knows I'm dangerous, and he best not fuck with me. At one point, Astarot sprints ahead and we follow, driven on by my need to be the only thing Mikkael sees when he looks behind him.

I'm so focused on him, I don't even notice the gigantic fucking eagle swooping toward us from a nearby ridge until he's nearly on top of us. My fingers dig into Ziselær's feathers, clinging more tightly to him before I realize how gods-damned terrified I am. Because that is a gigantic fucking eagle.

He doesn't want me, though, thank the gods. Instead, he aims at Astarot like an arrow, flying faster than many of Vanatia's dragons, as a memory teases at the edge of my mind. Sifa's red beast tries to spin away, but he's too slow. The eagle grabs Sifa and Mikkael in his claws and soars away at an impossible speed. My stomach drops as I watch him go and realize that Hræsvelgr—a shifter giant that can take a bird's form, who hasn't been seen in this land for more than a decade—has reappeared.

Because of course he has. This group has shit luck, and if I'm smart, I'll get the fuck away from them fast.

Astarot screams his fury at the sky, shooting toward the eagle that I swear to fuck is taunting the angry dragon. As Ziselær pivots to follow, his heart pounding and a tremble running down his spine, I realize that if Hræsvelgr drops his captives, we're the only dragon close enough to help Mikkael.

Thank fuck. I won't even have to kill the bastard. Hræsvelgr will do it for me.

I dig my hands into Ziselær's feathers and yank.

Don't you dare help that fuck. He should be dead already.

Necessary. I can feel his angst pummeling me through our bond, a hurricane beating at a window, drowning out everything else. He's desperate to save his destined rider but heeding my command for now.

Don't you dare. I won't tell you again.

Friend. My brittle beast is using Sifa and the others against me, reminding me that if I want to be part of their fucking rebellion, I can't just let Mikkael die.

I don't give a fuck. We don't owe that fraud anything.

Dani, Ziselær pleads. He's her mate and even if she hates him, it'll fuck her up to watch him die. They've already spent enough time together to give the gods-damned mating bond power over her. I can't have her fucked-up right now—obsessing over that bastard—when I *need* to fix things with her. It'll screw up everything.

Fuck me. A groan spews out of me as I admit to myself that my heartsick dragon is right about this. We've got to rescue the fuckwad. And I've already wasted precious seconds.

The Dróttning will kill us if she ever finds out.

Silence.

Silence or death.

Silence.

Fine. Go get him. I can feel my body tense, my teeth grinding together, as I give my dragon permission to save the male he should have killed weeks ago.

Ziselær's relief washes over me, a pail of cold water that drains away every emotion except my anger. He throws himself after the eagle, faster than he's flown in a very long time. We catch up with Astarot quickly, his weeks without the Dróttning's mash taking more and more out of him every day.

When we're nearly close enough to touch Sifa's dragon, the eagle's head spins toward us, his red eyes flaring in fury. He shrieks, a cry that shivers up my spine, and releases his captives. As they plummet to the ground, Hræsvelgr finds speed he couldn't reach with so much weight. I watch him go as Ziselær tucks his wings to follow Mikkael, my stomach plunging with my dragon.

We barely make it. Hræsvelgr was flying close to the ground so Mikkael didn't have far to drop. But Ziselær is a stubborn fuck. He finds the push he needs to reach the male and grasps him in his claws just before he crashes into the rocks beneath us. Snapping out his wings, Ziselær comes to an abrupt stop, hovering for a few seconds, before setting Mikkael gently on the ground. I turn to see Astarot do the same with Sifa. I have no idea how he made it to her in time, but dragons can find untapped strength and speed when their riders are threatened.

Land and get the fuck away from us. I'll speak with the male alone.

Ziselær doesn't respond, but he never does when I'm this angry. As soon as he's on the ground, he extends his wing, waiting for me to climb down before he turns and flies toward his mate, settling a dragon's-length away from us.

"Get your ass up," I bark at Mikkael, who's flat on his back sucking in deep breaths.

"Give me a gods-damned minute. That was as fucked-up as fucked-up gets."

"Get the fuck up," I repeat with a snarl, reaching for his arm to pull him to his feet.

But he snatches it away, sneering at me as it drops back down to the ground. "Was that an eagle?" he asks in a snide, self-satisfied voice. "It looked like an eagle."

"Fuuuuuuck!" I yell, throwing my hands into the air. "I just saved your miserable life. Get. Up."

"My dragon, that you happen to ride, saved my life," he responds with a smirk. "If I'd been riding him, I wouldn't have needed to be saved."

"Fine. Lay there like the lazy bastard you are." I spin to watch the others stride over, dropping my voice so they don't hear me threaten this male they've claimed as a friend. "You will get the fuck away from me today. I will not have you around my dragon any longer. If you're still hanging around tomorrow morning, I'll find a way to kill you."

"Ziselær just saved me, but you're gonna kill me anyway? You think that'll go over well with my dragon?"

"He's *my* dragon, you little prick," I grunt, knots forming in my chest and stomach as I try to ignore this asshole's taunts. "And if you don't get away from him and *my* female, I'll kill you just for the joy of watching the life drain away from those crap-colored eyes."

"Oh, relax," Mikkael says as he finally drags his ass off the ground. "I don't want to hang around Dani any more than she wants me around. Sifa said she'll drop me off sometime today."

"She better. I won't need much of an excuse to kill you."

The bastard steps in so close I can smell him, his eyes flashing as he stares at me. "You can try," he responds with a laugh as he claps a hand on my arm, plasters a smile on his face, and spins toward *my* female. "I knew the usurper likes me more than he'll admit," he says as she walks up and wraps an arm around me.

Sifa follows on Dani's heels, her face a mix of emotions I don't recognize. Taking a deep breath, she throws her arms around Mikkael, holding him for a few seconds before she does the same with me, grabbing Dani in the embrace.

Leaning back to capture my gaze, her eyes soften as she smiles at me. "Thank you. That required more than I thought you'd be willing to give. I am in your debt."

"It was a choice I didn't expect to ever make," I say at last, my pulse kicking up as I force myself to stop grinding my teeth together. I fucking hate the fact that my dragon was right about saving the bastard. "I know he's your friend and I couldn't let your friend die."

"Then I am even more indebted to you."

"We are," Fhord agrees as he walks up and pulls Sifa into a fierce hug. "That was too fucking close," he whispers before taking her lips in a kiss that probably should be confined to a bedroom.

"Did we just get captured by an eagle?" Mikkael demands, fixated like the simpleton he is on the gods-damned *type* of bird that just tried to kill him.

"That was Hræsvelgr," Sifa whispers, holding Fhord's gaze for a second more before turning toward Mikkael. "And everything I thought I knew about this world just changed."

"How do you know Hræsvelgr?" Fhord asks. "And why would his attack change your mind about anything? He hasn't been here for a while, but he's well-known in Vanatia."

"And in Njordheim," Dani adds.

"And in my worlds," Sifa murmurs, her gaze returning to Fhord's.

"Hræsvelgr visits your worlds?" Fhord's words barely disturb the still that descends on everyone, even the dragons, with Sifa's announcement.

I watch them for a few moments, waiting for someone to elaborate—because this clearly surprised them all—but nobody speaks.

"So?" If nobody plans to explain, I'll ask. "What does that matter?"

Sifa turns to blink at me, slowly, then shakes her head as if pulling herself out of a trance. "It doesn't," she lies. "It's just been a long time since I saw him. It surprised me."

"Why are you lying to me?"

"Don't be a dick," Dani urges from my side as the arm still wrapped around my waist squeezes me. "She nearly died.

Let's give everyone a minute to breathe before we start flinging accusations at each other."

I hold Sifa's gaze, wondering whether I'll give the Dróttning this information if I go back to her, then turn away to wave at Ziselær. "Let's get the fuck out of here," I mutter.

"Not yet," Fhord says. "We've ended up in an area too close to a rare plant to ignore. I want to harvest some of its leaves. Let's eat lunch and then we'll go."

"Good timing," Dani breathes from my side. "I'm starving." She turns and stalks toward Vulryn, grabbing the bag she packed earlier with our meal.

I don't follow her, not yet trusting myself to hold my tongue. Instead, I let my dragon come back to me, ready to deal with his bullshit. When he's close enough to reach out a tongue and taste my cheek—something he used to do when he was a hatchling but hasn't tried for decades because we are not soft—he stops, waiting for me to speak. I place my hands on either side of his snout and let him see the anger in my eyes.

This bond with your draikana is fucking with you. You're getting weak. I won't allow it. We will kill the beast and her rider and return to the Dróttning if I think they're gonna turn you back into the pathetic hatchling you used to be.

Strong, he assures, spitting a whisper of a flame from his nose.

Then why the fuck did I feel your fear for that bastard Mikkael? I demand. *Maybe you were right, and we needed to save him this time but not because you want him to live. He's just some fucker who doesn't mean shit. You are mine. Don't you ever forget it.*

He watches me for a moment, his eyes solemn. *Yours*, he says at last.

We will kill him. We can't do it now, but he must die. You know that, right? I'm holding his gaze, watching for any regret or uncertainty, but if he feels it, he hides it from me. I see the same resolve I feel.

Yours, he repeats, an assurance and a promise. When I decide the time is right, he'll kill Mikkael at my command. I've given the bastard a reprieve because Mikkael can't die quite yet. Soon, though.

Good. I don't want to have to kill you too, but I will. If I can't count on my dragon, I'll get another gods-damned beast.

Yours, he tells me for the third time. I can feel his resolve. Bastard's grown attached to me after a century. I know he's mine.

Go fly with your draikana. Maybe there's a herd nearby.

He drops his massive chin and spins his head, smiling at Vulryn when he finds her. I watch as Vulryn and Dani walk over to the others, probably to ask their dragons to fly. As soon as they're airborne, I turn my back and tramp away from them, searching for the privacy I need to take a piss.

And then the ground beneath my feet starts to tremble, a landshake deciding that now's the time to fuck up our world a bit more. Dropping to the ground, cursing to myself at the intensity of this shake, I cover my head with my hands and start counting, my heart beating so gods-damned loud it nearly drowns out the pounding around me. I've been in three of these and every single time, it's freaked me the fuck out.

The ground should not shake. That's gods-damned unnatural—evidence that gods still live and they're manipulating our lives for one fucking reason or another.

Twelve seconds after it started, it ends. I look around, thanking the gods that no tree or rock fell on me. Standing, I glance toward the others. Sifa, Fhord, Toffer, and the cat look as stunned as I feel, and I spin to search for Dani and the bastard.

They're not here, I realize, just as the others start to move rocks, frantically searching for something.

Gone, Ziselær screams at me, panic in his voice. Dani and Mikkael have disappeared. The rocks opened up and swallowed them. Nobody knows where they are, or how to get there.

CHAPTER TWENTY-THREE

DANI

TRAPPED, TOGETHER

"**Y**OU'RE A REAL BASTARD for making me save you. Again," I mutter as I wrap part of my coat around Mikkael's big head, trying to stanch the blood that was spilling from it when I woke up next to him in this cave.

The bastard smiles. I can barely see it in the dim cave, but light's seeping in from somewhere, thank the gods.

"Again?" he asks as the corners of his lips split his cheeks, and he opens his eyes to throw a lazy wink at me. But then his lips drop. "That hurts like a bitch," he groans as he glances down at himself and then at the chamber around us. "Where the fuck are we?"

I can't hold back my scoff. "Trapped. Together. Alone. Because the gods are fucking with us. The bastards."

"What do you mean alone?"

"What do you think I mean? You and me. Alone. Here in this cave."

Mikkael's eyes grow so wide I almost laugh before they narrow on me as if I'm to blame. "We can't stay here."

"I don't like this any more than you. Do you think I wanted to save your gods-damned life? Again?"

"Why do you keep saying again? When have you ever saved my life?"

"This is the third time," I declare, tugging the coat a little tighter around his thick skull. "I didn't kill you when Harald ordered it; my dragon convinced Ziselær to save you from plummeting to your death; and now this. Three times."

"He's my gods-damned dragon. That's why he saved me."

I glare at the stubborn bastard. "I'm going to give you some advice, just this once. You need to listen to me when I tell you Ziselær's not yours. He belongs to Matthias." I make sure he sees my eyes and the shit-eating grin on my face as I add, "Just as I do."

"You're mine too," Mikkael rumbles, lifting a hand to caress my cheek. I want to shrink from him. I need to hate his touch. I don't, though. My body craves it, and I can't pull myself away.

"But I'm not yours," he adds as he does what I couldn't, yanking his hand back. "Because I will never want you."

"You're the one who kissed me in that room," I remind him, the years-old memory of his lips on mine still stark in my mind.

"You're fucking crazy. You kissed me."

"Keep telling yourself that," I grunt. Twisting the coat into a knot, I push away from him and stand. "That should hold until they can get to us."

"Thanks," he gripes, holding my gaze for a moment before turning to look at the pile of rocks behind us. "How long do you think it'll take the dragons to dig through this shit?"

Are you safe?

I am, I assure her. *When will you be able to get us?*

Mikkael quirks an eyebrow at me, and I wave an arm at him to tell him to leave me alone.

"Are you talking to your dragon?" he asks.

Dipping my chin, I turn away, stalking a little deeper into the cavern as I wait for her response.

They are unsure whether we can reach you. The troll believes he can find another exit.

Why can't Fhord just move the rocks?

The wyrm would know if our male used the power he needs to open a tunnel. The other beasts and I have tried to dig for you, but the rocks are not stable. They fall too quickly into the hole we create. The troll fears we would bring the cave down on you if we continued.

Well, this is fucked. I spin to glance at Mikkael, who's still sitting on the ground watching me. *Toffer wants us to search for someplace else to get out?*

The troll believes he can find another exit, she repeats. *He will guide you as you walk to it.*

What if there's nothing close?

He will guide you, no matter the distance.

We've got no food or water down here.

The troll will lead you to creatures you might eat and water to drink. He is confident the caverns hold all you need to sustain you.

Fuck me. I cannot spend some unknown amount of time alone with this male. We'll kill each other. *Has everyone given up on digging us out?*

Wait, she tells me, an apology in her tone. I'm not ready to face Mikkael, so I lean against a nearby wall to rest my head against it. Matthias must be going crazy. He already was jealous of Mikkael, worried about some stupid fate-ordained bond. But he doesn't understand the depth of Mikkael's hatred for me or mine for him.

A minute or more passes before she tells me their decision. *My drake's rider believes we should continue to dig, but the others disagree. They will follow the troll's advice. He has decided the danger is too great. He will lead you as we search for an exit. He asks if you hunger now.*

Let me look around for my bag. I had a little food in there. Report when you have fully searched.

I will. I pause for a moment, wondering what Ziselær shared with her about Matthias. I'm almost afraid to ask. I don't want to know how crazy he's going up there. But he needs to know I'm thinking about him. *How is Matthias?*

Frustrated. And bitter. He would be there with you.

Tell him I wish it was him too. Mikkael won't replace him as Ziselær's rider or my lover.

As it should be.

Sucking in a deep breath, I turn toward the bastard I'm stuck with for who knows how long. This is going to be so fucked.

"The cavern's unstable," I tell him, trying my damnedest to keep my tone flat. "They're not going to dig us out. Toffer thinks he can lead us to an exit and help us find food and water along the way."

"You've got to be kidding me," he bellows.

"Do I look like I'm kidding?" I stretch my arms out and swing them around for the asshole. "Do you hear any digging? See any rocks falling while they try to get to us?"

"I. Don't. Like. You," he spits. "I can't stay in this cave with you."

"I don't like you either." My tone is rising, and I despise the female who appears when he acts like this. But she's here and I'm too angry to push her away. "Besides, we're not planning on staying, dipshit. Toffer will guide us toward an exit."

"I'll just go alone, then."

"Be my fucking guest," I snarl, flinging up an arm toward the dark cavern. "Find your own way out. I've got a dragon to tell me where to go and how to find food and water and you don't have shit. So good luck with that."

I almost laugh at the emotions that flicker over his face, with eyes narrowed in rage growing wide when reality sets in and then finally relaxing. "We're so fucked," he mutters at last.

"I hate this as much as you," I tell him, finally getting a grip on my emotions. "Let's just get it over with."

"Fine. Which way?" He sounds resigned to a miserable couple of days.

Same, asshole.

"First, we need to find something to use as a torch, and then look for my bag," I say. "It has food in it; maybe we'll get lucky and find it. I'm not looking forward to the worms or rats Toffer will lead us to if it's not here."

"He plans to look for worms and rats?" he demands, his tone rising again.

"He's gonna find anything we can eat. In Njordheim caves, that's worms and rats."

"Fuck me."

"Yeah, well, fuck me too. Let's just see if it's here and then get this over with."

It's not. We stumble around long enough to find a piece of wood and some dried grass we can wrap around it to burn and Mikkael, handy bastard that he is, pulls a flint out of his pocket. And then we dig until we nearly bring the roof crashing down on us, prompting a startled *Stop* from Vulryn.

The troll fears for the cave. He says you must stop. He will find food for you.

Soon? I'm starving, and I imagine the wanton male is too.

I will tell you when he believes food is near. She's quiet for a moment, then adds, *The troll says to follow the cavern to the right with the broad entrance. It goes up and to a larger system he believes will be more likely to lead to the surface.*

Please tell him thanks. Will you be walking along with us?

We will walk where the land allows. If the dragons must fly, the troll and a rider will follow the caverns on the ground as closely as they can.

Alrighty then. Let's go.

"This way," I tell Mikkael as I gesture toward the tunnel Toffer told us to take and trudge forward. I can hear him behind me, but I don't turn around. We're both going to pretend we're alone in this cave, and I'm fully on board with that plan.

We've walked for at least an hour, maybe more, when Vulryn's frustrated voice drops into my head.

Tell the wanton male to stop trying to speak with my drake. He will get no response, and it angers my drake's rider.

Why is he trying to speak with Ziselær?

My drake reports that the wanton male hopes to "get to know" him.

Yeah, I can see why that would anger Matthias. I'll speak with him. My stomach grumbles as I turn toward the arrogant male behind me, reminding me that Toffer has yet to lead us to food. *Any idea when we'll find a meal?*

I will speak with the troll. Vulryn's quiet for a moment. Her next words come with a laugh buried within them. *A pool is in your path, perhaps an hour ahead. The troll suggests you build a fire for whatever you find there.*

Great, I mutter, wondering how hard that will be. There can't be that much wood down here. But it doesn't matter. We'll figure it out when we get there.

I spin my head, catching Mikkael's gaze as I relay Vulryn's message. "Ziselær wants you to stop trying to speak with him."

"Why would I do that?" His eyes are playful, a smirk on his smug lips.

"Because your dragon asks it," I explain to the idiot. "Is that not good enough?"

"Z thinks he belongs to Matthias. I think once he gets to know me, he'll realize fate was right. He's mine. He just doesn't know it yet."

"Like you think I'm yours?"

"Like I know you're mine." Now he winks. Because he's a bastard who's determined to piss me off.

"Do you know what Vulryn calls you?"

"Let me guess. Z's rider-to-be?" he asks as an eyebrow cocks up. "Your mate-in-waiting?" He watches me for a minute as I let my scowl tell him exactly how I feel about his suggestions. "No? What?"

"The wanton male."

He barks out a laugh, looking up as if he could see my dragon if he tried and then back at me. "I like it. I've been known to let my cock lead me around. That's why I was so popular in Lumaria. I filled many beds, and women, with it in charge."

Bastard. I should have known he'd take it as a compliment. "She wanted to call you the angry male, but I told her we should find something more fitting. She said that's the only other name you deserved, given your reputation on the island."

"Were you asking about me, you sneaky spy? Jealous?"

"Fuck, no. I couldn't care less what you do with your cock. I just thought you'd like to know that none of those females you bedded gave a single shit about anything except your cock. You may be a good fuck, but that's all they wanted from you."

He tilts his head, crinkles at his eyes as he smiles at me. "I think you're jealous. I cuddled with some of them too, but it doesn't matter. We both know they've all had something you can only dream about, because this cock will never be yours."

"And we both know I don't want it."

"Keep telling yourself that," he whispers with an even bigger smile. "But why angry male? That doesn't suit me."

"You've been angry since I met you. You try to cover it up with this weird flirting shit..."

"Do you think I'm flirting with you?" Now, the corners of Mikkael's lips tip down, his eyes narrowing.

"What else would you call it?"

"I'm fucking with you," he tells me in a voice dripping with malice, "because you're a bitch and I'm going to do what I can to drive you crazy while we're stuck together. If I were flirting with you, you'd know it."

"Keep telling yourself that," I throw back at him. Two can play this stupid game. "And stop talking to Ziselær."

"Z's gonna love me as much as you do. Him, I'll take. Matthias can have you."

"His name is Ziselær. At least give him the respect of using his full name."

"That usurper Matthias calls him by his full name. When he's with me, he'll be a different beast. The dragon he was born to be. Not the bastard the usurper tried to create from my dragon. I won't use the same name for Z."

"You're so gods-damned difficult," I moan, sneering at him as I quicken my pace.

"You try being mated to someone like you," he yells at me as I stride away, "and watching a bastard like Matthias ride his dragon. You'd be difficult too."

He's quiet after that, thank the gods, as we trudge toward the pool that hopefully will give us a meal and something to drink. As Vulryn said, we find it within an hour, stepping into a vast cave. And I can't hold back my gasp, twisting to look at the majesty around me.

I've been in a lot of caves but never anything like this. It's lit somehow—the water seems to glow—and the cavern reflects the aqua that billows from the pool. As flat as my favorite Njordheim lake on a still summer morning, I wonder how I can possibly dip a hand into it and disturb its perfection. Although the sheen on the walls is a single color, the pool is rich with shades of blue. I see cerulean and cobalt deep in its midst, with cornflower and azure and royal blue shimmering and dancing above them.

The fish Vulryn mentioned float through the pool, their movements barely disturbing the water around them. Toffer suggested a fire, but I can't imagine anything impure living in that basin. I'd gladly eat them raw, to savor the delicacy of their flesh.

Lifting my eyes, I gaze at the stalactites that drop from the ceiling above. They shimmer with a medley of shades, reds and blues and oranges and purples reflecting the water to throw rainbows all around us. They're also enormous, reaching perhaps half the distance between us and the roof far above. Many drip onto stalagmites that have grown nearly large enough to touch their creators.

As I turn, my gaze finds Mikkael and, despite myself, I smile. I still hate the bastard, but I can't bring that hate in here. It feels sacrilegious, unholy. He must sense the same thing because he responds with a genuine grin, not the teasing smirk he's been wearing since he woke up trapped with me.

"It's almost worth getting stuck down here," he whispers, turning from me to explore the cave with his eyes. "Almost," he adds with his signature smirk as he looks at me again.

"But not quite," I respond, letting my smile stay for another second before turning away. "Vulryn said we should cook the fish," I tell him as I stride toward the pond and look in. "I wonder if we need to boil the water, or if it's safe to drink."

"I'll check," he says, walking over to sit next to me and pulling a vial of some sort from his coat.

"You have something for this?"

"I travel alone. I have something for everything."

"Well, shit. I guess I may have to admit to myself that you're handy to have around."

"You'll be admitting a lot more than that by the time we leave these caves," he tells me as he adds one drop of some green substance to the water, watching it carefully.

"What does that do?" I ask, ignoring his silly dig because that's probably exactly what I need to do with the insolent prick.

"It'll tell me if there's anything dangerous in the water."

"How?" That would come in handy.

He lazily spins his head to look at me, his eyes narrowing as his lips squeeze together. "Fuck if I know," he says. "I don't care as long as it works."

"So, is the water good?"

"Pure as the first virgin I fucked," he responds with a wink. "Until I fucked her."

"Great," I mutter, dipping my hands to bring a drink to my mouth. "Holy shit, that's good," I murmur as I drop my lips to the water and start sucking. When I've drunk my fill, I sit back on my feet, sighing as I finally start to feel a bit more normal. Turning to look around again, I find my gaze landing on Mikkael, who's staring at me with a smile that lifts just one side of his lips.

"You suck like a champ," he says, then yanks my coat from his wound and dunks his head into the water up to his neck, shaking like a gods-damned dog when he pulls up. "That is good." He drops his mouth to the water and sucks just like I did, smirking when he's done. "I suck good too."

"Fuck me," I mutter. "Is this what I have to look forward to while we're stuck down here? I thought you hated me."

All humor leaves his face as he stares at me, a muscle in his jaw twitching. When he speaks, his voice is cold.

"I hate you with a passion I've never felt for anybody before," he tells me, enunciating each word. "But you don't hate me because I didn't fuck you the way you fucked me. I didn't manipulate your lover's mind, convincing her to turn on you.

I may have been your weapon, but you killed Helga. I will not—I cannot—ever forgive you for that."

He stands, giving me his back as he strides away. "So I'm just gonna fuck with you. Remind you how gods-damned much you want me. That the usurper can never give you what I could. That you will never need him—you'll never crave him—the way you need and crave me. And then I'll fly away with my dragon."

Now he turns, glaring at me as he palms his cock. "Z's mine and you're stuck with me because Vulryn is his. Every single time Z and Vulryn fly together, I will fuck with you more. Not literally, of course. I will never stick my cock inside you. I'm just gonna use your *need* for me to make sure you live your life every bit as miserable as you've made me."

Spinning, he strides away, never looking back, as I crumple under the weight of his hate.

CHAPTER TWENTY-FOUR

FHORD

THE OLD GODS

"TELL ME ABOUT HRÆSVELGR," I ask Sifa as she drops next to me, reaching for my hand to link our fingers. We've finally broken away from Matthias—who is driving me absolutely fucking insane—so we can talk about the eagle and what his presence here means to Sifa's search for her home.

She doesn't answer right away, watching the creek bubble past us as she dips her feet in, sighing in relief after we tromped through the forest all day. We've spent the day following Toffer's instructions as he tracks the cavern Dani and Mikkael are stuck in, searching for a way out. He's certain we're making progress and thinks he'll lead them to an exit tomorrow.

"Let me ask first. Do you have giants here, like Hræsvelgr in his human form?"

"Our history holds mention of creatures like him, although few have the ability to shift, and they had a different name."

"What were they called?"

"Jötnar."

Sifa's eyes grow wide as the rest of her completely stills. She watches me in silence for a few seconds, then shakes her head and looks at her feet resting in the creek. "We have a common history," she says at last. "Are there still jötnar in Vanatia? Or Njordheim? I've never seen any."

"Only Hræsvelgr when he visits, which hasn't happened for ten years or more."

"Ten years? Did his visits stop when I arrived?"

I can feel my eyebrows slam together as I understand what Sifa's suggesting. She's right. It's been ten years since we saw Hræsvelgr. If they're connected in some way, his presence here after a decade must be significant. "They did," I tell her when my mind has finally caught up with hers.

"Does he ever communicate with anyone?"

"In the past, he's met with the Dróttning, and I assume Harald. The Dróttning has never invited anyone to join them, not even me."

"She knows about my worlds," Sifa murmurs. "I've been trying to get close to her, believing she'd have the knowledge I need to go back home, and it seems I'm right. She may not be the key, but she could help me find it." Her spine straightens as she throws her shoulders back and looks at me, squeezing my hand. "What if there's a window between worlds that opens occasionally, and my time to find it is limited?"

"What would you do if there were?" I know she'll never leave me—we're too connected for that—but I can't expect her to ignore this connection to her world. And I wouldn't want her to, especially if it would help her understand how she could regain the long life she would live there.

"I'd help Toffer get home if he wants to go," she tells me as she lifts a hand to caress my cheek. "And stay here with you to live as long as I can."

"Maybe we need to go there," I suggest. "If there are dragons in your worlds, ours would follow us."

She shakes her head, her dark eyes sad. "Joralf told me dragons can't pass between the worlds for some reason. At least, they couldn't in the downfall. The elves traveled to my worlds, but the dragons disappeared. Nobody knows where."

"There must be a way." My mind is spinning, the fantasy of a world without the Dróttning taking hold.

Sifa responds with the most adorable smirk ever. "You wouldn't want to live in my worlds. I miss a few people who were like family to me, a brother and sister and their father, more than anyone." She's quiet for a moment as she seems to consider something. "Freyja, the sister, has some shifter in her," she says at last. "She can't change fully, but her arms turn into wings. Our stories tell of shifters from the past—even dragon shifters—but not many remain in my worlds for some reason. Hræsvelgr was one of the few true shifters."

She falls silent again, staring into the creek. "I'd give nearly anything to know if Freyja and the others survived Ragnarök," she says at last. "But I'd never give up you or Astarot. I can't take you and I won't go back without you. *This* is my home. Besides, even if he could go, I wouldn't ask Astarot to live that life. Midgard evolved for millennia while dragons were trapped underground. It's a strange place for the beasts now."

"So we stay and you live a few decades? Fuck that," I snarl, a wave of revulsion pulsing through me at the thought of watching Sifa age and die. I rest my palm on her hand, making sure she sees the truth in my words. "I will live anywhere I must to be by your side. I will not watch you die. I will abandon this world and everyone I love if it means I'll be able to share one more day of my life with you. We'll figure out how to bring the dragons with us."

Sifa responds with one of those smiles that calms my soul. "The Dróttning has lived for centuries, although she's not an elf. What if there's something here—something she alone knows about—that gives her power and long life, like the gods in my worlds? There, it's a tree, Yggdrasil, that sits in Asgard. Its fruit gave power and endless youth to any who ate it. Asgard has the most powerful magic, but elves age slowly and have other gifts because our home is adjacent to Asgard, close to the tree. Its essence is everywhere, giving us what we need. What if this island is connected to Yggdrasil too, and we just need to find that connection?"

I lift my hand, caressing her cheek as her words settle in my soul. What if it is that simple? "If you're right, it's just another reason to destroy the Dróttning and claim whatever she's been hoarding."

"As if we need another reason," Sifa responds with a smirk. "But we'll worry about that tomorrow. Today, we're going to follow Toffer to the end of this cavern and get Dani and

Mikkael back. Then we'll deal with whatever is going to happen between the three of them—well, five of them if you count the dragons—until we can drop off Mikkael."

I dip my chin. She's right. We don't have to decide anything yet. And that bastard Matthias is a much more immediate problem. "Are we sure we want to drop him at the camp with Liv and Frida? They've just gotten back from Lumaria and didn't ask for this shit. We're putting them in danger."

She sucks in a deep breath, her eyes darkening as she holds my gaze. "I don't like it either, but they *did* ask for this. They've been working for Ulfhild and Bevin for a long time. Frida was Ulfhild's go-between with Knut—that bastard—and Troels. They want the same things we do, and we need them for this. Besides, I trust Vulryn, and Vulryn's convinced that Ziselær's sincere. If he's not, we'll kill him. We won't give him a chance to harm Liv or Frida."

"What if the dragon's sincere, but his rider isn't?" I can't stop myself from looking toward the others, as if I could see the annoying prick we're worried about. "He's so fucking sneaky. He could be hiding this even from his dragon."

"I think we have to chance it. We have to get Mikkael to a rebel camp, and this one is small, even if it is important to us." Another smile, as she looks in the same direction. "It helps that Liv and Frida are there. Mikkael will need friends after being trapped underground with Dani for a couple days. Plus, the Ætt provide some extra protection we'll need if Matthias does turn on us."

"And after we drop off Mikkael, do we find time to chase this window to your worlds, if it exists, and make sure Toffer can get through?" I bring my free hand to her chin, dragging my thumb along her bottom lip as I hold her gaze. "I don't want you to miss this chance to find something you've been seeking for so long."

"I don't want those worlds anymore, Fhord," she whispers, leaning forward to brush her lips on mine. "I'll talk to Toffer, but I think he'll agree with me. The Dróttning hurt him too. He's in this fight with us. Besides, your mother knows more than we ever realized. We need to focus on defeating her and forcing her to give us the answers I've been searching for."

"So, so dangerous," I rumble with a smile, my heart blooming as it sinks in just how much she's willing to give up to be with me. "I love you so fucking much, rabbit."

"I love you too," she whispers, taking my lips in a kiss that she quickly deepens, her tongue reaching for mine. Groaning, I open to her, savoring this moment alone with my mate. My cock decides to make itself known, responding to any hint that it might get lucky, but I ignore it as my tongue tangles with Sifa's.

"Toffer says we need to move," Matthias barks from behind us. "Dani and the bastard are done resting and they're walking again. Let's go."

"Asshole," I mutter as I break the kiss with Sifa and glare at him.

"Prick," he responds before turning and stalking away.

"Much as I'd like Dani and Mikkael to get along," Sifa tells me with a grin as she pulls her feet from the water and wipes them off, "I hope they don't do it while he's around. He's a bastard now. He'd be even worse of a dick if Dani and Mikkael hated each other a little less."

"I'd have to kill him," I agree. "Let's just pray to the gods that are always fucking with us that they don't fuck with Matthias any more until he's far, far away." Standing, I reach for her hand to draw her up, helping her pull her boots back on.

"One more thing," Sifa tells me, her voice dropping even more. "He keeps pushing Astarot to eat some of the Dróttning's mash. He says it's for Astarot's own good, but I think my dragon may be improving without it. He's not as pissy as he's been. And I was as surprised as you when he and Tindera flew together."

"A very welcome fucking surprise," I breathe, taking one more kiss from my mate as the memory of last night erupts in my thoughts. "I'm glad we were far enough away from the others to enjoy their flight too. We haven't done that since their first time."

"It did make for a ... memorable middle-of-the-night fuck," she purrs, wrapping her arm around me. "He hasn't been strong enough since they first flew, and that was driven by adrenaline. Last night, though, he felt vigor he hasn't in months."

"Do you think Matthias's interest in Astarot eating the mash is nefarious?" I ask, dragging my thoughts away from the feel of Sifa's naked body clinging to mine as our dragons flew.

"Should we rethink whether we trust him enough to join us in dropping off Mikkael?"

Sifa glances at me, then toward Matthias, standing next to Ziselær on the other side of the clearing. "I think we have to take a chance on him sometime. It's our best option for giving him a chance to prove he won't turn on us."

"Fuck," I mutter, flicking my gaze up to look at the asshole. "I don't like it, but I know you're right. I'll go talk to him, see if I can find a way through his shields, read his emotions before we do this."

Sifa nods, bending down to pick up the cat, who's sauntered over to rub against her legs. "Good luck," she says with a smirk, pulling Thor into her arms and scratching behind his ears as a low purr spills from his chest. "You'll need it to get anything from him."

I steel my shoulders and stride away, my mind whispering out toward the bastard. I've nearly reached him, my thoughts focused on him and the shield that's always been too gods-damned strong for a human, when a whispering at the edge of the trees claims my attention. My gaze spins toward Sifa and I can only watch as a wolf the size of a dragon hatchling launches itself from the edge of the forest very fucking close to my mate—and very gods-damned far from me—aimed directly at her.

My guts twist as I realize he's going to attack Sifa, and I can't do shit about it. Heart pounding in my throat, I start running toward her, but she's fast too, thank the fucking gods. She jumps away in time to avoid his gaping maw, dropping Thor to free her hands and yank the blades she always carries from their sheaths. But before she can attack the wolf, Thor does, springing forward with the most vicious yowl I have ever heard from any animal.

The wolf's confusion ripples through me as he bats away the ferocious beast Sifa and Toffer claimed, and he spins his head to watch the rest of us launch ourselves at him. He turns again toward Sifa, spewing out a growl that vibrates with frustration, and snatches Thor from the ground. And then the coward flees into the woods with the cat in its mouth.

What the fuck?

"Is that Sköll?" Matthias demands, rooted to the same spot as he stares at the wolf darting away.

Before I can answer, Toffer takes off running—that troll is gods-damned fast for a being with legs as short and thick as stumps—leaving us to race after him. And we do.

CAN WE FLY? Tindera screams into my mind as the dragons lead the pack, barely keeping up with the troll. I'm stunned by the depth of her emotion, a visceral fear for the cat rolling along our bond.

Toffer isn't the only one who fell under the spell of the bitchiest cat to ever walk this world.

Casting my mind as far as it will go, I search for any other beasts in the area. *Go,* I urge her when I confirm it's clear and we won't be seen by a rogue patrol. Almost as one, the dragons launch into the sky, darting after the beast that attacked Sifa, then stole Thor from within our midst. We chase after the wolf with the cat and the troll, leaping over fallen logs and twisting around trees as we travel deeper into the forest.

I'm so fucking pissed at myself. I need to pay more attention to the beings around us. Nothing should be able to get close enough to threaten Sifa and Thor. Maybe Matthias is right. Maybe that really is Sköll, and the old gods are emerging to suck us into their games as we throw ourselves into the rebellion and prepare to battle the Dróttning. Because that's exactly what those bastards would do.

But fuck them and fuck every single being that ever prayed to them. If we have to beat them all, we will. We *will* defeat the Dróttning, and Sifa and I *will* have a life together. I will not allow any other conclusion to the shitshow that has been the Dróttning's rule of Vanatia.

Close, Tindera tells me, her voice calmer in my mind. For now, at least, she's less afraid for the cat. Or resigned to its death. I can't tell which.

Is the cat alive?

Yes, she answers. Apparently, she can see the wolf and Thor, the cat standing on a log and hissing at the massive beast as if he could actually defend himself. I have no idea why the wolf didn't swallow Thor whole or how the cat got himself out of the wolf's mouth. Toffer will tell us, then Sifa will translate since nobody else can understand that gods-damned troll when he gets excited or scared or happy and starts talking in riddles.

A few seconds after Tindera told me what to expect, we come upon a clearing and watch as Sifa's cat hisses at a wolf that does look just like Sköll, although I haven't seen him in decades, maybe even a century. Toffer's halfway across the field, ready to throw himself at the beast terrifying his sidekick, as the wolf feints to the side, then launches at Thor. And that fucking cat holds his ground, slashing at the dog, who squeals like a whelp as blood spurts from his nose.

Holy fuck, life has gotten weird in the last week.

Khirta screeches at the troll and he skids to a stop, his entire body still as if he's frozen in place. He lifts his gaze to watch the dragons descend, surrounding the wolf, then stalks forward, his eyes never leaving Thor. Sifa and I follow, moving to flank Toffer.

Sköll, if that's who it is, doesn't even flinch. He stands to his enormous height and watches us approach. Toffer leans down and wraps the cat around his neck, then turns back to the wolf, eyes burning with a fury I've never seen from the troll.

"Why would you waylay my wildcat?" Toffer wails, his gaze focused on the beast a male's-height away. He turns to give Thor a kiss, then looks at us. "Our ferocious feline fought to be free. The savage spit him to the surface."

The wolf ignores Toffer and the cat, his attention focusing on Sifa. "We will return to your world together," he tells her. He doesn't move his mouth or speak out loud. Instead, the words drop into my head. They're in the strange language of the wolf gods, but I understand them as I always do when the wolves appear in our world.

"Are you Sköll?" Sifa asks, her hands resting on her blades as she steps between Toffer and the wolf.

"My name matters not, elf. It matters only that I am here to return you to Midgard. You are not welcome in this land."

"Who sent you?" Sifa takes another step forward and my hand whips out, grasping her wrist. "It's okay, Fhord," she tells me without looking back. "He's not taking me anywhere and he knows it. I suspect he didn't expect everyone to defend Thor the way they did. He must have hoped I'd chase him alone. But he understands now. These dragons will kill him before he gets close enough to try. And he might be able to give me answers I've been chasing for a long time."

"Your questions matter not," the wolf responds. "I come to offer you passage. Nothing else. Will you return with me?"

"I'm not going back home, although Toffer might."

"No, Sifa!" the troll huffs, his eyes enormous as his head spins toward her. "Your defender won't desert his damsel."

"You don't have to go if you don't want to, Toff," Sifa whispers, her gaze still focused on the wolf. "I just have no idea how long we'll live here. I don't want to keep you in this land if you're ready to go back home."

"Home is here with my heroes."

"I guess neither of us is going, then," Sifa says to the beast sitting in front of her. "But you can still tell me why you're in Vanatia, and who sent you. And why the fuck you attacked me, then took my cat."

"It matters not," the frustrating canine repeats. "It matters only that you do not belong here. This land bleeds with your presence. If you do not come willingly, she will kill you. Those are your options."

"The fuck they are," I snarl. "If the Dróttning sent you, tell her that Fhord said to fuck off. Sifa will never leave this world, and she is going to help me destroy my bitch of a mother. Sifa will be the cause of the Dróttning's fall, and when the time comes, I will hand Sifa the sword and give her the honor and the gods-damned pleasure of cutting off that cunt's head."

The wolf throws a dismissive glance at me before returning his gaze to Sifa. "You are warned," he says. "Return to Midgard with me or be killed." He holds Sifa's gaze for a moment, then lifts his chin to bay out his frustration and spins to lope into the forest. Tindera and Astarot shift away from each other to let him pass through them.

We all watch in stunned silence as he goes. And then Matthias turns to my mate, his skin blotchy as his nostrils flare. "What the fuck is going on with you people?" he yells, glaring at Sifa and me as if we had anything to do with this bullshit. "First Hræsvelgr and now Sköll? They're coming out of the shitting woodwork to attack you and your little gang of rebels. What did you do to piss off the old gods so fucking much? And why have I been dragged into this shit?"

Sifa's nearly as stunned as Matthias, her lips a thin line as her wide eyes watch the place where the wolf disappeared. "*Was* that Sköll?" she mumbles as she turns to look at me. She shakes her head twice, her lips tipping down at the ends. "Sköll is the grandson of Loki, the chaos god in my worlds," she says at last. "He wouldn't be here without Loki's consent. If that's him, it means the gods have a path to this world and we're fucked. Too many of the gods from my worlds are powerful and power-hungry. If they've allied with the Dróttning, I don't think we can win this fight."

"Who the fuck are you, elf?" Matthias's voice is sharp as steel, and I see red, my fists clenching as I turn blazing eyes toward him.

Nobody talks to my mate that way, especially not this ungrateful fuck. "It's none of your gods-damned business," I bellow at him. "She's mine. She will always be mine. If you so much as spit in her direction, I will take your head so I can offer it to her for the offense."

"Your female has powerful enemies, Fhord. You should think twice about taking her side."

"You're a disloyal bastard so you think everybody else is. I will bring this world crumbling down around us before I forswear this female. If you stand with us, you stand with her. There is no middle ground."

"That was Sköll," Matthias howls, flinging an arm toward the wolf. "A demi-god who hasn't been seen in this land during my lifetime—and probably my parents' lifetime—just tried to take your female. Then he stole a fucking cat so he could draw her into the forest. He's going to take her or kill her. Why in all the worlds would I want to stand with you?"

"Because if the wolf tries to take me, we'll destroy him," Sifa responds, her voice measured and calm as she throws her shoulders back and lifts her chin, "just as we're going to destroy the Dróttning and every being by her side when we come for her."

I suck in a deep inhale, wishing I could breathe in her calm along with the air.

She smiles, the look of a woman who knows exactly who she is, and who she's speaking to. "But you've already made your choice. Stand by your decision, whatever it is. Stay or go. If you stay, though, be prepared to join us in fighting old gods and new. If they come for us, we'll destroy them too. Nobody will stand in our way."

"Fucking lunatics," Matthias mutters, planting his hands on his hips as he turns and stalks away.

I watch him go, wondering when he'll abandon us, and what we'll have to do to stop him from betraying us when he does.

CHAPTER TWENTY-FIVE

MIKKAEL

I DON'T LOOK BACK

"I DON'T KNOW, ASSHOLE," Dani gripes when I ask again why she can't reach her dragon.

It's been an hour since she lost contact with Vulryn. Not a single word since then. Dani felt a flash of fear, which disappeared within minutes as Vulryn moved too far away for Dani to reach her.

"We're pretty deep underground," she says after a few seconds, "so she'd need to be directly above us to communicate. If they had to divert around some threat, she could be out of reach for a while."

"But you said she was afraid," I point out. "I've met your dragon. Nothing scares her."

"A moment of fear. That's what I said. She could have been surprised." She spins to look at me, her hands on her hips, and I feel it in my fucking cock, just like I always do when she turns my way. "Look," she says, "Vulryn's alive and unharmed. Even with the distance, I'd know if something happened to her. And

I'd feel her grief if Ziselær was harmed. She won't abandon us down here. Let's just follow this tunnel until we reach another branch, and if we haven't heard from her, we'll rest there until we do."

She's right. I know it, even if I fucking hate to admit it. Because she's right a lot, and I need her to be wrong. I keep reinforcing the walls I built after she killed Helga, but it gets harder every time. She's not a monster. She's a soldier who used her fucked-up talents to serve her monarch, like every other soldier does. If I could fuck with people's minds the way she can, I'd probably use it every chance I got to advance the rebellion.

"Lead the way," I mutter, angry at myself for letting her get to me.

We trudge along in silence for a while, as I fight the urge to speak with her. It's the mating bond, I know. It wants me to get to know her and I need to resist it.

Still, I can't deny I'm curious. I've never been to her land, and I've wondered about it for a long time.

I'm also bored as fuck and desperate for some conversation.

"Do you miss it?" I ask when I can't stand the silence any longer. "Your home?"

Dani turns to look at me, the light reflecting in her pretty blue eyes, a half-smile lifting her lips. For a moment, she holds my gaze, an inscrutable expression on her face. Then she nods and looks ahead again.

"Sometimes," she tells me, "but not often. I wasn't a happy child. Alone, bouncing around from home to home."

"We have that in common. I don't remember being young, but what I do remember—from the time I was fifteen or so—was chaos, uncertainty. Life in Revalle is harsh for orphans. I've spent my life alone, other than a couple of close friends. One of them dead now."

"And the lover I took from you," she murmurs.

"And the lover you took from me." I manage to keep my voice from revealing the pain and guilt I still feel.

"I am sorry, you know. I hated some of the things the Monarch asked me to do." She doesn't look at me this time and I wonder what I'd see if she did. Her shoulders are tight, back straight, as if she's reliving some of the fucked up shit the asshole demanded of her.

"Why'd you do them, then?"

"He was all I had," she tells me, her voice sad. "Him and the military. Abandoned children don't have a lot of choices in Njordheim. Women fight or fuck. Unless you're a drudge in someone's home or a trade-master deigns to apprentice you, those are your choices. I like sex as much as the next girl, but I wasn't going to spread my legs for any old asshole with coin. And I have a talent that's not shared by many others. I was a valuable soldier."

"It's like Sifa's, right?" We're still trudging through the cavern, and she hasn't looked back at me, but something inside me relaxes, even without being able to see her face. I hate it, but I crave moments like this, just being together and sharing parts of ourselves.

"She's much stronger than me. She can do a lot more than I can. But our magic is similar."

"Is that strange? That you both have this rare talent, and you both were destined for dragons?"

"It's not so rare," she tells me, and I can hear the shrug in her voice. "Elves have mind magic, although Sifa's is more powerful than most. Maybe fate gave us a similar talent because we were destined for dragons," she muses. "It might help us communicate with them. Or it's just coincidence. I have no idea."

"I can't do anything like it, and I'm destined for a dragon."

"I gave up trying to understand fate a long time ago." Now she turns to me, her eyes flat, brows drawn together, forming little wrinkles between them. "When I realized I'd just used my talent to force my mate to kill his lover—created a permanent enemy in the one male destined to be mine—I knew the fates or the gods or whoever the fuck is twisting our lives couldn't be trusted."

She pauses for a moment, holding my gaze as I stop too. Her eyes are bright again and I can't look away. "When he kissed me instead of digging the knife he held into my heart, then flung the blade across the floor and roared at me to go, I decided that destiny is bullshit. It paired me with a male who would always hate me, as he should, after what I'd done. I decided I would forge my own path, no matter what the fates decreed." She sighs, looking up to the rocks above us.

"When I bonded with Vulryn," she adds a few seconds later, "I wondered if I was wrong. Because she's exactly my kind of crazy. We're perfect together. That, at least, they got right. Then I walked into a cave in Revalle and my gods-damned mate was one of a dozen people sitting there. And now we're here, the only two people sucked into this cave. You hate me, and I get it, but fate's a stubborn bitch. She keeps pulling us together, even if we want nothing more than to push each other away."

My throat and chest constrict as I draw up images of Helga, focusing on those instead of the memories of Dani's lips on mine. Helga and I had been together for months when I killed her. I thought I might have loved her, even considered offering her a ring. I'd never been faithful to a female before her, and I haven't since. She was my friend as well as my lover. And fuck if I didn't betray her while her blood was still warm by kissing the female who'd just caused her death. Because I'm a disloyal bastard.

I'll never forgive myself for that. And I won't forgive Dani for causing it, no matter the reason.

"So, what do we do about it?" I grunt.

Maybe she senses the shift in my emotions. Her bright eyes shutter, and she steps back, crossing her arms over her chest. "We get through this and then try our damnedest to never see each other again," she says. "Ziselær belongs to Matthias and I'm starting to care for the male. Plus, he's a good fuck. Being with him, riding Vulryn, will give me a better life than I deserve."

I nod, smothering the ache in my chest and crush in my balls as I think about Dani and Matthias together. I don't want her.

I can't have her. But I fucking hate the idea of her being with another male, especially the bastard who rides my dragon and spews poison at and about me every chance he gets. Huffing out a deep breath, I start stalking forward again. She's right. We need to just get through this.

I have no idea how long we walk—and climb because the tunnel's ascending quickly—before Vulryn finally reaches out to Dani. I'm ahead of her in the cave, putting distance between us so her scent doesn't keep driving me fucking insane, when I hear her sigh of relief. Turning, I watch as she frowns, her fingers lifting to rest on her jaw as her eyebrows slowly pull together. And then she laughs, a burst of joy blooming within me at the sound, and shakes her head. When her gaze lifts to find mine, she smiles.

"Everyone's fine," she tells me. "A wolf attacked Sifa, then took Thor." This sounds like a question, although it's not. "I don't completely understand, but our connection is still a bit spotty. She'll explain when she sees me." She walks toward me, patting me on the chest as she passes. "You'll be rid of me soon," she says in a playful voice. "Toffer thinks we're a few hours from an exit."

"Thank fuck," I respond as I try to ignore the sparks her touch ignited. "Because I was gonna have to fight you or fuck you if we were stuck here together too much longer," I tease.

I don't know why in all the worlds these words keep spilling out of my mouth. I don't want to flirt with Dani. I told her it's because I'm determined to punish her, but that was a lie and she probably knows it. I want her to like me, for all the wrong reasons.

I want her to choose me over Matthias.

The child in me who remembers nothing of his youth except desperately needing connection and love *needs* my mate and my dragon to choose me. Not the bastard who's currently fucking my female and riding my beast.

And that's so fucked-up—such a betrayal of Helga—that I need to get away from Dani almost as much as I need to be stuck here with her for another week.

She turns at my words, lifting an eyebrow as she cocks her head. "You can try," she says after a moment with a wide smile, "but I don't like your chances."

"That's because I haven't tried yet," I tell her with a wink.

Fuck me. I just can't fucking stop.

She shakes her head at me, spinning to keep striding forward. I can't do shit but follow, so that's what I do.

When the ground collapses under her feet, sucking her into some kind of hole, my heart drops with her. The cave around me, the gods-damned air I breathe, all disappear as my soul searches for Dani. I'm scrambling to reach the narrow tunnel she fell into, desperate to be wherever she is, when I hear her.

"Don't come down here."

"Of course I'm coming down there. I need to get you out."

"It's not stable. It won't hold both of us." I hear a note of fear in her voice, but it's still firm and calm.

"Where are you? What do you need me to do?"

"Shine the light down here so I can look around."

I yank off my top shirt—the long sleeves will burn if I'm not careful, and the undershirt will hide my back. Dropping to my belly, I try to position the torch to throw as much light as possible on Dani. The flames flicker too close to my skin, but there's nothing I can do about that. Dani needs the light, and I'll heal.

She's at least a dragon's length below me, a steep cliff separating us. "Can you climb?" I yell down, my gaze searching the wall within arm's length for some hole or ridge I can set the torch on.

My skin is already starting to heat up, the fire sizzling some of the hair near my elbow, where the torch is closest. I've been burnt once before, and I always thought I'd do anything to avoid that pain. Now I know I was wrong. The burn that's already starting to pebble my skin is a nuisance. The only true pain I feel right now is the anguish of being unable to reach Dani.

"I sprained my ankle, maybe broke it," she tells me, her tone cool as she tries to keep me from freaking the fuck out. "Wish we had a rope," she mutters as the rocks around her jostle.

"What are you doing?" I demand, my heart pounding into my throat.

I'm about to be sick. She's the one trapped down there and I'm going to puke all over her.

That'll definitely win her heart.

"Trying to stand so I can put some weight on my ankle to test it out," she shouts up, knocking a few more rocks off whatever ledge she's sitting on, my stomach dropping to my feet with every clatter or crash.

"Just ... be careful. I'll never get out of here if you can't speak with your dragon."

Everything in the cave goes still. My heart beats so loudly, I wonder if she can hear it. Then her laugh floats up to me. "Is that really why you want me to be careful, Mikkael?"

"What other reason would there be, my sassy spy?" I can't keep the teasing note from my voice.

"My dazzling company, of course," she responds with another laugh. "You'd die of boredom down here if I wasn't around to be your punching bag."

Something about her tone settles in my gut, leaving me frustrated and a little ashamed. Maybe a lot ashamed. I'm speechless for a moment, the pain in her answer reminding me of everything I've done, everything I've said, since she walked into that cave with Fhord and Sifa. She's taken it all—each burst of anger, all of my threats and smears, every dismissal of the reason she did what she did—without complaint. And in return, she's taken care of me when I needed it. She's joined Sifa and Fhord in protecting me.

I'm such an asshole sometimes.

Maybe I don't hate her after all.

"I'm kidding, you know," she calls up when my silence lasts too long.

"I know," I tell her, forcing my voice to be light as I turn my attention back to the flame that's now causing real damage to my arm.

"My ankle's too weak." The voice that floats up to me can't completely hide her distress. "I don't think I can get back up to you. I'll let Vulryn know that Ziselær needs to speak with you so you can get out. Then they can come back with a rope."

"You want me to leave you here for hours?" I demand, not trying to hide my anger.

"It's the best plan."

"It's as fucked as any fucking plan can be. You're stuck on a tiny ledge. You won't make it that long."

"You can't come after me and we don't have a rope, so it's the only plan we've got."

"This is a good wall to climb," I tell her. "I'm gonna find a place to wedge in this torch then come and get you. I won't stand on the ledge since you said it's not strong enough. I'll get close enough for you to get on my back, then carry you up."

"No, you won't," she barks in an angry tone. "We'll both die if you try that."

"I can do this. I've climbed a lot of mountains wearing a heavy pack." I pause, struggling to keep my next words from spilling out. But I lose that battle. I need to say them. I need her to hear them. Because I've realized that I don't hate her. At all. I feel ... something ... for her, beyond the mating bond.

I like her. She's funny and sweet and eternally loyal.

Fucking gorgeous too. Exactly my type.

I want her to live. I want to explore this bond with her.

If she'll have me. Instead of the usurper.

"You're my mate, Dani," I tell her at last. "I can't let you be harmed."

"And you're my mate too. I can't let you kill yourself coming down to get me."

"You don't have a choice," I tell her in the carefree voice I usually use. "I owe you for the three times you've saved my life. I'm coming down."

"You're so gods-damned stubborn."

"Fuck yes, I am."

Moving the torch around—giving myself some relief from the blisters forming on my arm—I search for something that will hold it. When I finally find a large crack that will work, I huff out a sigh of relief. This would have been a short rescue mission without some light to guide me as I go.

Dropping into the cavern feet first, the torch in one hand, my other manages to hold me up while I make my way the short distance I need. When I reach it, I find a divot I can use to wedge the torch into the wall. Another sigh of relief bursts out when it stays, casting light far enough down for me to see Dani's wide, blue eyes.

Fuck, she's pretty. I never let myself *see* her, notice things like the eyes that shift colors the way the sea does or the smile she shares so freely. I pause, pretending to plan my path, and just watch her for a moment. Being so close—doing this for her—settles an uneasy part of me that never seems to rest.

I can do this. Down will be easy. It's the trip back up that may be tough, but I've got no choice. I can't abandon my mate here. Even if she'll never be mine—although the thought of her choosing the usurper instead of me twists my gut—I need to know she lives.

Dani berates me the whole way down, insisting I should have left her if she couldn't make it out herself, but I can feel her relief rippling through the shallow bond I've realized connects us. She knows this is the only plan that gives her a chance of living.

It doesn't take long to reach her, the wall giving me all the divots and clefts I need to descend. I find little shelves strong enough to hold me, and position myself just above the ledge Dani's on, extending my arms so my back is as close to her as I can get.

"Are you sure?" she murmurs, her hand resting on my shoulder. "I don't want to be the cause of your death."

"I'm sure." Spinning my head, I give her a smile of encouragement, then steel myself as she drags herself up—little groans erupting every time she puts pressure on her ankle—and wraps herself around me.

I feel her embrace in every part of my body. My skin tingles; my bones moan; my blood pulses. I still remember the sensation when I kissed her all those years ago, a jolt of pleasure in my lips flashing out to consume me. That kiss pales in comparison to having Dani's body flush with mine. She's a warm bath on a cold day, the whiskey that soothes me as its heat slides down my throat, a fire that melts my frozen heart.

I thought going up would be hard. I thought her weight would pull me down. But it lifts me up, giving me strength and energy and focus.

Which terrifies me. Suddenly, my *need* for her to choose me is primal. It consumes my gut, where a boy who lived his life alone, never accepted, never wanted, craves the approval of his mate and his dragon. It writhes and stretches and grows, pushing into that icy organ she's starting to thaw. It screams at me to fully let go of my anger and guilt and grief and see Dani for what she is. Let her be the mate destiny chose for me.

If she clings to me much longer, my frigid heart will be warm. Raw and vulnerable.

I can't let that happen. She belongs to Matthias, just like my dragon. She's never done anything to suggest she'd choose me over him. Everything she's said, all her actions, have made clear that if I open myself to her, she'll hurt me, like every other person before her, other than Johan and Sifa.

I scale the wall more quickly than I descended, desperate to put space between us. In a few minutes, we're at the top and Dani is grasping the ledge to pull herself up. She scoots out of the way and watches as I scramble over to retrieve the torch, then drag myself out. Flopping onto my back, I throw one arm over my eyes and lay there, trying to stuff all my emotions back into the box that's supposed to hold them before I have to touch her again.

"That was impressive," she whispers, her hand reaching for mine to squeeze it. "I didn't think you'd be able to do it."

I tolerate her touch for a second then pull away. "I've climbed a lot of mountains," I tell her again. Because she doesn't need to know how my body reacted to having her so close. "We should go." Standing, I pull on my shirt, then help her get up next to me and wrap my arm around her waist to hold her up. The ecstasy of having my mate so close drowns out every other sensation, even the burn of my scorched arm.

We've hobbled along for an hour or more—me studiously ignoring the comfort of her touch—when Dani's expression goes still, and she turns away from me as she listens to whatever Vulryn has to say. When she looks at me again, her face lights up with her smile.

"Maybe the gods are watching out for us after all," she says. "Whatever happened to the cave when I fell was widespread. Toffer felt a hole open up nearby. They didn't tell me because they didn't want to get our hopes up, but the dragons managed to dig a passage big enough to go through. They're in the cavern with us. We should see them any minute."

As if summoned, Fhord, Sifa, Matthias, and Toffer turn a corner, grins emerging as they do.

Everyone except Matthias. That bastard raises an eyebrow when he sees Dani and me holding each other.

"I sprained my ankle," Dani explains, an apology in her voice for some fucking reason. "Mikkael is helping me."

Matthias cocks his head, throwing a bitter glare at me before striding over to take her weight. For a moment, I think she's going to push him away, tell him I've got her. That she'll stay with me, let me support her.

Instead, she sighs, eyes turning to search mine as the corners of her lips drop. "Maybe we could be friends," she whispers. And then she leans toward Matthias. She tenses as his hand rests on her hip but doesn't stop the kiss he takes from her.

I move so the male my mate chose can take my place at her side, and turn away.

"Keep telling yourself that," I mutter as I stride into the cavern.

I don't look back. There's nothing behind me worth seeing.

And my heart grows cold again, exactly as it should.

CHAPTER TWENTY-SIX

DANI

THE SADDEST THING

A s I watch Mikkael walk away, my heart dropping into my feet, Matthias's hand snakes out, knuckles pressing against my chin to draw my gaze to him.

"Ignore him," he snarls. "He'll be gone soon enough, and it will just be us again."

I twist my head away, dislodging the hand trying to hold me in place, and glance at Mikkael one more time. "He saved me. I'll be his friend if he'll have me."

A deep groan rumbles from Matthias, and he reaches for my chin again, this time more gently. "He makes me crazy. We can't be around him. Any of us. It's too fucking confusing."

"And I told you, you need to be okay with him. Fhord and Sifa are part of my life and he's part of theirs. He'll be around. You can't lose it every time he is."

"Then tell him to stop his shit. You know what he was doing while you were down there, right? Trying to talk to my dragon. Acting like Ziselær would betray me, after a century together, if he just got to know Mikkael. Ziselær is mine. You are mine. He needs to accept that. All this bullshit he's throwing around is fucking with my dragon's head. I don't want it to fuck with yours too."

"Let me worry about that." Lifting my hand to rest on his cheek, I smile. "I'll ask Sifa to talk to him. And we'll drop him off today. She promised."

He jerks his chin down, a warning still embedded in the gaze that holds mine, then spins to start walking with me toward Vulryn. We'll wrap my ankle, and I'll ride her, even when we can't fly, until it can hold my weight again. I heal quickly, so it shouldn't take long.

What happened with Thor? I ask my dragon when Matthias settles me on the ground, my back resting against her as he goes to gather bandages. *You said something about a wolf?*

An old wolf-god attacked the starry female, but he could not capture her so he took the feline to draw the starry female away. The feline escaped the wolf's mouth...

Thor was in the wolf's mouth and got out?

The feline escaped the wolf's mouth.

Holy fuck. That's impressive. A laugh bubbles out of me as my thoughts form an image of Thor battling his way out of some enormous wolf's mouth. Everything and everyone in Sifa's life seems to possess wisps of her boundless strength and courage.

The feline has earned the respect of all the dragons. He is a ferocious beast.

Can you speak with him the way Toffer can?

The troll speaks for us. We know the feline. He belongs to us, as our male and the starry female belong to us.

Another laugh breaks free. The bitch of a cat, who hates everyone, somehow has won the hearts of four of the most dangerous beasts in this land. Or is it five? *Does Ziselær also care for Thor?*

My drake would fly through fire to save the feline. He belongs to all of us.

Fuck do I love every single one of these soft-hearted beasts. *So Thor escaped from the wolf? Then what happened?*

The feline repelled the wolf until we arrived...

What do you mean, "repelled the wolf"?

The feline has sharp claws. The wolf used surprise to capture him initially. When he no longer could rely on surprise, the wolf could not capture the feline.

Thor's a badass.

The feline is ferocious. It is how he earned our respect.

Okay, Thor escaped and repelled the wolf ... then what?

We arrived to find the feline and the wolf staring at each other. The wolf tried one more time to capture the feline, but the feline drew blood. The wolf then threatened the starry female, telling her she does not belong in this world and he had come to take her back.

He offered to take her back to her world? And Toffer too?

He did not offer; he demanded. She and the troll will not return to their world. He would take the starry female against her will.

They've decided to stay here?

They decided long ago to stay here. They will not leave our male or the fire beast behind.

How do you know all this stuff before I do?

I am more inquisitive than you. She's quiet for a moment before adding, *It is one of your failings, but I will gather the information you need.*

One *of my failings? How many other failings do I have?*

This pause is longer—is the uppity beast compiling a list? Finally, she snorts quietly. *My drake's rider returns.*

I turn my head to stare at her, gaze flat. *We'll discuss this some other time.*

Perhaps.

Stubborn beast. But gods-damn, I don't know what I'd do without her.

Matthias drags my attention away as he kneels next to me, lifting my foot to look again at the ankle. It's bruised, but we don't think it's broken. Thank the gods. Because that would be fucked. Gently, a little smile on his face the entire time, he pulls off my shoe, wraps my ankle, then tugs my pant leg over the bandage and puts my shoe back on. Neither of us speaks while he does it.

When he's done, he sits next to me, his back leaning against Vulryn, and takes my hand, linking our fingers. "If Ziselær and I left the group for a while, would you and Vulryn come with us?"

"We've talked about this. We're not ready to leave them yet."

"Just for a few days. I want to find our way back to who we were in the cove. When I'm alone with you, I can be myself. With the others—with that fucker Mikkael—I'm on the defense all the time. I'm one of the Dróttning's most trusted soldiers. I've spent more than a hundred years being the bastard she expects me to be. Maybe if we're alone, we can find ourselves again. I can find me again."

"You're right that I don't like the bastard that's been coming out. I won't be with that man. But I can't go yet. Let's see if it's better when we drop off Mikkael. We'll decide from there."

"I don't want to wait." Matthias's voice is firm, almost angry. "I want to leave today. Now."

"Then go. I'm not holding you back. I'm also not going with you."

"Fuck, you're hard-headed."

"You need to get used to that, too. I'm not some helpless female you can order around."

He stares at me, his eyes as fierce as his voice. "Ziselær needs to get away from Mikkael. We'll fly alone today. If we don't find you along the way, we'll meet you at the next cave tonight."

"Do you know how to find it?"

"I'll speak with Fhord, get the location from him."

Now it's my turn to watch him. Something feels off, but I can't read him when he's like this. He's right that we need to be alone again. We can't do it yet, but we will soon. "Be safe, Matthias."

"You too, my randy Dani."

I laugh and shake my head. "Asshole," I mutter as I lean forward to kiss him.

"Wench," he grunts before his lips take mine.

Mikkael's image, the long-ago feel of his lips on mine, the peace I felt when he carried me in the cave—like I was exactly where I was supposed to be after years of wandering lost—spill into my head, but I push them out. Matthias is my destiny now. I won't let Mikkael and the stupid mating bond confuse me.

Ziselær and Matthias are in the air within minutes, Vulryn and I watching in silence as they fly away.

I'm not sure if I trust him.

I trust my drake. That is enough for now.

It'll have to be.

We eat—thank the gods, because cave food is shit—and leave within an hour. It'll take a while to get to the rebel camp and drop off Mikkael, and I can tell everyone is hoping Matthias doesn't catch up with us until after we've done that. Sounds like he was quite the asshole while I was trapped with Mikkael, destroying some of the trust he'd earned.

When we're finally airborne and I'm settled into the rhythm of Vulryn's flight, I let myself glance at Mikkael, catching his gaze. He sneers and drops his eyes, focusing on Sifa's back for a moment before turning away from me. And my stomach drops. I know I need to be with Matthias. I know I can't bring Mikkael into my life, forcing Ziselær into an impossible situation.

But I want him. It's not just the mating bond, although that drew me to him initially. I like being around him. I love his teasing, and the flirting he swears isn't flirting, and the way he looks at me when he doesn't expect to be caught.

And while Matthias is handsome and sexy and a fun fuck, Mikkael is everything I've always wanted. He's dark where Matthias is pale; swaggers where Matthias stalks; and purrs where Matthias growls.

Matthias satisfies me. But my body craves Mikkael's touch.

Fhord's right. Fate, the gods—whatever is manipulating our lives—is fucked.

And I can't deny that Matthias is right too. I need to get away from Mikkael to get my head clear.

We've flown for two hours when Matthias returns, a smile on his face as Ziselær draws close to Vulryn.

Ask Ziselær why they're back so soon.

His rider wanted to be with you. He will fly with us for the rest of the way.

Ask your drake to tell him I'm glad he's back. It's not completely true—I wish we'd dropped Mikkael off first—but I'm happy he's dealt with whatever led him to fly away, and he's ready to be with us again.

She turns her head and I do the same, smiling at Matthias and his dragon. And we continue to fly.

The sun is high above us, beating down on the scarf I wear around my head to ride Vulryn, when my dragon tenses. I jerk my head up, looking around, and see all of them alert and focused. *What is it?*

Other dragons approach. Our male and the starry female also have sensed soldiers on the ground. They are closer than they should be. We should have recognized their presence before now.

Where do we go?

I am asking the fire beast and the sun beast. They will speak with their riders and direct us.

The next few seconds drag by, a lifetime of fears spilling out in a moment of time. Finally, Vulryn's words drop into my head.

We will fly to the west, away from the dragons and the soldiers. Many approach, moving fast. They will be difficult to fight, but too many soldiers blanket the ground. Our male believes the dragons hope to force us down, where the soldiers will kill or capture us. We are to stay airborne at all costs.

A strange mix of anticipation and dread washes through me, triggering tingles along my arms and legs, and bubbles in my gut. I don't know if I want to grin like the fighter I was born to be or get sick. Maybe both.

Would you forgive me if I puked on you?

The bitchy dragon gives me the cheekiest side-eye I've ever seen, and I barely hold back the laugh. *I would not.*

I'll do what I can to control myself, then.

Yes, you will.

I shake my head, enjoying a moment of levity before the shitstorm hits, then turn to look at Matthias. And I realize my laughter is the last thing he needs to see. He has defied the Dróttning, traveling with her fiercest enemies, and he's about to face her forces, and maybe her. Unless he betrays us right now, we've taken his choice from him. He'll be her enemy too.

Dipping my chin, I hold his gaze as I try to relay to him that I understand. I'm with him.

One side of his lips curves up—probably all the smile he can manage—and he nods back at me.

Everything is about to change.

Vulryn is throwing everything she can into the flight, the dragons holding a tight formation in the air, and I can't do anything except struggle to control the nervous energy rippling through me. My skin feels like it's covered in ants—little legs racing up and down every part of me—and the bubbles in my gut have turned into a swarm of butterflies. I'm so restless and anxious, I'm almost relieved when the dragons appear behind us.

Eight beasts follow us, all of them ridiculously fast. We'd hoped to outrun them, but we won't be able to, I can tell. The dragons will fight and many will die. I can only pray to the gods who abandoned me that our beasts survive.

Our male wants to turn and attack. We will grow too tired if we continue to fly.

Are we far enough away from the soldiers to risk it? What if someone falls to the ground?

The river beneath us runs fast. It will stop most pursuit.

Okay. Follow his lead and I'll hold on.

I will be very angry if you fall. Do not let me drop you.

I wouldn't think of it. I'll hold on.

Vulryn's quiet for a few seconds, then speaks again, this time her voice full of pride. *The starry female asks if you will share your memories with her. She believes she can attack the other beasts in their minds, confuse them in their assault. Your memories will help her.*

Maybe. I've never tried it, but I don't see why not.

She will have our male's power and asks to take yours as well. With you three, she may be able to hold images in all the dragons' thoughts.

Tell her I'll open myself to her as soon as we attack.

We fly for another minute, maybe more, and then as one, the dragons pivot in the air, holding their formation as they face the Dróttning's beasts and prepare to fight. I do the same, gathering my will as I harness the memories of my most gruesome kills to feed to the beasts, thankful to have something to do other than hold on.

The dragons must have decided already who they each would attack, because they move like dancers, spinning around the others in synchrony to face their enemies. Vulryn soars toward the largest beast—because she's a badass bitch—and I close my eyes to trust my dragon and do my part.

The process of feeding memories to strangers is so familiar after all these years, it's almost heartwarming. Almost. A rush of power washes through me as I begin, sending a shiver of excitement down my spine as Sifa's magic reaches out to me. I drop my shields to her, giving the ferocious elf everything she wants to take.

I tighten my hold on my dragon and start to replay my memories, getting sucked into them. Because to feed them to anyone, I must live them again. And some are fucked.

The male who'd eaten fruit from one of the Monarch's prized plants and gave it back only after I cut it from his stomach at the Monarch's order. I refused to dig inside him for it, so pried his stomach from his body—along with everything else in the area—and found the fruit's remnants in the midst of the liver he'd eaten for lunch.

Fuck, did that stink.

Another male, who'd forced his dick into the wrong woman, raping one of the Kastali's servants. My orders were to return with his cock. I did, after giving the poor girl a knife and time with him bound the way he'd bound her. She worked out an enormous amount of rage that day.

And walked away smiling.

The female who'd demeaned the Monarch's mother decades ago, then disappeared before the Monarch could take his vengeance. She'd called the petite queen regnant a "titless witch" and lost her tits as a result. The Monarch wanted her alive when I took them and forbade me from causing any other injury. She lived for hours as her blood slowly seeped away.

I don't know what the Monarch did with the tits, and I don't want to know.

I'm snapped from the reverie that always consumes me when I manipulate minds with Vulryn's frantic screech. *No!*

My eyes fly open, and I search the air, trying to figure out who lives ... and who doesn't. Tindera is right in front of me, attacking a massive purple beast with a viciousness I couldn't have imagined. She's the only one fighting, Astarot hovering next to her, flame rippling from his snout. They're alone in the sky so my eyes track down to the ground.

Eight dragons lay beneath us, their bodies broken.

When I see why Vulryn cried, my eyes fill.

Seven of the beasts belong to the Dróttning.

One belongs to us.

Khirta is on her back, her eyes wide and unseeing, her throat destroyed. If Tindera's anger is any indication, the purple dragon tore out Khirta's throat as one of the last attacks in a battle our dragons nearly had won.

My heart is in my throat and twice its size as I gulp down the bile pushing up from my stomach. Memories of the green dragon fill my thoughts and pull the tears from my eyes. I don't try to stop them. Khirta deserves the tribute of my tears.

I can only watch as Tindera uses a move she learned from Vulryn, spinning beneath the other beast and then feinting to her side, latching on to the wing exposed as she tries to follow. When Tindera's claws have captured the wing completely, destroying the dragon's ability to fly, she spins again, leveraging against the dragon's body—well out of reach of teeth desperate to dislodge the gold dragon—and pulls.

It's not a fast death. Tindera is frantically beating her own wings to hold herself aloft as she slowly yanks the dragon's wing from its side. A screech from the purple beast turns into a wail and then a moan. When the wing rips free, sending the purple beast plummeting to the ground, Tindera screams her anger and grief into the air.

Fhord's gaze is locked on Sifa's, tears rolling down her cheeks too, as their dragons close the gap between them and Astarot nuzzles Tindera's cheek. I drag my eyes away and look around for Matthias, wondering where he and Ziselær are.

My drake and his rider are not here. I do not know when they left or where they are.

I'm disappointed, but I can't blame him. If he'd stayed here, he'd be fighting against the Dróttning before he's decided whether he'll stand with her or us. I'd probably have left too if I were him.

Maybe he'll still meet us at the cave.

My drake will find us. If not today, soon. I am sure of it.

My eyes fall to Khirta again, and I struggle to stop the flow of tears. I can cry more later. Now, I need to be strong for my dragon.

She never got a chance to meet her destined rider. For some reason, that's the saddest thing of all. Khirta had one rider—an evil bastard—and didn't meet the male or female the fates had chosen for her.

The clover dragon killed her destined rider. At her rider's order.

What?

Many years ago, the clover dragon and her rider came across her destined rider. As the wyrm demands, her rider ordered the male's death and the clover dragon complied.

Fuck. That's horrific.

The clover dragon never forgave herself for heeding the command to kill her destined rider. She spoke of it occasionally. She suffered much when that male died. It is why she refused to kill our male and the others when her wyrm-chosen rider demanded it. She would not inflict that pain on the sun beast. The clover dragon and the sun beast were strong allies.

I turn to look again at the brave green dragon as our beasts turn to leave her behind. I wish we could give her a proper burial. She deserved so much more than to be left in a field to rot.

This is why we fight.

And this is why we must win.

MATTHIAS

DID YOU KNOW?

"**Y**OU TOLD ME I'D be able to capture them if I attacked with sufficient force."

The Dróttning's angry enough to flay me herself. She lost eight dragons today—eight of her fiercest beasts—and watched Fhord and the others slip through her fingers again. I'm just as pissed because Dani got away too. I lied to her about a lot of shit, but I told the gods-damned truth about one thing. She's mine and I will get her back. Next time, though, she won't be leaving this Nest.

I'll be on the rack if I can't talk myself out of this, but maybe I'd welcome it. That northern bitch has gotten under my skin. A bit of torture might be just what I need to fix my shit—take back the control that wavers too gods-damned much around her—and be the soldier the Dróttning needs me to be. For a moment, I'd even considered abandoning my liege to join the traitors. Thank fuck that lunacy disappeared when we left the cove. One mental caress from the Dróttning smacked my shit into place, reminding me where my loyalties lie and why.

Ziselær's pissed at me—I've never seen the bastard so angry—but he'll get over it. I hid my plans from him, communicating with the Dróttning in the way she taught me to evade even my dragon's knowledge. He would have turned on me and deserves the punishment he'll receive today for ceding his balls to his draikana.

If he doesn't get his shit together after that, I'll make him wish for today's penalty the next time. I need him to fight with me for the Dróttning, but after we put down this puny little rebellion, he'll be on the chains long enough to crush that pathetic heart he's developed since his mating.

If he can't be the dragon I need with Vulryn in his life, I'll put her down.

I might keep her rider, though. She's got quite the cunt. And like I told her, she's mine for as long as I want her. She'll fight me at first, but I'll enjoy a defiant Dani more than a willing one. I like a little fight before a fuck. Or, better yet, a lot of fight.

The Dróttning's waiting for my answer, so I drag my thoughts away from Dani's cunt and focus on staying off the rack. "The elves have learned to whisper into dragons' minds," I report. "Neither my dragon nor I knew this. I'm certain Vulryn didn't know. She wouldn't have kept this secret from her drake. I suspect Vulryn's rider also was ignorant. I couldn't have learned this fact before I came to you."

"Couldn't?" she spits, flecks of her slaver sprinkling my face. I ignore it because she will fuck me up if I try to wipe it away, and hold her gaze. "You said they'd accepted you, even planned to take you with them to a rebel camp. I'd have waited and attacked overnight if you hadn't convinced me otherwise."

"Your plan would have been the wiser one," I agree, dropping my head to stare at my feet. "I am yours to punish as you will for my lapse in judgment."

"I don't want your blood. At least, not yet," she adds with a hint of a smile. "I want you to fix this. How did you err so badly?"

"They hadn't previously used this new mode of attack, and as I said, I'm certain Ziselær's draikana and her rider didn't know. Perhaps they attempted it for the first time today. We'll be ready for it next time."

"Did it impact your dragon as well?"

"It didn't. They were able to focus their illusions on the attackers alone. Ziselær learned of it from another dragon."

"Tell me exactly what my dragons experienced. None were coherent enough to relay information, even to their riders, as they fought the elves' manipulation."

"Ziselær was close enough to experience some of it with them, as they opened their minds to each other, trying to join together to fight. They failed."

"What?" she demands, her voice a pitch higher as her frustration seeps through. "What did the elves do?"

"They used their magic on the dragons. The mind manipulation they've been able to do on humans..."

"One of the reasons elves are so dangerous and must be imprisoned," she interjects, as if she's trying to convince me of something.

"Proof of your wisdom those many years ago," I agree, pausing to let her say more if she wants. She's impatient, though, waving at me to continue.

"The elves manipulated the dragons' minds. Ziselær recognized his draikana's rider as they fed the dragons memories of her kills. They were vicious but the dragons weren't bothered by that. The problem was they lost the ability to concentrate on their fights. The illusions in their minds occupied too much of their focus. The rebel dragons are skilled, and your dragons couldn't beat them, even with their better numbers."

She watches me for a long time, perhaps deciding whether or not to punish me. She should have attacked overnight, as she planned, but I worried Ziselær and I wouldn't be able to leave the cave without somebody noticing. This gave us the best chance of slipping away, to join the rebels again when the Dróttning chooses to send me—if Ziselær can keep our secret to himself.

I'll make sure he does. My punishment will remind him he's mine and must always choose me and the Dróttning over his draikana. I'm looking forward to it. It's been too many months since I heard him scream.

When the Dróttning speaks again, her voice is soft. She's setting a trap for me, and I hope I find my way out. "Did you want me to succeed in this attack, Matthias?"

My heart pounds out of beat seven times as I watch her, scrambling to think of the best response. My throat suddenly is so dry, I'm not sure I'll be able to swallow again. She waits in silence as I take two deep inhales and finally open my mouth to respond.

"I would never suggest an attack I believed might fail, my liege. Ziselær and I want nothing more than to see those rebels dead and to bring his draikana and her rider back to the Nest. I have failed you too many times since Ziselær recognized his draikana. If my survival were not so important to you now, I would willingly take my own life as penance. Once we've defeated the rebels, I will offer it to you, if you would have it."

"That's a very nice sentiment, rider," the Dróttning says as she lifts a hand to pat my cheek, hard. "But you can see why I would question you. You even admit it. Since Vulryn and Dani entered this land, you and Ziselær have become weak. I cannot trust you. I wonder if I shouldn't rid myself of both of you. Slowly, of course. You do not deserve a quick death."

"I would ask for a reprieve, my liege. Let us fight for you. Let us join you in squashing the rebellion that would thrust you from your gods-given throne. When we have succeeded—when Fhord and the elves are in Helheim or the elven prison, where they belong—my life is yours. Take it in any way you see fit."

Again, the Dróttning simply watches me, her eyes inscrutable. Finally, though, she dips her chin.

"Granted. This time. If you fail me again, you'll go to the rack and Ziselær to the chains. I won't give you another chance."

"I would not deserve another chance if I failed you again."

"Good. Go to the dragon-master. Report your dragon's experience and your knowledge of the rebels. Be available to her as much as she needs to plan our next attack. The dragons must be prepared to protect their minds from those wicked elves."

I bow deeply, my gaze cast to the floor, and wait for her to release me. She holds me there for a long time before muttering, "Stand" and spinning around to stride away from me. I watch her go, thanking the fucking gods I'm still alive and free.

Time to go fuck with my dragon.

He knows what to expect when I walk into the chamber in which dragons are punished, where I told him to go when we got back to the Nest. His gaze holds mine, anxiety rippling off him in waves instead of the anger that grew as we came here. He's never learned to appreciate pain, even after a century of it. It's one of the things that makes disciplining him so fun. Most beings eventually enjoy the pain I give them, and then I have to move on to someone else. It's no good for me if they like what I'm doing.

Did you know? I demand. I wasn't completely honest with the Dróttning, but I'm often not. I learned long ago to tell her whatever I must to walk out of the room unharmed. I told her what she needed to hear—that neither my dragon nor I realized what the elves would do. If Ziselær did know, I'll have to make sure he *never* tells the Dróttning. That would piss her right off.

No! His response is emphatic. He's convinced Vulryn had no idea. He got hints of her surprise and pride when she spoke with Astarot before they attacked the Dróttning's beasts but no specifics. He would have told me if he knew.

Do you trust your draikana?

Yes. This time he's a bit less emphatic, but I sense no doubt. She wouldn't keep something like this from him.

I hold his gaze for a moment, letting him see the anticipation I'm positive brightens my eyes. And then I grin and watch him collapse, as he always does. His back sways as he closes his eyes, dropping his chin to the ground and releasing a heavy sigh.

What have you done wrong this time? We always start this way. It's important for him to acknowledge how he erred, the reason he's being punished. He won't learn otherwise. And this is all about teaching him. Even if I do enjoy the fuck out of it.

Mikkael. He tries to inject his response with ire, but I can see through it. That bastard wormed his way into my dragon's heart—the gods-damned heart I've been trying to beat out of Ziselær for decades—and clung there. Twice, my dragon refused to do what the Dróttning demands and kill his destined rider. And then he convinced me to save the fucker's life.

I still can't believe I fell for it. His frailty infected me too. I'm getting rid of all that shit today.

How should I discipline you? This is always the most important question. Ziselær tries to walk the line between proposing enough and too much. If he doesn't offer something sufficiently harsh, I go overboard, inflicting more pain than he deserves because he misjudged the severity of his failure. But I always do at least as much as he suggests, so sometimes I go overboard in this way too.

It's all good by me. Ziselær's the only one with regrets if the punishment outweighs the offense.

He plasters himself to the ground and extends his wings, giving them to me as he did to that little green dragon. Fuck, am I glad she's dead. At least one good thing came out of today's fuck-up. Khirta would have been a constant reminder to Dani that I can be a cruel male. But she'll learn that enough soon anyway.

Which reminds me. *Did you tell your draikana that we weren't honest with the green beast? That your actions were at my command, not the Dróttning's?*

He's silent for a long time and I feel guilt wash through him. Dragons are honest with their mates. It's a crushing betrayal to lie. Still, he responds as he must. *No.* He kept my secret. I don't give a shit about Fhord and his elf, but Dani cared about Khirta. I want her to warm up to me again at some point, even if I will enjoy the fight until then. She'd probably never forgive me if she knew I'm the one who demanded every single thing Ziselær did to the little dragon.

What should I do to your wings? I ask as I accept this part of his proposed penance—one of the most extreme, because he knows how badly he fucked up—and step toward the table that holds the blades, selecting two of my favorites.

Again, he's quiet. Finally, he shares a memory with me of the third time I disciplined him, when I carved off his wingtips. He shrieked like a hatchling while I did it and then wailed for days. I'm pleased with his offer. If his reaction—and the reaction of every other dragon I've punished this way—is any indication, that shit hurts. Not quite as bad as other things I can do, but enough. And he was smart to choose a sanction that will cause tremendous pain, while still allowing him to fly. It'll sting like a bitch when the wind passes over his wounds at the speeds we'll need to travel, but that's true of anything I would do.

Both of them? I ask. I'll do both, whatever his answer. The only question is whether I'll stop there.

Both, he responds, his voice small. Another reason this is necessary. My dragon should never be small.

Good, I tell him, walking over to praise him for doing so well. This is the only time I'll give him that kind of approval, and it's only because the dragon-master has assured me it's an important part of training.

I do listen to some females, despite what Dani says about me. I may not like it, but one or two of the Dróttning's cunts earned my respect.

Well, maybe it's just the one. The dragon-master is damned good at what she does.

I don't bother sharpening the blades. Other riders might—because they're feeble and emasculated, too soft to their beasts—but I think it's important to take my time as I carve. Sharp blades sometimes move too quickly, and they always cut too cleanly. I like needing to put my back into the punishment, maybe even having to saw at Ziselær a little bit. He learns his lesson well on those days. It's good for both of us.

I approach him slowly, letting him feel my disappointment in him. *I'm only doing this because I must*, I remind my dragon. *I'd prefer an obedient beast, who always heeds my commands. When you defy me, you defy the Dróttning. And she does not tolerate defiance.*

Atone, he responds, stretching his wings further. He may hate the pain but at least I've taught him to crave the correction. He knows I do this because I care for him. It's the only expression of love—or as close to that emotion as I can feel—that he'll ever receive from me.

I nod, finally dropping to my knees to get to work. A grin emerges on my face with the first cut, and I grunt as I work the blade through the feathers, finally meeting skin. Running the blade back and forth along the path I've chosen, savoring the whimpers tumbling out of Ziselær's mouth, I start to carve.

What have you learned today? I demand. It's important to make him talk through the pain. I can't let him get lost in emotions as I work, so I focus him on the things that matter.

Yours, he tells me. The fates can fuck themselves. He's mine, regardless of what they say. Just like Dani is.

And what will you do the next time I order his death?

Comply. He's not able to eliminate the sorrow from his response but I'd have been a fool to expect it. I understand the dragon-rider bond. He's connected to that bastard and while Mikkael lives, Ziselær will feel for him. I just need to make sure he fears and respects me enough to kill those feelings dead. A couple of wingtips should do it but if not, I'll take a lot more next time.

You're going to slay Mikkael, I agree as I work my way through the wingtip. He hasn't sniveled yet, but it's coming. I can feel the agony wrapping around his limbs and squeezing him, as his sensitive wings trigger nerves throughout his body. I'm getting covered with blood that spurts out as I carve, and I'm starting to get hard already, thinking about my bloody cock plunging into ... someone. I haven't decided who yet.

I'll focus on that when I'm done. I'm here for my dragon this afternoon.

The time hasn't been right yet so I've let you get away with disobeying me, but it won't happen again. We probably won't kill him in front of your draikana or her rider because we're still trying to be nice to them. But we'll get that fucker alone sometime and when we do, you will burn him.

Comply, he repeats, this time with a little less emotion. He's already beaten, the weak-ass bitch.

I finish with the first wingtip, yanking it away to break the last few strands of sinew holding it to his body, and fling it toward him. Nice shot, I tell myself as I watch it flop directly in front of his snout, splashing blood onto his feathers. He flinches, closing his eyes as his breaths grow heavier, and I can't hold back the laugh.

One more to go, I announce, standing to stride over to his other wing, patting him on the nose as I go. *You'll thank me when I'm done*, I remind him. *We're doing this for you.*

Yes, he responds, finally managing to calm himself.

Dropping down, I grab his wing and get started on the second tip. He gasps weakly, holding his breath for a moment, then exhales. His eyes open and he looks at me, an apology in their depths.

My blade really needs to be sharpened, but I can't stop now. Pushing and pulling to get through this one, I begin again with my training. *You know you'll need to destroy that bastard Mikkael, but I don't think you've accepted what else you'll have to do if you flout my order again.*

No. This is a whisper, barely reaching me.

Yes, Ziselær. It's necessary. Our loyalty is to the Dróttning. Vulryn and her rider have proven they don't share our allegiance. They will never fly for the Dróttning, so they are of no value to her. Such beasts are not allowed to live.

I pause for a moment, gritting my teeth as I force my blade through one of the bones, sawing at the stubborn bastard. At last, a minute or more after I started, my knife slices completely through. And Ziselær finally starts to scream. He held out for a while this time. The screams always come, though.

When he's done squealing like a bitch and I'm nearly finished with this wingtip—just a few more inches to go—I turn to catch his gaze so he sees how serious I am.

You need to understand what will happen if you rebel again. I'm going to bring them to the Nest so they're here for us when we want them. I like your draikana's rider—she's a good fuck—but I don't give one little shit about the dragon. When I tell you to kill Mikkael, you will *kill him. If you don't, I'll do it myself, and then I'll take you to your draikana's cage and order you to destroy her. If you refuse again, I'll butcher her while you watch, then give you to the Dróttning. Your draikana can die fast by your fire or slowly by my hand. Your choice.*

Ziselær doesn't respond, the pussy. He's lost his fight. *That copper hussy is fucking with your head and she's fucking with your loyalties. I won't tolerate it. I'd sooner kill Vulryn than lose you to her.*

I rip away the second wingtip and toss it at him. This one hits his snout—a patch of red against his blue feathers—before falling to the ground. Barking out a laugh, I walk over and run my hand through his blood, then turn and walk away.

I don't look back. My cock's hard and I'm gonna get fucked.

CHAPTER TWENTY-EIGHT

SIFA

WHERE DO WE START?

T HE CAVE FEELS EMPTY without Khirta. She'd become one of us, every bit as much as Astarot, Tindera, and Vulryn.

Tindera managed to save Toffer and Thor, thank the gods. She'd just killed one of the final dragons when she turned and saw the purple beast—Fafnir—fighting Khirta. She nearly made it in time to save our little green dragon, but Fafnir managed to rip out her throat before Tindera could get there. Tindera's claws caught Toffer and Thor before they fell; she settled them behind me on Astarot and then attacked Fafnir.

It all happened so fast, and now Khirta's gone. I'm still numb. I don't think I've fully processed the loss. But that will come, probably in a wave of emotions when I least expect it.

We went to a different place than where we planned to meet Matthias. Fhord saw him nod to one of the other riders and leave as soon as the fighting started. Maybe Dani's right and he left because he's not yet ready to commit to our cause.

Or maybe he betrayed us. Either way, we're not giving him a chance to send the Dróttning's forces after us tonight. We're in a large cave hidden in a small island just offshore that nobody ever visits. It took us a while to get here, but it's worth it.

I turn my head to look at Fhord as he steps behind me and wraps his arms around my waist. "How are you?"

"I don't know whether I'm more angry or sad. Khirta didn't need to die."

"None of them did. Tindera's devastated about her and also buried in guilt over how many of the Thunder we killed today. Beasts she once considered family. Dragons shouldn't be fighting other dragons."

"We need to put an end to it."

"It's time to get serious about gathering others who might be sympathetic to our cause. We'll sleep tonight—because we all fucking need to sleep—and tomorrow we'll go first thing in the morning to the dragon we think is most likely to turn. He's close, which is part of the reason I led us here. We can probably track down three a day if we really push ourselves. Then we attack the dragon training center. Free the beasts being held. Show the Thunder we're fighting for them."

I turn, wrapping my arms around his neck. Smiling as I draw his lips to mine, I whisper, "Good fucking plan, Fhord."

"We'll destroy her, dragon by dragon," he responds before closing the distance between our lips.

We're well rested when we take off in the morning. Mikkael's flying with me and we've decided not to drop him off, for now. Matthias is gone and we can use another fighter. Vulryn's worried about Ziselær—something happened to him, and she felt echoes of her drake's intense pain yesterday—but he's alive. He's too far away to speak with her and it's driving her a little mad. There's nothing she can do about it now, though, so we're moving forward until we can find Ziselær and Matthias again.

Toffer and Thor ride with Vulryn because she's worried about them after what happened to Khirta. She doesn't trust the other dragons to protect them. She's so fierce with such a soft heart. I've really grown to love that copper beast.

As Fhord promised, the first dragon is close. This time, he's with his rider because both are on the Dróttning's list as possible sympathizers with the rebellion. Like before, the dragons drop us off and then approach the beast, Glabor, and his rider, Bella. We wait in silence; I'm too lost in my thoughts to speak and assume that's true for everyone else. The loss of Khirta weighs on me, and I'm not sure I'll ever get over it.

Come, Astarot says, just as Fhord and Dani lift their heads to listen to their dragons. He's pleased and knows we will be too.

"I've been wondering when you'd start approaching other dragons," Bella says as we stride forward. She's standing next to a beast as white as snow, hands in her pockets and no blades on her belt. I glance down to see them lying on the ground next to her feet. She smiles when she catches my gaze. "I wanted to make sure you know I'm no threat to you."

"Nor are we to you," I tell her, removing my hands from my blades, where they usually rest when I meet strangers. "So, you were expecting us?"

"We know what happened with Iyanshe."

"How? I took her memories of the meeting."

"She shared it with an ally while you were meeting with her. The dragons were connected when the Dróttning dropped in, and you started yanking out Iyanshe's memories."

"Is she okay?" My heart's in my throat as I ask this question. I don't know if I want the answer.

"She is," Bella tells me with a smile. "She slept for two days, but you did her no permanent harm."

A knot in my gut unwinds as I release a soft breath I didn't realize I was holding. "I hated that I had to do it," I murmur as my lips tip up at the sides.

"We know why you did it. And we're grateful you were so careful. We've told Iyanshe what she needs to know. She's made a decision. We all have."

"Who is we?" Fhord's voice is tense. He suspects a trick, and I don't blame him. But I sense no deception from Bella. She's eager and relieved. Also very happy. She's been waiting for us.

"Everyone on the list you received," she responds with a grin.

"How do you know about that?" Now Fhord's really suspicious.

"One of us planned to travel to Lumaria when we learned you were there, but you left before we could. Friends on the island told us you were going to Revalle to deal with Aksell."

She smirks as she glances at her dragon. "I'm so fucking glad he's gone. It's about time."

She shakes her head, turning back to look at us. "We'd been searching for a way to reach you without the Dróttning learning of it. Couldn't do it, so we decided to encourage you to come find us. We threw together a list of dragons we knew to be sympathetic to the rebellion. A connection to Aksell got the list into his hands. It was a risk. We had a plan to retrieve it if you delayed a day, since we couldn't take a chance the Dróttning would get it. But you went as planned and set this in motion."

"Why didn't Iyanshe tell me that when we approached her? She seemed surprised and hesitant about committing to a cause Dagny might not support." Now I'm suspicious. Iyanshe didn't know about the outreach.

"We had to work quickly and hadn't spoken with everyone yet." She smiles, a hint of regret in her gaze. "I wish you'd started elsewhere, but the dice fall as they will. Iyanshe is a shy and nervous beast. She reached out to an ally as soon as your beasts approached, leaving her thoughts open as you spoke. We think the Dróttning must have sensed it. It wasn't a coincidence she focused on Iyanshe while you were meeting with her."

"Who else on the list is uncommitted?"

"At this point, nobody. We've had time to talk to everyone, and they're all prepared to join you. We've been breaking away from the Thunder when we can to create opportunities for you to come to us. I'm glad you found me first." Now her gaze bounces between us, sorrow in her eyes. "We wanted to fight before yesterday. Now we're hungry for it. We all loved Khirta. We're eager to avenge her death."

"How do we know this isn't a trap?" Fhord's voice is steel.

"The Dróttning isn't here. She would be if Glabor or I reached out to her." Bella gestures to the ground. "I've laid down my knives, but I'll do better." Turning to me, she smiles. "I know of your magic. Enter my thoughts. Go anywhere you'd like. See for yourself."

I turn to Fhord. "Does she have skills that might be a problem?"

"None. To my knowledge, she's as human as they come."

"I am," Bella affirms. "But bind me if you want. Do whatever you must to make yourself comfortable with my offer."

"I don't need to bind you. But I appreciate the gesture. Relax your thoughts. This won't take long."

Fhord reaches out to me, asking to go along for the ride. I smile and draw his mind into mine, then carry us toward Bella. As she promised, she's fully exposed and relaxed about it. I don't sense a hint of fear or subterfuge. I shuffle through her memories quickly, gathering the ones she wants me to see—confirming what she's just described—then search for those I need to give her our trust.

Bella's initial allegiance to the Dróttning, strong enough to eventually win a dragon, emerges first as I start digging. I see her belief in the Dróttning's cause, and then bounce through the events that changed her mind. I can't hold back the smile when I realize how much of an impact Astarot had on her—his rebellion and the torture he suffered as a result. Tindera's there, too, a beast everyone loves who's punished severely for Fhord's allegiance to me. Memories of Khirta filter in, shaded by the love Bella and Glabor felt for the little dragon.

Their commitment to the Dróttning started faltering years ago, but it was Vulryn's presence in Vanatia that brought it crashing down. She showed everyone that dragons can live without the Dróttning controlling their lives. They'd been under her thumb for so long, it felt inevitable. Impossible to escape. And along comes a confident—okay, cocky—female, mated to Ziselær, who refuses to bow to the Dróttning. And always wins.

It changed everything. The plan to join us started to form.

I've seen enough, Fhord. You too?

Me too, rabbit. Take us out.

I withdraw our thoughts, caressing Fhord as I release his mind. We turn to each other and grin like little kids.

"We might win this," he rumbles as his thumb comes up to stroke my jaw.

"We're gonna win this," I whisper, placing my hands on his cheeks. "She's harmed too many lives. That ends now."

"Fuck yes, it does."

"Fuck yes." Turning as I take Fhord's hand and link our fingers, I give Bella my smile. "So, what now?"

"Three others are gathering nearby with their riders. Glabor reached out when he sensed your dragons. They're the only ones able to get away without drawing the Dróttning's eyes. We'll meet them and talk about next steps." She pauses for a moment, holding our gazes. "We're at your disposal. We have a suggestion but you decide. You've come this far; we're just trying to help you win the battle you've already started."

"Let's go make a plan," Fhord declares, spinning to give me a quick kiss and then striding over to Tindera.

We all mount our beasts and fly south, but not for long. Glabor and Bella lead us to a cave only a few vikus away. Casting my thoughts out as I feel Fhord do the same, I search for life outside the cave but find only the three dragons and riders inside. I don't know them, but I can tell immediately that Fhord does. He's happy about someone waiting for us.

When we stride in, Fhord laughs, throwing his arms open as a petite female with skin as dark as mine flies into them. I can only watch as they cling to each other and her laugh joins his. Tindera strides over to a dragon whose feathers resemble the sea we flew over this morning with Astarot on her heels. The other riders gather around Fhord and the female, smiles on their faces.

Fhord looks up to find me and my heart flutters in my chest. He's so fucking gorgeous when he's happy. There's a lightness to him—as if his hopes have come to life in this little cavern—that I don't see often. He waves me over and I nudge Dani to join us, motioning to Mikkael, Toffer, and Thor to do the same.

"Nalani, this is my mate, Sifa," he says as his arm wraps around my waist and he pulls me into him. "She freed Astarot and rides him." Turning to me, he cocks an eyebrow. "And as you'll see, she's wrought a bit of a change in me since she captured my heart."

"It's nice to meet you, Sifa." Nalani's voice is surprisingly deep for such a small female. She extends her hand, her eyes open and welcoming.

"It's nice to meet you too," I tell her, taking her hand. "I haven't seen Fhord this happy in a while."

"Sifa lies," Fhord whispers dramatically. "She's discovered the way to make me very happy. We just don't share our secrets with others."

"You're such an ass," I mutter, smacking him on the chest as my grin emerges.

"But I'm your ass," he responds before pointing at Dani and the others, introducing them in turn, then looking back to Nalani. "Nalani and Vyara helped Tindera when I couldn't be at the Nest with her. They got her through some tough times. I'll always be in their debt."

"Then I'm also in your debt, as is Astarot."

Nalani shakes her head. "Help us escape the Dróttning and we'll owe you. We've been waiting for this for many years."

"It's time," Fhord declares as he gives me a squeeze. "Everything's in place." Now his gaze lifts to the other riders. "Including the dragons."

"We've heard nothing to explain how Vulryn—and now Astarot—can defy the Dróttning's commands. And how the dragons survive outside the Nest. Vulryn's presence here proves there's a way. She's turned everything we thought we knew upside down. But are you certain *Vanatian* dragons can survive without the Dróttning?"

"We are," Fhord says with a quick glance at the group. "You've been to Lumaria so you may already suspect the dragons need the water available there. There's a large source in each Nest—probably the reason the dragons chose those caverns as their homes so many centuries ago—and the Dróttning thinks she controls the only sources in Vanatia. But it's also available in a place I discovered many years ago, near the northern border. We can give the dragons as much access to that water as they need. That's one part of it."

"And what's the other part?" Nalani quirks her eyebrow as she tilts her head to the side, her lips drawn into a fine line.

"The mash," Fhord responds with a smile. "It has a magic we don't fully understand, but we do know that while dragons eat it, the Dróttning has the ability to control them, and if they go without long enough, she loses that ability."

Nalani scoffs. "That's it? A food?" Now she looks really skeptical. And who could blame her?

"It seems too easy, but we've seen the evidence. Giving up the mash is difficult—Astarot suffered when his body craved it, and he received none. He was weak, and for a time, certain he would die. But those cravings are gone, and he's found his full strength again."

Nalani shakes her head. "I'm not sure I believe that's all it would take to break free of her grasp." Shaking her head again, she turns to the other riders and then back to Fhord. "My questions won't stop us, though. We're ready to trust you ... to fight with and for you." She pauses as her gaze rests on each of us for a moment, her lips tipping up. "Let's introduce everyone and get to work."

"Before we do, are you all sure?" Fhord looks around the cave, his brow furrowed as he scrutinizes the riders and their dragons in turn.

The females nod their heads, their eyes solemn. The male just smirks. "Have I told you my story, Fhord? The reason I oppose the Dróttning?"

Fhord turns to me, then the others. "This is Gorm. He rides Khanti, the pink beast. He's like me, one of the few who rides a dragon the fates chose for him, instead of the Dróttning. Aquina is his consort," he points to the other female, a tall woman with a narrow body, brown hair and sharp purple eyes, "and Aquina rides the yellow dragon, Sunni, who is mated to Khanti."

"Nice to meet all of you." I glance at Mikkael, but his eyes are guarded. Dani's movement to the side of me draws my gaze. She's moving away from Mikkael, her gaze focused on Gorm.

"Tell us your story, rider."

"Let's sit," he says, gesturing to a fire with a large pot bubbling above it, prompting a grumble from my stomach. He smiles as he glances at me. "We'll serve the meal soon and talk until it's ready."

We gather on the waiting logs—Mikkael and Dani as far apart as they can be without having to look at each other—and watch as Gorm turns toward Aquina, reaching for her hand. She responds with a reluctant nod and then walks over, sitting next to him. They hold hands for a second, but then she releases his, clasping hers in front of her as she stares at the fire.

"It took a while for Aquina and me to accept our relationship," Gorm says as he straightens his back, crossing his arms over his chest. "It started in trauma, as happens too often in this land. Heart-breaking loss for Sunni and me that Khanti and Aquina experienced through our bonds."

He takes a deep breath, closing his eyes for a moment, then letting his shoulders drop as he looks at us again, one by one. "We first encountered each other when Khanti recognized his fate-chosen rider, Kat, and circled around to find her. Kat and I were having a picnic to celebrate." He gazes at Aquina, giving her a sad smile, then shakes his head again and returns his attention to us.

"Kat was pregnant." His voice is soft, like he's loath to give this memory life, drag it back into the relationship he's forged with Sunni's rider. "We'd been mated for a couple of years and trying nearly the whole time to have a child. We had so much love to share, it seemed wrong to keep it to ourselves. We'd only learned that day." He pauses as he stares into the fire. "That child was never born."

"Fuck, no," Mikkael snarls from my side. I think he knows what Gorm's going to tell us.

Gorm's gaze snaps to him, widening as he sees the veins throbbing in my friend's neck, his hands clenching and unclenching. "You're fated to ride a dragon."

Mikkael responds with a quick jerk of his chin, his eyes full of an apology I can see, but only because I know him so well.

404 ROCHELLE L. WILCOX

"Did he recognize you?"

"He did."

"Yet, you live."

"He has refused to kill me twice and saved me once."

"Treachery." Gorm smiles. "But we're all traitors here. Who's your dragon? Perhaps he can be persuaded to join us."

"I should ride Ziselær," Mikkael mutters, glancing toward Dani for just a moment and then back to Gorm.

Gorm notices, his eyes following Mikkael's glance. "You ride Vulryn."

"I do."

"And she's mated to Ziselær."

"She is."

"But you are with Matthias."

"I am."

"We don't like each other," Mikkael mutters, lifting a glare to Dani.

"Hate and love are but sides of the same coin." Gorm's lips lift into a half-smile.

"Yeah, well, we still don't like each other. The fates are just fucking with us." Now Mikkael shakes his head, then looks up at Gorm. "Finish your story." His voice is flat, cold.

Gorm's silent for a long time, his gaze shifting between Mikkael, Dani and Vulryn. But then he turns to Aquina and nods before staring again at the fire. "There's little more to tell. Sunni abided by Aquina's demand..."

"The Dróttning's demand," Aquina interjects, reaching for Gorm's hand. "I was an obedient soldier. The person I was never would have disobeyed in something like this."

"I know, my love." Gorm reaches out, wrapping his hand around the back of her neck to hold her gaze to his. "I know." His words are emphatic, full of a love grown out of conflict and loss.

Sighing, he turns back toward the fire. "I'd stepped away to get a blanket. Kat was cold. I suspect I'd be dead too if I'd been next to her. For a long time, I wished I was. It was quick. Sunni didn't burn her, and I'll be eternally grateful for that. It would have been such a painful way to die. She came up from behind her and clipped her head with a claw."

Gorm looks at Mikkael. "In the Nest, the dragons teach each other to do that. The dragon-masters don't know. They'd forbid it if they did. But not all dragons want to cause pain. The older dragons can tell who in the Thunder they can trust. Who would want to kill their destined rider without pain. They share their knowledge, as they did with Sunni."

His next words are a mumble, like he's still living the pain of that moment. "I watched her fall. And there was nothing I could do. She was dead by the time I reached her. My mate and our child."

"When did you bond with Khanti?" Dani's voice is so soft.

"Khanti and I had bonded long before that. He was in the Nest while Kat and I picnicked alone. Sunni came from the Northern Nest, and her path had never crossed Khanti's. The next day, they found each other. Sunni was suffering from having killed Kat, and Khanti found himself drawn to her strong emotions. He never left her side. I tracked him down a week later—after I buried Kat—to meet his mate. I felt the loss of my mate and child all over again when I realized I'd be forever bound to the dragon who killed them."

"That's why we're here," Aquina says, her tone fierce. "I love Sunni, and Gorm and I have learned to love each other. I'm grateful to the gods for both of them. But nobody should experience the loss Gorm and Sunni did. The Dróttning has destroyed too many lives. It has to end."

"It has to end," Mikkael agrees, his voice just as fierce.

"Where do we start?" I ask, drawing every eye toward me.

"The training center," Gorm declares, Fhord's gaze flicking up at his suggestion. "Most dragons detest what happens there. We'll free those beasts and create an army to defeat her."

"We're of the same mind," Fhord tells him, a broad smile lifting his cheeks and crinkling his eyes. "It must be the right move. Is tomorrow a good day?"

"It's the best day. The Dróttning's still in the southern Nest, looking for people she can punish for yesterday's loss. It's as good an opportunity as any we'll have."

"Tomorrow, then," Fhord declares, tugging me closer to him, "we start the revolution."

CHAPTER TWENTY-NINE

DANI

A BAD IDEA

I DON'T EVEN KNOW what to think about the dragons and riders who joined us and their devastating story. I could feel Mikkael's heart break as they told it. Because that was his destiny too. Ziselær refused Matthias's demand only because he'd found Vulryn and she opened his eyes to the power of the mating bond. He'd be dead without that.

Gorm and Aquina love each other, even after she killed his mate. The dragon bond is that powerful. It's why I know I made the right decision in going to Matthias. Even though I could feel how much it hurt Mikkael and crave my mate more than I ever could have anticipated.

I knew when I bonded to Vulryn that she'd come first in everything. She must come first in this too. What I want can't matter.

Are you ready? Her voice erupts in my thoughts. She's eager. She loves a good fight.

As ready as I'll ever be.

We fly.

Vulryn lost her fight with Toffer about leaving Thor behind, where he wouldn't be in danger. We're carrying them—the only compromise my demanding dragon would accept—and Mikkael is with Sifa, as he usually is. I have to constantly fight to stop my gaze from finding him. I'm worried about my mate and really wish I wasn't. I want to let him go and be happy with Matthias.

I'm also certain that bringing him along is a bad idea.

It doesn't matter now, though. He's going. And he'll be good to have in the battle that's coming.

Has Fhord confirmed the Dróttning isn't nearby?

Our male did not sleep. He and the sun beast flew south far enough to confirm the wyrm remains in that Nest. They waited to make sure she did not sense his presence and follow him back. He is confident she cannot return in time to help if we move with the speed we must.

We're in the air within a few minutes, flying north to approach our target from over the mountain. We'd talked about using a tunnel to get in but decided the blunt attack would be best. The training grounds are close to the surface—well within Fhord's powers—and we'd have to travel too far, and probably kill too many people, to get access from one of the caverns. This will draw the Dróttning, but anything we do would. Once we're in, she'll be racing to this Nest anyway.

As we'd hoped, the Dróttning doesn't expect an assault from this direction. We don't find anyone, and the dragons patrolling the area are all too far south to sense our presence.

We reach our destination, flying high so we're not seen, and wait for Fhord to give us instructions.

Our male is ready to begin, Vulryn tells me before long. *We are to hasten to the mountain and hover just above ground in a hidden area close to the training grounds while he opens our path.*

Let's hasten, then, I drawl as Vulryn tucks her wings. Toffer tightens his hold on me and down we go. If my stomach wasn't already twisted—the pre-battle angst bringing it to life, as it always does—it would be now. I love these dives, but it's a struggle to keep my breakfast down if they last too long. And this one lasts a long time. I hold on—my gaze finding Mikkael only once, the *need* to see his face as we descend too strong to resist—and focus on how pissed Vulryn would be if I spewed on her.

She'd never forgive me if she entered this battle covered in my vomit.

Finally, she snaps out her wings, levels herself a man's-height above the mountain, and floats down. Toffer's giggle fills the space behind me as he relaxes his grip.

I'd have slammed us into the rocks if I were in charge. She's very good at this whole flying thing.

Our male is ready to begin, she announces, just as I feel Fhord's magic ripple around us. He's ridiculously powerful. The mountain starts to tremble beneath the strength of his will within a few seconds, rocks tumbling away from the hole he plans to create. I smile, my thoughts dragged from our impending battle for a moment, as many roll uphill, even gravity bending to Fhord's command.

And then the landshake really starts. The rumble turns into a roar, swallowing us with the cacophony of the mountain breaking apart. I'm awestruck, my mind focused on this alone, as he methodically opens a chasm into the training center. The reality of the war we're starting settles into my skin, pressing like a blanket that will smother me if I can't control it.

When the hole is big enough to see inside, I count a dozen trapped beasts, all of them terrified—the trauma of the Dróttning's "training" suddenly eclipsed by the mountain parting above them. But none are harmed. I realize as the mountain splits beneath us that nothing is falling into Fhord's hole. He's pulling out every rock and boulder and puff of dust, to scatter the ground around the crack he's creating. As I watch, the dragons' terror turns to excitement.

Although they didn't know how we'd come, they're expecting us. The Dróttning isn't, or she'd have been here. But they knew, and they're ready.

The "trainers" are ready too. Three dozen soldiers are spread about and half of them scramble for the dragon bolts that are their best defense. Sifa and I respond as planned. I open my mind to her and she takes me along as she plants herself within the minds of each one. I'm ready to get lost in my first memory, letting her take over as I spin them out, when the trainers attack.

We're so fucked, I realize as I double over, clinging to Vulryn, trying to stop myself from sliding off. Because our job was to eliminate them and the threat of the dragon bolts, and we won't be able to do that if we can't find a way past the agony they're throwing at us.

My dragon screams—her fear over my pain visceral and all-consuming—but it's a whisper I barely notice. The torture I felt in the Nest, when that bastard of a guard tried to rape me, is a shadow of the anguish pounding through me now. That was a campfire; this is an inferno. Every bone in my body is twisting in place, even my fingers and toes flinging so much torment through me, I'd sooner cut them off than experience another second of it.

It stops suddenly and my head jerks toward Sifa, desperate to know if she's okay, and if she has any idea what in Helheim just happened to us. She's breathing rapidly, her chin on her chest, fingers wrapped tightly around Astarot's feathers. Three times, she sucks in a deep breath, and then her head twitches and she looks at me.

The fire beast asks whether you know what caused the pain.

I don't have any gods-damned idea. I was hoping she did.

The starry female also is not sure. It ended when she stopped trying to feed the soldiers your memories.

It's like the pain inflicted by that button they have in the Nest. But a thousand times worse.

Vulryn's quiet for a moment, then responds in a flat voice. *Our male believes it is the same. He thinks the Dróttning has modified it to use against you and the starry female, that she's turned the mind connection you wield as a weapon into a weakness. We will proceed without it.*

How the fuck do we get past all the dragon bolts? I'm sure I fail miserably at keeping the worry from my voice.

Carefully, is Vulryn's only response. But like always, it's spoken with a confidence that only my belligerent beast could muster in the face of more than a dozen weapons aimed at us.

Let's go carefully, then.

Vulryn leads the group—and I wouldn't expect anything else—twisting to approach from the side instead of directly above. She doesn't go in right away, giving the soldiers some time to search for their attackers and start to fear. When she decides the time is right, she doesn't make a sound. Instead, she gathers the speed she needs to soar through the hole, holding her wings outstretched as she approaches and then tucking them at the last minute to spiral into the training grounds.

My stomach spins with her, coming much too close to dislodging my last meal. But then relief washes through me as we make it inside safely, and Vulryn flings herself at the closest bolt-wielding soldier. The next minute is a blur. He turns toward her a few seconds before she'd have burned him alive, hoisting his weapon to aim it at her. She lurches at the last minute, barely avoiding the arrow he managed to launch.

Out of the corner of my eye, I see the other dragons following on Vulryn's heels, one of them twisting just in time to avoid a massive hole in her head, but I can't even turn to look. Vulryn is spearing toward the rocks below to drop us off—the plan for each dragon and rider—so we can fight on the ground while they attack from the sky. Toffer and I don't waste any time dismounting; my dragon's airborne again moments after our feet land.

Toffer turns to me with a vicious grin—murderous creature that he is—while Vulryn throws herself into the sky. Thor's golden gaze scans the cave, as if he's here to choose Toffer's kills. "We'll end our enemies for eternity," Toffer declares, his eyes bright as his smile grows even larger.

I nod, clap his arm quickly, and spin to run toward the soldier lifting his bolt to aim it at my dragon. He's concentrating, doing his damnedest to follow her spirals in the sky as he pulls back the string to fire. Throwing myself at his feet, I toss him to the rocks beneath us just as he releases the arrow. It flies wide, barely, slicing through the edge of Vulryn's wing without doing any real damage. Thank fuck.

I'm vaguely aware of the new dragons who soar into the cavern from one of the adjacent tunnels—some of the Dróttning's drudges, no doubt—as the soldier I'd flung to the ground attacks me. He's too fucking good to ignore, and it's all I can do to stop the punches and kicks from ending my fight before I had any fun. Throwing myself to my feet, I reach for my sword and sneer at him. He pulls his blade from its scabbard, growls, and attacks.

For the next minute or more, I'm fighting for my life. His sword nearly takes my head twice, drawing blood once, to spurt out and down my neck. Both times, though, I manage to fling my blade up just in time to stop him. I'm dancing back, trying to find an advantage against him, when I realize his left side is weak. Nearly every swing of his blade has come from the right.

Twisting myself around him—spinning to his left when he expects me to go right—I stab his shoulder. He squeals, his blade clattering to the rocks below, and I pull my other sword to flick at a wrist, exposed for a moment as he pivots to try to protect his wound. His hand and weapon fall to the ground together as his squeal turns into a shriek. I end that with a slice of his throat, leaving him to gurgle behind me as I look for my next kill.

Dragons litter the rock and dirt around me, many dead, others fighting on the ground instead of in the air. Their riders are fighting, but there aren't as many of the Dróttning's soldiers as we'd expected. Our beasts need help, not the riders. We didn't discuss releasing the chained dragons to join the fight, but we should have. Many look hungry to take their vengeance. Grasping at the dead soldier's pockets, I breathe a sigh of relief as I find a bundle of keys.

Twisting, I run toward the closest one—a gray beast who seems healthy enough to fight and eager for his freedom. Holding his gaze for a moment, I smile. "If I free you, will you fight with us?"

He shoots out fire, blue eyes blazing with hatred and fury. A sharp dip of his chin and another burst of flame is all the answer I'll get, but it's enough. He's on our side.

It takes me so fucking long to find the right key. My breath is rasping through my throat, the bile forcing itself up again as a fist seems to wrap around my chest. Four times, the dragon strains at his chains to extend over my trembling body, protecting me from flames and blades. But never a dragon bolt. Our dragons can be killed. These are the Dróttning's, and she's trying to salvage them for riders obedient to her.

Her arrogance will be her downfall. These beasts are eager to join the rebellion and finally break free of her iron fist. And I hope to whatever gods still give a shit that I get to watch when it sinks in that her beloved son and a few elves defeated her.

Finally, long minutes after I started searching, I find the right key. Fumbling too much before it finally slides into the lock, I groan as I strain to turn it, exhaling when I hear the click and watch the manacle fall from the dragon's leg. He spins to offer me the other one, protecting me the entire time. This goes more quickly—the same key works for both locks—and then he's free.

"The copper dragon's mine," I bellow as he swings his snout to look at me. "Protect her if you have a chance."

Dipping his chin once, he blinks and throws himself into the fight.

And I go free another dragon.

I'm racing toward my third chained dragon, scrabbling with the keys in my hand as I search for one I haven't used yet—because the second beast's chains required a different key, that took for-fucking-ever to find—when Vulryn's cranky grouse interrupts my thoughts.

I do not need to be protected.

A little busy here ...

Do not tell these beasts to protect me—she spits out the last two words, like they're poison—*and I will not need to correct you.*

I laugh. Because of course that would piss off my dragon. What the fuck was I thinking? *You're the strongest and smartest beast here*, I assure her. *I wasn't thinking. Let me concentrate on this, please.*

Do not let it happen again.

I can't stop myself from finding my angry, uppity beast and winking at her. A massive flame emerges in response, her eyes narrowing dangerously at me, before she spins around to attack another dragon.

The orange beast I'm approaching grunts at me, his gaze swinging toward his chains. "Yes, you're next," I mutter, a little annoyed at the demanding asshole. I'm doing my best here. It takes three times to find the right key, and this dragon doesn't protect me the way the others did, 'cause he is an asshole.

At one point, I'm forced to scramble behind him, letting him take the brunt of the impact from a dragon fighting with Khanti. The chained dragon rasps out his complaint, and I wonder if he really is just an asshole, or if he's still committed to the Dróttning and pissed at me for joining the group freeing him. But then he barks at the Dróttning's dragon, drawing his gaze and giving Khanti a chance. He rips out the exposed throat of the Dróttning's beast then roars at the chained beast and throws himself into the air to chase someone else.

Any doubts I had about freeing this beast slip away. He may be a bastard, but he saved Khanti, so he must be our bastard. I move back to the stubborn lock around his ankle. Finally, the lock clicks, drawing a gust of relief from me, and I move to the second ankle, unlocking it too. "You're free," I mumble as he turns to glare at me, as if I've done something wrong, and bays his fury at … something. "Go," I tell him with a wave of my arm. "Get one of the dragons trying to keep you chained."

But the mother fucker doesn't do that. He looks directly at my dragon and flings himself into the air, propelling himself toward her at an impossible speed.

Vulryn, I shriek, terrified about what I've just unleashed. *Watch out.*

Her head swivels toward me, her eyes bright, as the dragon she's fighting drags itself from the ground and poises to attack. And then both dragons are on her, frantic in their strike.

"I saved you, you bastard," I yell at the orange dragon as my heart pounds in my throat. What the fuck was I thinking? My heart is dropping into my stomach as the magnitude of my stupidity settles on me. Of course there would be dragons here committed to the Dróttning. I needed to let Fhord and the others do this. They'd have known who they could trust and who they couldn't.

I should be doing something—anything to help our fight—but I can't drag my eyes away from Vulryn. I'm empty, my body hollow as my chest squeezes me so tightly, I'm not sure how I'm still breathing. So, I slink back to the nearest wall and stand there, motionless as my gaze tracks my dragon.

The Dróttning's beasts work together in a brutal assault. I can tell by watching them how badly I fucked up, because the dragon I just freed anticipates Vulryn's moves. He's been trapped here since Fhord ripped open the mountain, and he must have quickly realized how dangerous Vulryn is, focusing on her. Three different times, the fucker nearly captures one of Vulryn's wings. Every time, my scream into her thoughts—*Left*, *Behind you* and *Left*—draws her attention just in time for her to throw herself away.

Finally, though, Vulryn gets the advantage she needs. The weaker dragon tries for her wing, but he doesn't know how to do it safely. He stretches too far, exposing his neck to Vulryn. She doesn't hesitate, whipping her head forward as her teeth grasp skin and bone and cartilage. And then she twists. He topples to the ground, dead before he lands, as Vulryn hurls out his remnants and turns toward the orange bastard.

He's good but not good enough to fight her alone, and my lungs start to expand as I realize she's going to survive. It only takes her a few minutes to force him onto his back, his wings fluttering helplessly as he tries to right himself. Before he can, though, her claw digs into him, opening his flesh from the base of his neck nearly to his ass.

Serves him right, the bastard.

Vulryn turns to me, a dragony smile lifting her lips. And then she looks up. Her voice, smug and pleased, drops into my mind. *He has come.*

What?

My drake has come to join our fight.

I spin my gaze to the ceiling and watch Ziselær soar in through the hole, his wide eyes fixed on Vulryn.

Thank fuck.

We need another dragon on our side.

CHAPTER THIRTY

MIKKAEL

BITTER VICTORY

I FEEL HIS APPROACH. Every nerve in my body, each muscle, all of the blood pulsing through my veins, cries out to my dragon. I can't see him yet, but he's close.

When Z appears above me, hovering as he stares at Vulryn, I nearly lose my head to the idiot attacking me because I can't drag my gaze away from his eyes, even if they're not looking at me. He's so fucking magnificent. My heart grows, warmth spilling into my veins, at the knowledge that the fates chose me to ride him.

But I need to keep my shit together because I'm still in the middle of a fight for my life and I damn sure better win. I block the sword swinging at my neck—again—and start to get serious. I have no idea how long Z will be here, and I won't be able to watch him if I'm stuck fighting these assholes the whole time.

Two more weak parries from my opponent follow, another aimed at my neck—because that's how this male fights—and one at the belly that's never once been exposed and isn't now. Fucking idiot. When he tries again for my neck, I fling my sword up to disarm him and follow with a backswing that takes his head. Glancing around quickly to make sure nobody else will come after me right away, I look up again at my beast.

He must feel me ogling him. When he drags his gaze away from Vulryn, he turns to me. His eyes are dull, as if they've been drained of their life. *Leave*, he grunts at me. Our connection is so much stronger now than it was when I first saw him. I feel the emotion and understand the nuance in his word. I also can tell he's trying to keep both from Matthias. Z's horrified I'm here. He wants me to escape before Matthias realizes it.

His terror for me is a palpable thing, and for a moment, I feel like I'm swimming through it.

I'm here to fight, Z. Like you are. I can't leave.

Please. Shame coats his plea because if I'm to die today, it will be by Z's fire.

And I understand. I'm so gods-damned lucky I'm still alive, and I'll never blame him if he does what he must. What the Dróttning demands.

I'm not going to hide from Matthias. If that means you have to kill me, then do it. I know you've chosen him, and I get it. I really do. But while I live, I need to see you. In my soul, you're mine. I can't stay away.

He puffs out flame just as Matthias looks in my direction. Even from this distance, I can see the anger the bastard wears like a weapon. His eyes are impossibly wide, and his hand tightens around Z's feathers as he yanks at them. Z glances back, his movements slow and hesitant, and then looks down. He tucks his wings to spear toward Sunni, who's just gutted one of the Dróttning's dragons.

For a moment, I think Z's going to help in some way. Because he can't be attacking Sunni. Matthias was nearly one of us. We were going to take him to the camp with Liv, Frida, and the Ætt. He chose Vulryn and Dani.

But he still belongs to the Dróttning. He pivots in the air just above Sunni and snags the base of her wings, digging his claws into them in a hold Sunni won't be able to break. And then he leverages his body to begin pulling the wings out of Sunni's back.

I'm running toward Z before I realize I made the decision, pivoting around dead dragons and leaping over soldiers' bodies. Z's head spins toward me once, flame licking through his teeth, and then he turns to concentrate on the dragon beneath him.

The usurper's gaze, though, follows him to me and then never leaves. I'm still running, desperate to get to Z before he does something he'll always regret, when Matthias's gods-damned voice drops into my head.

Leave this beast. Kill your destined rider.

Z's grip on Sunni grows slack and he lets go, flinging himself back as he twists his head to glare at his rider. I watch the yellow beast for a minute, making sure she's alive, and then look for someone who might help her. Everyone's trapped in their own battles, though. Vulryn alone knows that Z's here to kill us, and she's fighting two large dragons.

Please. Z's plea snaps my gaze back to him. He's begging that bastard for my life. But I'd rather die than let my dragon debase himself to that fucker for me.

Don't beg him for anything, Z. He's not worth it. He's not worthy of you. I can think of no better death than by your flame. Take my life if that's what you must to be happy.

I won't tell you again, Ziselær. The usurper's voice is cold, no emotion to interfere with his command.

Gods, do I hate the male.

Please. This time, the word comes alone. It warbles with emotion—dread and anger and sadness packed into that single syllable. And my heart breaks.

I stride closer to my dragon, flinging my arms open to stand before him, ready. *Save yourself, Z. Don't take his anger for me.*

You know what will happen, Ziselær. You kill him or I will. If I have to do it, Vulryn and Dani will be next. They will die because you're too weak and emasculated to do your duty.

Don't you fucking dare, you bastard. This is between us. If you think you can kill me, come try. I don't think you'll even come down here, though. I think you're too much of a pussy to fight your own battles.

Land. Matthias snarls this command, some emotion finally entering his voice. He's pissed, but so am I. This has been too long coming.

Z doesn't comply immediately, his head spinning toward me and then back to the usurper.

One of us needs to die, Z. Bring him to me. Let us fight it out.

Z rasps out a little wail, drawing Vulryn's gaze to him for a moment, and then flutters down to land a dragon's-length away. Before he can even stretch out his wings—that bear horrific injuries, as if someone carved off their gods-damned tips—Matthias is dropping to the ground, his hands on his swords and his gaze never leaving me. I draw my blades from their scabbards and stride forward, my fury at the Dróttning and this gods-damned usurper driving me. This mother fucker took Z back to her, subjected my loyal, kind dragon to her torture, and I am going to dance in his blood.

Visions of his severed head bounce through my thoughts as I attack. Matthias barely frees his sword in time, swinging it up nearly to his face to clang against mine. I step back and swing toward the small space between his breastplate and tasset, but he spins and blocks that strike as well. Twisting his blade—thinking he could disarm me—a ghost of a smile appears on his lips as he flicks, but I respond by slamming my blade into his, digging it into the ground.

Our swords clash, echoing around us, as we dance and parry and thrust. Twice I manage to throw him to the rocks below, but he sends me down three times. Neither of us can take advantage as we scramble up or away from the other before a blade can find its mark. I sense Z nearby, his emotions swinging wildly, but he can't do anything except wait to see which of us will die.

And then Z's low whine draws my gaze toward him, and I duck when I should have spun. Matthias's sword digs into my side, dropping me to my knees and then my back as he lands on top of me, his steel at my neck. My hand wraps around the gaping wound, trying to stanch the blood gushing out of me, as I search for my dragon. He's so close. His eyes are so tormented.

It's okay, I tell him with a smile, hoping he believes me.

Finally, I twist to look for Dani. Because as much as I hate her, she's my mate and I need to see her before I die.

She's still fighting her own battle, just like everyone else. Nobody even realizes what's happening over here—that I'm going to die today. It's just as well. This is between Z and Matthias and me. As it should be.

Matthias doesn't take the killing blow, though. Instead, a chilling smile twists his face. He spits on me, his slaver dripping along my cheek—I can't even lift my gods-damned hand to wipe it off—then stands to step away.

Burn him now, Ziselær, and I may let you keep your draikana and her rider.

It's okay, Z, I tell my dragon as I spin my head to gaze at him again. *I've had a good life. I'll die happy because the fates chose me for you.*

Z's responding whine rips my heart out. He's bonded to me, just as he is to Matthias. Our link may not be as strong, but it matters to him too. This will hurt him.

I'm so sorry I tried to make you mine. I don't wish this pain on you.

Now, Ziselær, the usurper snipes. *Don't make me tell you again.*

Z looks at Matthias, back at me, and gives his wings one strong flap. I close my eyes, wondering how he'll kill me. I hope it's fire. I don't want the quick death that would come with a clip to the head.

I feel Z's decision when he makes it, slamming my eyes open to stare at Matthias—his pupils blown wide in shock—as Z pivots and stretches his claws toward his Dróttning-chosen rider. The keen that erupts from the beast as he rakes one talon across the back of Matthias's head echoes around the massive cavern.

My world breaks in two, my dragon's anguish pulsing through me, all the power and rage of an ocean trapped within a thimble, pounding, demanding an escape. I don't know how to breathe. I don't know how to move. I can only feel grief and terror and such deep and suffocating agony, it's a wonder Z could survive it.

Z lands next to Matthias as the male's body collapses to the floor then grows still, my dragon's tongue the only movement as it snakes out to turn Matthias onto his back and touch his cheek. Part of me is aware of the fight around us, stunned the world continues to turn, oblivious to Z's heartbreak. This is how it should be, though. With Matthias gone, this is between Z and me. He needs this time alone.

But Z isn't alone. I feel the shift in Vulryn's energy before I see her. Maybe through Z; maybe through Dani. I have no fucking idea, and it doesn't really matter. Nothing matters except Z's grief. Out of the corner of my eye, I see Vulryn drop from the sky to land next to Z, her bloody maw nuzzling into the side of Z's neck as a low, deep squall spills from her.

And then I hear Dani's cry. Spinning my head, I see her next to Vulryn, her eyes focused on Matthias.

She doesn't even see me. She hasn't looked once, has no idea I'm bleeding like a stuck pig. Because she doesn't give a shit. She chose him. And with him dead and me bleeding all over the gods-damned floor, her gaze is on him alone.

I stand, needing Z. I'll never have Dani, but that doesn't matter. Z is my dragon. He chose me. That's my only truth right now.

When I take a step toward him, my hand on my side as gore eeks out of me—that pain a whisper of the torture I feel from my dragon—Z's head spins toward me. His eyes are fire, full of hate and betrayal and sorrow. Spewing out a stream of flames, he stops me in my tracks.

No! Z's anger at me consumes his soul. This is my fault. I erupted in his life, twisting what he knew so well before me. I refused to leave him alone, filling his head with traitorous thoughts. I forced him to choose, and he chose wrong. Matthias had been his rider for a century. I am nothing and I will never ride him.

I collapse again, this time from a heartbreak that sucks all the air from my lungs, leaving me gasping for breath. My gaze never leaves Z, though. *I'm sorry. I wanted you to take my life. I didn't want you to suffer like this.*

Shaking his head, Z turns again to look at Matthias, then gently lifts him into his mouth, flaps his powerful wings, and soars through the hole above us.

He never looks back.

Dani stares after them for long seconds. When she turns to me, tears stream down her cheeks.

"You're hurt." Her voice is so soft, I barely hear it.

She stands, stumbling in my direction, but I don't want her anywhere near me. I dig my heels into the dirt and rock beneath me, pushing away from her. "Don't come near me."

"Let me help you, Mikkael."

"You chose him. Even now, with him dead, you chose him. That's all I need to know. It's all I ever need to know."

"You don't understand." I barely hear her, even as the clamor around us starts to die down.

"Fuck, no, I don't understand. He just turned on us. Took the Dróttning's side and attacked our beasts. And you still chose him." I spit at her, shoving myself farther away. "I'll never understand."

Sifa strides toward me, dropping down to shove her shoulder under my arm. "We need to go. The dragons are free and more of the Dróttning's fighters are on the way. We only have a couple of minutes to get out of here."

I look at her, still lost in Z's grief and Dani's betrayal, my head spinning as it tries to catch up with Sifa's words. "Did we win?" I ask after a moment. "Are we done?"

"We've freed the dragons. The ones on our side will come with us. And all our dragons and riders live. It's everything we hoped to do."

Nodding, I let her drag me up. Dani stands to stride over to us, but I bark at her. "Get the fuck away from me. I don't ever want to see you again."

"Please, Mikkael. Give me a chance to explain." Her eyes are the sea at sunset, darker than I've ever seen them before, as she lifts a hand toward me.

"Get the fuck away from me, Dani. Don't make me tell you again."

She nods, holding my gaze for a moment before nodding again. Spinning, she strides over to Vulryn, climbs to her back, followed quickly by Sifa's troll and the gods-damned cat, and launches into the sky. She doesn't look back either.

Sifa helps me onto Astarot—the gaping hole in my side a little drop in the bucket of Z's pain, still beating through me—and settles in behind me, wrapping a cloth around me to slow down the blood. "It'll work out," she tells me, her voice full of pain, "even if it doesn't feel like it now."

But it won't. When it mattered, my mate chose that bastard over me. And while Z may have killed Matthias in a moment of weakness, my dragon despises me now for forcing him to make that choice. Nothing could ever fix that.

I'm alive, but I'll never be whole. Two-thirds of my soul rejected me when I needed them the most.

It's a bitter, bitter victory.

Astarot launches into the sky, Sifa's arms holding me in place atop her dragon.

I don't look back. There's nothing left for me to see.

VULRYN

IT'S MY FAULT

I HAVE LOST HIM.

My drake's grief consumes him, destroying every emotion he might once have felt for me. All that we'd done, each of our promises, every moment together, is lost in the hurricane of his pain.

It's my fault. I know it as well as him. And I know he will never forgive me. He chose to save his fate-chosen rider the first time, believing I would want it. I rewarded him because he was right. I did not want my rider's mate, my drake's fate-chosen rider, to die. I believed it would cause too much pain—to my rider and my drake. I asked him to let his fate-chosen rider live.

I did not know my drake would bond so strongly to that male. That it would create such conflict. That the fates would step in and stop my drake from killing the male they had chosen for him. That faced with an impossible choice, my drake would be compelled to kill the male who had ridden him for a hundred years—the rider my drake had chosen—and spare the life of his fate-chosen rider.

I cannot change the past, although it will destroy the future, and all hope I ever had for a life with my drake.

I can only ask the fates to take away my drake's pain.

To help him find joy again, even if I am not destined to share it with him.

The End,

For Now ...

Sifa, Fhord, Dani, Mikkael, and their dragons
are waiting for you in *Mythical Menace,*
Book IV of *Tales of the Vanir.*
Get your copy here.

Thank You

Thank you for reading *Divine Dilemma!*
I hope you're enjoying *Tales of the Vanir*,
and I would appreciate it so much if you could
take the time to leave a review on Amazon,
Goodreads, or wherever you review books!

AUTHOR'S NOTE

I'M SO LUCKY TO be able to do what I love, supported by family and friends. Thanks to my hubby Al, our boys Albert and Stephen, and the amazing friends who have been cheering me along.

Thanks also to everyone who read *Divine Dilemma* and shared their thoughts with me, starting with my alpha reader Cynthia, who's read all my books and given me great feedback.

With this series, I relied heavily on beta feedback.
Many thanks to Cindy Ray Hale and Keele Publishing,
Kaitlin Slowik, and Keeya Marquez
for all of their comments and suggestions.

And last but definitely not least, thanks to everyone who gave this series a try. I fell in love with this world and hope you do too. As an indie author, your support means everything. I'm grateful to everyone who talks about my books, through a review or on social media, and just as grateful to everyone who reads them. Thank you!

Also by Rochelle Wilcox

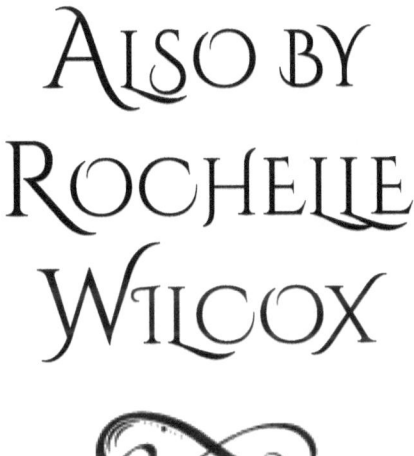

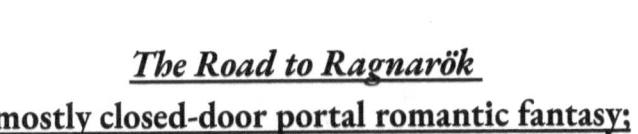

The Road to Ragnarök
(mostly closed-door portal romantic fantasy; *Heavy Heart* has one spicy scene)

Fickle Fate
(the spicy prequel, available to subscribers
to my newsletter at RochelleWilcox.com)
Lost Long
Enemies Eternal
Alive Again
Heavy Heart

ABOUT THE AUTHOR

Rochelle Wilcox is happily retired from practicing law, focused on writing what she loves to read. You can find Rochelle at rochellewilcox.com and at any of the social media sites below:

amazon.com/stores/Rochelle-Wilcox/author/B007PEWME6

goodreads.com/author/show/6951175.Rochelle_Wilcox

bookbub.com/authors/rochelle-l-wilcox

facebook.com/TheRoadToRagnarok

instagram.com/rochellewilcoxauthor/

tiktok.com/@rochellewilcoxauthor

www.ingramcontent.com/pod-product-compliance
Lightning Source LLC
Chambersburg PA
CBHW030328120726
47901CB00007B/1719